Virgin Brides

These brides have kept their innocence for their perfect husbands-to-be…

*Praise for three bestselling authors –
Miranda Lee, Sharon Kendrick and
Kate Walker*

About Miranda Lee:
'Ms Lee outdoes herself in this vibrant tale
packed with emotional intensity, a dash of
intrigue and scorching sensuality.'
—*Romantic Times*

About Sharon Kendrick:
'Sharon Kendrick transports readers to a fantasy
land with rich, indulgent characters and an
overabundance of romance.'
—*Romantic Times*

About Kate Walker:
'…Kate Walker will tug at your heartstrings
with intense romance, great character
development and heartfelt dialogue.'
—*Romantic Times*

Virgin Brides

THE VIRGIN BRIDE
by
Miranda Lee

ONE BRIDEGROOM REQUIRED!
by
Sharon Kendrick

NO HOLDING BACK
by
Kate Walker

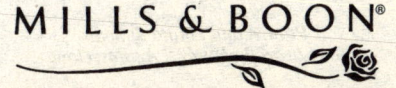

DID YOU PURCHASE THIS BOOK WITHOUT A COVER?
If you did, you should be aware it is **stolen property** as it was reported *unsold and destroyed* by a retailer. Neither the author nor the publisher has received any payment for this book.

All the characters in this book have no existence outside the imagination of the author, and have no relation whatsoever to anyone bearing the same name or names. They are not even distantly inspired by any individual known or unknown to the author, and all the incidents are pure invention.

All Rights Reserved including the right of reproduction in whole or in part in any form. This edition is published by arrangement with Harlequin Enterprises II B.V. The text of this publication or any part thereof may not be reproduced or transmitted in any form or by any means, electronic or mechanical, including photocopying, recording, storage in an information retrieval system, or otherwise, without the written permission of the publisher.

This book is sold subject to the condition that it shall not, by way of trade or otherwise, be lent, resold, hired out or otherwise circulated without the prior consent of the publisher in any form of binding or cover other than that in which it is published and without a similar condition including this condition being imposed on the subsequent purchaser.

MILLS & BOON and MILLS & BOON with the Rose Device are registered trademarks of the publisher.
Harlequin Mills & Boon Limited,
Eton House, 18-24 Paradise Road, Richmond, Surrey, TW9 1SR

VIRGIN BRIDES © by Harlequin Enterprises II B.V., 2005

The Virgin Bride, One Bridegroom Required! and
No Holding Back were first published in Great Britain by
Harlequin Mills & Boon Limited in separate, single volumes.

The Virgin Bride © Miranda Lee 1999
One Bridegroom Required! © Sharon Kendrick 1998
No Holding Back © Kate Walker 1995

ISBN 0 263 84473 0

05-0305

Printed and bound in Spain
by Litografia Rosés S.A., Barcelona

Miranda Lee is Australian, and lives near Sydney. Born and raised in the bush, she was boarding-school educated and briefly pursued a career in classical music, before moving to Sydney and embracing the world of computers. Happily married, with three daughters, she began writing when family commitments kept her at home. She likes to create stories that are believable, modern, fast-paced and sexy. Her interests include meaty sagas, doing word puzzles, gambling and going to the movies.

**Look out for the next sizzling read
by Miranda Lee:
BOUGHT: ONE BRIDE
Coming in July 2005, in Modern Romance™!**

THE VIRGIN BRIDE
by
Miranda Lee

CHAPTER ONE

WHAT a glorious day, Jason thought as he stepped outside. Spring had finally come, and with it that delicious sunshine which encompassed just the right amount of warmth. The town had never looked better, nestled at the base of now lush green hills. The sky was clear and blue. Birds twittered happily in a nearby tree.

Impossible to feel discontent on such a day, Jason decided as he walked down the front path and out onto the pavement.

And yet...

You can't have everything in life, son, he heard his mother say.

How right she was, that wise old mum of his.

His heart turned over at the thought of her, and of her wretched life: married at eighteen to a no-good drinker and gambler, the mother of seven boys by the time she was thirty, a deserted wife by thirty-one, worn out and white-haired by fifty, dead five years ago of a stroke.

She'd only been fifty-five.

He was her youngest, a bright and affectionate boy who'd grown into a discontented and fiercely ambitious teenager, determined to be rich one day. He'd gone to medical school not because of a love of medicine, but because of the love of money. His mother had worried about this, he knew. She'd argued that money wasn't the right reason to become a doctor.

How he would like the opportunity to tell her that he'd finally become a good doctor, and that he was quite happy, despite not being rich at all.

Not perfectly happy, of course. He no longer expected that.

'Morning, Dr Steel. Nice day, isn't it?'

'It surely is, Florrie.' Florrie was one of his patients. She was around seventy and popped into the surgery practically every week to discuss one of her wide range of ailments.

'Muriel's having a busy morning, I see,' Florrie said, pointing to the bakery across the street. A bus was parked outside, and people were streaming out from the shop's door, their arms full.

Tindley's bakery was famous for miles. It had almost single-handedly put the little country town back on the map a few years ago, when it had won first prize for the best meat pie in Australia. Travellers and tourists on their way from Sydney to Canberra had begun taking the turn-off from the main highway, just to buy a Tindley pie.

In response to the sudden influx of visitors, the once deserted shops which fronted the narrow and winding main street had thrown open their creaking doors to sell all sorts of arts and crafts.

The area surrounding Tindley had always been a haunt for artists because of its peaceful beauty. But before this new local market had become available they'd had to sell their wares to shopkeepers situated in the more popular tourist towns over on the coast.

Suddenly, it wasn't just pies which attracted visitors, but unique items of pottery and leather goods, wood and home crafts.

In further response to this popularity, even more businesses had opened, offering Devonshire teas and take-away food. Tindley now also boasted a couple of quite good restaurants, and a guest house filled most weekends with Sydney escapees who liked horse-riding and bush walks as well as just sitting on a wide verandah, soaking up the valley views.

Over a period of five years Tindley had been resurrected from being almost a ghost town into a thriving little community with a bustling economy. Enough to support two doctors. Jason had bought into old Doc Brandewilde's general practice five months ago, and hadn't regretted it for a moment.

Admittedly, he'd taken a while to settle to the slower pace after working twelve-hour days in a gung-ho bulk-billing surgery in Sydney. He'd found it difficult at first to resist the automatic impulse to hurry consultations. Old habits did die hard.

Now, he could hardly imagine spending less than fifteen minutes to treat and diagnose a patient. They were no longer nameless faces, but people he knew and liked, people like Florrie, here. Having a warm, friendly chat was a large part of being a family doctor in the country.

The bus started up and slowly moved off, happy faces peering out of the windows.

'I hope Muriel hasn't sold my lunch,' Jason said, and Florrie laughed.

'She'd never do that, Doctor. You're her pet customer. She was saying to me just the other day that if she were thirty years younger, you wouldn't have to put up with Martha's matchmaking, because she'd have snapped you up already.'

Now Jason laughed, though a little drily. Matchmaking wasn't just Martha Brandewilde's domain. All the ladies in Tindley seemed to have got in on the act, his arrival in town causing much speculation among its female population. Apparently, it wasn't often that an attractive unattached bachelor under forty took up residence there. At only thirty, and better looking than average, he was considered ripe and ready for matching.

Not that they'd had any success, despite Jason being invited to several dinner parties where lo and behold, there had just happened to be a spare single girl placed right next to him. Jason suspected he'd been a severe disappointment to his various hostesses so far. Martha Brandewilde was particularly frustrated with him.

Still, he found it reassuring that, despite his apparent lack of enthusiasm for the young ladies served up to him on a platter, there had never been the remotest rumour or suggestion he might be a confirmed bachelor. This was one of the things he found so endearing about Tindley's residents. They held simple old-fashioned views and values.

Florrie gave him a frowning look. 'How old are you, Dr Steel?'

'Thirty, Florrie. Why?'

'A man shouldn't get too old before marrying,' she advised. 'Otherwise he gets too set in his ways. And too selfish. Still, don't be pressured into marrying the wrong girl, now. Marriage is a serious business. But a fine, intelligent man like you knows that. Probably why you're being so choosy. Oh, goodness, look at the time! I must go. *The Midday Show* will have started and I do so hate to miss it.'

Florrie hurried off, leaving Jason to consider what she'd said.

Actually, he agreed with her wholeheartedly. About everything. His life *would* be complete if he could find a good woman to share it with. He might have come to Tindley disillusioned with a certain lady doctor he'd left behind, but his disillusionment hadn't extended to the whole female race. He wanted to marry, but not just anyone.

He shook his head at how close he had come to marrying Adele. What a disaster that would have been!

Admittedly, she'd been a very exciting woman to live with. Beautiful. Brilliant. Sexy as hell. He'd been blindly in love with her, right up till that awful day when the wool had finally fallen from his eyes and he'd suddenly seen the real woman beneath the glittering façade: a coldly unfeeling creature who'd been capable of standing there and dismissing the death of a child with such chilling nonchalance, taking no blame whatsoever for her own negligence, saying that was life and it wouldn't be the last time such an accident happened.

He'd decided to walk away from her then, as well as from his own increasingly selfish and greedy lifestyle. And it had cost him plenty. Rather than fight

Adele in court for his half, he'd given her the place at Palm Beach, and the Mercedes, walking out with little in the way of material possessions. After paying Doc Brandewilde for his half of the practice, Jason had arrived in Tindley with nothing but his clothes, his video collection and a car which was as far from a red Mercedes sports as one could get. White, four-doored and Australian-made. Reliable, but not flashy. The sort of car a country doctor should drive.

Adele had thought him insane, had given him six months to come to his senses. But Jason knew he'd already done that. He wanted no more of the fast life, of the obsessive acquiring of wealth, or even the sort of wild, often kinky sex that women like Adele liked, and demanded. He wanted peace of mind and body. He wanted a family. He wanted marriage to a woman he could respect and like.

Being in love, however, he could do without.

Naturally, he wanted to *want* his wife. Sex was as important to Jason as any other red-blooded man. The town wasn't the only thing being warmed up by spring, and, quite frankly, his celibate lifestyle was beginning to pall. He needed a wife and he needed one soon!

Unfortunately, his chances of marrying the only girl to seriously catch his eye since he'd come to Tindley were less than zero.

He glanced down the road to the small shop on the corner. Its doors were still firmly shut. Understandable, he supposed. Ivy Churchill's funeral had only been last week.

Would Emma stay on and run her aunt's sweet

shop? Jason wondered. Even if she did, where would that get him? Her heart belonged elsewhere, stolen by some local creep who'd done her wrong and left town some time back. According to her aunt, she was still madly in love with this rotter, and probably waiting for him to return.

Jason had been told these scant but dismaying details on his second home visit to the old lady, perhaps because he'd cast one too many admiring glances Emma's way during his first visit.

Not that the girl had noticed herself. She'd seemed oblivious of his admiration as she sat by the window in her aunt's bedroom, doing some of her much admired tapestry work.

It had been impossible, however, not to look at her. Jason's eyes had been drawn again and again to the exquisite picture she'd made, sitting there with her long, slender neck bent in an elegant arc, her eyes downcast, long curling eyelashes resting against her pale cheeks. She'd been wearing a white ankle-length dress with a lacy bodice and a flowing skirt. The setting sun's rays had been shining over her shoulder, turning the soft fair curls hanging around her face into spun gold. A gold chain had hung around her throat, falling slightly away from her skin, swaying with each movement of the large needle she was moving in and out of the canvas.

Jason could still recall how he'd felt as he'd watched her, how he'd ached to slide his hand up and down the delicate curve of her neck, how he'd imagined taking that chain and pulling it gently backwards till her head tipped up and back. In his mind's eye, he'd bent his lips to her startled mouth, before something his patient said had snapped him out of his dream-like, yet highly erotic reverie.

His thoughts had aroused him then. They aroused him now.

Scowling, Jason launched himself across the road and up onto the verandah of the bakery shop. But as he reached to open the shop screen door, he swiftly replaced the scowl with a more pleasant expression.

One minor drawback to life in Tindley was that nothing went unnoticed, not even a passing scowl. He didn't want it getting around town that poor Dr Steel was having personal problems. He also knew not to ask any questions which might be misinterpreted. He was dying to enquire about Emma's intentions, but suspected this might raise a few eyebrows.

'Mornin', Dr Steel,' Muriel chirped straight away on seeing him. 'The usual?'

'Yes, thanks, Muriel.' And he threw her a smile.

By the time he'd selected an orange juice from the self-serve fridge in the corner, his 'usual' of a steak and mushroom pie along with two fresh bread rolls was perched in paper bags on the counter. He was about to pay for it and just go, when curiosity got the better of him.

'I noticed the sweet shop's still closed,' he said, as casually as he could.

Muriel sighed. 'Yes. Emma said she just couldn't face it this week. I feel so sorry for that girl. Her aunt was all she had in this world and now she's gone too. Cancer is a terrible disease. Truly terrible!'

'That it is,' Jason agreed, and handed over a five-dollar note.

Muriel busied herself at the cash register. 'When I go, I'd like to pop off in my sleep with a nice heart attack. Nothing slow and lingering. Frankly, I was surprised Ivy lasted as long as she did. When Doc Brandewilde sent her up to that hospital in Sydney last year for chemotherapy, I wouldn't have given her more than a few days. But she lingered on for over a year. In a way, I suppose it's a relief for Emma that she's finally gone. No one likes to see someone they love in pain. But she's going to be awfully lonely, that girl.'

'I suppose so,' Jason said. 'Er...it's surprising that a pretty girl like Emma doesn't have a boyfriend,' he ventured, trying to look innocent.

Muriel shot him a sharp look. 'Surely you've heard about Emma and Dean Ratchitt. I would have thought Ivy would have said something, what with your visiting her so often these last few months.'

'I don't recall her mentioning anyone by that name,' Jason said truthfully. Dean Ratchitt, eh? The only Ratchitt he knew was Jim Ratchitt, a cranky old so-and-so who lived on a run-down dairy farm just out of town. 'Is he related to Jim Ratchitt?'

'His son. Look, you might as well know the score,' Muriel said as she handed over the change. 'Especially if you're thinkin' of casting your eye in *that* direction.'

'What score do you mean, Muriel?'

Muriel gave him a dry look. 'About Emma and Dean, of course.'

'They were lovers?'

'Oh, I don't know about *that*. Dean liked his girls free and easy, and Emma's not that way at all. Ivy brought her up with solid old-world standards. That girl believes in white weddings and the sanctity of marriage. Still...who knows? Dean had a way with women, there's no doubt about that. And they *were* engaged, however briefly.'

'Engaged!' Ivy hadn't mentioned any engagement.

'Yes. Just before Ivy went up to Sydney last year. Took the town by surprise, I can tell you, since Dean had been squiring another girl around town the month before. Anyway, Emma was sporting his ring just before she went up to Sydney with Ivy. By the time they got back, a couple of months later, it was all over town that Dean had got the youngest Martin girl in trouble.'

'The girl he was seeing before Emma?'

'Oh, no, that was Lizzie Talbot. Anyway, he didn't deny sleeping with the Martin girl, but refused to acknowledge the child, saying the girl was a slut and he wasn't the only bloke who'd been having sex with her. Emma and he had this very public row, right outside Ivy's shop. I heard some of it. Heck, the whole *town* heard some of it!'

Muriel lent on her elbows on the counter, enjoying herself relaying the gossip. 'Dean had the hide to still ask her to marry him, you see. Emma refused and he lost his temper, claimed that everything was her fault, though how he figured that I'd like to know. I remember him yellin' at her that if she didn't marry him as planned, then they were finished. She yelled back that they were finished anyway. She threw his ring back in his face and said she'd marry the first decent man who asked her.'

'Really?' Jason said, unable to hide his elation at this last piece of news.

'Don't go countin' your chickens, Doc,' Muriel said drily. 'She was only spoutin' off, like women do. Pride and all. Her actions since then have been much louder than her words. It's been a year and she hasn't gone out on one date, despite being asked many times. No man'll ask her to marry him when she doesn't let them get to first base, will he? We all know she's just waitin' for Dean to show up on her doorstep again. If and when he does...' Muriel shrugged resignedly, as though it was a foregone conclusion that Emma would fall readily into the arms of her long-lost lover.

And he *had* been her lover. Jason didn't doubt that. Women in love were rarely sustained by old-fashioned standards.

Still, the thought of Emma falling victim to such a conscienceless stud churned his stomach. She was such a soft, sweet creature, warm and caring and loving. She deserved better.

She deserves *me*, Jason decided. Modesty had never been one of his virtues.

'What happened to the girl?' he asked. 'The one Ratchitt got into trouble.'

'Oh, she moved away to the city. Rumour has it she got rid of the baby.'

'Do you think it *was* his?'

'Who knows? The girl *was* on the loose side. If it was Dean's child, it's the first time he slipped up that way. Odd, since over the years he'd made out with just about every female under forty in town, married *and* single.'

Jason's eyebrows lifted. 'That's some record. What's he got going for him? Or dare I ask?'

Muriel laughed. 'Can't give a personal report, Doc, since I'm headin' for sixty myself. But he's a right good-lookin' lad, is our Dean.'

'How old is he?'

'Oh, a few years younger than you, I would say, but a few years older than Emma.'

'And how old's Emma?'

Muriel straightened, her expression reproachful. 'Doc, Doc...what have you been doin' these past few months during your home visits? You should know these things already, if you're serious about the girl. She's twenty-two.'

Jason frowned. He'd thought she was older. There was a maturity and serenity in her manner which suggested a few more years' experience in life. Hell, at twenty-two she was barely more than a girl. A girl who'd lived all her life in a country town. An inexperienced and innocent young girl.

Emma's brief engagement to Dean Ratchitt came to mind, and Jason amended that last thought. Not so innocent, perhaps. Nor quite so inexperienced. Men like Ratchitt didn't hang around girls who didn't give them what they wanted.

'Do you think Ratchitt will come back?'

'Who knows? If he hears about Ivy passin' on and Emma inheritin' the shop and all, he might.'

Jason didn't think Emma inheriting that particular

establishment would inspire even the most hard-up scoundrel to race back home. The small shop had provided the two women with a living, he supposed, but only because they didn't have to pay rent. The shop occupied the converted front rooms of an old weatherboard house, as did most of the shops in Tindley. But it was smaller and more run-down than most. As real estate went, it wasn't worth much.

Jason couldn't imagine Ratchitt returning for such a poor prize. But who knew? Those who had nothing...

'If he did come back, do you think she'd take up with him again?' Jason asked.

Muriel pulled a face. 'Love makes fools of the best of us.'

Jason had to agree. Just as well *he* wasn't in love with the girl. He wanted to make his decisions about her with his head, not his heart.

'See you tomorrow, Muriel,' he said, and gathered up his lunch. He'd already tarried far too long in Tindley's bakery. Muriel was going to have a field-day gossiping about what she'd gleaned.

Not that it would matter. Jason had made up his mind, and he would make his move this evening, after afternoon surgery. He had no intention of waiting till the dastardly Dean showed up. He had no intention of wasting time asking Emma for a date, either. He was going to go straight to the heart of the matter...with a proposal of marriage.

CHAPTER TWO

Jason was beginning to feel a bit nervous, a most unusual state for him.

But understandable, he decided as he opened the side gate which led round to the back of Emma's house. It wasn't every day you asked a woman to marry you, certainly not a woman you didn't love, whom you'd never even been out with, let alone slept with. Most people would say he was mad. Adele certainly would.

Thinking of Adele's opinion had a motivating effect on him. Anything Adele thought was insane was probably the most sensible thing in the world.

Determined not to change his mind, Jason closed the gate behind him and strode down the side path to Emma's back door. A light was shining through the lace curtains at the back window, he noted with relief. Some music was on somewhere. She was definitely home.

There were three steps leading up to the back door, the cement worn into dips in the middle. Jason put one foot on the first step, then stopped to straighten his tie and his jacket.

Not that any straightening was strictly necessary. He was wearing one of his suavest and most expensive Italian suits, a silk blend in a dark grey which never creased and always made him feel like a million dollars. His tie was silk too, a matching grey with diagonal stripes of blue and yellow. It was smart and modern without being too loud. He'd even sprayed himself with some of the cologne he was partial to, but kept for special occasions.

Jason knew his mission tonight was a difficult one and he was leaving nothing to chance, using everything in his available armoury to present an attractive and desirable image to Emma. He wanted to be everything he was sure Dean Ratchitt wasn't. He wanted to offer her everything Dean Ratchitt hadn't. A solid, secure marriage to a man who would never be unfaithful to her, and whom she could be proud of.

Taking a deep, steadying breath, he stepped up, lifted his hand and knocked. In the several seconds it took for her to come to the door, a resurgence of nerves set his empty stomach churning. He should have eaten first, he thought irritably. But he hadn't been able to settle to a meal before hearing Emma's answer.

That *she* might think him mad as well suddenly occurred to him, and he was besieged by a most uncustomary lack of confidence.

She'll turn you down, man, came the voice of reason. *She's a romantic and she doesn't love you.*

The door handle slowly turned and the door swung back, sending a rectangle of light right into his face. Emma stood, silhouetted in the doorway, her face in shadow.

'Jason?' came her soft and puzzled enquiry. It had

taken him weeks of visiting Ivy to get her to call him Jason, he recalled. Even then, she still called him Dr Steel occasionally. He was glad she hadn't tonight.

'Hello, Emma,' he returned, amazed at his cool delivery. His heart might be jumping and his stomach doing cartwheels, but he sounded his usual assured self. 'May I come in for a few minutes?'

'Come in?' she repeated, as though she could not make sense of his request. He hadn't been to visit since her aunt's death. He'd attended the funeral, but not the wake, an emergency having called him back to the surgery. She probably thought that their friendship—such as it was—had died with her aunt's death.

'There's something I want to ask you,' he added.

'Oh...oh, all right.' She stepped back and turned into the light.

Jason followed, frowning. She looked more composed than she had the day of the funeral, but still very pale, and far too thin. Her cheeks were sunken in, making her green eyes seem huge. Her dress hung on her, and her hair looked dull, not at all like the shining cap of golden curls which usually framed her delicately pretty face.

It came to him as he glanced around the spotless but bare kitchen that she probably hadn't been eating properly since her aunt's death. The fruit bowl in the centre of the kitchen table was empty, and so was the biscuit jar. Maybe she didn't have much money to spend on food. Funerals and wakes did not come cheap. Had it taken all her spare cash to bury Ivy?

Damn, but he wished he'd thought of that before.

He should not have stayed away. He should have offered some assistance, seen to it she was looking after herself. What kind of doctor was he? What kind of friend? What kind of man?

The kind who thought he could bowl up here out of the blue and ask this grief-stricken young woman to marry him, simply because it suited his needs. He hadn't stopped to really consider *her* needs, had he? He'd arrogantly thought he could fill them, whatever they were.

God, he hadn't changed at all, he realised disgustedly. He was still as greedy and selfish as ever. When would he learn? Would he ever really change? Hell, he hoped so. He really did.

But knowing what he was didn't change his mind about his mission here tonight. He decided he was still a good catch for a girl whose circumstances weren't exactly top drawer.

'I'll get us some coffee, shall I?' she said dully, and without waiting for an answer moved off to fill the electric kettle and plug it in.

It wasn't the first time she'd made him coffee. She'd done the honours every time he'd come to visit Ivy. She already knew he liked his coffee in a mug, white with one sugar, so she didn't have to ask.

Jason closed the back door behind him and sat down at the old Formica-topped table, silently watching her move about the kitchen, seeing again what he'd seen that first time. The unconscious grace of her movements. The elegance of her long neck. The daintiness of her figure.

Once again, he felt the urge to touch her, to stroke that tempting neck, to somehow seduce her to his suddenly quite strong desire, a desire as strong and almost as compelling as he'd once felt for Adele.

Yet she was nothing like Adele, whose dark and very striking beauty had a sophisticated and hard-edged glamour. Adele's long legs and gym-honed body had looked incredibly sexy in those wicked little black suits she wore to work. And what she did for a red lace teddy had to be seen to be believed.

Somehow Jason couldn't see Emma dressed in either red or black, or having the body to carry off the kind of sexy lingerie Adele had been addicted to.

But, for all that, he found the delicacy of her shape incredibly sensual, as he did the feminine free flowing dresses she favoured. He imagined she probably donned long frilly-necked nighties for bed. But he wouldn't mind that. There was something perversely alluring in a woman covering up her body. It gave her a sense of mystery, a touch-me-not quality that was challenging and arousing.

Jason realised he had no idea what Emma might look like naked, other than slender. Her breasts looked adequate in clothing, but who could say what was bra and what was not? Not that he found small breasts a turn-off. He liked tiny, exquisitely formed things.

She was petite in height as well, head and shoulders shorter than his own six feet two, unlike Adele, who in heels matched him inch for inch. To be honest, he rather liked Emma having to tip back her head to look up at him. He liked everything about her. And, whilst he had no doubt now that he was still a selfish man, Jason vowed never to do anything to deliberately hurt her, anything at all.

'Sorry I haven't got any biscuits or cake to offer you,' she apologised as she carried the two mugs over to the table and sat down opposite him. 'I haven't felt like shopping. Or cooking. Or eating, for that matter.'

'But you should eat, Emma,' he couldn't help advising. 'You don't want to get sick, do you?'

A wan smile flitted across her face, as though she didn't think her getting sick was a matter which would overly trouble her at that moment. Jason frowned at the awful thought she might do something silly. She had to be very down and depressed after her aunt's death.

Yet he could not think of the right thing to say. It seemed his newly acquired bedside manner had suddenly deserted him.

They both sat for a few moments, silently sipping their coffee, till Emma put hers down and looked over at him.

'What did you want to ask me?' she said in that same flat, bleak voice. 'Was it something about Aunt Ivy?'

She wasn't really looking at him, he noted. He might have been wearing anything, for all she cared. Her lack of interest in his swanky suit and spruced-up appearance didn't do much for his already waning confidence.

'No,' he replied. 'No, it wasn't about Ivy. It was about you, Emma.'

'Me?'

The soft surprise in her voice and eyes showed she was taken aback by his displaying any personal interest in her at all. But he'd gone too far in his mind to back down now.

'What are you going to do, Emma,' he asked gently, 'now that Ivy's gone?'

She sighed heavily. 'I have no idea.'

'Do you have any other relatives?'

'Some cousins in Queensland. But I don't know them very well. In fact, I haven't seen them for years.'

'You wouldn't want to move away from Tindley, anyway,' he argued. 'All your friends are here.'

And *me*.

'Yes,' she said, and sighed another deep and very weary sigh. 'I suppose I'll open the shop next week, and just...go on as before.'

Go on as before...

Did that mean waste her life waiting for Dean bloody Ratchitt to return? Didn't she know any relationship with him was a dead loss, even if he did come back?

'I see,' Jason said. 'And what about the future, Emma? A pretty girl like you must be planning on marrying one day.'

'Marrying?'

He saw the pain in her face and wanted to kill that bastard. 'You would make some man a wonderful wife, Emma,' he said sincerely.

She flushed and looked down into her coffee. 'I doubt that,' she muttered.

'Then don't. I think any man you agreed to marry would have to be very lucky indeed.'

His words sent her head jerking up, and Jason saw the dawning of understanding over his visit. Shock filled her eyes.

'Yes,' he said before his courage failed him. 'Yes, Emma, I'm asking you to marry me.'

Gradually, her shock gave way to confusion and curiosity. Her eyes searched his face, looking for God knew what.

'But why?' she said at last.

He should have expected such a question, but it threw him for a moment. *Don't lie,* his conscience insisted.

'Why?' he stalled.

'Yes, why?' she insisted. 'And please don't say you're in love with me, because we both know you're not.'

Jason was tempted to lie. He knew he could be very convincing if he tried. He could say he'd hidden his feelings because Ivy had warned him off. He could say a whole load of conning garbage. But that was not what he wanted. If and when he married Emma, he wanted no lies. No pretence. From either of them.

'No,' Jason replied with a degree of regret in his voice. 'No, I'm not in love with you, Emma. But believe me when I say I find you very pretty and very desirable. I have right from the first time I saw you.'

He took some comfort from the colour which zoomed into her cheeks. Had she been aware of his admiration all along? If she had, she'd never given him any indication, although, to be fair, she'd always been prepared to spend time with him after he'd visited her aunt, always offered him coffee and conversation.

'A man like you could have any girl he wanted,' she countered. 'Ones far prettier and more desirable than me. There's not a single girl in the district who wouldn't throw herself at your feet, if you turned your eye her way.'

But not you, it seems, Jason thought. Damn, but this was not going to be one of his greatest moments. Failure was always a bitter taste in his mouth. In the past, there hadn't been a girl he'd fancied whom he hadn't been successful with.

Keeping his voice steady and calm, and his eyes firmly on hers, he went on. 'I don't want any other girl in the district, Emma. I want you.'

Now she flushed fiercely, and his confidence began to return.

'As I've already said, Emma, I think you'd make a wonderful wife. And a wonderful mother. I watched you with your aunt. You're so kind and caring. So patient and gentle. In the weeks I've known you, I've come to like you very very much. I thought you liked me in return. Was I mistaken?'

'No,' she returned, although warily. 'I *do* like you. But just liking someone is not enough for marriage. Neither is finding them attractive.'

So she found him attractive, did she? That was good. That was very good.

'You think you have to be in love?' he probed softly.

'Well, yes, I do.'

'Six months ago I might have agreed with you,' he said ruefully, and her eyes narrowed on him.

'What do you mean? What happened six months ago?'

Jason hesitated, then gambled on telling her the complete truth. There was a bond in revealing one's soul to another. And one's secrets. He wanted no secrets between them, not if they were to be man and wife. And, by God, they would be, if he had anything to do about it.

'Six months ago I was working with and living with a woman in Sydney. A doctor. I was madly in love with her and we were planning to be married this year. One day, one of her patients died. A little boy. Of bacterial meningitis.'

'Oh, how sad! She must have been very upset.'

'One might reasonably have thought so,' he said bitterly. 'I have no doubt you would have been devastated in her position. But not Adele. Oh, no. The child's death meant nothing to her, other than a slight blow to her ego. She was briefly annoyed she hadn't matched the child's symptoms with the cause, but then how could she, in a mere five minutes' consultation?'

'Five minutes?' She was shocked, he could see.

'That was the average length of a consultation in our surgery. Get 'em in and get 'em out as quickly as possible. Turn-over meant money, you see, and money was the name of the game. Not people. Or lives. Just money.'

She was staring at him, perhaps seeing the truth behind that vitriol, that it wasn't just Adele who'd been greedy and heartless in those days. He'd been just as bad.

He sighed. 'Yes, it's true. There, but for the grace of God, go I.'

'Oh, no, Jason,' she said softly. 'Not you. You're not like that at all. I watched you with Aunt Ivy. You're a very caring man, and a very good doctor.'

His heart squeezed tight. 'You flatter me, Emma. But I would like to think I finally saw the error of my ways and made changes for the better. That's why I left the city and came here, to find my self-respect again, and to find a better way of life.'

'What about your relationship with this Adele?' she asked, her expression thoughtful.

'I could hardly continue to love a woman I despised,' he said.

Her laugh startled him. 'Do you think love is finished as easily as that? Do you think finding out something unpleasant—or even wicked—about the person you love, smashes that love to smithereens? Believe me, Jason, it doesn't.'

Her words were like a kick to his stomach. She still loved Dean Ratchitt, regardless of his faithless character. And she believed he still loved Adele.

Jason tried to give that concept some honest thought. Perhaps he *did* still love her. He certainly thought about her a lot. And he missed her, especially in bed.

But neither of these factors would deter his resolve for a future between himself and Emma. Nor would he let her think he wasn't aware of her unrequited passion for another man.

'I've heard all about Dean Ratchitt,' he said abruptly, and her green eyes flared wide with shock.

'Who from? Aunt Ivy?'

'Amongst others.'

'And what...what did they say?'

'The truth. That you were engaged to be married and he betrayed you with another girl. That you argued and told him you would marry the next man who asked you.' He set steady eyes upon her own stunned gaze. 'So I'm the next man, Emma, and I'm asking you. Marry me.'

Jason was taken aback when her shock swiftly became anger. 'They had no right to tell you that,' she shot back at him. 'I didn't mean it. I *never* meant it. I can't marry you, Jason. I'm sorry.' And she tore her eyes away from his to smoulder down into her coffee.

Her passionate outburst stripped away the cool, calm façade Jason had been hiding behind. He was never at his best when his will was thwarted, especially when he believed what he wanted was for the best for everyone all round.

'Why not?' he demanded to know. 'Because you're waiting for Ratchitt to return?'

'Dean,' she snapped, glittering green eyes flying back to his. 'His name is Dean.'

'Ratchitt matches his character better.'

Her gaze grew distressed and dropped back down. 'He...he might come back,' she mumbled. 'Now that I'm alone, and...and...'

'An heiress?' he supplied for her cuttingly. 'I don't think this place will bring him running, Emma.' And he waved around the ancient and shabbily furnished room. 'Men like Ratchitt want more out of life than some old house in a country backwater, even if the front rooms have been turned into a sweet shop.'

She was shaking her head at him. 'You don't understand.'

'I think I understand the situation very well. He stole your heart, then broke it, without a second thought. I've met men like him before. They can't keep their pants zipped for more than a day, and they love no one but themselves. He's not worth loving, any more than Adele was. I've consigned her to my past. The best thing you can do is consign Ratchitt to your past, and go forward.

'Marry me, Emma,' he urged, when her eyes became confused. 'I promise to be a good husband to you and a good father to our children. You do want children, don't you? You don't want to wake up one day and find that you're a dried-up old spinster with nothing to look forward to but loneliness and rheumatism.'

She buried her face in her hands then, and began to cry. Not noisily, but deeply, her shoulders shaking. Jason was moved as he'd never been moved before. He raced round the table to squat down beside her chair. He reached out to take her small, slender hands in his and turned her tear-stained face towards him.

'I won't hurt you like he did, Emma,' he promised her with a fierce tenderness. 'I give you my word.'

'But it's too soon,' she choked out.

Jason wasn't sure what she meant. 'Too soon?' he probed. 'You mean since Ivy's death?'

'Yes.'

'Are you saying you might marry me later on?'

Her eyes lifted, betraying a haunted, hunted look. She was tempted to say yes, he could see. But something was stopping her.

'A month,' she blurted out. 'Give me a month. Then ask me again.'

Jason sat back on his heels and exhaled slowly, his surge of elation dampened by a prickle of apprehension. It wasn't a long time, a month. But it worried him. He didn't believe the wait had anything to do with Ivy's death. It was all to do with Ratchitt. She still hoped he'd come back for her.

The possibility of that scum showing up again was slight, Jason believed. But even that slight possibility sickened him. The thought of Emma falling back into his filthy arms sickened him even further.

And it did something else. It sparked a jealousy which startled him.

He'd never been a jealous man before. Not even with Adele. Emma was evoking emotions in him that were alien to all his previous experiences with women. Along with the jealousy, he also felt fiercely protective.

Still, he would imagine most men would feel protective of a girl like Emma. She was so fragile-looking. And so sweet. Someone had to stand between her and the Ratchitts of this world. She wasn't experienced enough to see just how bad his type were. How depraved and conscienceless.

'All right, Emma,' Jason agreed. 'A month. But that doesn't mean I can't see you during that month, does it? I'd like to take you out on a regular basis. We could get to know each other better.'

'But...but everyone with think that...that...'

'That you're dating Dr Steel,' he finished firmly. 'What's wrong with that? You're single. I'm single. Single people date each other, Emma. That's hardly grounds for gossip.'

Her eyes almost smiled through their wet lashes. 'You don't know the good ladies of Tindley.'

'Believe me, I'm beginning to. So what about dinner tomorrow night? It's Friday, and I always eat out on a Friday. We could drive over to the coast if you don't want to be seen with me here in Tindley for a while.'

She blinked the last of her tears away and looked at him with that searching gaze he found quite discomfiting. 'Are you going to try to get me into bed afterwards?'

Jason had trouble stopping the guilt from jumping into his eyes. Not that he'd had seduction on the menu for tomorrow night. He'd actually been going to leave that course of action for a week or two.

'No,' he said, with what he hoped was honest-sounding conviction. 'No. I wouldn't do that.'

She looked at him with frowning eyes. 'Why not?' she posed in a puzzled tone. 'You said you found me pretty and desirable. You also asked me to marry you. I imagined you fancied me, at least a little.'

'I *do* fancy you. And more than a little. Hell, Emma.' He stood up and raked his hands back through his hair. She'd thrown him for a loop by being so sexually direct. He hadn't expected it from her. Did she *want* him to try to seduce her or not?

'It's perfectly all right, Jason,' she said calmly. 'I've been brought up in a country town, not a convent. I'm well acquainted with the way men think and feel when it comes to sex. I know you haven't had a girlfriend since coming here to Tindley, and I'm sure you're fairly frustrated by now. I just didn't want to give you false hopes if I agreed to go out to dinner with you. You're a very attractive, experienced man, and I'm sure you know how to get to a girl. But I have no intention of sleeping with you. Not this side of a wedding ring, anyway.'

He stared at her, and her chin tipped up, revealing a side to Emma he hadn't seen before. A very stubborn side. A decidedly steely light gleamed in her green eyes and her attitude was definitely defiant.

One part of him admired her strong old-world standards, till he remembered Ratchitt. He'd bet London to a brick on that she hadn't given *him* the same ultimatum.

Or had she? he suddenly revised. Was that what

had happened between them? Had she refused to sleep with Ratchitt till he'd walked with her to the altar? Had he given her an engagement ring, then simply had other girls on the side till the prize would finally be his without any more arguing, for ever and ever?

'Do you want to take back your proposal now?' she asked challengingly. 'And your dinner invitation?'

'No,' he said slowly. 'But I would like an answer to one simple question.'

'What question's that?'

'Are you a virgin, Emma?'

CHAPTER THREE

THE following day felt interminable to Jason. Several times his mind wandered to that moment the evening before when Emma had looked him straight in the eye and told him the truth. Yes, she was a virgin. So what? Did he have a problem with that?

Did he have a problem with that?

Yes, and no.

Virginity wasn't something he'd encountered before in his personal life. Not once. Adele hadn't been a virgin. Not by a long shot. None of his other girlfriends over the years had been virgins, either.

The thought of making love to a virgin was a little daunting. Unknown territory usually was.

At the same time, the thought of making love to an untouched Emma on their wedding night appealed to a part of him he'd never known existed. He'd never thought of himself as a romantic before. But with Emma he was a different man. He recognised that already. She brought out the best in him.

And perhaps the worst.

Possessiveness and jealousy in men weren't traits he'd ever admired. He didn't like the way such men treated their girlfriends and wives. The females in their lives were flattered for a while—seeing their partners' passion as evidence of the extent of their love. Till reality set in and the flattery gave way to fear. He vowed to fight the temptation to be like that with Emma. He wanted her to be happy as his wife, never afraid.

And she *would* be his wife. He felt confident of that now. It was just a matter of time.

Time...

Jason glanced up at the clock on the wall. Five o'clock. And the small waiting room was still full of wheezing, sneezing patients. The beautiful spring weather had brought a rash of hay-fever sufferers, along with the blossoms.

Sighing, Jason rose from his desk and went to call in the next patient.

'I hope to heaven that's it, Nancy?' Jason said at long last, popping his head around the consulting-room door and sighing with relief when he spied the empty waiting room. The clock on the wall now said five to seven. Surgery usually finished around five-thirty and, whilst it sometimes ran late, it was rarely this late.

'Yes, all finished for the day, Dr Steel,' Nancy returned, in a sighing tone which Jason knew didn't denote tiredness, but a reluctance to leave the love of her life and go home to an empty house.

Not him. The practice!

Nancy had been Doc Brandewilde's resident receptionist - cum - secretary - cum - book - keeper - cum - emergency nurse for the past twenty years. She worked six days a week—seven, if and when required—and overtime without ever asking for an extra cent. Rising sixty now, she was as healthy as a horse and would probably be presiding over the practice for another twenty years at least.

She'd been a bit pernickety with Jason when he'd first arrived, till he'd discovered through Muriel that Nancy was afraid he'd fire her, if and when Doc retired, and Jason took on a new partner. Once Jason had reassured Nancy the job was hers for as long as she wanted it, their relationship had improved in leaps and bounds, although there'd been a temporary hiccup when Jason had suggested they get a computer system for the files and the accounts. He'd made the mistake of saying a computer would be more efficient and cut down on her workload. He hadn't realised, at that point in time, that Nancy didn't *want* to cut down on her workload.

Nancy had gone into an instant panic, then flounced home in a right snip, saying if Jason thought a machine could do a better job than twenty years' experience, then she didn't want to work for such a fool. After one day's mayhem in the surgery, Jason had gone crawling on his hands and knees, begging for her to return. He'd grovelled very well, calling himself an idiot from the city who didn't understand the workings of a country practice, saying if she could be gracious enough to forgive his ignorance and help him wherever possible, he was sure to get the hang of things in due time.

After that, they got on like a house on fire, even though Nancy maintained an old-fashioned formality in addressing him as Dr Steel all the time, which sometimes irritated Jason. Still, that seemed to be the way with people in country towns. They held their doctors in high esteem. Put them on a pedestal, so to speak. And while that was rather nice, Jason sometimes felt a bit of a fraud. If they knew his original motives for choosing medicine as a profession, they might not be so respectful.

'Sorry to love you and leave you, Nancy,' he said briskly, when it became clear she was going to linger, 'but I have to go upstairs and change.'

'Going out for dinner, Doctor?'

'Yes, that's right.'

'Where are you off to tonight?

'I thought I might drive over to the coast.'

'Seems a long way to go to eat alone,' Nancy returned on a dry note.

Jason opened his mouth to lie, but then decided against it. The people of Tindley would like nothing better than to see their second and much younger doctor safely married to a local girl. Doctors were as scarce as hen's teeth in some rural areas. They would exert a subtle—or perhaps *not* so subtle—pressure on Emma, to be a sensible girl and snap up the good doctor while she had the chance.

'Actually, no, I'm not going alone,' he said casually. 'I'm taking Emma Churchill.'

If he'd been expecting shock on Nancy's face, then he was sorely disappointed. Her smile was quite smug. 'I suspected as much.'

'You sus—' Jason broke off, grimacing resignedly. The small town grapevine never ceased to amaze him. 'How on earth did you know?' he asked, with wry acceptance and a measure of curiosity. No way would Emma have told anyone.

'Muriel said you were asking about Emma yesterday. Then Sheryl spotted you going through Ivy's side gate last night. Then Emma dropped in to Beryl's Boutique at lunch-time and bought a pretty new dress. On top of that, you've been clock-watching and jumpy all day. It didn't take too much to put two and two together.'

Jason had to smile. Jumpy, was he? You could say that again. He'd hardly slept a wink last night for thinking about Emma.

'And what will the good ladies of Tindley think about such goings-on?' he asked, still smiling.

Nancy laughed. 'Oh, there won't be any goings-on where Emma is concerned, Dr Steel, so you can save your energy and keep your mind above your trouser belt till the ring's on her finger. You *are* planning on proposing, aren't you?'

Jason saw no point in being coy. 'I am...but that's doesn't mean she'll say yes.'

'She will, if she's got any sense in her head. But there again—' She broke off suddenly, and frowned.

'If you're thinking about Dean Ratchitt, then I know all about him,' he said brusquely. 'Muriel filled me in.'

Nancy's expression was troubled. 'He's bad news, that one. Emma was really stuck on him. Always was, right from her schooldays.'

'I hear he's very handsome.'

Nancy frowned. 'Not handsome, exactly,' she said. Not like you, Dr Steel. Now, you're handsome in my book. But he has something, has Dean. And he has a way about him with the women, no doubt about that.'

'So everyone keeps telling me,' Jason said testily. 'But he's not here in Tindley, Nancy, and I am. So let's leave it at that, shall we? Now, I must shake a leg or I'm going to be late.'

'What time did you say you'd pick Emma up?'

'Seven-thirty.'

'Just as well she lives down the road, then, isn't it? Off you go. I'll lock up here.'

Jason dashed up the stairs, stripping as he went.

Like Ivy's sweet shop, the surgery was part of an old house which fronted the main street of Tindley. But where Ivy's place was small and one-storeyed, the house Doc Brandewilde had bought thirty years before was two-storeyed and quite spacious. Doc and his wife had raised three boys in it.

But they'd always wanted a small acreage out of town, it seemed, and once Jason had expressed interest in the practice Doc had bought his dream place and moved, leaving the living quarters of the house in town to his new partner.

Jason had been thrilled. He'd liked the house on sight. It had character, like those American houses he'd often seen in movies and which he'd always coveted. Made of wood, it had an L-shaped front verandah, with wisteria wound through the latticed panels, and a huge front door with a brass knocker and stained glass panels on either side. Inside, the ceilings were ten feet high, and all the floors polished wood. A wide central hall downstairs separated two rooms on the left and two on the right. It passed a powder room under the stairs, and led into a large kitchen which opened out onto a long, wide back verandah.

The two rooms on the left—which had once been the front parlour and morning room—had been converted into the waiting room and surgery. The two on the right remained the dining and lounge rooms.

Upstairs, there had been four bedrooms and one bathroom till a few years back, when Doc's wife, Martha, had brought in the renovators and combined the two smallest bedrooms on the right into a roomy master bedroom and *en suite* bathroom.

Jason rushed into this bathroom now, snapping on the shower and reaching for the soap. No time to shave, he realised. Pity. He'd wanted to be perfect for Emma. Still, he wasn't one of those dark shaven men who grew half a beard by five o'clock in the afternoon. His father had been dark—according to his parents' wedding photos. But his mother fair. He'd ended up being a mixture of both, with mid-brown hair, his father's olive skin and his mother's light blue eyes.

And a blessed lack of body hair, he thought as he lathered up his largely hairless chest.

With time ticking away, he didn't shampoo his hair. No way did he want to front up with wet hair. Snapping off the taps, he dived out of the shower, grabbed a towel and began to rub vigorously. Five minutes later he was standing in his underpants, scanning his rather extensive wardrobe.

No suit tonight, he thought. Tonight called for something a little less formal, which didn't really present a problem, except in making a choice. During his days as a dashing young Sydney doctor, he'd bought clothes for every occasion.

His eyes moved up and down the hangers several

times. Damn, but he had too many clothes! Finally, he grabbed the nearest hanger to his hand, and had already dragged on the cream trousers, pale blue silk shirt and navy blazer before remembering Adele had chosen that very outfit the last time they'd gone shopping together. She'd said it made him look like a millionaire, fresh from winning the Sydney to Hobart yacht race. She'd liked the image, said it turned her on. Nothing turned Adele on, Jason thought ruefully, like the thought of money.

He scowled at the memory, but had no time to change, consoling himself with the thought that at least the woman had had taste in men's clothes.

She came to mind again as he slipped on the sleek gold watch and the onyx dress ring he always wore. Both had been presents from Adele, bought in the first year of their three together. She'd given him quite a few personal gifts in those early days, mostly to enhance his new status as her partner.

Jason felt no personal attachment for the gifts any more. Usually he wore them without a second thought. But it didn't seem right to wear them when he was going out with the woman he was going to marry. He compromised by leaving the ring off but wearing the watch, because he liked knowing the time. Still, he determined to buy himself another watch in the morning. Something less flashy.

Scooping up his wallet and car keys, he turned and went forth to make his destiny.

Emma was ready and waiting for him, as pretty as a picture in a dress just made for her pale colouring and willowy slenderness. Round-necked and long-sleeved, it was mainly cream, but tie-dyed with splashes of peach and the palest orange. The material was light and crinkly, the style on the loose side, skimming over the gentle rise of her bust and falling in soft folds to her ankles. Her fair curly hair had obviously been shampooed and especially conditioned, for it shone in contrast to the previous night's dullness. Her face had some colour too—thanks to some lipstick and blusher, perhaps? Her eyes looked huge, even though he could see no visible make-up around them. When her neck craned back to look up at him, a faint smell of lavender wafted from her skin.

She looked like something from another world. A unique treasure to be cherished and cared for.

Was that how Ratchitt had seen her when he'd pursued her? Or was Emma just another notch on his belt? Had her purity enraged or enslaved him? Jason couldn't see the rotter who'd been described to him as having any sensitivity. He'd probably only asked Emma to marry him because he thought she'd come across once a ring was on her finger.

Jason was glad he'd failed to get what he wanted. He didn't deserve her. Men like him didn't deserve any decent woman, let alone *his* Emma.

And that was how he saw her now. *His* Emma.

'You look lovely,' he said, his eyes raking over her with what he hoped wasn't too impassioned a gaze. But, dear heaven, he *did* desire her. Yet so differently from the way he'd desired Adele.

Adele, he'd wanted to ravage. With her, he'd wanted to take, never to give. After all, Adele was one of those liberated females who shouted to the rooftops that they were responsible for their own orgasms, and she *had* been, at times. He and Adele hadn't made love, he now saw. They'd had sex. Great sex, it was true. But still just sex, the only aim being mutual physical satisfaction.

Emma made him want to give. Jason had no doubt that his priority when he made love to her would be to give her the most wonderful experience in her life, an experience which would banish Ratchitt from her mind for ever. His own pleasure would be secondary...which was an extraordinary first for him when it came to sex. Maybe he *had* changed, after all!

'You look very nice yourself,' she was saying. 'Very...handsome.'

At least she hadn't said rich.

'Thank you. Shall we go? My car's out in the street. There again,' he added, smiling a wry smile, 'my car's always parked out in the street.'

That was one thing his new house didn't have. A garage. There was room in the back yard, but no access down the side.

You can't have everything in life, son...

Jason glanced over at Emma, and his smile softened.

Maybe not, Mum. But I'm getting closer.

CHAPTER FOUR

'WHAT happened to your ring?'

Jason was about to fork a honeyed prawn into his mouth when Emma posed the unexpected query. Slowly, he lowered his fork to the plate, and looked across the table into her big, luminous green eyes.

Her asking such a question was telling, he thought, for it revealed she'd noticed his always wearing the ring in the first place. He reasoned that you wouldn't notice such a thing—or its absence—if you hadn't been watching a person fairly closely.

The thought flattered his ego.

He was also grateful that their conversation had finally become a little more personal. During the drive over to Bateman's Bay, Emma had been quiet and tense. Jason had had the awful feeling she was regretting coming with him, regretting having anything to do with him at all. Sensing her mood, he hadn't pressed her with any questions of his own, keeping the conversation light and inconsequential. He'd tried amusing her with an account of his relationship with Nancy so far, but, whilst she'd laughed at the right moments, he'd suspected her mind was elsewhere. Ratchitt, probably.

Now he wasn't so sure. Her eyes were focused on *his* face with a concentration which was total and exclusive. He almost preened under the triumphant and very male feelings her intense gaze evoked.

'I took it off,' he said. 'And left it off.'

'But why?' she asked, perplexed. 'It was a beautiful ring.'

'Adele gave it to me.'

'Oh,' she murmured, and looked down at her largely untouched Mongolian lamb.

'She gave me this watch too,' he added matter-of-factly. 'And it's going to be replaced in the morning as well.'

Her eyes lifted, confusion in their depths. 'You sound so calm about it.'

'I *am* calm about it. They have no meaning for me any more. I don't want anything of hers around me,' he finished with a betraying burst of emotion.

Her smile was rueful. 'You still love her.'

'Maybe. But I certainly won't for ever. Time cures all wounds, Emma.'

'That's a simplistic statement for a doctor to make, Jason. Time doesn't always cure. Some wounds fester further. Some become ulcers. Some turn into gangrene, and ultimately kill.'

There was a moment's stark silence between them. Jason was horrified at the depth of her pain over that creep. God, how she must have loved him! Was he foolish in thinking she would ever get over him, that they could be happy together? Was his ego overriding reality?

'What are you going to do with them?' she asked abruptly. 'The ring and the watch.'

'I'll post them to one of my brothers. Jerry, I think. He'll love them.'

'One of your brothers,' she repeated slowly, and shook her head. 'I'd forgotten you would have a family somewhere. I'm used to being alone, you see. I forget other people have parents and brothers and sisters.'

'Actually, I don't have any parents any more. My mother's dead and my father's God knows where. He ran out on Mum the year I was born. I don't have any sisters, either, but I do have five older brothers. I had six till Jack was killed in a motorbike accident, which leaves James, Josh, Jake, Jude and Jerry, working from the eldest down. I'm the youngest. Mum liked boy's names starting with J, as you can see.'

She smiled at that. 'And where are they, your brothers? What are they doing?'

'Scattered to the four corners of the earth. Since Mum died we don't keep in touch much. Typical boys, I guess. But Jerry's closest to me in age and I have a soft spot for him. He's not too bright, works in a clothing factory in Sydney and doesn't earn much. He's not married and lives in a boarding house. I send him some money sometimes. And clothes and things.' Actually he hadn't sent Jerry anything for ages, not since his break-up with Adele. His mind had been elsewhere. He vowed to do something about that, come Monday.

'I would have liked a big brother,' she said wistfully. 'But I was an only child. My parents were getting on when they had me. Aunt Ivy was my Dad's sister.'

'Ivy mentioned your parents were killed in a helicopter crash.'

'Yes. A joy flight. Ironic term, don't you think?'

'Tragic.'

'We were holidaying at this resort on the Gold Coast. I was ten. I was going to go up in the helicopter with them, but I'd eaten too much rubbish earlier, which hadn't agreed with me, and they left me behind because they thought I might be sick all over them. I actually saw the helicopter crash. It clipped the top of a tree as it was taking off and just tipped head-first into the ground.'

'What a dreadful thing for you to witness,' he sympathised.

'It was, I suppose. But, to be honest, I wasn't as devastated at some children might have been. I never felt my parents really loved me. I was an unwanted pregnancy, you see. Totally unexpected. Mum often said to Dad in my presence that they were too old to have a child, that I was a nuisance and she should have had an abortion.'

Jason didn't know what to say to that. He'd never felt his father's rejection because his father had never been around. To be constantly told you weren't wanted must have been awful. And not too good for your self-esteem. He might have been dirt-poor, but he'd always known he'd been the apple of his mother's eye.

'Anyway, when Aunt Ivy took me in,' Emma went on, 'I finally knew what it was to be loved and wanted. She was so good to me. So very, very good...'

Tears welled up in her eyes, but she staunchly blinked them away and wiped her eyes with the red serviette from her lap. 'Sorry,' she muttered, scrunching up the serviette and lowering it to her lap again. 'I promised myself I would be good company for you tonight. But I haven't been, have I? I won't blame you if you never ask me out again, let alone ask me to marry you again.'

He stared at her. What was that odd note in her voice? Had she had second thoughts since refusing him last night? Had she decided she was a fool to wait any longer for Ratchitt's return?

'I wouldn't worry about that, if I were you, Emma,' Jason said. 'I *will* ask you out again. And I *will* ask you to marry me again. Again *and* again. I intend asking you till the answer is yes.'

Her intake of breath was deep, but she let it out slowly. Her eyes never left his, as though she could plumb the depths of his soul if she looked long enough and hard enough. 'You're very strong-minded, aren't you?' she said.

'I know what I want. And I want you, Emma.'

Her face twisted into a tight grimace and he thought she might cry again. But she didn't. 'I...I don't think I'd make you a wonderful wife at all,' she said in a wretched voice.

'Why's that?'

'I... I...' She shook her head again and fell silent, her eyes dropping. But not before Jason glimpsed something that looked like guilt.

'Tell me why, Emma?' he demanded to know. If there was one thing he could not stand, it was being kept in the dark about something. He always needed to know the truth, no matter how unpalatable. He could cope with the truth. What he could not cope with was deception and evasion.

'Emma, look at me,' he ordered, and she obeyed, however reluctantly. 'Now, tell me why you said that. And be honest. Don't be afraid. Nothing you say will shock me, or make me angry.'

'You won't want to hear *this*.'

'Try me, Emma.'

She remained silent.

'*Trust* me.'

'Even if I agree to marry you,' she confessed on a whisper, 'I know I'll never forget Dean. And I'll never love *you* while Dean's here in my heart, no matter how much I might want to.'

Jason sucked in a sharp breath. He had guessed that was what might be troubling her. But still...hearing her say the words hurt far more than he could ever have imagined. He supposed at the back of his mind he'd hoped that eventually she would learn to love him, as he was sure he would learn to love her. He might still be in love with Adele at the moment, but he believed time would definitely cure *that* particular wound.

Time...

Of course! That was the crux of all his problems with Emma, he realised on a wave of relief. Time.

She might believe with all her heart in what she was saying, but that was now, this very minute, tonight, not tomorrow, or next month, or next year. Young love could be very intense, but young love, like a young plant, didn't survive indefinitely without being fed and watered. In the end it withered and died.

When Ratchitt didn't come back, Emma's love for him would wither and die as well, replaced by a new love, for her husband. Emma was too sweet and caring a person to deny affection if he was kind and attentive to her.

When she placed her crumpled serviette beside her plate on the table, he reached across and took her hand in his. She immediately stiffened under his touch, but he persisted, stroking the length of her fingers with gentle fingertips. 'You let me worry about what kind of wife you'll be to me,' he said softly. 'It's my job to make you happy, Emma. I think I can do that. In fact, I—'

He was startled when she snatched her hand away and put it back in her lap. 'I don't want you touching me like that,' she snapped, but would not look at him. There was a high colour in her cheeks which he found encouraging.

'I'm sorry,' he said, though he wasn't sorry at all.

Perhaps his lack of sincerity echoed in his voice, for her eyes swung back to glower at him. 'Don't ever say sorry to me when you're not! And don't ever, *ever* say you love me when you don't!'

He was stunned by her attack. He hadn't known she had that kind of spirit. Or such a temper!

'All right,' he agreed, still a bit shell-shocked.

Her fierce expression suddenly sagged, as did her shoulders. 'I'm sorry,' she said. 'I'm being a right bitch.'

He almost smiled. She had no idea what a 'right

bitch' was really like. Adele would eat her for breakfast.

'Why don't we stop apologising to each other,' he said, 'and eat up our dinner? You said you liked Chinese, remember? That's why we came here, and not that nice little Italian restaurant down the road.'

'I should have let you have your way,' she said as she toyed with her meal. 'I don't have much of an appetite lately. Do you like Italian food an awful lot?'

'Love it. But I also like Chinese, as well as German, French, Asian, Thai and Japanese. Fact is, I like food, period. As long as I don't have to cook it.'

'Normally, I love to cook,' she said.

'That's good.'

Her glance was sharp. 'I haven't said I'm going to marry you yet, Jason,' she reprimanded rather primly.

'I can live in hope, can't I?'

Her face clouded. 'They might be false hopes.'

'I'm willing to risk it.'

She stiffened in her chair. 'You don't think he'll ever come back, do you?'

'If he loved you, nothing would have kept him away. There again, if he loved you, he would not have done what he did in the first place.'

'You're so black and white,' she said, and sighed. 'I know what Dean did was wrong. And I can't condone it. But I also know he loved me. That's what makes everything so hard. Knowing that.'

'I see.' And he did.

When he'd told Adele he was leaving her, she'd been angrier than he'd ever seen her. How could he leave her when they loved each other so much? When she loved *him* so much? She'd tried everything to persuade him differently. She'd appealed to every weakness she thought he had. His ambition. His greed. His supposed love of city life.

And sex, of course. She'd thrown everything at him in that regard, tried everything, done everything.

And he'd let her, to his discredit. But he'd still walked away in the end. No, he'd run, before she could persuade him differently.

What would he have done, he wondered now, if she'd come after him? If she'd shown up during his first few weeks here in Tindley, when he'd thought he'd made the biggest mistake in his life, before he'd got used to the slower pace, before the town and the people and the peace and quiet had seeped into his soul.

Maybe—just maybe—he'd have allowed himself to be seduced back to Sydney, despite his better judgement.

So he *did* understand how Emma felt.

But people like Adele and Ratchitt didn't love as deeply or as long as others. Adele hadn't run after him, and Ratchitt had not come back.

He looked at Emma's depressed face and decided a change of subject was called for.

'Do you want dessert, perhaps?' he asked. 'I can see you're not going to eat that. But something sweet usually goes down easily.'

'All right,' she agreed, brightening. 'I wouldn't mind some ice-cream.'

'Is that all?'

'Yes, but with lots of flavouring.'

'Your wish is my command.' And he signalled the waitress.

He kept the conversation off lost loves for the rest of the night, and the drive back to Tindley was much more relaxed than the drive over. He regaled her with tales of his days at university, including some of the jobs he'd done to pay his way through.

By the time he eased his car into the kerb outside the sweet shop, Emma was laughing. 'You really worked in a gay bar?'

'For one evening only,' he returned drily as he switched off the engine and unclicked his seat belt. 'I didn't know it was a gay bar when I applied. I was walking past and saw a sign in the window saying 'Drinks Waiter Wanted'. I went right in and was hired on the spot.'

'When did the penny drop?'

'I realised my mistake pretty quickly that night, but I decided I could cope when I saw the size of my tips.'

'And?'

'I lasted three hours before I admitted defeat and quit. It seemed I wasn't as money-hungry as I'd thought I was. I had to leave, or end up in jail. Because, believe me, if one more guy had squeezed my buns as I walked past, I was going to give him a mouthful of fist.'

'Oh, that's so funny! Still, I'll bet you were a very cute young man.'

'Cute!' God, but he hated that word.

She laughed some more, her mouth falling open and her eyes dancing over at him.

He didn't mean to do it. He really didn't. But she was so lovely and he'd been so lonely. Before he knew it he was twisting in his seat, leaning over the gear lever, cupping her face and kissing her.

She didn't resist him, despite the firm pressure of his mouth on hers, despite his tongue taking advantage of her parted lips, despite all those old-world values of hers.

Oh, yes, there *was* a fleeting moment when she froze beneath his kiss, and her hands *did* flutter up from her lap to lie, palms flat, against his chest. But she didn't press him away, or try to shut her mouth. She accepted the intimate invasion of his tongue, and even moaned a soft moan of pleasure.

It was that soft moan of pleasure which opened the floodgates of his suppressed passion and showed Jason that his notion of always wanting to 'give' when making love to Emma was a fallacy. All of a sudden, giving had nothing to do with his feelings. Seduction became the name of the game. Seduction, and coercion, and possibly corruption. He wanted to make her moan again, wanted to make her forget who she was with, wanted her to surrender blindly to his will.

His mouth ravaged on while his right hand lifted from her face in search of her breasts. He found one through her clothes, warm and soft and surprisingly full. He kneaded it with his fingers, his thumb pad feeling for, and finding, the nipple. She moaned again, a muffled, choked sound which spoke of a pleasure which both shocked and delighted her. Her back arched away from the seat slightly, pushing her breast more firmly into his highly experienced hand.

Jason became so caught up in her responses—not to mention his own galloping arousal—that he didn't at first feel her pushing against his chest. It wasn't till her struggle turned panicky that he registered she was no longer wanting him to continue.

He'd never encountered resistance to his lovemaking before. Not at this advanced point. It stunned him, when, for a split second, he couldn't—or wouldn't—stop.

But then he did, his mouth wrenching from hers as he slumped back into his seat. His right hand, which moments before had been teasing her nipple into taut erection, lifted to comb his hair back from his sweat-beaded forehead.

'Sorry,' he muttered, furious that he might have just jeopardised his chances with her. But, hell on earth, she could have stopped him sooner.

She didn't say a word, just sat there, staring out of the passenger window with her hands clenched tightly in her lap. He saw that her breathing was still erratic and her cheeks were flaming.

'I said I was sorry, Emma,' he repeated tautly, his own breathing only now calming down. The rest of him wasn't in good shape, either, and promised a sleepless night ahead. Either that, or several cold showers. Any other alternative repulsed him these days. He wasn't a randy adolescent with no self-control. He was a man, a man who wanted a woman, not self-gratification.

Her head slowly turned and her eyes were wide and glazed-looking.

'You don't understand what you've just done,' she said shakily.

'What? What have I done?'

'You've shattered everything I've always believed about myself.'

'Which is?'

'That I would only ever feel like this with Dean...'

'Like what, exactly?'

'Like this...' And, taking his hand, she placed it on her breast again, so that he could feel the still hard nipple, plus the mad pounding of her heart beneath.

The extent of her sexual naivety really hit home. Jason conceded that he could use her lack of experience to bend her to his will—this very night, if he chose. But he knew she would regret it bitterly in the morning. And blame him.

He wanted her respect, as well as her body. Above all, he wanted her as his wife. So it was against his best interests to seduce her. But he wasn't going to let her go on believing his hand on her breast was anything more than it was.

'Love and sex do not have to go hand in hand, Emma,' he murmured as he knowingly and ruthlessly caressed her breast once more, watching in dark triumph as her lips gasped apart. 'What you're feeling is simply a matter of chemistry, and hormones.'

Abruptly, he removed his hand, more for his own benefit at that point than for hers. There was only so much he could take.

'You're a grown woman, Emma,' he said a little harshly, 'and you're probably as frustrated as I am.'

'But I thought that...that...'

'That frustration was a male domain? That nice girls didn't want or need sex?'

'No. Yes. No. I don't know. I...I thought nice girls had to be in love to want to make love.'

'I'm sure being in love would enhance the experience emotionally, but making love without love can still be...extremely satisfying.'

She stared at him, and he could almost read her mind. She was thinking what it might be like to make love with him. She'd enjoyed his kiss, thrilled to his hand on her breast over her clothes. How much more pleasurable to have his hands on both breasts, naked, to have his hands all over her, inside her, to have *him* inside her.

He had difficulty controlling the surge of arousal which threatened to make him throw all caution to the winds. He managed by focusing on what it would be like to have her on their wedding night, to have her every night afterwards, and whenever he wanted.

'We're sexually in tune, Emma,' he argued, in a desire-thickened voice. 'I can feel it. *You* can feel it. Marry me and I can promise you that that part of our lives will be very fulfilling.'

'You...you think our marriage could really work?'

'I know it could,' he reassured her firmly.

'But we don't love each other.'

'Love is no guarantee of happiness in a relationship, Emma. Surely you can see that. We like each other, and we want each other. We can plan things together with cool heads, instead of hot and sometimes ill-judged hearts. We'll make a great team.'

'You're very persuasive.'

'And you're very lovely.'

She flushed. 'You confuse me.'

'I want you.'

'I'm still not sure why you do.'

'You underestimate yourself.'

'No, I don't think so. I know what I am, and I know I'm not the sort of girl a man like you would normally look at twice. You've asked me to marry you on the rebound, Jason.'

'That's not true. I've asked you to marry me because you're exactly what I want in a wife.'

She frowned at this statement, and in truth it *had* sounded rather cold. Jason regretted it immediately. He leant over and laid a gentle palm against her cheek. 'So what's your answer to be, lovely Emma?' he asked softly. 'Will you marry me or not?'

'You...you were going to wait a month before asking me again,' she replied a little shakily, her eyes searching his as though in fear he was about to kiss her again.

'I've changed my mind. I don't want to waste another moment. Even if you say yes, it will take several weeks to arrange things. The licence alone takes a month, and the banns, three more weeks.'

'Banns?'

'In the church. I'm going to marry you before God, Emma. I'm going to promise to cherish you till death do us part. And you're going to walk down that aisle to me, wearing white, as befits your beautiful innocence.'

'Oh!' she exclaimed, her eyes flooding.

'Don't cry,' he murmured. 'Just say yes, and I'll spend the rest of my life making you happy.'

'You...you promise you'll never be unfaithful?'

'Never!' he vowed heatedly.

'If you are, I'll leave you.'

'If I am, then I'll deserve leaving.'

'So be it. Then, yes, Jason. Yes, I'll marry you.'

CHAPTER FIVE

'WELL?' was the first thing Nancy said to him the following morning. It was his weekend for Saturday morning surgery, unfortunately, otherwise he would have taken Emma engagement-ring-shopping. New-watch-shopping for himself as well.

He contemplated not telling Nancy, but discarded that as futile since he had a fatuous smile plastered all over his face. 'Can you keep a secret, Nancy?' he asked with stupid optimism.

'Dr Steel! What a silly question! Of course I can.'

'She said yes.'

Nancy clapped excitedly. 'Oh, that's wonderful news! Wait till I tell—' She broke off and looked guilty. 'I mean...how long do I have to keep this a secret?' she asked painfully.

'Do you think you might manage till Monday? That's when I'm going to take Emma shopping for a ring.' Whichever doctor took Saturday surgery had Monday off.

'I guess I could,' she said, if a little unhappily. 'But what if Emma tells someone herself beforehand?'

Jason almost laughed. What a terrible disaster that would be. Poor Nancy—to have a scoop and have to sit on it!

He thought about the situation and relented. 'Oh, all right, Nancy. Just let me pop over to the shop and let Emma know I've told you, then you can tell whomever you like.' In truth, he'd already rung Emma once this morning, to make sure she hadn't changed her mind overnight. She hadn't, but had sounded a bit dazed still. She was going to cook him dinner that night, but that was half a day away. A personal visit ASAP would clearly not go astray.

She was just opening the shop when he arrived, her eyes lighting up at the sight of him, before turning a little worried. 'Is there anything wrong?' she asked.

'Not at all. Shall we go inside, or shall I kiss you right out here in the street?'

Her look of shock-horror amused him. 'There's no use thinking you an keep our engagement a secret here in Tindley, Emma,' he said, smiling. 'Nancy already knows. I told her.'

'You *told* her! But why?'

'Because I want everyone to know. Don't you?'

He could see by her face she didn't, and his happy mood immediately deflated. 'What's the problem?' he demanded to know, his ego wounded. 'You're afraid Ratchitt will somehow get to hear you're marrying another man?'

She didn't deny it, and he had difficulty controlling his temper. Taking her elbow, he shepherded her into the privacy of the shop. The last thing he wanted was all of Tindley to overhear their arguing.

'Look, Emma,' he muttered once they were safely alone. 'I thought we had this out the other night. The man's a rotter. And he isn't coming back. When will you get that through your head? Stop being a masochist, for pity's sake, and give yourself a decent chance at happiness.'

Her eyes flashed at him. 'You think I *want* him to come back now?'

'Yes, I do. I think you're fixated on the creep and you won't be happy till you see him again. One part of me wishes he *would* come back, so that you could see just what you've been pining for. My guess is you've romanticised Ratchitt for far too long. If I knew where he was, I'd send him a damned wedding invitation.'

She paled. 'You wouldn't.'

'Too right I would. You think I'm frightened of him? I'd pit myself against the Ratchitts of this world any day, and I know who'd come out on top. Stack us up side by side, Emma, and love or no love, I know who you'd choose in the end!' His voice softened when he saw how stricken she was looking. 'He's low-life, darling. You deserve a lot better than that.'

'You...you called me darling,' she said shakily.

'And so you are,' he crooned, and drew her into his arms. She went willingly, her mouth soft beneath his. He kissed her just long enough and hard enough to make her breathless, and to show her just why she'd agreed to marry him. When he released her, she looked up at him with gratifyingly enslaved eyes. If he felt a tiny stab of guilt for using her blossoming sexuality to his own selfish advantage, then he argued it away in his mind. He was the man for her, wasn't he? He would make her happy, not Dean Ratchitt.

'Now, let's have no more foolish talk,' he said

firmly. 'I'm going to marry the loveliest girl in Tindley and I don't care who knows it!'

The next few weeks were the most amazing in Jason's life. His relationship with Emma deepened considerably with their time spent together. They discovered surprisingly similar tastes in books and movies, both liking character-driven plots you could really get your teeth into. Neither had any patience with mindless violence or horror stories. Science fiction only got the thumbs-up if the characters were believable and didn't have unpronounceable names. Jason had always read a book or watched a video to wind down after a long day's doctoring, and whilst he always bought new books—and only read them once—he liked nothing better than to see a favourite movie several times.

When he'd showed Emma his video collection, she'd expressed delight at spotting some favourites of her own, and insisted they watch every single one together. Over the past month or so they had, and then had such fun listing their top five in order of preference. Jason had been astounded at how close their lists were. They both put *Witness* at number one, and, whilst the next three had been in different order, they'd both selected *Braveheart*, *Chariots of Fire*, and *Tootsie* for numbers two to four. Only in the fifth selection had they differed, Emma liking Jane Austen's *Emma*—which he'd laughingly pronounced a form of nepotism—whilst he'd put in *Blade Runner*.

Yes, Jason was delighted at how the woman he'd chosen with his head and not his heart was working out. Just talking to Emma was great. And with any serious lovemaking sidelined till the wedding, they had a lot of time for just talking.

He discovered that his fiancée, whilst not academically brilliant, was creative, intuitive and sensitive, holding interesting opinions on a wide range of subjects. In the year she'd nursed Ivy, she'd read her aunt the newspaper every day from cover to cover, and had acquired a general knowledge which was surprising. Her memory was excellent. She still read the paper over breakfast every morning, she told him with pride.

Jason also admired her cooking skills, whilst she, in turn, simply admired him. He could feel it, and it fed his confidence where she was concerned. Once their wedding day was on the horizon, he really didn't care if Ratchitt returned.

The trouble was...it wasn't Ratchitt who showed up to spoil things. It was Adele.

It was two weeks before the wedding, a coolish Friday in late October. Doc was taking surgery that afternoon, and Jason was out on house calls. He'd just finished his last call and was heading back to Tindley when his mobile beeped. It was Nancy.

'A call came through for you, Dr Steel,' she said, a bit snippily. 'A lady doctor, no less. She said it was an emergency and she needed to contact you immediately.'

Jason felt his stomach flip over. 'Did she leave her name?'

'Yes. Dr Harvey. She said you would know her numbers off by heart,' Nancy added, suspicion in her tone. 'Anyway, she wants you to ring her back straight away.'

'Right. Thanks, Nancy. Dr Harvey's an old colleague from my Sydney days. Must have a medical problem she needs consulting on,' he found himself babbling. Hell, he could feel Nancy's dark disapproval down the line. The possibility—however remote—of her spreading a rumour around Tindley that Dr Steel was no better than Dean Ratchitt, and had some lady-friend on the side whilst he was courting Emma, brought panic. Emma was so vulnerable in that regard.

'Damn you, Adele,' he growled as he pulled over to the side of the road and dialled the number of the surgery first.

She wasn't there. She was on the road somewhere. Would he like her mobile number?

He said he knew it, which he did. He'd rung the darned thing a million times in his day.

She answered on the third ring.

'Jase?'

He ignored the jolt the sound of her voice made, not to mention the way she shortened his name. She was the only person who'd ever called him that, and he'd liked it straight away. Perhaps she knew the effect it had on him, for she'd always used it a lot, especially in bed. It had been *Yes, Jase; please, Jase,* and *Oh, God, Jase*, all the time, in low, husky whispers. It sent shivers down his spine just thinking about it.

'What do you want, Adele?' he said, quite coldly, determined not to let her see she affected him in any way. But the length of his celibate state didn't help. Only by reminding himself that he was just two weeks from marrying Emma could he keep the image of a nude Adele gyrating on top of him from exploding to the forefront of his mind.

But then she spoke again, and he was in imminent danger of being mentally unfaithful.

'It's great to hear your voice, Jase. I've missed you, darling. Have you missed me?'

Jason cursed her to hell in his mind.

'My secretary said you had an emergency,' he ground out in what he hoped was his best no-I-haven't-missed-you voice.

'It's your brother, Jase. Jerry.'

Jason snapped to attention. He'd sent Jerry the watch and ring, as planned, as well as a wedding invitation, and had received a small thank-you note, but a regret about the wedding. Jerry was chronically shy and didn't like formal dos.

'What about Jerry?'

'He came into the surgery last night with severe abdominal pains. Just by chance, I was the doctor allotted to him. I didn't want to take any chances so I had him admitted to hospital. Thank God I did, because he had a pretty bad night. They've done tests and he has some form of obscure food-poisoning. He's not critical, but he's a very sick man. The specialist said he won't be in the clear for a couple of days. I thought you might want to be with him.'

'What hospital?'

'Royal North Shore.'

'I'll come straight away.' Doc wouldn't mind taking over for the weekend in this situation. Jason had done the same for him when he'd had to go to a funeral in Brisbane a couple of weeks back.

A funeral...

Dear God, he hoped Jerry didn't die. 'How did you find my number, Adele?' he demanded to know.

'Oh, Jase,' she said, and he could hear the smile in her voice, that slow, sexy smile she used to give him as she undulated towards him across the bedroom, peeling off her clothes as she went. 'I've always known where you were. I was just waiting a while till you came to your senses. Six months I was going to give you, remember? It's been more than that now.'

Bulldust, he thought. She hadn't been going to contact him at all, not till this business with Jerry had made it necessary. She just couldn't resist playing *femme fatale*.

'I'll bet you're bored to tears down there in Hicksville,' she went on a droll tone. 'Country towns and country girls just don't have what it takes to keep a city boy happy. And you're a city boy, Jase,' she said, with a low, wicked little laugh. 'Through and through.'

He knew that. It had been a battle to adjust. But he *had* adjusted, and he *liked* his new life. Okay, so it wasn't wildly exciting. There were no first nights at the opera; no dinner parties in penthouses overlooking the harbour; no all-night sex sessions to drive him out of his mind.

But such things were just passing moments of pleasure. They weren't *life*, not the kind of life he wanted.

'Actually, I'm not bored at all,' he countered

coolly. 'I love it here. Fact is, I'm going to be married a fortnight tomorrow.'

She hardly missed a beat. 'No kidding? What happened, Jase? Get some poor little country girl in trouble, did you?'

'Trust you to think something like that. No, Adele, Emma isn't pregnant.'

'Emma. What a sweet goody-two-shoes name! Does she have a sweet goody-two-shoes nature to go with it? Or is she just a little bit naughty sometimes? Does she do for you what I used to do for you, darling? I can't imagine you doing without *that* once in a while.'

'Emma's a nice girl, Adele,' he said icily.

'Nice, is she? Oh, poor Jase. I think you *are* going to be bored. But you can always drop up to Sydney once in a while. Make some excuse to the little wife. A conference is always good for a weekend away.'

'I have no intention of doing any such thing, Adele. I left you seven months ago and you're staying left.'

She laughed. It wasn't a nice laugh. 'You won't forget me that easily, Jase. You might pretend to, but when you're lying in bed with your nice little wife, and having sweet goody-two-shoes sex every night, you'll think of me. I'll guarantee it.'

'I wouldn't count on it, sweetheart,' he snapped back. 'Thank you for doing the right thing by Jerry. It surprises me you didn't just give him an antacid tablet and send him home to die. I guess even the worst doctor in the world gets it right occasionally. Don't call me again, Adele. Goodbye.'

He was shaking by the time he hung up. Literally

shaking. He dropped the phone on the passenger seat and lowered his sweating forehead onto the steering wheel, glowering down at his lap and the evidence of what she'd done to him with just her voice.

Slowly, he pulled himself together, and put his logical mind into gear. Old tapes playing in his head, he decided. Not love. He'd lived with the woman for three years, made love to her countless times, become addicted to her brand of sex. Hard to wipe out any addiction in a few months. She was like a bad habit which was difficult to toss. Yes, his body had responded—out of habit, not out of true feeling. He refused to believe differently.

You won't forget me that easily, Jase...

He groaned, gunned the engine and headed for Tindley.

He didn't tell Emma the woman doctor who'd called was Adele. He wouldn't have told her it was a woman doctor at all except Nancy knew. And what Nancy knew the whole of Tindley would know, eventually. Thank God Adele hadn't given her Christian name!

He lied to Emma a second time as well, saying this particular lady doctor was a colleague from a different surgery from the one he'd worked at. She'd been given his number by Jerry, he said. Women doctors were common amongst GPs, he'd added, when she'd looked worried.

They weren't evil lies, he reasoned. Just little white lies so that Emma would not feel badly or think worrying things while he was away for the weekend.

He might have taken her with him, except he didn't

trust Adele not to show up at the hospital some time. He wasn't fooled by her nonchalant attitude over the phone. Adele hadn't taken at all well to the 'woman scorned' label. After his verbal insults today, he had no doubt she would love the opportunity to put a spanner in the works of *his* happiness. He didn't think she'd go out of her way to do that—such as a trip to Tindley—but his coming to Sydney was an opportunity she might seize. Someone as soft and sensitive as Emma would be a perfect victim for her brand of malice. Adele would leave no stone unturned to cut away at any confidence Emma had in their marriage working.

No, Emma and Adele had to be kept apart.

Fortunately, Emma was up to her eyes making her wedding dress, and was planning on finishing it that weekend. Jason was glad he didn't have to argue against her coming with him, as that might have made her suspicious. She didn't seem to mind his going, either. She could be a very independent little thing, happy with her own company.

Jason liked her independence. And her lack of material greed. He'd offered to buy her a dress if she couldn't afford one, but she'd refused. She'd given him a warm look at the time and said no, she *wanted* to make her dress. She was a good seamstress, she'd said, and he didn't doubt it. Her tapestries and collages were incredible, and snapped up by buyers the moment they were displayed on the sweet shop walls.

Not that she made much money out of them. The materials and framing ate into her profit. But it was a satisfying hobby and one which had brought in some good pocket money over the years, she'd explained when he'd wanted to discuss her financial situation. Not that he wanted any of her money, he'd quickly added. Whatever she earned was hers to do with as she pleased. Plus anything she inherited from Ivy. He wanted none of it.

She'd listened carefully, then told him Ivy hadn't owned much except the house and shop. He'd been dead right about the shop not bringing in much income as well. Less than twenty thousand a year. Still, Emma said she wanted to keep on working in the shop after their marriage, at least till she had a baby to care for, after which she'd find someone to run it. She didn't want to sell, or even rent out the rest of house. She was going to turn those rooms into a craft club, where the local women could come and work and chat and have a good time.

Jason thought that was a great idea, and said so. He supposed she wouldn't have got much for the rent, and what was money, anyway? It didn't make you happy. He was seeing that more and more these days.

Of course, it wasn't good to be poor, either.

But enough was enough.

'When will you be back?' Emma asked him as she watched him pack. She was sitting on the bed which would eventually be their marriage bed, a huge high brass number which had the comfiest of mattresses and didn't squeak, thankfully.

He looked at her sitting there, swinging her dainty feet, and felt an overwhelming surge of desire. What would she do, he wondered, if he started making love to her, not gently, but fiercely? If he pushed her back on the bed and mercilessly took her past the point of no return?

He could do it. He knew he could.

He'd felt the rising sexual tension in her over the weeks of waiting, weeks when he'd kissed her and held her, cuddled and caressed her till they were both breathing heavily and both wanting more. Last night, however, she'd totally lost it, which had been good for his ego but bad for his own level of frustration. She'd actually begged him not to stop, and it had taken one heck of an effort to deny her, with his hand sliding up under her dress at the time.

But he had, telling her highly agitated self that he knew she'd hate him afterwards if he went on. They only had to last two more weeks. What was two weeks when compared to a lifetime?

She'd shaken her head at him, her face flushed, her whole body still trembling. 'I wish I'd never started this nonsense.'

'It's not nonsense, Emma. It's sweet, and it's special, as you are special. I can't say I was thrilled by the idea in the beginning. But now I wouldn't have it any other way.'

She'd looked up at him with something close to love in her eyes, and he'd been blown away. He thought of that look now and abandoned all plans of a forced seduction. She would not look at him like that afterwards. He was sure of that as well.

'I can't say when I'll be back,' he told her truthfully. 'It'll depend on Jerry's condition. But I'll keep you posted. I have to be back to do morning surgery on Monday. At the very latest I could drive back very early Monday morning. At least the traffic wouldn't be so bad then.' With the advent of warmer weather, the tourist season was on the move again, and the Princes Highway was always busy.

'I'll miss you,' she said softly. He glanced over his shoulder at her and their eyes locked. Hers were like large, shimmering green pools, and he felt himself dissolving. Her mouth looked soft and inviting, as did her whole body, clothed as usual in one of her softly flowing feminine dresses. It was a simple and sweet style, with tiny mauve flowers all over it.

He wanted to rip it to shreds.

'I'll miss you too,' he returned, but stayed with his packing. Hell, if he kissed her now...

She fell silent, and he glanced over his shoulder a second time. Her hands were in her lap and she was twisting her engagement ring around and around. The diamond sparkled in the sunshine which was coming in the window and slanting across the bed. It wasn't a huge diamond, but it was what she'd chosen. Four smaller emeralds flanked the shoulders, the same green as her lovely eyes. He planned on giving her a matching eternity ring on their wedding night. The jeweller had secretly made it up for him after she'd chosen her engagement ring and he was to collect it next week.

'Is there something wrong, Emma?' he asked.

She looked up and smiled a taut little smile. 'No, I suppose not. I'm being silly. It's just that I had this feeling. You know...like someone was walking over my grave? A premonition. You...you will be careful, won't you, Jason? I mean, driving around those busy Sydney roads.'

He came over and sat down beside her, taking her by the shoulders and looking deep into her eyes. 'I'll be very careful,' he promised. 'Nothing, and I mean nothing, is going to stop me coming back to you.'

'You promise?'

'You have my solemn oath.'

Her sigh was deep. 'That's all right, then.'

Without kissing her, he rose and returned to his packing.

The trip up was a nightmare. Too many cars and trucks, and too many hold-ups. The road being dug up in too many places.

And then it started to rain.

It was well after dark by the time he turned his car into the hospital car park, later by the time he found Jerry's ward. His new watch said ten to nine as he strode up to the ward work station where he introduced himself as a doctor as well as Jerry's brother, thereby stopping any officious nonsense about it being after visiting hours. Then he asked if he could speak to the specialist in charge of Jerry's case.

The sister, who was an attractive woman in her thirties, smiled at him and said that unfortunately he wouldn't be able to speak to that particular doctor till morning. But Jerry's GP was somewhere in the building. Also unfortunately, they'd given his brother a sedative not long before, and he was probably asleep. But he was welcome to sit by his brother for as long as he liked. He was in 4F, last room down on the left.

Jason walked down the highly polished corridor to 4F, a long thin room which had six beds, though only four were filled. Jerry was lying in the furthest bed from the door. He had a window with a view over the city, but Jerry wasn't seeing any view at the moment. He *was* sound asleep.

Adele, Jason saw with some relief, was nowhere in sight. But he had no doubt she would show up soon. The thought rattled him somewhat.

He found thankful distraction in his brother's condition, inspecting Jerry's pupils and taking his pulse. When he read the chart at the foot of the bed, Jason felt momentarily nauseous at how touch and go it had been. Jerry's blood pressure had been appallingly low at one time, his temperature sky-high. He'd had seizures during the night as well.

No doubt he should have been in an intensive care unit, but he was a non-paying public patient, so what could you expect? Not presidential treatment, that was for sure. Still, things seemed to have stabilised, and he would probably pull through. He looked like hell, though.

Jason put the chart back and walked over to the window. He stared down at the city lights. Pretty spectacular-looking. Certainly not the unsophisticated colonial outpost the rest of world occasionally imagined. Sydney throbbed during the day, and hummed at night. It was an exciting and beautiful city, full of exciting and beautiful people.

'Hello, Jase... I've been waiting for you...'

Her husky voice curled around his gut and pulled him slowly round.

The sight of her, however, had a surprisingly different effect.

She was standing there at the foot of Jerry's bed, wearing one of those sexy little black numbers which had always turned him on. Not a suit, this time, but a dress, a short, chic crêpe sheath which looked as if it had been sewn on, it was so tight. The blatant outline of erect nipples shouted she wasn't wearing a bra, which wasn't a surprise. When did Adele ever wear a bra?

The shortness of the skirt suggested she'd opted against suspenders in favour of sheer shiny black pantyhose, the expensive kind which never ran, no matter how many times they were man-handled. Her feet were shod in the sort of sexy strappy high heels guaranteed to raise most men's blood pressure.

Jason's heart didn't miss a beat.

She sashayed a little closer, perhaps to show him she could walk in them quite well.

Practice did give one a wide range of professional skills, he thought cynically, as his eyes raked over her.

She took his thorough appraisal for interest, fairly preening before him. What she didn't know was the reality of her had had the opposite effect of her voice over the phone. That had stirred old memories, those old tapes in his head. Powerful old tapes. Adele in the flesh stirred nothing in him but a rueful surprise that he'd ever found her attractive, let alone addictive.

After being with someone as genuinely lovely as Emma—inside and out—Adele looked the hard piece she basically was. Her short dyed black hair was too harsh around her too pale make-up. She was wearing too much black around her eyes, too dark a lipstick on her full mouth and too much perfume all over her body. It fairly swamped him in its overpoweringly musky scent.

Sure, she still had a striking figure, with legs up to her armpits, but even that was now too much. He preferred Emma's tiny daintiness. He preferred Emma's lack of artifice. He preferred everything about Emma.

The worry that he might still be harbouring a lasting passion for Adele disappeared like a magician's assistant, and the relief was overwhelming. He was free of her at last. Free to forge a future with Emma without any hangovers from the past. His elation produced a real high.

He looked up at Adele's sultry face and laughed.

She pouted angrily. 'Why are you laughing at me like that?'

'I wasn't laughing at you, Adele. I was laughing at myself.'

'Meaning?'

'Meaning I've been a fool. Look, I don't hold any malice towards you, Adele, but you're wasting your time here. Go and find yourself another poor ignorant idiot you can infatuate with your undoubtedly skilful technique. I don't want it—or you—any more.'

Disbelief soon gave way to a dark determination. 'Give me five minutes and I'll bet I could change your mind about that.'

'Five minutes? Here and now?'

'Right here and right now,' she mouthed provocatively. 'Jerry's unconscious. We could pull the curtain around his bed.' She began to do just that, the action bringing her closer.

He snatched the curtain out of her hands and threw it back, eyeing her with a savage look which rooted her to the spot. 'Now listen to me, you miserable excuse for a human being and a doctor,' he hissed. 'I wouldn't let you touch me if you were the last woman on earth and the existence of the human race depended on it. You make my skin crawl, do you know that? Which is what you should be doing. Crawling, like the low-life serpent you are. Go crawl on back into your hole, darling, and give us decent folk some fresh air to breathe.'

She didn't say a word, just stared at him, her cold black eyes filling with hate.

He knew he'd gone too far. Far too far. But it was too late now.

Still without saying a word, she spun round on those dangerously high stilettos, and, without teetering a millimetre, stalked from the room.

Jason was left to watch her go, and to worry about what form her vengeance might take.

CHAPTER SIX

IT WAS a worrisome weekend, despite Jerry making a good recovery on the Saturday, and despite several phone calls to Emma eliciting a happy brightness from her which Jason doubted could be faked. The dreaded Adele had clearly not zapped down to Tindley during his absence to stir up trouble.

Each phone call home should have brought relief. Instead, it created more tension in him, an irrational fear that everything he'd been working towards and looking forward to was about to be destroyed. His relationship with Emma. Their marriage. His future.

He set off for the five-hour drive back to Tindley mid-afternoon on Sunday, leaving behind a much improved Jerry, but taking with him an escalating tension. He had to stop himself from speeding, only his promise to Emma to drive carefully holding him back.

But he wanted to see her for himself and make sure everything was all right. He drove into Tindley shortly after seven, parked outside the sweet shop and went straight round to her back door, knocking impatiently.

The moment she opened it, he knew he was too late. For as long as he lived Jason would always remember her expression at that moment. Never had he seen such dismay and despair. Her face was dead white, her eyes red-rimmed. That she'd been crying for hours was obvious.

He reacted as any man would. With a helpless, hopeless fury.

'What, in God's name, did that vicious, vindictive cow say to you?'

Her chin came up, as it did sometimes, and she eyed him suddenly with a chilling dislike. 'I presume you're speaking about Adele. Dr Adele Harvey, to give her her full name. The woman you lived with for three years. The woman who rang you about your brother on Friday. The same woman you made love to for hours on end this weekend.'

'No!' he burst out, and, launching himself into the house, he grabbed her upper arms and kicked the door shut behind him. 'No, no, no!' he repeated loudly, shaking her. 'A thousand times no!'

She glared down at the brutal grip on her arms till he released her.

'Which part is wrong, Jason?' she asked coldly. 'Which one of the many lies you told me isn't a lie?'

He grimaced at how bad things must look to her. 'Look, I only lied about who rang me because I was afraid you'd think the wrong things. And I was right, by the look of things. You did. You *do*! Damn it, Emma, I didn't sleep with Adele. I saw her briefly at the hospital on Friday night, and, yes, she did make a pass at me, but, no, I didn't touch her. And, no, I'm not still in love with her. In fact, I said some pretty nasty things, and I knew afterwards that she'd get even. And she has. She's rung you up and fed you a whole truckful of lies.'

Emma said nothing, just looked at him and started shaking her head.

'I did not sleep with her!' he shouted.

'I don't believe you. By the way, she didn't ring, Jason. She came in person. She was here, this afternoon, in this very kitchen.'

'Oh, God,' Jason groaned.

'Seeing her was worth a thousand words. She's everything I could never be. Strikingly beautiful. Incredibly smart. Stunningly sophisticated. No man would choose me over her if he had a real choice.'

Jason was appalled. Adele must have really put on a show. Toned down the make-up. Dressed more sedately. Acted as though she had feelings.

'You *had* to get out of Sydney, didn't you?' Emma threw at him, and he gaped. 'It was your patient who died. It was you who was shamefully neglectful, not Adele. She told me all about it.'

Jason's mouth finally snapped shut. 'Really?' he grated out. 'Do go on. I'm fascinated to hear the rest of the script of the best performance since Scarlett O'Hara in *Gone With The Wind*.'

'You can scoff all you like, but I know the truth when I hear it. She was crying,' Emma flung at him with a wealth of emotion. 'Crying her heart out. She told me she'd never loved any man as much as she'd loved you. But after what happened with the little boy she just couldn't work with you any more, or be with you any more. She finally told you to leave, and you did, without a backward glance.'

Jason could hardly believe his ears! He might have laughed if he hadn't been seeing his life go down the tubes at a frightening rate.

'She knew then that you'd never loved her at all,

that all you'd ever wanted was success and sex. She said your greed and ambition knew no bounds. You were eaten up with the idea of money because you'd once been so poor. She said she thought she had no feeling left for you, but when she saw you on Friday night, and you looked so upset about your brother, she felt sorry for you. And, of course, you *are* a very handsome man, Jason. No one could deny that.'

Well, thank heaven for small mercies, he thought bitterly.

'She asked you back to her place, just to give you a place to sleep for the night, but when you started making love to her she just couldn't resist. She said you always were a wonderful lover. Very...skilled. The next morning she wanted to tell you to go, and not come back that night, but she didn't have the strength of will. She hadn't had a lover since you left, and she's been so lonely.'

Jason was shaking his head in disbelief, but Emma just ignored him, determined, it seemed, to relay every lie Adele had fed her.

'By this morning she felt bitterly ashamed, even more so when you told her you were going to be married, to a simple country girl who would look after you like a king but never question what you did or where you went. She said you told her sex with me would bore you to death, but you aimed to supplement your bland day-to-day diet with more exotic fare from time to time. Women you'd met over on the coast. A widow or two you'd met during your rounds. The occasional trip to Sydney—and her.'

'Oh, *please*,' he groaned, but Emma swept on, regardless.

'She said after you left for the hospital this morning she kept thinking about me, a fellow woman, about to be used and deceived so cruelly. She drove down to apologise for what she'd done and to warn me to break off my engagement to you. And that's exactly what I'm going to do.' Her eyes filled and she began to take off her ring.

'You stop that right there!' Jason raged.

And she did, wide, tear-filled eyes flying to his.

'She lied to you, Emma. Can't you see that? Hell, I can prove that boy wasn't my patient. There are records. Documents. Death certificates. Besides, don't you think Doc Brandewilde had me checked out before he took me on as a partner? My reputation as a doctor is second to none. I can also prove where I stayed on Friday and Saturday night. In a hotel in North Sydney. Nowhere near Adele's place at Palm Beach. The man at the desk would remember me. I had breakfast in the public dining room both mornings. If you like I'll take you up there personally, so that you can ask around.'

Jason saw he was beginning to get through to her. Her mouth was dropping open and a big dollop of doubt was muddying that shimmering but clear green gaze.

'Then there's my calls to you,' he argued with ruthless logic. 'All made either from the hospital or the hotel. Phone records would prove that. None were made from Adele's number. You know how often I rang you. If I was supposed to be in bed with Adele half the weekend I would have had to call you some of the time from her place, wouldn't I? Think, Emma. Don't let her do this to us. Don't let her spoil what we have, which is something very special. Very precious. That's what's killing her. That I don't love her any more and that I've found happiness with someone else. She doesn't really want me, but she doesn't want you to have me, either. I promised you I would never be unfaithful to you and I haven't.'

'But how...how can I be sure of that?' she cried plaintively. 'There's no proof. If it were me who'd been unfaithful to you, at least there'd be proof!'

'You shouldn't need proof, Emma, not if you know me at all. You have my word.'

'Your word...'

'Yes,' he said. 'Or isn't that good enough?'

When she didn't say anything, his shoulders sagged, all his energy suddenly draining out of him.

'That's it, then,' he said wearily. 'We have no future anyway, if you don't trust me.'

When he went to walk away she grabbed his shoulder. 'If what you say is true...then that woman is truly wicked.'

'She is, Emma. Believe me.'

'Then how could you ever have loved her?'

'I thought you said someone being wicked was no barrier to love?'

'No, I meant *doing* something wicked. Not *being* wicked. Truly wicked.'

'Ahh... So your beloved Dean isn't truly wicked? He just made one mistake. That's a joke, Emma, and you know it. He'd been sleeping around in this town for years before he turned his attentions to you. And he didn't confine himself to single women, either, from what I've heard. Nothing's sacred with him, provided he gets his end in!'

'Don't be disgusting!'

'You have to be disgusting when you're talking about men like him, and women like Adele. They're both tarred with the same brush. They're selfish and amoral and mean. What they want, and can't have, they try to destroy.'

Her face began to crumple. 'I...I suppose you're right...'

He stepped forward and folded her into his arms before she could burst into tears, holding her close and stroking her hair. 'We can't let them spoil things for us, Emma. We have to stay strong. And stick together.'

He felt her lungs fill on a deep breath, then empty in a series of small, quivering shudders. 'It's so hard,' she said.

'Life *is* hard, Emma. But people sometimes make it harder by picking the wrong partners. Dean was as bad for you as Adele was for me.'

She drew back and looked up at him with glistening green eyes. 'Did...did you still find her attractive, Jason?'

'No. Not one little bit.'

'I find that hard to believe. She's very striking-looking. And so tall and stylish.'

'I much prefer you, Emma.'

'Do you still want to wait till our wedding night?'

'Yes.'

Perversely, she looked put out.

'Do *you*?' he asked gently.

'Yes. No. Oh, I don't know.' She pulled out of his arms and began to pace agitatedly around the kitchen. 'I don't know anything any more. All I know is that I can't stop thinking about it.'

'It?'

She ground to a halt on the opposite side of the table and threw him a reproachful look. 'You know very well what I'm talking about, Jason. Don't be cruel. It's all very well for you. You've been there, done that. You don't know what it's like to lie there in bed at night and wonder and worry.'

'What do you wonder and worry about?'

'Everything!'

Jason wasn't about to tell her he was a bit worried himself. He wanted to make their wedding night wonderful for her, but her virginity might prove a problem. From what he'd gleaned, a first-time experience could be pretty painful. Yet he wanted to give her nothing but pleasure. She deserved it. He would have to use every bit of knowledge and skill he had to ensure that she would experience *some* pleasure at least.

But first he had to allay her fears. Fear caused tension, and tension often caused more pain.

'It's going to be fine, Emma,' he said softly. 'You're a very responsive girl. Worrying isn't going to help things. Making the sex good is *my* job. Leave it up to me.'

Emma stared at him. 'She...she said you were a wonderful lover...'

'How nice of her,' came his frosty reply. 'Are you worried she was lying about that as well?'

'No. I'm worried you're going to find me a very big disappointment.'

'I doubt that, Emma.' Hell, he'd been aching to make her his own for weeks now. He'd enjoy himself, no matter what! 'Just don't expect too much too soon. Really good sex can sometimes take a little time.'

She frowned.

'And talking about it is the kiss of death,' he added with a wry smile. 'So shall we stop, and curl up together on the sofa and watch the Sunday movie? It's going on eight-thirty.'

She looked at him as though he was insane. 'No, no, I don't think so, Jason. I've had a pretty upsetting day, and my mind is too full to watch a movie.'

'Oh. Oh, all right.' He could never get used to the way women liked to wallow in their feelings. Now that she knew Adele had been lying, she should be happy. *He* was. 'I'll drop in for breakfast, shall I?'

'If you like.'

He frowned at her coolness. 'You're not still angry with me, are you, Emma?'

'You *did* lie to me, Jason.'

'But with the best of intentions, darling.'

His using that term of endearment did not go down well at all. 'Don't try to soft soap me, Jason. You lied. You didn't trust *me* to trust *you*. I hope you won't make a habit of that.'

He blinked at her stern tone, and the uncompromising glint in her eyes. She was a lot tougher than he'd realised. And quite stubborn about some things.

But so was he. 'I repeat, Emma. I did what I did because I didn't want you to worry. People tell little white lies sometimes.'

'I understand that. But I won't be taken for a fool. Or some simple country girl who won't ask questions.'

Jason sighed. It seemed Adele's malicious lies could not be wiped away so easily. He would have to win Emma's trust back with actions, rather than words. He vowed never to go anywhere without her for a long, long time. Not that he should have to. Soon, they would be married, and then they would spend every spare moment together.

His loins leapt at the thought. He could hardly wait!

CHAPTER SEVEN

'JASON, do stop fidgeting!' Martha hissed from the front pew. 'It took me ages to arrange that tie for you and it's perfect. Leave it alone.'

Jason lowered his hands, which were shaking slightly.

This marriage business wasn't as easy as he'd thought it would be. Certainly not this part, with him standing alone at the foot of the altar and a whole churchful of people staring expectantly, first up at him, then down the still empty aisle.

No best man stood by his side to calm him. He didn't have one, hadn't thought he needed one. Emma had decided against bridesmaids. She didn't have any girlfriends her age, she'd explained, her intensive nursing of Ivy preventing her from socialising this past year or so. She didn't have any close relatives, either. No one she could ask to walk her down the aisle and give her away.

Doc had agreed to do the honours, and he and his wife, Martha, were going to sign the certificate as witnesses. They weren't having a formal reception, either. Officially it was a quiet little wedding, but they'd issued a general invitation to everyone in town to come to the church, where Jason had organised for drinks and sandwiches to be served outside afterwards, weather permitting. Then, after photos were taken, the wedding cake would be duly cut and small speeches made under the large oak tree near the church steps.

Once tradition was satisfied, Jason was going to whisk Emma straight off on their honeymoon, an unknown destination on the coast where they would spend a week before they had to be back. Jason hadn't felt he could take any more time off than a week after only being at the practice for so short a time.

A quick glance at his new watch showed him it was twenty-five past three, yet the wedding had been booked for three.

Where in heaven's name *was* she? It wasn't as though she had to go far. The church was right in town, less than a minute's drive from the sweet shop. You could walk the distance if you had to!

Linking his hands agitatedly behind his back, he moved from foot to foot, and waited. The minutes dragged on. It had to be three thirty by now, and still...no sight of her.

She's changed her mind, he thought. She isn't coming.

Jason closed his eyes as the ghastly possibility took shape in his mind. She'd been different since the disaster with Adele. Quieter and more distant. She hadn't wanted to watch movies with him, hadn't wanted him to touch her or kiss her. Sometimes he'd caught her looking at him with watchful eyes, as though she didn't know what he was any more.

He'd done his best to reassure her. But the bottom line was their relationship had been damaged by what he'd done. He should have been honest with her. He could see that now. He was going to pay for his mistake, and pay dearly. She wasn't going to marry him.

'She's here,' Martha whispered to him, and Jason's eyes flew open in time to see that the minister was in place in front of the altar and everyone else's heads had swivelled round to face the back.

He felt sick with relief.

The organ started up with the 'Bridal March' and there she was...his bride...his Emma, floating down the aisle towards him in the most gloriously feminine wedding dress he'd ever seen, a fantastic concoction of chiffon and lace which fitted tightly around her bust before flowing right down to the ground in soft folds. The neckline was dangerously low-cut, displaying more of her breasts than he'd ever seen—or even felt—before. Tight lace sleeves encased her arms, in which she carried an elegant sheaf of white lilies. The soft folds of the skirt swirled around her legs as she walked, clinging to her slender thighs in the most tantalising fashion. A pearl choker adorned her elegant neck. A short lace veil covered most of her pretty face. A long, lace-edged net veil trailed out behind her, completing the truly stunning image.

That she had made her dress and veil awed him. That she would make such a sexy style surprised and aroused him.

He would have liked to see her eyes as she approached, but they were hidden from him by the veil. Only her mouth was visible.

It was totally unmade-up, he noted with some surprise. She usually wore lipstick, if only a pale colour. Had she forgotten to put it on? He could appreciate that nerves could make one forget anything. *He'd* had to go back for their rings. And arranging a simple tie had been beyond him.

He smiled a little nervously at her, but she didn't smile back. Neither did Doc.

Jason's stomach dropped to the floor. Something was wrong. He wasn't sure what, but something…

He frowned at Doc, but he was already turning away to join Martha in the front pew. When Jason took Emma's hand, it was trembling uncontrollably.

He wanted to ask her what was wrong, but the minister had already started the simple and traditional ceremony they'd chosen. Soon, Doc was coming forward to say his bit, and they were both vowing, 'I do.' Jason tried to sound cool and confident, but Emma's voice was small and strained.

The exchange of wedding bands was similarly tense, with Emma's hands shaking so badly he had to help her slide the ring on him.

Nothing, however, had been as fraught with danger as the part where the minister had asked if there was anyone here who knew of any reason why these two should not be declared man and wife. Jason had been holding Emma's hand at the time, and felt her fingers flinch, then freeze, felt her holding herself so stiffly that he worried she was on the verge of a faint.

And then it came to him. Why she was late. Why she was still in such a state.

She'd been waiting one last time, hoping that Ratchitt would return at the last moment to save her from marrying a man she didn't love.

Jason's emotions began to churn as he watched her

stiffly held form. What was she thinking or silently hoping for at this moment? That her long-lost love would suddenly stand up there in the organ loft, screaming at her not to do it? And if he did, what would *she* do? Pick up the skirt of her wedding dress and run away from him into her lover's arms, drive off into the sunset in the old rust-bucket of a utility he was sure to drive?

Perhaps. Jason didn't know. And he could hardly ask. All he could do was hold his breath, as she was holding hers, and wait till the ghastly moment passed.

It did, and he could almost feel the huge sigh of relief which rippled through the congregation.

Damn it, what did they know that he didn't?

They knew Ratchitt; that was what. Knew how crazy Emma had been about him. Knew the sort of man he was. Jason accepted that if and when he *did* turn up it would not be a good day.

But he refused to worry about that today. Today was his wedding day. Today, Emma was marrying *him*.

'I now pronounce you Man and Wife!' the minister said loudly, and the congregation burst into spontaneous applause.

Jason was stunned. His head turned to see a sea of smiling faces. They were genuinely happy, he realised. Happy for him and his bride. Happy for the little local girl with the broken heart who'd finally found a decent man to stand by her side. He felt humbled again, as he had several times since coming to Tindley. He hoped he would never let his lovely bride or this town down. He sure as heck aimed to give both his best shot.

He suddenly realised the minister had said he might kiss the bride.

Filled with resolve to be everything she could want in a husband, he turned to her with a warmly confident smile on his face and lifted the lace veil. Her eyes speared him with doubt. For they were shimmering with tears and clinging to his with a pleading desperation he could not understand.

What was it she wanted him to do?

'Emma?' he whispered on a puzzled, pained note.

'Just kiss me, Jason. Kiss me...'

So he did. Gently. Sweetly.

But it seemed that wasn't what she wanted at all, for she reached up and cupped his face with determined hands, digging her fingertips into his cheeks and drawing his mouth more firmly down upon hers. Parting her lips, she sent her tongue forward as she had never done before, entwining it around his in an erotic dance.

It blew him away, and before he knew it it was *her* face imprisoned within *his* hands, and he was kissing her as a lover might before sweeping his woman under him in bed, his tongue surging deep into her mouth.

By the time he released her, his ears were ringing and hot blood was thrumming through his veins. He stared with wide eyes down at her, expecting he knew not what.

She stared back up at him, her glazed gaze gradually clearing to an expression of the most heart-felt relief and heartbreaking gratitude. Jason almost reeled under its impact, and its implication. She was grateful to him. *Grateful!*

Hell on earth, he agonised with a flash of stark realisation. He didn't want her gratitude. He wanted her *love!*

Jason almost laughed. He'd thought he'd worked it all out. He'd thought he'd got round the problem of falling madly in love with a woman. The insanity of it all. The blindness. The uncontrollable passion. And the ultimate pain.

Yet he'd done it again. Not only done it again, but done it much more dangerously than ever before, because he not only loved this woman, he liked and respected her, wanted and admired her.

He would *never* fall out of love with Emma.

Yet she would *never* fall in love with *him*.

She'd told him. Quite emphatically.

Of course, underneath, he hadn't really believed her. He saw that now. His ego had fooled him, letting him think he could win her heart in the end. But after today's performance he doubted that would happen. Ratchitt had her heart. He would always have her heart...

The hurt was unbearable. He could not stand it. *He* wanted her heart. He wanted all of her. Oh, God!

You can't have everything in life, son...

'Jason?'

He blinked, his eyes clearing to see she was now looking up at him with worried eyes.

Gathering himself, he found a smile from somewhere. 'It's all right,' he said softly, and patted her hand. 'I just need something to eat.'

'We have to sign the register first.'

'Yes, of course.'

'And the photographer wants some extra shots in the church.'

'Ahh...'

Somehow he made it through everything. The signing. The photos. The cake-cutting and the speeches. At last he was helping Emma into the car and climbing in behind the wheel. Doc obligingly removed the tin cans which some boys had tied to the bumper bar. Jason told him to leave the 'JUST MARRIED' sign stuck on the back window. That could easily be removed once they were out on the road.

His mood brightened once they were on their way, the despair which had been hovering lifting. Logic came to his rescue once more. He'd overreacted back there in the church. Seen things with an overly black pessimism.

So he loved her. That wasn't bad. That wasn't wrong. She was his wife, after all.

Okay, so he couldn't tell her he did. Not yet, anyway. She wouldn't believe him at this stage. She'd warned him never to tell her he loved her when he didn't.

But he could *show* her he loved her. By his actions. By being whatever she wanted him to be.

His mind flew back to the way she'd kissed him in the church, and the penny dropped. She didn't want *too* much tenderness in his lovemaking. She wanted passion. She wanted to be swept off her feet. She didn't want to think, or to remember...

Jason gritted his teeth as the spectre of Ratchitt loomed once again in his mind. In a way, it would have been better if he *had* showed up some time. Jason could fight a real live man, but not a romantic memory. Ratchitt was like an evil spirit hovering over their life together, a third party trying to climb with malicious intent into their marriage bed.

Well, there would be no third party tonight, he vowed. Emma would know who was in bed with her, know who was her first lover, if not her first love.

Jason Steel. That was who. Her husband, and the man who *really* loved her.

CHAPTER EIGHT

'You were fairly late arriving at the church,' he said, lightly, and not at all accusingly.

They were barely ten minutes into the drive and she hadn't said a word. Jason had just climbed back into the car after ripping off the 'JUST MARRIED' sign. Emma had spent the short stop taking off her veil and laying it carefully on the back seat. Now she was back, facing the front, pulling at the pins which had anchored her hair up on top of her head. It tumbled down around her ears and neck in a mass of silky blonde waves.

Jason believed she'd heard him, but was pretending not to.

'Last-minute nerves?' he suggested, his hand reaching for the key but not turning it yet.

Her sidewards frown seemed innocent enough, but her hands were twisted tightly in her lap. Far too tightly.

'The reason you were late,' he repeated calmly, even while his own stomach clenched down hard.

'Oh. Yes. Nerves.' And she looked away from him through the passenger window.

Jason decided the only way to defuse the power this man had over Emma—and himself—was to bring him out in the open. 'Emma,' he said gently, his hand lifting from the ignition, 'let's not keep secrets from each other.'

Her head whipped round, her face flushing with guilt. 'What do you mean? Secrets?'

'Look, I know you were thinking about Ratchitt this afternoon in the church. I dare say he's the reason you were late, because you had some last-minute doubts. It's perfectly understandable and I'm not upset at all.'

What a pathetic liar he was! It had turned him inside out. Even Emma gave him a look which suggested his lack of anger was incredible.

But to tell her the truth—that he'd been beside himself with the blackest of jealousies—would not help him achieve his goal of taking away the mystery and the magic of this man whom Emma thought she still loved.

'I won't be angry with you,' he said, all the while mentally gnashing his teeth. 'I promise. So you can admit it. You *were* thinking about him, weren't you?'

'Yes,' she confessed in a strangled voice.

Jason swallowed. 'Tell me about him.'

Her eyes widened, then jerked away. 'No,' she said agitatedly. 'No, I don't want to. You can't make me.'

Jason had never felt so angry. Or so impotent.

Slowly, she turned back to face him, her expression quite determined. 'I've made my choice, Jason,' she told him. 'And it's you. Believe me when I tell you that if Dean had come to me today, before the wedding, and begged me not to marry you, but to marry him instead, then my answer would have been no. I would still be sitting here with you. So please...don't spoil our honeymoon by bringing Dean up again.'

Jason wasn't sure whether to be pleased or not. If only she hadn't sounded so bitter. If only her voice had been warm and passionate, and not so chillingly valiant, as though such a decision would have entailed an awful sacrifice on her part.

'I don't know what to say,' he said, truthfully enough.

She stared at him for a few seconds, then smiled a strange little smile. 'You could tell me you like my dress. You haven't mentioned it yet. Not once.'

And he hadn't. He'd been so rattled by what had happened in the church that he'd hardly been able to think straight afterwards, let alone remember his manners. Her gentle reproof reminded him how much such compliments mattered to women at the best of times. That he'd forgotten to voice his delight in her wedding dress was unforgiveable.

Saying sorry was highly inadequate, so he let his eyes speak volumes as they roved hotly over her, lingering on the provocative curves of her tantalisingly exposed breasts. How her nipples hadn't popped out was a downright miracle. He gulped down the lump in his throat, his follow-up words thickened with a maddeningly uncomfortable desire.

'When I saw you coming down the aisle in that dress, I thought I'd died and gone to heaven. Never has a bride looked so radiantly beautiful. Or so damned sexy,' he added drily. 'And then, when you kissed me like that...' He shook his head. 'You've never kissed me like that before, Emma.' She'd accepted his tongue in the past, but never used hers. Just thinking about the way it had snaked around his was turning him on again.

'Yes, I know,' she said, her eyes never leaving his. 'But you're my husband now. And I'm your wife. There's no reason for either of us to hold back any more, is there?'

'Hell,' he said. 'Don't say things like that, or I'll make love to you here and now.'

'If...if you like...'

He blinked at her. She could not possibly want him to make love to her here, in the car, in broad daylight. The thought that she'd been brought up to believe marriage entailed a female sacrificing herself on the altar of forcible conjugal relations repulsed him. His face must have revealed his thoughts because she looked distressed.

'Don't you want to make love to me, Jason?'

'Yes, of course I do. But I know women. They like making love in more comfortable conditions than this. You said the other week you were worried about what our wedding night would be like for you. Trust me when I tell you it's better we wait till later, when we have total privacy.' A car zoomed by at that moment, then another, highlighting the unsuitability of this setting for any form of real intimacy.

'Yes, I guess you're right...'

Now she looked disappointed. He didn't know what to do for the best.

'Emma, trust me.'

'I do, Jason.'

'Good. Then we wait a little longer.' Even if it killed him.

Against his better judgement, he leant over and kissed her, just to take that hurt look off her face. Her mouth was soft and melting under his, and his heart turned over and over. He could not help it. He pried her lips open again and waited to see if she would do it again.

She did, even more sensually than before, her tongue an erotically lethal weapon as it explored his whole mouth. Hell on earth, he thought, and abruptly lifted his head.

Her lips remained provocatively open for a few seconds, her mouth wet and inviting, her eyes tightly shut. Her sigh, when it came, was long and shuddering.

He turned from her to start the car, but not before he vowed to make her shudder again tonight, often, and with satisfaction, not frustration.

The unit he'd booked for their honeymoon was in Narooma, a small seaside town south-east of Tindley and only an hour's drive away. Narooma was quite a popular tourist spot during the summer holidays, being exactly halfway between Sydney and Melbourne, with a kind climate and lots to do. Fishing. Swimming. Boating. Bushwalking.

Restaurants were plentiful, as were clubs which provided plenty of entertainment.

And then there was the golf course, for which Narooma was quite famous. It was listed amongst the top ten courses in Australia, with several holes overlooking the Pacific Ocean, and one providing a chasm to drive over from tee to the green. Jason enjoyed a game of golf occasionally, and Emma had agreed to caddy for him.

Not that Jason had planned on too many outdoor activities. Now that his love for Emma had surfaced he planned on doing even less. He wanted her all to himself. Her desire had been palpable just now. Whether it was for him or just for sex was immaterial at this point in time. Beggars couldn't be choosers. Either way, he aimed to take full advantage of her blossoming sensuality during this coming week, to bind her to him as woman had been bound to man for centuries. With a baby.

He knew for a fact this week was right in the middle of her cycle. She hadn't wanted a period to spoil their wedding day and had chosen a safe date. She'd also said she wanted to try for a baby straight away herself. And why not? In her eyes, this was hardly the love match of the century. It was a marriage made with heads, not hearts. A marriage based on liking and friendship, caring and commitment. Having a family was a natural progression of such a marriage. Months spent just blindly making love simply for the sake of expressing one's love for each other was not on the agenda.

Jason almost groaned aloud at the thought. What he would not give...

'What a pretty place!' Emma exclaimed as they drove into Narooma. 'I love Tindley, but this could become my second most favourite town.'

'Become?'

'We'll have to come back every year to celebrate our anniversary.'

'We haven't celebrated the original yet,' he returned drily, his own frustration beginning to bother him. So many months without sex was enough to bother any man, he reckoned.

'I can't wait to get this dress off,' she said.

'Neither can I,' he muttered, and she laughed.

It broke his tension, that laugh, and he laughed too. Their eyes met and he could have sworn he saw love in hers.

But of course that was just wishful thinking. Still, he could pretend, couldn't he?

'Bags the bathroom first,' he said, and she pouted at him. 'Only joking,' he added. 'The place I booked has two bathrooms.'

'Two! But what for?'

'For impatient people?' he suggested, and she laughed again.

'No,' he explained, 'it's a holiday unit, and most don't come any smaller than two-bedroomed. According to the agent, it also has a fully equipped kitchen, L-shaped lounge-diner, a lock up garage, and a balcony with a view second to none. How does that sound, Mrs Steel?'

'Heavenly,' she said, smiling. 'The unit sounds pretty good, too.'

He almost said it then; he almost opened his mouth and told her he loved her. But he didn't. He didn't dare. She might think he was lying, or trying to emotionally blackmail her, or manipulate her. Better they continue as they were, as good friends and soon-to-be lovers.

'I have to collect the keys from the agency,' he explained when he pulled over to the kerb in the small hilly main street. 'Won't be a minute.'

He dashed in, ignored the stares of the two girls behind the desk, collected the keys and dashed out again. Several other passersby raised their eyebrows as he ran around and jumped into his car. He supposed it wasn't every day they saw a man in a formal black dinner suit dashing about the streets in daylight. But, hell, he was in a hurry.

The unit lived up to the wraps put on it by the travel agent, being very stylish, with great cane furniture and all the mod cons. Air-conditioning. A spa bath in the main bathroom. A huge television and video.

It was one of two units on the second floor of a brand-new block, tucked in behind the shopping centre and overlooking a park, with the small harbour beyond. Further out lay the breakwaters, and then the ocean. The balcony was totally private, with side walls. An outdoor table and two chairs in green ironwork sat in one corner, potted palms in the other.

When Emma slid back the large glass door and wandered out to admire the view, a cool breeze swirled the filmy curtains. Jason stayed inside, watching her and thinking she looked like an angel—or perhaps a ghost—standing out there in her long white dress, its full skirt whipped back by the wind, her fair hair lifting from her pale throat. The pearl choker gleamed in the dusky light, reminding Jason of the first time he'd seen her.

On that occasion her elegantly sensual neck had been enhanced by a gold chain. He recalled wanting to pull her head back with it so he could kiss her. He found the pearl choker infinitely more erotic. Why that was, he wasn't sure. Maybe because it looked like a collar, and evoked images of bondage which appealed to his dark side. He could almost understand why men of yore kidnapped fair damsels and kept them enslaved in dungeons for their pleasure, and theirs alone. There was something deeply primitive about such an action. And deeply arousing.

He'd waited long enough.

'Emma!' he called out sharply, and she whirled around, her hair whipping across her face.

He didn't have to say another word. She came back through the open glass door and slid it shut. Turning, she came to him across the thick blue carpet and slid her arms up around his neck, reaching up on tiptoe till her mouth was a breath away from his.

'Yes?' she whispered, her lips falling softly apart.

He groaned, and took what she offered, all his good intentions of focusing on her pleasure alone disintegrating under the wild passion of her response. For a few mad moments he was hers for the taking, not the other way around. But then she wrenched her mouth away and stepped back from him, flushed and trembling.

When her hands lifted to reach blindly behind her in search of her zipper, he swiftly pulled himself together. He had to take charge of his emotions, take control of the situation, or all would be lost.

'No,' he said firmly, forcibly ignoring his own fierce arousal. 'Let me...'

CHAPTER NINE

HE MOVED behind her and placed his hands on her shoulders, running them down then up her lace-encased arms, feeling her tension, deliberately stoking it as he repeated the action. Only when she trembled did he reach for and pull the zipper slowly down her back, bending at the same time to kiss the small span of flesh between the top of that tantalising necklace and the lobe of her ear. The zipper undone, his lips travelled upwards to that lobe, and then up to her ear, breathing softly into the soft, sensitive well.

'Oh,' she gasped, and a shiver ran down her spine.

He sent his tongue where his breath had been and she shuddered, her head twisting away from him so that his mouth connected with the pearl choker. He resisted the temptation to remove it, choosing instead to peel back her dress and expose her back, her stunningly bare back.

For a few seconds he thought she wasn't wearing a bra, but when he trailed a fingertip down her spine he saw she was actually wearing one of those strapless corsellettes which dipped dangerously down at the back in a deep V, the hooks connecting just above her waist, pulling that waist in tightly, forcing her slender hips to flare out more than her natural body shape.

The corset was white, and made of satin and lace. Boned at the front, no doubt, the kind of exotic, erotic contraption which pushed the breasts up and together, and gave any woman wearer a shape so feminine and desirable that just looking at her was enough to send any red-blooded man's desire meter sky-high.

Jason's was already off the planet. How he was going to control himself here, he had no idea.

Her dress suddenly slipped from his fingers and pooled on the carpet, and his heart jolted at the sight before his eyes. Oh, God! The corset had suspenders, and lacy stockings, and nothing to cover her bottom but a tiny thong of satin between the two most delectable buttocks he'd ever seen.

He turned her to face him, because that was safer. Or he thought it was till he did it, only to find himself confronted with even more torment. Her breasts pouted up at him, erect nipples half escaping the provocative push-up cups. The front was as dangerously cut as the back, lower down displaying an R-rated amount of smoothly shaven flesh. On top of that she was looking up at him with huge liquid eyes, as though he were some Greek God and she his sex slave.

If only she knew. *He* was the slave, not her. He would do anything for her. Anything.

'You are so beautiful,' he murmured, his gaze hot upon her. 'And so incredibly sexy.' He'd mistakenly thought she would never wear provocative underwear. He'd foolishly imagined he would prefer her in flannelette, instead of satin and lace.

Stupid, stupid Jason!

'I had to order it from a catalogue,' she said, blushing wildly. 'It...it only came this week.'

'It's...fantastic.'

'You really like it? I...I hoped you would.'

'I love it.'

'Do...do you want me to take it off?'

'Hell, no,' he said, and pulled her into his arms, kissing her ravenously, sliding his hands down her back to cup her buttocks and press her hard against him. The cool-headed part of him warned him to slow down; the rest ignored any such advice and just did what came naturally.

What came naturally was to pull her down onto the carpet, laying her beneath him as he ravaged her body with his mouth and hands. The flimsy lace cups were no barrier to his desires, easily pushed aside so that his hungry lips could claim the evidence of *her* arousal.

Emma's first gasp was followed by a low moan, then another gasp as he moved over to her other nipple.

The desperate sounds she made only inflamed him further as he licked and sucked both peaks into twin points of exquisite torment. Instinct and experience told him when to move on, breathing hot breaths over her satin-covered stomach while his hands found and unsnapped the press-studs between her legs. He peeled the scraps of material back and bared her to his questing lips. When she gasped and wriggled, he pressed one palm firmly down on her stomach while his other hand stroked her quivering thighs further apart.

He knew exactly what to do, and when to do it, ignoring her one feeble, fluttering protest, taking her swiftly beyond embarrassment to a world which knew no such inhibitions, only the most incredibly addictive compelling pleasure. He felt her surrender to its power, felt her lose herself to a rapidly rising rapture. She struggled for breath, sucking in deeply over and over as her body melted with heat. Her cries were sometimes gasps, sometimes moans.

And then she was really crying out, sobbing and shuddering as everything broke within her, her flesh spasming wildly under the most intense orgasm he'd ever given a woman.

Jason collapsed beside her on the carpet, her pleasure having unexpectedly become his pleasure, shocking him. He'd never known anything like it.

He lay like that for several minutes, before levering himself up on one elbow to look down at her. Her arms were flung out, palms up, by her sides. Her eyes were shut and her lips still agape.

He left her there and made his way into the bathroom, stripping as he went and stepping into the shower. Five minutes later he was back, scooping her up into his arms and carrying her towards the main bedroom.

Her eyes opened on a low moan.

'You're not going to sleep yet, Mrs Steel,' he told her mockingly. 'That was just the entrée. Now we're moving on to the main course.' And, laying her face down in the bed, he proceeded to unhook the corselete and strip her totally, even dispensing with the pearl choker this time. His movements were swift and impatient, his inadequately subdued flesh already on the rise again. 'Did you think your wifely duties were over for the night?' he asked as he snapped on a bedside lamp and rolled her over.

'Oh,' she gasped. 'You're naked!'

'And so are you, my lovely,' he said, and climbed onto the bed beside her.

Her blush was charming. But she made no move to cover herself. He propped himself up on one elbow and began to touch wherever his eyes travelled. She had a lovely feminine shape, even without the help of underwear. Breasts just full enough. A tiny waist. Slender hips and thighs. It was her skin, however, which fascinated him, with its satiny softness. Even her pubic hair was soft, curling damply between her legs. He stroked those legs apart once more and watched her while he explored every inch of her body. Her breathing quickened once more. Her eyes closed and her lips fell slightly apart.

His own pulse was racing, but he remained in control. What had happened earlier had calmed him somewhat.

He slipped one finger inside her and her eyes shot open. Again he knew exactly where to touch, searching for and finding that elusive G spot. Her eyes widened and her lips fell further apart on a low moan. He kissed her while one finger eventually became two, then three. She was opening for him, her flesh growing slick and eager. The moment she started grasping and releasing his fingers he stopped kissing her, his head lifting.

Till that moment he'd deliberately avoided thinking of his own arousal, so he was astonished to find he was bigger and harder than he'd ever been in his life. Not good, he thought, but what could he do about it?

'Jason,' she moaned when his hand withdrew.

'It's all right,' he muttered, and levered himself over, between her legs. Straight away she lifted her knees and wrapped her ankles and arms around him. Hell, she was a natural, he thought, as she rocked slightly back and forth, rubbing her moist flesh against him.

His aim was to penetrate her as gently as possible, so as not to hurt her. It was both agony and ecstasy as he eased his aching flesh inside hers, for whilst she was deliciously tight, her sharp intake of breath indicated that he *was* causing her some discomfort. She was tensing up; he could feel. He was losing her.

'Oh, God,' she cried painfully, but he simply could not stop at that point. What good would it have done, anyway?

'I'm sorry,' he rasped, and wondered if it might be better to do this more quickly.

Her resistance was surprising him. He'd thought he'd prepared her well. Or was his extra hardness the trouble? Whatever, his own pleasure at being sheathed inside her was incredible. He'd never felt anything like it. That, combined with the knowledge that she was finally his, that he was one with the woman he loved, broke his control.

He drove in to the hilt.

She didn't cry out. But she seemed stunned, lying motionless beneath him for a while, but then slowly, as he began to move, she came to life beneath him, moving with him, her nails digging into his back. He had her again. Clasping her tighter, Jason thrust harder and deeper.

'Oh,' she cried, but not from pain. From pleasure. He could hear it, feel it. And then she was coming around him, her muscles contracting wildly. He was powerless to last any longer, his seed racing towards her waiting womb, exploding deep within her. His groan was primal, his back arching with the force of his climax. He came and came and came.

Towards the end of his ecstasy, Jason realised his bride was crying, sobbing into his chest with he knew not what emotions. Regret that he wasn't Ratchitt?

Jason's stomach lurched, all pleasure ceasing.

It tore him apart that the reality of what had just happened was too much for her, that in her heart she still wanted Ratchitt. Jealousy ripped through Jason as he imagined she might have responded so intensely because she'd been pretending it was *Ratchitt's* arms around her tonight, *his* mouth pleasuring her, *him* buried deep inside her.

It took every ounce of maturity not to act like some stupid, self-destructive fool. Maybe she would have preferred Ratchitt, but she'd married *him*, hadn't she? He was the man lying in bed with her tonight. He would be the man in her bed every night. The man who would father her children. Ratchitt was the stupid fool!

So he pushed aside his futile thinking and held her to him till she stopped crying and fell asleep. Only then did he slide from underneath her and try to sleep himself. But he remained, wide-eyed and awake, till the wee hours of the morning, thinking of his mother's words once more.

You can't have everything in life, son...

She'd never been so wrong. Or so right.

CHAPTER TEN

JASON woke to a gentle hand on his shoulder.

'What?' he said, sitting bolt upright and almost upsetting the tray Emma was carrying.

She stepped back and stood there, smiling shyly down at him, all dressed and pretty in pale pink. 'It's almost eleven,' she said.

'Good Lord!' He rarely slept in like that.

'I've been up for hours,' she went on. 'Been shopping too, as you can see. There wasn't anything in the cupboards except tea, coffee, sugar and toilet paper. I thought you would need something more substantial than that.' She smiled and bent to place the tray on the bedside table. 'I know you usually have muesli for breakfast, but I didn't think honeymoons were the right occasion for the mundane. I looked for something more decadent. Did I do right?'

His eyes swept over the breakfast tray, with its grapefruit juice, bacon and eggs, fried tomato and sautéed mushrooms. Two slices of perfectly browned toast rested on a bread plate along with a dollop of butter. Two pretty paper serviettes were tucked underneath.

'You did very right,' he said, levering himself up to sit back against the headboard, careful to arrange the sheet over him so she wouldn't be embarrassed by his nudity. He could see the morning had brought back some of her ingrained innocence. The sensual partner of the night before had been put to bed, and in her place was the Emma he'd first met. A little shy. A little prim. A lot old-fashioned.

He was dying to go to the bathroom, but decided that could wait till she was gone. 'This is fantastic, Emma. You shouldn't have.'

'But of course I should! You're my husband.'

Something squeezed tight within him. He wasn't sure if it was satisfaction, or the beginnings of despair. Was that all he would ever be to her, her husband?

Probably, he decided, and tried not to look wretched. At least she couldn't claim last night had been for duty alone. She'd enjoyed it, even if she *had* cried afterwards.

Jason decided not to cry for the moon himself. He'd made the decision to marry with his head, and not his heart. Well, that was what he'd got. A wife who'd married *him* with her head and not her heart. He should be thankful she found pleasure in his body.

That was if it *was his* body she was finding pleasure in.

'I'll bring your coffee in a little while,' she said sweetly. 'Meanwhile, I'll unpack your clothes.'

'No!' he jumped in, quite sharply, and she looked alarmed. 'No, I don't want you to do that, Emma,' he went on more calmly. 'Look, I don't know what that aunt of yours brought you up to think a wife should be, but I don't expect you to be my maid. I can look after myself very well. I can look after my own clothes too. I can even wash and iron with the best of them. Not that I have to, in the main. I have a woman come in Mondays and Thursdays who takes care of that, plus the general cleaning. You know her. Joanne Hatfield. She's a single mum and can do with the money. I have no intention of letting her go just because I'm married now.'

Emma didn't seem to know what to make of his speech, looking confused and distressed.

'I married you for *you*, Emma,' he insisted, 'not to get a free housekeeper. Of course, I don't mind if you cook, since you're so good at it, but I'll be doing the washing-up every night.'

She looked horrified. 'I can't let you do that. I mean…what would everyone think?'

'I don't give a stuff what they think. You said you were going to go on working in the sweet shop. Working couples share the chores these days.'

'But you'll be working much longer hours than me some days.'

His smile was soft. She really was very sweet. 'Then on those days I'll let you spoil me and wash up as well, okay?'

Her smile was uncertain. 'If you say so…'

'I say so. Now…what would you like to do today?'

Jason was startled when her gaze instinctively moved over his naked chest, then over the rumpled bedclothes. Her cheeks were pink by the time her eyes lifted back to his. 'I don't really know,' she said, but her face told a different story. She wanted to spend the day in bed with him. She was just not bold enough to say so. 'Anything you like,' she added.

Anything he liked...

Now that was an invitation no man could turn down, let alone one in love with the lovely young woman making the offer. Any spoiling thoughts about Ratchitt were firmly pushed aside in favour of the reality of the moment, which was that Emma desired him. *Him.* Her husband.

But there were things he had do first. Breakfast. The bathroom. But after that...after that he'd do what she wanted. And how!

'Give me half an hour,' he said, his eyes holding hers. 'Then we'll see what I can come up with.'

'Darn!' Jason exclaimed, and sat up abruptly in bed. 'I forgot to do something.'

Emma glanced up at him. 'I can't think what,' she said in all seriousness. 'Is there anything else?'

He grinned, then dropped a kiss on her pretty pink mouth. 'That's for me to know and you to find out.'

They'd been making love on and off all day. At least, *Jason* had been making love to *Emma* on and off all day, and he had no intention of changing that formula at this stage. He certainly wasn't going to urge her to take the reins where lovemaking was concerned, not even in foreplay. He definitely shrank from suggesting she manually or orally arouse him. Whilst he enjoyed both activities a lot, he knew some girls never took to doing either, and he didn't want to risk repulsing Emma this early in their marriage. She was so responsive when he made love to her. Silly to spoil things by asking for more than she was ready to give.

There was plenty of time to become adventurous later in their marriage, he reasoned sensibly.

Besides, he didn't want another Adele, did he? He wanted his innocent and inexperienced Emma, who gained the most intense satisfaction from the simplest of lovemaking. He glanced at her now, with the sheet modestly pulled up over her bare breasts, her face still slightly flushed from her last orgasm.

'You stay right there,' he said as he scrambled out of bed. But when he walked round to the foot of the bed, where he was sure he'd dropped his clothes, they weren't there! 'Now where is that darned dinner jacket of mine?'

'Oh...I...er...hung it up. Before you asked me not to,' she added swiftly. 'It was lying on the floor, along with all your other things.'

He glared at her in mock exasperation, then laughed. 'You're forgiven. Where did you hang it?'

She nodded towards the wardrobe door on the right. He dived in and quickly retrieved the dark green velvet box, hiding it behind his back as he turned to face her.

'What are you hiding?' she asked eagerly.

'Not much,' he countered wryly, glancing down at his naked self with its surprisingly semi-aroused equipment. When he looked back up he was touched to see she was blushing. Not once, in all the years he'd been with Adele, had he ever seen that woman blush. He doubted she knew how.

Emma smiled. 'Stop embarrassing me and tell me what you have there.'

'Shall I bring it over to you?'

'Yes,' she said, then added impishly, 'All of it!'

'You saucy minx!'

'If I am, then you're to blame,' she accused. 'You make me think things and want to do things I've never wanted to do before.'

Jason liked the sound of that. 'Tell me more,' he said, and came over to sit on the side of the bed.

'Only after you've shown me what you have behind your back.'

'It's a deal.' And he produced the green velvet box. 'I meant to give you this on our wedding night. But I got waylaid by a wanton lady in wicked white suspenders.'

She frowned down at the box, then up at him. 'It looks like a ring...'

'Why don't you open it and find out for sure?'

She did, gasping at the sight of the diamond-and-emerald-encrusted band. 'Oh, Jason, it's lovely! Why, it matches my engagement ring exactly.'

'That was the idea.' He took it from the box and slid it on her finger.

'And it fits exactly!' she exclaimed delightedly.

'It's called an eternity ring,' he explained. 'Which means you're mine now, Emma...for ever and ever.'

She touched the ring as though it were the most precious thing in the world. 'For ever and ever,' she murmured, before looking up, her eyes clouding a little. 'That's a long time, Jason.'

His heart lurched, but he kept his face steady. 'For ever with you won't be long enough, my darling girl,' he whispered, and, bending, kissed her tenderly on the lips.

When his head lifted, her eyes were swimming.

'If you cry again,' he warned, wagging his finger at her, 'I will have to take stern measures.'

She smiled through her tears. 'Such as what?'

'Such as making you stay in bed with me for the rest of the day.'

'Oh, dear. Such a terrible punishment.'

Jason loved the way her lips started twitching as she struggled not to laugh or smile. She had a wicked little sense of humour at times. He'd found that out when they'd watched movies together.

He kept a straight face himself with great difficulty. 'Wives must be taught their place, right from the word go!'

'And where is that?'

'Under their husbands, of course. So tell me, wife,' he said, deliberately keeping things light and teasing, 'what are these wicked things I make you think of and want to do?'

Her eyes slid away, and the colour zoomed back into her cheeks. 'I...I don't like to say...'

'Emma, darling, there should be no secrets between husbands and wives, especially in the bedroom. Tell me. I won't be shocked.'

She opened her mouth, then closed it again, shaking her head. 'Oh, I simply can't.'

'Of course you can. I'm a doctor.' And he grinned at her.

'This is serious, Jason!'

'No, it's not, Emma. Not always. Sex can be fun too, you know. The trouble is people get all uptight about it. Like you did before our wedding. They wonder and worry too much. If you want me to do something, or vice versa, then you must say so. I know it can be a bit difficult, but once you've expressed your desires out loud the first time, you'll find it easier the next time. Try it. Tell me one thing you want to do. Just one thing.'

She stared at him, then visibly swallowed. 'All right...I'll try...' Her eyes shifted from his, and her cheeks glowed pink. 'Sometimes,' she said huskily, 'when I look at you, I...I want to touch you so badly. Like now...with you sitting there like that...I want to reach out and...and...'

He could see her courage was failing her, so he took her hand and placed it in his lap. Her soft fingers rested against his semi-erect penis. 'Oh!' she gasped, staring down at him as it began to swell further. Carefully, gently, he moved her hand so that she was stroking the rapidly lengthening shaft. Without being told, she suddenly encircled it totally with her hand and exerted a wonderful pressure.

He could not help it. He groaned. Her hand froze and her eyes flew up, their expression a mixture of confusion and fascination.

'Did I hurt you?'

'God, no,' he rasped. 'Keep going.'

'I...don't really know what to do.'

'You're doing wonderfully.'

'It...it feels lovely,' she whispered, once he was fully erect. 'So strong and smooth. And this bit is like satin...'

He sucked in a sharp breath when her fingertips grazed over the head. Her eyes came up again, and this time they were knowing upon him. 'You like that, don't you?' she murmured as she repeated the action over and over.

He must have choked out something.

'Tell me what else you like?' she insisted.

Jason was tempted, but he knew it was too soon. Besides, he was fast reaching the point of no return. So he whisked her hand away and whipped her under him on the bed. 'This,' he growled, and surged deep inside her. 'This is what I like.'

The week went quickly, but perfectly. Jason could not have been happier. Emma was everything he'd already known she was, and everything he'd hoped she'd be. Giving and loving, warm and quite wonderful. And that was *out* of bed.

In bed, she was just so beautiful, and flatteringly insatiable for him. Soon, she seemed to want him as much as he wanted her, and that was saying something, since he wanted her all the time. All those wonderful holiday activities Narooma was famous for swiftly went by the board in favour of traditional honeymoon activities. They did leave the unit to dine each evening, and they did sleep for a few hours each night, and sometimes during the afternoon, but that was about it. The rest of the time was spent making love.

On their last afternoon, Emma insisted on a visit to the golf course. 'You told me last week how much you were looking forward to playing a round here. Besides,' she added, 'I'd like to learn to play myself. Do you think you could teach me?'

Jason was surprised. Most young women didn't care for golf at all. 'Sure I could, but do you really want to play?'

'Married couples should do things together,' she stated simply. '"Whither thou goest, I will go".'

Jason liked the image of togetherness this projected, but not the reference to the dutiful wife, Ruth, in the Bible. Emma's penchant for duty rather irked him when applied to their personal relationship. He wanted her to do things with him because she enjoyed them, never because she thought it was her job. 'You should only play golf if you really enjoy the game, Emma.'

Her frown was thoughtful. 'I suppose so,' she agreed, then flashed him a sweet smile. 'But how will I know I enjoy something if I don't try it?'

Jason could not complain about the logic in that. 'Fair enough. Do you have any clothes suitable for golf with you? You can't play in a dress.'

'Will shorts and T-shirt do?'

'Fine. What about on your feet? You can't wear sandals. They'll slip.'

'I have some sandshoes.'

'They'll do. For now. But if you like the game I'll buy you some proper golf shoes.'

'I can afford to buy my own shoes,' she said, then hurried off to dress, leaving Jason to throw a rueful look after her. What a contradiction in terms she was sometimes! Wanting to be an old-fashioned wife to him, yet at the same maintaining a very modern financial independence.

Jason wasn't sure if he liked either, which was perverse. What was not to like?

Emma was a bit quiet on the drive to the golf course, her face turned away from him. She might have been admiring the scenery—the view of the blue Pacific beyond the emerald-green fairways *was* spectacular—but he had a feeling her mind was a million miles away.

'Is there anything wrong, darling?' he asked softly, after he'd parked the car and she was still sitting there, totally unaware that they'd come to a standstill and he'd turned off the engine. Her head jerked round, a stiff smile hiding whatever emotion she'd swiftly wiped from her face.

'No. Not really. It was just thinking...we have to go back tomorrow, and I...I can't say I want to.'

Jason sighed with relief. So *that* was it! She didn't want their honeymoon to end. An understandable reaction, but nothing to worry about. For a moment there...

He reached out to lay a gentle hand against her cheek. 'I know how you feel,' he murmured. 'It would be lovely to stay here for ever, wouldn't it? Just you and me and no one else.'

Her hand came up to cover his and she leant her cheek into his palm. 'Yes,' she said simply, and looked deep into his eyes, her smile soft and full of tenderness. Jason's body immediately began to ache for her again.

'Time for golf, I think,' he said, and abruptly withdrew his hand, turning his head away.

Teaching Emma to play golf was a welcome distraction. So was her aptitude for the game. 'You're going to be a handy little player with some practice,' he complimented her when they were well into the second nine.

'But I've lost nearly all of your balls!' she wailed. 'Two in the ocean and three in that awful lake back there!' And she pointed angrily at the wide water hazard now behind them, her face still flushed with frustration. Stubborn by nature, she'd been determined to hit over it and not around, and three times her ball had gone to a watery grave.

'There are worse things in the world, Emma,' he commiserated, 'than lost balls. I still have two left; one for you and one for me.'

She stared at him, then burst out laughing. Only then did he realise what he'd said, and he grinned. 'Yes...well, shall we call it a day and go home?'

'No fear! I'm determined to finish. And to get better.'

'You're darned good for a beginner already.'

Her surprised pleasure touched him. Hadn't anyone ever told her how good she was at anything before?

'Really?' she asked.

'Really.'

'I suppose I've always been pretty good at doing things with my hands.'

'Mmm. So I've noticed,' he murmured.

Her blush was instantaneous, her gaze skittering away from his. Jason could not help but smile. When her eyes returned to his, he was surprised to see they carried a slight frown. Her mouth opened to say something, then shut again.

'What?' he queried.

More colour, but this time she held his gaze and spoke. 'You once told me I shouldn't be scared to tell you anything...or ask you anything... About sex, that is.'

Jason tried not to look surprised, or alarmed. 'That's right.'

'What you said just now about my being good with my hands... I've been thinking... I mean... Oh, dear, this is difficult.' And she glanced around to see if anyone was nearby. There wasn't, the back nine of the course almost deserted at this late hour in the afternoon.

Jason waited patiently for her to get over her embarrassment and continue.

She bit her bottom lip and refused to look at him, instead finding a target for her eyes somewhere on the grass before going on in halting whispers. 'I've been wondering...why you haven't asked me...to...um... do *more*...in bed.'

'More?' Jason repeated a little numbly while his heart raced. 'What, exactly, do you mean?' he asked.

Her eyes swung to his, glittering now within their bright pink setting. She'd never looked so embarrassed, or so incredibly desirable. 'Oh, Jason, please don't make me spell it out. You must know what I mean. You're an experienced lover. And, while I'm not, I *have* read all those magazine articles which go on about the things men most like in bed. There's one especially, which crops up all the time. I've been wondering why you haven't asked me to do...that. You said I was to always ask for things I wanted. Why haven't you? Wouldn't you like me to...to do that to you?'

Her questions flustered him almost as much as they were flustering her. 'I...well...yes, of course I would. But I didn't think you'd want to. I mean...women usually only do that when they...er...um...'

'When they're madly in love with their partner?' she finished for him.

'I guess so,' he agreed uncomfortably, although he'd been going to say when they'd been having sex a little longer than a week.

'What about wives? Wouldn't wives generally do it for their husbands?'

'Emma, I don't feel comfortable with this conversation.'

'Why not?'

He was beginning to get irritated. *Why not?*

Because it smacked of the same thing as her wanting to unpack his clothes and iron his shirts and bring him breakfast in bed. He didn't want her thinking she *had* to do things like that, just because she was married to him. Fellatio was not part of her job description as his wife!

'Did Adele do it?' she demanded to know.

Hell, what was he going to say to that?

'Not often,' he mumbled.

'Did you like it when she did?'

Hell on earth! *'Yes,'* he bit out.

'Then I want to do it too,' she said stubbornly. 'I want to do everything you like. Do you understand me, Jason? I want to.'

He understood, only too well. And, while it pained him, he knew he'd be too weak to say no.

Besides, he thought with a bitterly ironic twist on what she'd said earlier, how did he know she wouldn't enjoy it, if he didn't let her try?

CHAPTER ELEVEN

JASON woke to an empty bed. Light was filtering in through the curtains, but it felt early. Rolling over, he picked up his watch from the bedside table and looked at the time. Only ten past five.

He glanced around, looking for Emma. The *en suite* bathroom door was wide open. She wasn't in there. Possibly she'd gone to the toilet in the main bathroom, so as not to wake him. That was the sort of sweet thing Emma would do.

The memory of her last night, however, did not conjure up thoughts of sweetness so much, but the most incredible passion. She'd been shy at first, though clearly determined. Any worry Jason had had over how he might react to such an intimacy was soon obliterated. He'd been so turned on he'd ended up demanding all she had to give. And more!

He hoped he hadn't shocked her.

She hadn't seemed shocked. She'd curled up to him afterwards like a cat who'd licked up all the cream, a purring, contented cat. Yet now she was gone from the bed, when she should have been still beside him, sleeping the sleep of the sated.

Throwing back the covers, Jason walked, nude, out into the living room. A pre-dawn glow was shining through the open glass doors and onto the blue carpet, the rectangle of light broken only by the figure on the balcony. Emma was standing there, leaning against the railing, watching the sun rise, wearing his navy silk bathrobe.

His mouth was creasing into a relieved smile when, suddenly, her head dropped into her hands and her shoulders began to shake.

Appalled, Jason rushed across the room and wrenched open the glass door. With a strangled sob, she whirled, and he saw the devastation in her face. The utter, utter devastation.

'My God, Emma,' he cried. 'What is it? What's wrong?'

'Oh, Jason!' She was shaking her head and crying at the same time.

He came forward and took her in his arms, oblivious of the cool dawn air pricking his skin into goose bumps. 'Tell me,' he insisted.

'I don't know how to,' she choked out, and buried her face into his chest.

He put a finger under her wobbly chin and lifted it so that she had to look him straight in the eye, even though hers were flooded.

'You must tell me what's wrong, Emma. You can't cry like this without telling me what's the matter.'

'It...it's Dean,' she confessed, bravely blinking back the tears. 'He's back.'

His hands dropped away from her face as though stung. 'Back? What do you mean, back? You mean in Tindley?'

She nodded, her eyes wide and frightened.

Confusion warred with apprehension within Jason. 'How could you possibly know that?' he asked. 'Did someone ring here during the night? Did you ring someone in Tindley?'

She shook her head. 'No.'

'Then make sense, damn you,' he snapped, and she flinched. He hadn't meant to swear at her, but God in heaven, he was only human. His worst nightmare was happening and he couldn't even get a handle on it.

'He...he came back the day of the wedding,' she said on a raw whisper, fear still in her face.

Jason was staggered. 'On the day of our wedding? When? Where? Where did you see him?'

'Please, let's go inside. I don't want to discuss this out here.' And she bolted from the balcony into the living room. He followed, slamming the glass door shut behind him.

'You *saw* him, didn't you?' he flung at her, and she flinched again. Oh, yes, she'd seen him, he suddenly realised. Nothing short of a personal visit could have rattled her like this.

And then the penny dropped, and a chill rippled through him.

'You don't have to say anything,' he said coldly. 'I get the picture. He showed up at your place just before the wedding. That's why you were late at the church. So what did he want? As if I don't know!'

'Oh, Jason, please don't be like that! Oh, God, this was what I was afraid of all this week. How you would react.'

'You should have told me, Emma.'

'When? When could I have told you without spoiling our wedding, and then our honeymoon? I wanted to give us a chance to start right. I didn't want you to…to…'

'To what? To know you were thinking of Ratchitt every time I made love to you? To worry that you might have married me just because you thought it was the right thing to do, or because you didn't have the guts to call the wedding off at the last moment? You haven't done me any favours, Emma, marrying me when your heart is breaking over another man. Which reminds me, just who *were* you going down on last night? Me, or Ratchitt?'

Her hand cracked across his face with such suddenness and such force that he reeled backwards, staring at her as his hand came up to gingerly touch his stinging cheek. Her look of indignant outrage might have convinced someone else, but not him, not when his stomach was reeling at the thought of the way her eyes had always closed last night, every time she'd taken him into her mouth.

'How dare you say that to me?' she exclaimed, her voice shaking. 'I chose to marry *you*, not Dean. What I told you in the car after the wedding was the truth. Yes, Dean came and asked me not to marry you but to marry him instead. I said no. I chose you, Jason. I did what you told me to do. Made the decision not to choose a partner who was wrong for me. When Dean came back after all this time, I began to see him as I'd never seen him before. He swaggered in, all macho selfishness, explaining nothing, caring about nobody but himself. It didn't bother him that he might be spoiling our wedding day. He was simply intent on grabbing what he wanted with no thought for anyone else but himself.'

'And did he?'

'Did he what?'

'Grab you?'

'Yes, he grabbed me. And he kissed me. He even told me he still loved me.'

'Did you believe him?'

'As you said, if he really loved me he'd have come back sooner. Dean arrogantly thought I'd still be waiting for him. He thought I'd still be in love with him.'

'And are you, Emma?'

'I don't know, Jason. I honestly don't know. All I can say is I'm not blind to him any more. And I don't want to marry him any more. I'm not sorry I married you. Not for a moment.'

A few seconds' elation was soon replaced by what Emma had left unsaid. She might not want to marry Ratchitt, but that didn't mean she didn't still want him. Jason could not get out of his mind the way her mouth had been totally devoid of lipstick at their wedding. That had taken a lot of kissing.

'Did you like it when Ratchitt kissed you?' he asked, sounding quite calm. But inside he was churning.

She could not meet his eyes, and he knew the truth.

Jason wanted to kill them both. 'So what was the outcome? What did he say to you when you knocked him back again? And I want the truth, Emma. No prevarications, and no watered-down words. What, exactly, did he say?'

'He...he said I was welcome to marry you, but that

one day we would be together, and nothing and nobody could stop that, certainly not some stupid fool of a husband I didn't even love.'

'Really? And how did he know that you didn't love me? Could it be because of the way you kissed him back?'

She went bright red. 'I didn't mean to, Jason. It was like I was in shock, or on auto-pilot, or hypnotised. When he pulled me into his arms, for one mad moment it was just like it used to be. I forgot…everything. By the time I woke up to reality, he was smiling smugly down at me. I…I wiped my mouth so many times after he was gone, you've no idea. I can assure you, Jason, that when you kissed me in the church that day, I…I liked it just as much.'

'Good God, am I supposed to be grateful for that?' He was shaking his head at her, fearing that he'd been right all along. She'd spent her entire honeymoon thinking of Ratchitt, trying her heart out to be a good wife, but wondering in the back of her mind if it might have been better with him.

His sigh carried defeat. 'I don't know what to say to you.'

'Tell me you you're glad I chose to marry you. Tell me you care about me. Tell me you trust me!'

'Hard for a husband to trust his wife when she's in love with another man, don't you think?'

'You knew that when you married me.'

Jason's mouth curled into a bitter little smile. 'True. I thought I could handle it when he was a mythical person. A memory. It's slightly different now that he's a real live man living in our town and vowing he won't rest till he seduces my wife!'

'He won't succeed in that, Jason.'

'Oh? Pardon me if I don't feel too confident of that. From what I've heard, Ratchitt would run rings around Casanova himself in the lovemaking department.'

'I wouldn't know about that,' she muttered.

'But you'd like to, wouldn't you?' he accused nastily, jealousy a festering sore in his heart. 'I'll bet you wished you hadn't been Miss Purity a year ago. I'll bet you wish you'd let him do what he wanted back then.'

'Yes, I do, in a way,' she confessed, totally blowing him away. 'But not in the way you think. Look, you've always wanted to know about my relationship with Dean. Maybe it's time I told you.'

'Maybe it is!'

'All right, then,' she snapped, green eyes flashing. 'But not till you've put something on. I can't stand here talking to you when you're in the nude. It's too...distracting.'

Jason didn't know whether to feel flattered or furious. Arching his eyebrows, he strode down to the bathroom where he wrapped a blue bathsheet around his hips. 'This do?' he asked caustically on returning.

'A bit better,' she said agitatedly, and walked over into the compact U-shaped kitchen. 'I think I'll make us some coffee while I talk.'

'Do that,' he bit out, and climbed up on one of the kitchen stools at the small breakfast bar.

She didn't say anything till the electric kettle was

on, and the mugs were all ready, then she turned to face him across the counter.

'I first became infatuated with Dean when I was twelve and he was seventeen. I was in my first year at high school, and he was in his last. Practically every girl in school was mad about him. He was just so sexy-looking and so...oh, I don't know. Dangerous, I guess. He did things other people didn't dare to do. He was always being hauled up in front of the principal. He was labelled a troublemaker, but back then he just seemed exciting. As the years went by he seemed even more exciting, and highly unattainable. He went off to Sydney for ages, then came back riding a motorbike. You know the type. He had an earring in one ear, a tattoo on his arm. He wore tight jeans and a sinful-looking black leather jacket.'

Jason could not believe Emma could have been taken in by such superficial garbage! Till he thought of his relationship with Adele. When had he ever done more than scrape the surface of her personality? He'd been attracted to the glamorous façade, and her animal sensuality. How could he blame Emma for finding Ratchitt attractive when *he'd* been guilty of a similarly shallow infatuation?

But couldn't she see that was all it was? Not love, but the combination of misguided hero-worship and sexual attraction.

A dangerous combination, though. He did concede that.

'But it wasn't just what he looked like,' she went on. 'He had a way of focusing his attention on you sometimes which made you feel so...desirable. And he used to say things. Sneaky little compliments whispered in your ear which made you feel wickedly sexy. Not just to me, of course. He said things like that to any female he fancied. I used to watch him with other girls and ache to have him ask me out. But I didn't think I was his type. Oh, he would flirt with me sometimes, but that was as far as it went. When he finally asked me out, I nearly died. I just couldn't handle it. I lost my head over him. I admit it.'

'Not enough to sleep with him, though?' Jason pointed out testily. He had to say something to bring this paragon of rampant sexuality and charismatic machismo down to size!

Emma sighed. 'You have no idea how hard that was.'

Jason had a pretty good idea how hard it had been for Ratchitt, if Emma had been as responsive to him as she'd been this past week. Not that he had any sympathy for Dean Ratchitt. Hopefully, some day soon, some jealous husband or boyfriend would do the world a favour and castrate the creep!

'I know you think I didn't sleep with Dean because of my old-fashioned stance about sex before marriage,' she elaborated, 'but that had nothing to do with it. Oh, yes, Aunt Ivy did bring me up to think that way, but that's not the real reason I held out. I wanted to go to bed with him like mad. But I was afraid if I did, he'd lose interest in me, as he always lost interest in every female he slept with. I thought keeping him dangling was my only chance to get him to marry me. Which was what I wanted at the time.'

Jason thought he did well to sit there and listen to

his wife tell him of the extraordinary lengths she'd gone to to get Ratchitt to marry her.

'Is that why you didn't sleep with me?' he couldn't resist asking, his voice scornful. 'Because you were afraid I wouldn't marry you if you did?' He didn't imagine that for a moment. He didn't rate such measures.

Strangely, she looked guilty as hell. 'No. I...I stupidly believed that if I hadn't let Dean make love to me this side of marriage, then no way was I going to let someone who...who...'

'Whom you didn't love,' he sneered.

'Oh, that sounds terrible! And it's not how I feel now. I mean...'

'Don't go saying you love me, Emma,' he snapped, 'just because you think you've hurt my feelings! Let's go on as we began, for pity's sake, and not pretend. We went into this marriage with our heads firmly screwed on. Don't let a week of sex confuse you. Not that it wasn't fantastic sex. I have to give credit where credit is due, Emma. How you kept your virginity with Ratchitt is a damned miracle. I just hope that now you don't have any virginity to protect you, your resistance to him finds a new reason.'

'I would never be unfaithful to you, Jason.'

'Are you sure, Emma? Are you sure it won't eat into you that you can still have Ratchitt if you want to. I know human nature. I have an awful feeling that in the end you'll be compelled to turn your romantic fantasies into reality. After all, how would I ever know? There'd be no physical proof now, Emma, just as there wasn't any proof with me and Adele.'

She drew herself up straight, shooting him a proud, yet hurt look. 'You'll just have to trust me, won't you? As I trusted you with that woman. I repeat, Jason, I married you, not Dean. I don't regret that. Not for a moment.'

'Is that why you cried on our wedding night?' he flung at her. 'Because you weren't regretting it was me in your bed and not Ratchitt?'

'My crying that night had nothing to do with Dean.'

'Then what did it have to do with?'

'With you,' she said. 'And me. With our being married and making love on our wedding night and not being in love. I thought that was rather...sad. I guess I *am* a silly romantic at heart. It took me a while to come to terms with the sort of marriage I'd agreed to. But I don't find it sad now, Jason. I think it's fine. Just fine. *More* than fine.'

She was trying to be conciliatory. But the word 'fine' was lukewarm at best. Being the person she was, Emma would continue to try to be a good wife to him, but the reality of her emotions hadn't changed. She would never forget Ratchitt, and never fall in love with *him*.

Which meant she would always be vulnerable to Ratchitt's attentions. If the creep hung around long enough, it was inevitable that one day—perhaps when their marriage was going through a bad patch—she would surrender to her unrequited passion for him. Then where would that leave him?

'Fine,' he bit out, and, whirling, stalked from the room.

He was in the shower when she came into the bathroom and stood outside the shower recess, staring at him through the glass.

'I do not want Dean like I want *you*, Jason. Haven't I shown you that this last week?'

A type of fury ripped through him. A fury born of fear and frustration, a fury rooted in his male ego and sexuality, in everything that had gone before and everything he feared might happen in the future.

He shot back the shower glass and grabbed her nearest wrist, yanking her into the shower with him. The jets of hot water plastered the silk robe around her body, revealing every curve and dip in her body. He didn't remove it, just wrenched it apart, then gobbled in her wet nakedness till he was fully erect. She gasped when he pried her legs apart and pushed up into her where she stood.

He didn't know if she was ready for him or not. There was too much water streaming down over their bodies to tell. Perversely, he didn't want her to be ready, or to find pleasure in his body. He wanted to use her, as men once used their wives of old, without asking permission, without having to care about their satisfaction.

How much of what had happened this week had been real? he agonised as he pumped up into her. And how much was pretence? Since she didn't love him, then what did it matter either way, as long as she let him do what he wanted, whenever he wanted it? She'd made her bed and now she was going to have to lie in it.

Except when the place of copulation was a shower, he thought bitterly. Then she could stand. His eyes flashed to hers and his thoughts were venomous. Why aren't you coming, wife? What's wrong with you this time? Not thinking of Ratchitt enough?

No sooner had this last thought intruded than she closed her eyes with a raw moan, sliding her arms up around his neck, reaching up on tiptoe and urging him on to a more powerful rhythm. Swearing, he hoisted her up off the floor, turning her and pressing her up against the tiles for better support. He hated her when her legs wrapped voluptuously around him, when her mouth gasped wide, when she came with the sort of violent contractions that could *not* have been faked.

It crossed his mind as he shuddered into her that *he* was the one being used here, not the other way around.

CHAPTER TWELVE

'JASON,' she said sternly. 'We *have* to talk.'

He looked up at her from where he'd been eating the mouth-watering casserole she'd served up to him fifteen minutes earlier and which he'd been eating in a brooding silence.

They'd been back at Tindley for ten days, and during that time their marriage had gone from bad to worse. He knew it was mostly his fault, but he couldn't seem to help it. His jealousy of Ratchitt was poisoning his love for her, making him surly and suspicious.

Their sex life had changed considerably since that last tempestuous time in the shower at Narooma. He still made love to her every night, but selfishly and savagely, uncaring if she came or not.

But she always did.

He began to hate her for that. He would have preferred her not to, so that he could imagine she was finding satisfaction elsewhere. His insecurities were beginning to feed upon themselves, and every day he wallowed in all sorts of disgusting scenarios where Ratchitt and his darling wife were concerned.

The worst had seemed to become concrete that very day when he'd gone into the bakery to get his lunch, and Muriel had given him an almost pitying look, followed by a most uncustomary lack of conversation.

'I don't know if should tell you this,' she'd finally said when she handed over his change, 'but Dean's been droppin' in at the sweet shop every time you go out of town on your rounds. I'm not spyin' on Emma, mind, but it's hard not to hear that bike of Dean's. It's very noisy. I...I just thought you'd like to know, Dr Steel. I'm sorry.'

He'd thanked Muriel politely, saying not to worry, he'd handle Dean Ratchitt.

Muriel had still looked worried.

Jason looked at Emma now across the dining-room table and knew his face was closed and cold. He wondered sourly if she was about to come clean, to confess all. Somehow he doubted it. Adultery was much more fun when kept secret and hidden.

'What's there to talk about?'

'I'm not pregnant,' she said. 'My period came today.'

His disappointment was fierce, as was his simmering fury. 'So?'

She winced at the word. 'I think it might be a good idea if I went on the pill for a while.'

'Oh, you do, do you?'

'Yes.'

'Why?'

'Because I don't think I want to bring a baby into this marriage yet.'

'Wise woman,' he said caustically. 'Husbands have a natural aversion to supporting other men's children.'

She looked terribly hurt. 'Oh, Jason... Don't...'

'Don't what? Don't face the truth? You think I don't know about Ratchitt dropping into the shop all the time? Parks his bike out the front and bowls up whenever I'm out of town, so Muriel tells me.'

'I didn't ask him to, Jason, if that's what you're thinking.'

'You have no idea what I'm thinking,' he snapped.

'I have a pretty good idea. But you're wrong. He only stays a few minutes. He just says the same old thing, then leaves.'

'Which is?'

'That he still loves me and he's there for me, when and if I ever need him.'

'In that case, why didn't you tell me?'

'I...I didn't want you thinking things,' she said wretchedly.

A memory shot out of the past, of his doing and saying exactly the same thing when he'd had that encounter with Adele. Emma had trusted him then, but he couldn't seem to find it in his heart to trust her. Perhaps because he loved her so much, and he knew she didn't love him back.

He put down his fork and pushed his plate away. 'Sorry,' he bit out. 'I don't feel hungry tonight. I think I'll go read a book. Don't wait up. I have a feeling I'll be very late to bed.'

'Jason, please don't leave me alone tonight.'

'Sorry, darling, no can do. You have your period, remember? Or were you think of offering me some other service in lieu of the real thing?'

'Why are you doing this?' she cried.

'What?'

'Spoiling everything. I...I can't go on like this.'

'Can't you? And what do you intend doing about it?'

'I don't know.'

'Let me know when you do.'

He whirled and walked out the room, beginning the worst week of his life. She didn't speak to him. Not once. Not a word. Every night she lay next to him in bed like a corpse, and he dared not even put his arm around her. Every morning she set out his breakfast before silently leaving to go to the shop. Every evening she cooked his meal, and even did the washing up, perhaps because she didn't want to ask him to.

And every other day Ratchitt called in at the sweet shop, according to Muriel.

The tension in the house grew till Jason knew he had to say something.

But she beat him to it.

'I've decided what I'm going to do about it,' she said abruptly as the evening meal drew to its usual silent end. 'I'm going to stay at the shop for a while. In my old room.'

He stared at her, his guts in instant turmoil. She was leaving him. Less than a month into their marriage and she was leaving him. A dark suspicion formed in his jealousy ridden mind when he realised her period would have finished about now.

'How convenient for Ratchitt.'

His snarled remark brought a look of despair. 'You

once said I'd be miserable married to Dean,' she told him bleakly. 'You promised to make me happy. I'm not happy, Jason. I'm more miserable than I've ever been in all my life.'

'I see.'

'Oh, no, Jason. You don't see at all, but I'm not about to explain. You'll only say more nasty things. You have a cruel streak in you, you know. And there I was, when I married you, thinking you were perfect.'

She stood up, and looked him straight in the eye. 'The washing up's yours tonight. And so is everything else till you come to your senses, Jason. I'm not leaving you. Not permanently. I take my marriage vows seriously. But you have to know I won't put up with this. Think about things, and when you want to talk— I mean *really* talk, not throw around useless accusations—then I'll come back. Meanwhile, you can abuse yourself instead of abusing me! As for food, I'm sure Muriel can always provide you with something to eat at night. Or Nancy, or any of the other women in town who still think the sun shines out of your bum! I know better!'

She spun on her heels and walked out on him. He just sat there for a long while, thinking about what she'd said, guilt consuming him over his abominable treatment of her. He knew in his heart she hadn't been unfaithful to him. Emma would not do that. If she was going to go with Ratchitt, she'd say so first. But that didn't mean the creep wasn't waiting in the wings, watching for his chance.

And he was about to get a big fat one, with Emma having moved out.

Finally, he jumped to his feet. What in hell was wrong with him? What was he doing letting someone like Ratchitt ruin his marriage? He should be fighting for his woman, not giving another man every chance to steal her away from him.

And 'fighting' was the operative word! Men like Ratchitt didn't understand polite conversation. They needed to have a fist shoved down their throats before they took any notice. Jason hadn't been brought up in the outer Western suburbs of Sydney for nothing. He might *seem* like a civilised man on the surface, with an educated voice and fancy clothes, but underneath he was still the same streetwise kid who'd had to stand up for himself with his fists more times than he could count.

Time for action. Time to bring things down to Ratchitt's level. Snatching up his car keys, he stormed from the house, slamming the door behind him.

Jason knew where he lived. He'd paid a house call to his cantankerous old man.

In took ten minutes to cover the distance from Tindley to the run-down old farmhouse which housed the Ratchitt men. Despite it being nearly eight o'clock by the time he turned into the rutted driveway, it was still light. With daylight saving, the sun was only just setting. A dark-haired man was tinkering with a mo torbike parked in the front yard. A vicious-looking black dog was barking insanely and jumping up and down on the end of a chain nearby.

As Jason drove up, Ratchitt unfolded himself from his hunched-down position, snarled at the dog to shut up, then turned to face his visitor.

Jason eyed his competition as objectively as possible. He wasn't handsome. Muriel was right about that. But he had those dark, bad-boy looks women seemed to go for in a big way. Long black hair which fell in rakish waves to his shoulders. Deep-set black eyes. And almost feminine lips. He wasn't overly tall, but his physique was all macho perfection, displayed overtly in tight stone-washed jeans and a chest-hugging black T-shirt. Jason could see without looking too hard that he was well built everywhere.

Ratchitt eyed him back as he climbed out of the car, a smug smile pulling at his full lips.

Jason wanted to wipe that smile from here to Broken Hill. But he wasn't a fool. He suddenly saw what might happen if he smashed the cocky creep's teeth in. Emma might not be impressed at all. She might tag *him* as a violent man, and run to Ratchitt's side, offering sympathy and solace.

Ratchitt's increasingly triumphant smirk told its own tale, and Jason suddenly realised he'd made a mistake in coming here. He'd fallen right into this devious fellow's hands. But it was too late now. No way was he going to back down and go off with his tail between his legs.

'The good Dr Steel, I presume?' Ratchitt drawled as Jason walked up to him.

'And the not so good Dean Ratchitt,' Jason countered drily.

Ratchitt grinned. 'The one and the same. To what do I owe the honour of this call?'

'I want you to keep away from Emma.'

'I imagine you do. But what you want and what I want are two different things, Doc.'

Jason didn't doubt it. 'She doesn't want you any more.'

He laughed. 'Is that what she told you?'

'In a word...yes.'

'Emma's always had trouble admitting what she wants.'

Jason was having trouble keeping his temper. 'I think you've lost touch with what Emma wants.'

'I don't think so, man. Her mouth *says* one thing but it *tells* you a different story. She's a good little kisser, isn't she? I taught her how. I'd have taught her a hell of a lot more if she'd let me. But that's beside the point. The point is what Emma wants.'

Jason was beginning to realise Ratchitt wasn't as dumb as he'd thought he'd be. He was a very street-smart and cunning fellow.

'You think I haven't always known what was going on in her life?' Ratchitt scoffed. 'I have eyes and ears all over Tindley. I know she never went out with anyone in all the months I was away. She was waiting for me to come back. And she'd have said yes, lickety-split, the next time I asked her to marry me. I was just biding my time. But then you came along, Doc, and cruelled all my plans. I made the mistake of not contacting home for a couple of months and what happened? She upped and got engaged, without so much as a single date beforehand. I'd like to know how you managed that, Doc?'

'I'll bet you would. For the record, though, I was her aunt's doctor during Ivy's last months, and a regular visitor to Emma's home. We got to know each other *very* well during that time.' And he could read into that whatever he liked!

'Oh, yes,' he sneered. 'Dear old Aunt Ivy. The stupid old bag, filling Emma with all that nonsense about no sex before marriage. She must have been out of the Dark Ages. If it hadn't been for her, Emma would have been *my* wife now, and I'd be living in clover.'

Jason frowned. In clover? What on earth was he talking about? He could not possibly think living in the back of the sweet shop would be living in clover. Or maybe he could, he rethought, glancing around at the dump he was living in.

When his gaze moved back to Ratchitt he saw that he himself was on the end of a wry appraisal.

'You know, when I first found out about you, I wondered what a fancy-pants doctor from Sydney wanted with my Emma. It couldn't be her stunning beauty, I told myself. She's a pretty little thing, but can't hold a candle to that brunette chick you used to live with.'

Jason gaped at him, and Ratchitt grinned with malicious pleasure.

'Yeah, Doc, I checked you out while you were away on your honeymoon. I checked *her* out as well. Thought it only fair. Now there's a top sort, and bloody good in the cot, even if I say so myself. Hardly had to do a thing. She told me a lot about you, too. How ambitious you were. How much money means to you. That's when it all clicked. I dare say old Aunt Ivy told you about Emma's trust fund while she was dying. It was from her parents' estate. It comes to her when she turns twenty-five, or when she gets married. Which ever happens first. Look, I don't blame you, Doc. Really I don't. But you should never poach on another man's property.'

Jason could not hide his shock. Not about Adele. He didn't give a damn about her. But about this trust fund. Emma had never mentioned it.

Any shock quickly gave way to a startling realisation.

'Good Lord! You were going to marry Emma for *money*,' he said.

Ratchitt looked taken aback by his attitude. 'Yeah, sure. Why else would anyone marry a silly little bitch like her? You didn't think I was in love with her, did you? I'm just like you, Doc. Love doesn't come into it. But I don't even have to marry her now, thanks to you. The money's there for the taking. She won't be able to deny me a thing, not once she lets me give her a bit of the old Ratchitt magic.'

Jason felt his hands begin to ball into fists.

'I hope you've done a good job in my place,' Ratchitt taunted. 'Virgins are notoriously easy to spoil, you know. They're a bit like a new bike,' he drawled, stroking the shiny black metal side as though it were a woman. 'You have to run 'em in kinda slow, or they're just never any good. Have to keep 'em well oiled too, or you're in for a bumpy ride.'

Something exploded in Jason's brain. Something white-hot and violent. Ratchitt was on the ground and out for the count before he knew what had happened. Jason was grimacing and shaking his bleeding knuckles when the cattle dog which had been chained up suddenly leapt at him, its fang-like jaws closing over his clean white shirt-sleeve, just below his elbow.

CHAPTER THIRTEEN

'Now you know what it's like to be on the other end of sutures,' Doc said as he pulled the cotton tight and reached for the scissors.

Jason had called his partner from his mobile phone, after old Jim Ratchitt had pulled the dog off him and he'd escaped into the sanctuary of his car. They'd met up at the surgery in town. No point in going to Doc's house, since it was a good fifteen-minute drive on the other side of Tindley.

Jason gritted his teeth. 'Do you have to be so rough?'

'Grown men who brawl like louts don't deserve to be treated with kid gloves.'

'A dog did this,' Jason growled. 'Not a man.'

'So you told me. You up to date with your rabies shots?'

'*What?*'

'Only joking,' Doc said, smiling through his white moustache. 'But a booster for tetanus might be a good idea. And I'll shoot you full of antibiotics for good measure.'

'How's Ratchitt, do you know?' Jason asked as Doc went about his business.

'Have no idea. What's your guess?'

'I only hit him once, but he went down like a ton of hot bricks. Must have a glass jaw.'

'Or a coward's heart. When some men go down, they stay down, till the danger's past.'

'Mmm. Do you think he might press charges?'

'No. His type don't go to the cops. They simply have you beaten up in retaliation one quiet night. Or they seduce your wife.'

Jason glowered at him. 'This town knows too damned much about everyone else's business.'

'True. But you just have to live with that. So what's the situation? Emma still hung up on that low-life?'

'Your guess is as good as mine. She says not, but the evidence isn't all in. On top of that, he's hanging around the shop and bothering her. Given his reputation with women, I find that a bit of a worry.'

'I'd be worried too. Speaking of Emma, where is she, exactly? Hard not to notice the little wife isn't here in the house, offering succour and comfort to her wounded husband.'

'She's spending a few nights at the shop. We have some things to work out.'

When Doc arched his bushy white brows, Jason gave him a narrow-eyed glare. 'And will that piece of news be on the village grapevine tomorrow?'

'Lord, Jason, you're way behind the action. That will have already done the rounds, the moment Emma's old bedroom light behind the shop went on earlier this evening.'

'I don't believe this,' he muttered.

'Then believe it. Oh, and by the way, the going odds on you and Emma divorcing are about even money. But don't worry, lad, my money's still on you. There! All done. You'll be as good as new by morning surgery.'

'Thanks a bunch.' Jason sat up and began rolling his shirt-sleeve down, till he saw it was ripped and bloodied. Muttering under his breath, he ripped the thing off and threw it in the corner, which was a pity, since it had cost a hundred bucks.

'Tch-tch,' Doc said as he tidied up the consultation table. 'Emma won't like that. She's a meticulous girl, is Emma.'

'Well, too bad! She isn't here to notice anyway, is she? I can be a slob if I want to be.'

'You can be an idiot if you want to be too. Why don't you go down there and tell her you love her?'

Jason's eyes whipped round to stare at him.

Doc shrugged. 'We all know your marriage wasn't a love match in the beginning. But I'm betting you love her now. She's a treasure, is our Emma. Only selfish, ignorant bums like Dean Ratchitt can't appreciate that.'

Jason considered the suggestion for what it was worth, then discarded it. 'She won't believe me.'

'Why not?'

'Partly because she thinks I still love another woman.'

'Just like you think *she* loves Ratchitt. Looks like we have two fools here instead of one.'

Jason frowned. Could Doc be right? Could Emma have fallen in love with *him*?

'Don't let too much water run under the bridge before you tell her, Jason. Dean won't be. You mark my words. I didn't like to mention this before, but I heard a motorbike rumble down the street a little while back. You were in too much pain to notice. If you don't want to lose Emma for good, then I suggest you hotfoot it down to the shop before this evening's incident is given a slant you won't recognise.'

Jason felt sick at the thought, but confused at the same time. 'How would he know she was there and not here...with me? She only left at tea-time.'

'I dare say he got the news from Sheryl.

'Sheryl lives on the other side of the sweet shop,' Doc elaborated when Jason looked even more confused. 'She's a legal secretary, works for Jack Winters, Ivy's solicitor. Went out with Dean, briefly a couple of years back. She's a good bit older than Dean but not bad looking. And she's never married. Probably still fancies him.'

Jason thought of Dean's boast that he had eyes and ears all over Tindley. Who better to tell him about Emma than a next-door neighbour?

'I have to go and get a fresh shirt first,' he said, heading for the door.

'Don't go getting into another fight!'

'I'll do what I have to do to protect Emma from that creep.'

Doc sighed. 'You do realise I'm getting too old for all this drama.'

'Then retire, and I'll get myself a new partner,' Jason tossed over his shoulder as he hurried from the room.

'You and what army?' Doc called after him.

Jason grabbed the first shirt he could find. It just happened to be a black designer number which had probably cost more than Ratchitt's whole bloody wardrobe. He was still tucking it into the waistband of his grey trousers as he bolted down the stairs and ran from the house.

He didn't knock on Emma's back door. He bowled straight in, sucking in a sharp breath when he saw a decidedly worse-for-wear Ratchitt sitting at the kitchen table. The right hand side of his chin was swollen, and there was an ugly bruise spoiling his macho perfection. He'd never seen a better target for a woman's pity, whereas *his* wounds were well hidden.

Emma was at the kitchen sink when Jason burst in. She whirled, worry filling her face as her eyes searched *his*.

'See?' Ratchitt taunted straight away. 'Not a mark on him. He jumped me when I wasn't looking, Emma. The man's mad. And violent. He tried to kill me. If it wasn't for my dog, he might have.'

'The world wouldn't be any the less for your death, Ratchitt,' Jason grated out. 'But it won't be me who does the deed. You're not worth spending twenty years in jail for. Emma, don't believe a word he tells you. The man's totally without conscience. He told me this evening that his only interest in you was money, some trust fund you came into when you married. He called you a silly little bitch and said he'd never loved you. He also bragged that now he wouldn't have to marry you to get the money. He thinks he can seduce you, then con you out of it.'

She didn't say a word, just stared at him with startled, disbelieving eyes.

'Just about word for word, wasn't it, honey?' Ratchitt drawled, rising to his feet and going over to a frozen Emma, placing a triumphantly possessive arm around her shoulders and drawing her to his side. 'But it wasn't me saying any of that filth, you bastard,' he sneered at Jason. 'It was you, as you very well know.'

Ratchitt tipped Emma's face up to his with a gentle little gesture. 'He boasted to me that he'd twist it all around and make out I said I wanted to marry you for the money,' he told her, stunning Jason with the passionate sincerity in his voice and eyes. 'But honest, Emma, I didn't know anything about this trust fund. You think your aunt would have told *me* about such a thing? She might have told *him*, though,' he went on, pointing an accusing finger at Jason. 'He probably got her to confide in him when she was in a morphine daze. And what did he do? As soon as she was dead, he proposed. That proposal was a shock, wasn't it? He hadn't given you any indication that he cared for you before, had he?'

Jason watched, appalled, as Emma slowly shook her head.

'I thought not. He lied to me about that, too. When I tackled him on the suddenness of your engagement, he said it wasn't at all sudden, that you'd become great friends during his visits to your aunt. More than friends, actually. He implied you'd become lovers.'

Her eyes flew to Jason's, pained and reproachful. Groaning, he did his best to adopt an aggrieved expression, but he had a feeling he just looked furious.

'I didn't tell you this earlier, Emma,' Ratchitt was

saying, 'but after you went away on your honeymoon I went to Sydney to check up on this man you married. I was worried about you. What did you know of him, really? I found this colleague of his, who turned out to be his old girlfriend, and what she told me about him made my hair curl. The man's a cold-blooded, mercenary monster. Money is his god, Emma. He'd do anything for it. Say anything. Marry anyone. On top of that he's violent, as you can see. I still love you, Emma, despite everything. But he doesn't. He'll hurt you, Emma. Let me move in here to protect you from him. Let me look after you and love you as you deserve to be loved.'

'No!' Jason cried.

'It's not up to you, Steel,' Ratchitt snapped.

Jason looked straight at Emma with an imploring gaze. 'Please, Emma, I beg of you. You don't have to come back to me yet, if you don't want to, but don't let him into your life, not for a moment.'

'How...how did you know about the trust fund?' she choked out.

Jason grimaced. 'I didn't. Not till Ratchitt told me tonight.'

'Yeah, right,' Dean sneered. 'As if I'd do that if I *did* know.'

'You knew all right,' Jason said with sudden inspiration. 'Your friend Sheryl told you. She works for your aunt's solicitor, Emma, and lives next door. Doc told me she and Dean were lovers once. She's still crazy about him and would tell him anything he wanted to know. She must have told him you were here, and not up at my house. Why else did he come *here* tonight, instead of the surgery? Someone had to tell him. I certainly didn't. Did you?'

'N...no.'

'Then ask him. Ask him why he came here.'

'Dean?'

'He's grabbing at straws, Emma. Sheryl didn't tell me anything of the kind. *He* did. That's why he came looking for me out at the farm. Because you'd left him and he was worried stiff you'd find out he never loved you.'

'Jason never promised to love me,' she said in a puzzled voice.

'And neither will he,' Ratchitt insisted. 'Ever!'

'That's not true,' Jason denied with an anguished groan. 'Not true,' he repeated, his shoulders sagging as his heart began to despair. 'I *do* love you, Emma. I love you with all my heart. I didn't marry you for any money. I knew nothing of any trust fund till I heard about it from Ratchitt tonight. He thinks all men are tarred with the same brush. He couldn't seem to imagine my actually loving you. Yet I cannot imagine *not* loving you. I certainly can't imagine my life without you.'

Jason knew he wasn't being very impressive with his declaration of love. His voice sounded tired and defeated, probably because of the look on her face. The shock and the patent disbelief. He was wasting his breath. Totally wasting his breath.

'I can't make you love me back,' he continued, driven on by desperation, not any real hope. 'I can't make you come home with me. I can't make you stay away from this...creature. All I can do is appeal to your common sense. I know you have heaps. Think, Emma. Think and judge. A man is known by his actions, not his words. Would I have acted as I have acted this past few weeks if I hadn't been sick with a very real jealousy? And would Ratchitt have acted as he has acted this past year if he really loved you?'

She didn't say a word, just kept staring at him.

He sighed. 'That's all I have to say. That's all there *is* to say. I'm going home now. I'll wait for you till morning. If you don't come, I won't be staying in Tindley. I couldn't bear it. You can have a divorce. You can have *him*, if he's what you really want. I won't stand in your way. But God have pity on your soul if that's the way you choose, Emma, because he'll destroy you.'

'Don't listen to him, Emma. He's the one who'll destroy you. He's evil. And clever. Far cleverer than me. I don't have his power with words. Or his fancy education. I only have what's in my heart. Feel this heart, Emma,' Dean Ratchitt said, taking her hand and placing it on his chest. 'It's beating for you. I know I hurt you a year ago. I was wrong. All I can say is that I was lonely for you, and that girl threw herself at me. But that wasn't love, Emma. That was just sex. Surely you can see what I mean now. You've been to bed with this man. You've had sex with him. But that's not making love. That doesn't come from the heart. When we're finally together, *that* will be making love. It'll be incredible, princess. I promise you...'

She was staring up into those penetrating black eyes of his as though hypnotised, seemingly unable to break away from the sexual spell his words and his presence were casting over her body. Jason could not bear to watch it any more. His heart was breaking.

He turned and walked through the back door, stumbling a little on the steps. Somehow, he made it back up the street and into the surgery.

Doc had left, thank God. He would not have wanted another man to see the tears streaming down his face. He made it into the living room, where he slumped into the big armchair to the right of the empty hearth. He didn't turn on the reading lamp next to it, just sat there in the semi-darkness staring into nothingness, the tears slowly drying on his face as the minutes ticked away. For a while his ear strained to catch the sound of Emma's steps on the front porch, his heart aching with one last, final, futile hope.

How could she not see the truth? How could she be taken in by that creep?

Easily, Jason finally accepted. As easily as he had been taken in by Adele all those years. Both of them had outer physical attractions which could mask the ugly person inside. Both were clever and cunning. Both dared to do what decent people would not even dream of doing. They conned and corrupted. They seduced and schemed.

Jason's thoughts finally turned to Emma, and he knew he shouldn't sit by and let Ratchitt taint such a beautiful person. But what could he do, short of killing the bloke?

Nothing, really. In days gone by he could have kidnapped her and carried her off to some faraway land, but not nowadays. Nowadays, that would land him in jail. But wouldn't jail be preferable to this agony of doing nothing to save her from a fate worse than death?

He was still sitting there, mentally tossing up between murder and kidnapping, when he heard the sound of the front door opening.

CHAPTER FOURTEEN

JASON'S hands balled into fists on the armrests of the chair. He dared not get his hopes up. What if he was wrong? What if she'd just come home to get some clothes? What if it wasn't Emma at all?

He sat there like a block of stone, petrified.

'Jason?' Emma called softly. 'Where are you?'

He didn't answer. Couldn't.

He listened to her walk up the stairs and call out to him there listened as she walked slowly back down. 'Jason, where *are* you?' she cried again at the bottom of the stairs, sounding almost despairing.

'I'm in here,' he said at last, but his voice sounded odd. Empty and hollow.

She switched on the light, then just stood there in the doorway, looking over at him. He didn't know what he looked like, but it must have been pretty terrible by the expression on her face.

'Oh, Jason,' she groaned, and ran over to squat down by the chair.

'I'm sorry,' she cried, her green eyes filling while his remained strangely dry and distant. 'So very sorry...'

Jason's chest was aching. She was sorry. Sorry about what? Sorry she was leaving him?

That had to be it. She'd taken too long to come home for the outcome to be otherwise. It was agony thinking of what she and Ratchitt had been doing during that time.

'Just get whatever it is you've come for,' he said flatly. 'And go.' He no longer had any stomach for his earlier violent solutions. If she was fool enough to want Ratchitt, then let her be destroyed. Why not? He was.

'But I've come home, Jason,' she said. 'I chose you.' And, reaching out, she touched him on the arm, right where the dog had bitten him.

He wrenched his arm away, his moan a mixture of emotional and physical pain.

'What is it?' she said, her eyes instantly stricken. 'What's wrong with your arm? Show me!' Already she was undoing his cuff and gently peeling back the sleeve. Her gasp was horrified. Jason looked down at it closely for the first time himself.

It *did* look pretty nasty, despite Doc's expert handiwork. Much worse than Ratchitt's face. He would carry scars for the rest of his life.

'Oh, Jason...'

'It'll be all right,' he said sharply.

Their eyes met, but he still could not quite believe what she'd said. 'You meant it?' he rasped. 'About coming home? About choosing me?'

She nodded, and two big tears trickled down her face.

'What about Ratchitt?'

'I sent him away.'

'You sent him away,' he repeated dazedly.

'I don't love him any more, Jason. I don't even want him any more.'

'You don't?'

'No. I'm sure of that, Jason. Quite sure.'

He couldn't say anything to that, his heart too awash with emotion.

'You...didn't just say that about loving me, did you?' she asked. 'You did mean it, didn't you?'

'Yes.' That was all he could manage. Just yes. His relief was too intense, his exhaustion total.

She nodded. 'I didn't think you would lie about something like that. Not you.' And, taking the hand of his good arm, she began tugging him to his feet.

'What are you doing?' he choked out.

'I'm taking my husband upstairs to bed. He looks tired.'

'Tired' did not begin to describe the state he was in.

He let her lead him upstairs, let her sit him down on the side of the bed while she knelt down at his feet and began taking off his shoes and socks.

He wanted to ask her what had happened with Ratchitt after he left. He wanted to ask her about the trust fund. But he didn't have the energy. Or the will. Instead, he watched her tend to him with a sweet gentleness which threatened to embarrass him for ever in front of her. Only with the greatest force of will did he keep his own tears at bay.

At last he was naked, and being tipped back under cool sheets. 'Can I get you anything?' she asked. 'A glass of water? Some painkillers?'

'Painkillers would be good. There are some extra strong ones lying on my desk in the surgery. Just bring me the packet.'

He closed his eyes after she left the room and began counting to ten. If he got to ten without crying, he thought, everything would be all right.

He didn't cry. But he didn't get to ten, either. Something very strange happened to him around eight. He fell asleep.

Jason woke to the feel of Emma's arm sliding around his waist, plus the tips of her breasts pressing into his back. For a moment, everything inside him leapt, till her deep even breathing told him she was actually asleep. Understandable, he accepted, after a quick glance at the bedside clock.

It was five past two.

For a long while, he lay there in the dark, mulling over everything that had happened the night before, still stunned by the outcome. Emma had chosen *him*, not Ratchitt. She didn't love Ratchitt any more.

It was almost too good to be true. What had changed her mind about Ratchitt? What had happened after he'd left them alone together?

Her apology when she'd first come home took on a sinister meaning. What had she been saying sorry for? Had she let Ratchitt make love to her, only to find out her fantasies about him had been just that—fantasies?

Something must have happened during the time which had elapsed. He couldn't see Ratchitt wasting time just talking to Emma. That was not his style.

But being unfaithful wasn't Emma's style, either. He knew that, down deep in his heart. No, something else had happened to make her see the light.

And the light was what? *He* was a better bet for

the future than Ratchitt? Jason dared not hope she'd suddenly discovered she loved him. That was the hope of fools. More likely she'd chosen the lesser of two evils.

He still felt terrible about the way he'd acted since they'd arrived home in Tindley. He could not blame her for leaving him. He'd treated her without consideration and without respect. Without love.

Emma stirred against his back, snuggling in closer, murmuring his name in her sleep. When she lifted her leg to hook it over his, Jason was taken aback to discover she was totally naked. She hadn't come to bed like that since their honeymoon, he recalled.

Back then, he'd rolled over many times during the night to make love to her. And it had been so wonderful. At least in bed he could make her happy.

He went to roll over right then and there...till the pain in his arm momentarily stopped him.

But only momentarily. It seemed an aching arm was no deterrent to the waves of desire which began flooding through him. Jason suspected his arm could be falling off and nothing would stop him wanting to make love to her.

Slowly, carefully, he rolled over. Instinctively, she rolled too. Yet she was still asleep. Jason curved himself around her, keeping his damaged arm out of harm's way. He slid his other arm under her, tipping her slightly backwards against his chest, bringing her breasts within easy reach.

She woke slowly, voluptuously, arching her back into his hands, showing him with her body language that she liked what he was doing. More than liked it.

Her arms lifted above her head to find and wind around his neck, leaving both her breasts, and the entire front of her body, unhindered for his pleasure. Her right knee lifted up onto his right thigh, opening and offering herself for whatever he might want.

Her attitude of total sexual surrender sent his desire for her off the Richter scale. Not to mention his love. Even if she didn't love him back, she'd chosen him. And she wanted him, wanted him more than a man she'd claimed she would always love and *never* forget. Surely that must mean it was only a matter of time before she was his, totally. His heart swelled with passionate determination. He would make love to her with every ounce of skill he had, showing her that, despite his own runaway passion, *her* pleasure would be his first priority from now on. He wanted to wipe away the memory of the past couple of weeks when he'd been so abominable to her.

Carefully, he eased himself inside her, his hands splaying across her stomach to keep her still against him. But her insides weren't still, and for a panic-stricken moment he feared disaster. Hell, he was drowning in her heat, being seduced by her pulsating muscles. The pleasure was dizzying, and potentially destructive.

No way could he last.

But he was going to, no matter what!

'Emma, be still,' he warned her sharply, when she began squeezing and releasing him between frantic little wriggles of her bottom.

'I can't,' she gasped, and came with an intensity which threatened his resolve to give her the experience of a lifetime. It took every ounce of his will not to let everything come to a swift and premature end right then and there.

Gradually, her spasms died away, and he set to making love to her seriously, with a steady rhythm, using his hands to re-arouse her. Her second climax was gentler on him, but no less difficult to ignore. He ploughed on, taking her on to the highest of pleasure zones, where her whole body was so sensitised that the slightest touch of his knowing fingertip had her quivering with delight. Only when he knew he could not last another moment did he take her with him to a third full-blown orgasm.

'Oh, Jason,' she cried afterwards as he cradled her to him, her body still trembling. 'Jason…'

'Hush, my darling,' he murmured as he rocked her gently to and fro. 'Relax… Go to sleep…'

'I can't. I… I…'

'Shh. Don't talk. Just take deep breaths, then let go all your muscles.'

She did as he suggested, scooping in then letting out several huge, shuddering sighs. Her arms and legs finally went very limp.

'Sleepy,' she mumbled.

'Yes,' he agreed, stroking her hair.

Once she was unconscious, Jason eased himself from her. Rolling over, he reached for the painkillers she'd left on the bedside chest and which he hadn't taken earlier. He took three. Hell, he needed them. His arm felt as if a mad dog had mauled it, and the rest of him wasn't much better.

But he was content. More content than he'd ever

been in all his life. She might not love him yet, but she would…in time. Ratchitt was history.

Carefully, he rolled back over onto his side and curved his aching arm around the sleeping form beside him.

She didn't stir an inch. Thank God.

CHAPTER FIFTEEN

JASON woke to the dawn...and more pain. His arm felt as if it had been put through a shredder. His head was aching, as was his whole body.

A sidewards glance showed a curled up Emma, sleeping like a baby.

'It's all your fault,' he muttered under his breath, but with a wry smile forming. 'You've totally wrecked me.'

The wreck struggled out from under the covers and staggered downstairs to the surgery, where he dressed the wound, gave himself another shot of antibiotics and swallowed some bigger pain-killing bombs. Only his nudity prevented Jason from wandering out onto the front porch and watching the sun rise. He didn't want to scandalise the people of Tindley any more than he'd already scandalised them. No doubt the news of the night before would be doing the rounds of the town with a speed and inaccuracy which would rival Peyton Place.

Oh, well. At least everything had come out all right. In a fashion. Emma was back home in his bed and Ratchitt was...gone, he hoped. Permanently.

Jason levered himself back upstairs, where he literally ran into Emma, hurrying through their bedroom door in her birthday suit.

'Oh, there you are, Jason!' she exclaimed. 'I woke

up and you were gone. I was worried. What have you been doing downstairs? Did you want something? A cup of tea, perhaps? Some breakfast?'

She was babbling, he could see. And blushing. God, he liked it when she blushed.

'Let's go back to bed,' he said, taking her arm and praying those painkillers kicked in shortly.

Her upward gaze betrayed she was not averse to his suggestion. 'But...but what about your poor arm?' she protested feebly.

His smile was wry. 'You weren't too worried about my poor arm in the middle of the night.'

She blushed some more, but her eyes carried warm memories of their lovemaking. 'That was...incredible, Jason. But then, I knew it would be.'

His eyebrows lifted. 'You did? How come?'

'Oh, Jason...' She placed her hands, palms down, upon his chest, reaching up to kiss him lightly on the mouth. 'You were the one who said sex could be extremely satisfying without love, remember?'

His insides tightened. 'Yes,' he said tautly. 'I remember.'

'But you added that being in love would enhance the experience.'

He stared down at her, that horrible thing called hope doing awful things to his stomach. 'What are you trying to say, Emma?'

'I love you, Jason.'

He swallowed a couple of times. 'You...you wouldn't say a thing like that unless you meant it, would you?'

'Never in a million years, my darling.'

Oh, God...

Only her lips saved him, her lovely, loving lips, kissing away the shock, taking him back from the threshold of total embarrassment to that place reserved for lovers where their bodies and hearts beat as one and nothing existed but their love and need for each other. They moved together onto the bed to show that love and satisfy their need as man and woman had since the garden of Eden. Afterwards, they lay locked in each other's arms, basking in the afterglow of their lovemaking.

Jason felt no pain, only the sweetest of pleasures and the deepest of wonders. Emma loved him. Everything *was* going to be all right.

'When did you know you loved me?' he asked her, wonder still in his voice.

'I suspected as much after that incident with Adele,' came her astonishing reply, 'but I wasn't certain till last night.'

'When last night?'

'I'm not sure when, exactly. Last night carried a lot of confusion. Your declaration of love stunned me, Jason. I could not quite believe it. To be honest, I've had trouble believing in our relationship from the word go. It all seemed rather...unreal.'

'Unreal, Emma? In what way?'

'Do you have no idea, Jason, how you present yourself to others? Or how you might look to a simple country girl? That first day you came to visit Aunt Ivy, I took one look at you and I thought...wow!'

Jason was staggered. 'But you didn't even *look* at me!'

'Oh, yes, I did. Sneakily. And I thought about you afterwards. But not in any real way. You were like some movie star. Way out of my league, but nice to dream about. I found myself looking forward to your visits, just so I could look at you some more. I used to wonder what you were doing here in our little country town, with your trendy clothes, your city sophistication and your incredible style. I tried to picture what kind of woman you'd end of marrying if you stayed. That was why I was so shocked when you asked me. I didn't fit the image I'd made up for your wife in my mind...

'But Adele did,' she went on. 'She fitted it like a glove. God, that weekend was ghastly. I don't know how I survived it. I'd been wanting you to make love to me so badly, and I was missing you terribly, when suddenly there was this gorgeous woman standing in my dreary little shop, telling me you would never be faithful to boring little me and that she'd spent most of the weekend in bed with you. When she left I wanted to smash everything in sight. I was so eaten up with jealousy, I couldn't see straight. Nothing else she'd said seemed to matter, only that you'd made love to *her*, and not me. In the end, I just cried and cried and cried. That was when I knew I was far more emotionally involved with you than I'd realised.'

Jason could empathise with everything she felt—and he did. 'I was the same, believe me,' he said feelingly. 'The panic I felt when I found out Adele had been to see you was incredible. I should have known I loved you back then. Instead, it didn't hit me till I saw you walking down the aisle on our wedding day. I was quite blown away, I can tell you.'

Emma shook her head. 'I probably would have felt the same way about you that day, if I hadn't been worried sick about Dean causing trouble. It wasn't till we were well away from Tindley that I could relax and begin to enjoy being married to you. And I did enjoy it, Jason. Even when I didn't know I loved you.'

'The sex, you mean?'

'Yes. Was that wicked of me?'

'Not at all. Just human. You were ripe and ready to be made love to, Emma. I thank my lucky stars that I came along at the right time in your life.'

'I'm glad I waited for you, Jason. I'm glad to never made love with Dean. I love you much more than I ever loved him.'

His heart tripped over. 'You make me ashamed of myself for the way I've treated you these past couple of weeks. My only excuse—and it sounds pathetic— is that I was crazy with insecurity and jealousy.'

'You need never be jealous of Dean again, Jason. I despise him. I'm well aware that everything he ever told me was a lie, including what he said about you last night. Not that I didn't already suspect as much.'

'But I thought you were totally taken in by him! The way you were looking up at him, like you were hypnotised.'

'Not hypnotised, Jason. Shocked. Too much had happened too quickly. I felt totally disorientated. It was only when you walked out that my mind began to clear. I still wasn't convinced of your love for me. I was worried you might just be trying to get me back with words. But I began to see that everything you'd said about Dean did make sense. His past actions certainly weren't those of a man genuinely in love. His attitude once you'd left didn't endear him to me, either. He became insufferably smug and presumptuous. When he started manhandling me, and telling her how much he loved me, I found myself rejecting his declaration of love much more strongly than I had yours.'

Jason frowned. 'What do you mean...manhandling you?'

'Oh, you know. Hugging me and kissing me.'

'You let him *kiss* you?'

'I didn't *let* him do anything. He just did it.'

'I'll kill him!'

'No, you won't. I don't want you going to jail over that trash. Look, I'm glad I let him kiss me one last time, Jason, because I didn't like it one bit. In fact, I found it quite repulsive. I knew then I felt nothing for him any more, not even a sexual attraction. When he kept insisting that my inheritance meant nothing to him, I just knew he was lying. I wanted him out of my life, and out of Tindley. For ever. But I knew he was not about to give up, not while he thought I was rich. There was no use just saying go away, that I didn't love him any more. Frankly, Jason, I'd already said as much to him on our wedding day, and he simply took no notice. So I told him I was relieved he wasn't interested in my money, because the trustees of my fund had invested all my money into the Asian money market and they'd lost the lot in the 1997 crash.'

'And had they?'

'No, of course not. But that's beside the point. Once I said that, you should have seen him back-pedal as fast as he could. Suddenly, my irresistible charms became very resistible. He started talking about how it might not be a good idea if he moved in with me just yet because it might ruin my reputation, and he cared about me too much to do that. He said it might be better if we waited till I got a divorce. When I calmly told him I had no intention of getting a divorce, and that I'd decided to go back to you, he blustered a bit about women never knowing their own minds, and that he would never have come back to Tindley except for me. I then told him that perhaps it might be better if he left Tindley, after which he pretended to be angry and stormed out of the house. He was riding off down the road without a backward glance as I walked up here to you. I doubt he'll be back. He's exhausted Tindley's supply of eligible females. I think he'll try greener pastures.'

Jason didn't doubt it. With a bit of luck, he'd go back to Sydney and look up Adele again. They deserved each other.

He thought of telling Emma about Ratchitt and Adele, but decided there was no point any more. Besides, the last thing he wanted was to keep bringing up old history. Let sleeping dogs lie...

'Three million,' Emma said abruptly, interrupting his thoughts.

'Three million what?'

'Three million dollars. That's how much my trust fund is worth, give or take a few thousand.'

Jason saw the worry in her face and understood it.

'I knew nothing about this trust fund, Jason,' she elaborated, 'till after Aunt Ivy's death. She left me a letter in her will about it. She also advised me strongly never to tell anyone about the money. Not till after I was safely married, anyway.'

Jason could appreciate Aunt Ivy's common sense. But Emma's eyes still bothered him. 'She never told me about it, Emma,' he insisted. 'Honest.'

'Oh, I know that. I'm just worried the money might change things between us.'

'I see...' And he surely did. Money corrupted. 'Give it away, Emma,' he said firmly. 'Donate it to some charity. Cancer research, perhaps.'

Her sigh carried a telling amount of relief. 'I'm so glad you said that. I was thinking the very same thing. Of course, I might keep a little nest-egg, just for emergencies. But the bulk of it can go.'

'Splendid idea!'

'Oh, Jason!' she cried, hugging him tightly. 'I do so love you. I felt so terrible when I came home last night and saw you sitting in that armchair, looking so devastated. I think that was the first moment I really believed you loved me.'

'And you, Emma? Did you know then that you loved me back?'

'I'm sure I did, but I just couldn't seem to face it. I don't know why. Perhaps I was afraid to. Then, later, when you made love to me like you did, I...I was just...overwhelmed. But I knew how much I loved you the moment I woke and found you gone. Oh, I knew it then, Jason.'

He could understand that. There was something

about loss—even a temporary one—which stripped the wool from one's eyes.

'I love you with all my heart,' she said sincerely.

His own heart filled to overflowing. 'Tell me again.'

'I love you.'

'And I love you, dear, sweet Emma. I love everything about you, even your stubbornness.'

Her eyes flickered with surprise. 'My stubbornness? I'm not stubborn.'

'Oh, yes, you are, my darling. But that's all right. I wouldn't want you too perfect.'

'I'm far from perfect.'

'Not too far,' he murmured, and his mother's words echoed in his mind once more.

You can't have everything in life, son.

But he knew that you could, if what you wanted were the simple things in life. And if you were lucky enough to marry a girl like Emma.

'Jason…'

'Yes?'

'I…um…didn't go on the pill.'

'That's good.'

'You know, it worries me a bit, not getting pregnant after all the sex we had. Do you think something could be wrong with me?'

Jason felt his heart catch. But he kept quite calm. Worry and tension were not advisable when a couple were trying for a baby. 'Now why should there be something wrong with you?' he said reassuringly. 'Or me, for that matter? These things take time, love.' And he gave her a comforting squeeze.

'Oh!' she gasped, and smiled a wide smile up at him. 'That's it, Jason!'

'What's it?'

'Love! Before, we were just having sex. But now...now we're making love. We'll make a baby this month. I'm sure of it.'

He forced himself to smile. 'I'll certainly give it my best shot.'

It was the most difficult month of Jason's life. Keeping his emotional cool while making love to Emma till he was exhausted. As the day approached when her period was due, he was beside himself with tension. Which was crazy. Because what he'd said to her was true. These things *did* sometimes take time. Lots of it. To put this kind of pressure on himself at this stage was silly, and potentially destructive.

D-day arrived and went. No period. Another day. Then another. And another. Jason knew he could do a pregnancy test on her—they were accurate far earlier these days—but he didn't dare suggest it. That would betray his escalating tension. And make a big issue of her conceiving.

He was getting ready for afternoon surgery the next day when Emma suddenly burst in, waving something in her hands. 'It was positive, Jason!' she cried excitedly. 'We're pregnant! I bought a test from the chemist. The one being advertised in all the women's magazines. It said you could tell at ten days, and I'm well over that.'

Joy and relief exploded through his chest like a

fireworks display. He hadn't realised till that moment how much having a family of his own meant to him.

Unable to express his feelings in words, he scooped her up into his arms and kissed her over and over.

'Just as well Nancy's stepped outside to do some shopping,' he said breathlessly, when he finally put her down again. 'Otherwise the whole of Tindley would know the news before this day was out.'

Emma gave him a pitying look, then laughed.

'What are you laughing at?'

'Jason, everyone already knows.'

'But how? Did you tell them?'

'No. But they're past masters at putting two and two together. Not that it would have been hard. There's only one chemist shop in Tindley. What would you think if a recently married person—namely me—came in and bought a pregnancy testing kit, then half an hour later went running from her shop up the street like a madwoman into her doctor husband's surgery?'

Jason pulled a face. 'She's pregnant?'

'Exactly!'

He sighed. 'Maybe you shouldn't bother to have an ultrasound at four months. We'll just ask the good ladies of Tindley. No doubt they'll operate a book, giving odds on the sex, the due date, weight length and name! Did you know we were even money on getting a divorce at one stage?' Jason began shaking his head. 'That's the only drawback to living in Tindley. That infernal grapevine!'

'True,' Emma said, nodding sagely. 'But it's much

better than living in the city. You can't have everything in life, Jason. Everyone knows that.'

He blinked at her, then laughed.

'What did I say that was so funny?'

'Nothing.'

She gave him a suspicious look. 'You're not keeping secrets from me again, are you?'

'Never! It's just that that was what my mother always used to say. That you can't have everything in life.'

'And it's true.'

Jason looked at this beautiful girl who loved him and who was carrying his child and drew her into his arms once more.

'No, it's not, my darling. Not in my case. Because I have you, and you are everything.'

She looked up at him with wonder in her eyes. 'Do you want our baby to be a boy or a girl?'

'I don't mind either way. Do you?'

'No. Any child of yours will be special. Thank you for marrying me, Jason. Thank you for saving me from myself.'

Jason knew who should be thanking whom, but he was a man, after all, and allowed his ego to wallow in her lovely words. 'You're welcome, my darling,' he murmured, and slowly, gently, covered her mouth with his.

It was a girl. Emma named her Juliette, in keeping with the Steel tradition of using names starting with J. Only one person in Tindley collected on the name. A charge of 'insider information' was directed at

Nancy, but she claimed innocence. She'd simply chosen the most romantic name she could think of!

Juliette's christening was an all-town affair, with Jason's brother, Jerry, and the Brandewildes the proud godparents. Jerry had come to Tindley at Emma's instigation, late in her pregnancy, when she'd said she needed help in the shop. Jerry had proved to be a born sweet-seller, his shyness eventually evaporating with life in a smaller and much friendlier community. Emma had given him the rooms behind the shop to live in, shifting her plans for a craft club to the local hall.

At Juliette's christening, her proud dad brought forth his new video camera, bought for him by his doting wife from that little nest-egg she'd put aside. Emma was always buying Jason things. A lovely sapphire dress ring. The latest VC player. A super-soft leather reading chair with footrest. He loved being spoiled by her, and loved spoiling her back again in his own special way!

The people of Tindley counted their blessings every time they saw the happy family walking down the main street together. Dr Steel was going to stay, the men of Tindley finally agreed. No doubt about that.

The matter was deemed as settled, and money changed hands. The odds on Jason staying had been a generous four to one when the bets were first laid eighteen months before.

Doc Brandewilde really cleaned up.

Sharon Kendrick started story-telling at the age of eleven and has never really stopped. She likes to write fast-paced, feel-good romances with heroes who are so sexy they'll make your toes curl! Born in west London, she now lives in the beautiful city of Winchester – where she can see the cathedral from her window (but only if she stands on tip-toe). She is married to a medical professor – which may explain why her family get more colds than anyone else on the street – and they have two children, Celia and Patrick. Her passions include music, books, cooking and eating – and drifting off into wonderful daydreams while she works out new plots!

**Look out for Sharon Kendrick's next sexy story:
THE FUTURE KING'S BRIDE
On sale April 2005, in Modern Romance™!**

ONE BRIDEGROOM REQUIRED!
by
Sharon Kendrick

PROLOGUE

THE wedding dress gleamed indistinctly through its heavy shrouding of plastic.

It was an exquisite gown—simple and striking and fashioned with care from ivory silk-satin. Organza whispered softly beneath the skirt and the matching veil was made of gossamer-fine tulle.

At a little over twenty years old, it was ageless and timeless, a future heirloom—to be passed down from bride to bride, each woman adapting it and making it uniquely hers.

But for now it remained locked in a wardrobe, hidden and protected and unworn.

And waiting....

CHAPTER ONE

LUKE GOODWIN stood in front of the big, Georgian window and gave a sigh of satisfaction which not even the bleak November day could dispel. He stared at the unfamiliar landscape before him. It was a loveless time of year in England, once the last of the leaves had fallen.

The sky was as grey as slush and the clouds had an ominous bulge which spoke of heavy rains to come. It was as unlike the golden and blue African skies he had left behind as it was possible to be.

Yet the green chequerboard of fields which stretched as far as his eye could see was now his. As was this graceful old house with enough bedrooms to sleep a football team. His hard mouth softened into a smile as he tried to take it all in, but it was hard to believe that this, all this beauty, now belonged to him.

Oh, a different type of beauty from the one he was used to, that was for sure. His beauty had been searing heat and blazing cerulean skies. The scent of lemons and the puff of fragrant smoke wafting from the barbecue. There had been bare rooms where giant fans cast their flickering circles across bleached ceilings—so different from the elegant Georgian drawing room in which he now stood.

He had been here only eight hours and yet felt he knew the house as intimately as any lover. He had arrived in the middle of the night, but had walked the echoing floors in silence, examining each room and reacquainting himself with each chair, each moulding. Running his long fingers along their pure, clean surfaces with the awe of a mother studying her newborn.

His heart sang with possession—not for the house's worth, but for its link with the past, and the future. Like a rudderless boat, Luke had finally found the mooring of his dreams.

He let his eyes grow accustomed to the view. Through an arched yew hedge was a clutch of thatched cottages, a pub, a few tasteful and essential shops—as well as the added bonus of a village green with accompanying duck pond. England at its most picture-perfect. His senses were stretched with fatigue, and the soft beauty of his childhood home had never seemed quite so poignant.

Next month Caroline would arrive from Africa, in time for Christmas. Caroline who, despite her associations with that country, was the epitome of an English rose. Caroline with her soft, understated beauty and her unflappability and her resourcefulness. Not his usual kind of woman at all...

Somehow, God only knew how, she had arranged for a woman to come and clean the house for him. She hadn't let the matter of a few thousand miles affect her organisational skills!

He guessed it was yet another indication of how much his tastes had matured. Luke's wild and rollicking adventuring days were over, and he was ready to take on all the responsibilities which his inheritance had brought. Sometimes your life changed and there wasn't a damned thing you could do about it.

Luke smiled the contented smile of a man who had found what he was looking for.

Life, he decided, was just like a giant jigsaw puzzle, and the last piece had just slotted effortlessly into place.

Holly clicked off the ignition key just before the engine cut out of its own accord in the middle of the narrow village street. Number ninety-nine on her list of things to do, she thought with dark humour—change her car.

If only she didn't love it so much! An ancient old Beetle which she had lovingly painted herself, because that was the kind of thing that students did. It was just that she wasn't a student any more...

She slowly got out of the car and stood on the pavement, staring up at the empty building with eyes which half refused to believe that this shop was now *hers.*

Lovelace Brides. The place where every bride-to-be would want to buy the wedding outfit of her wildest and most wonderful dreams. Where she, Holly Lovelace, intended to transform each woman who set foot over that threshold into the most amazing bride imaginable!

Holly shivered. She should have worn her thermals. The November air had a really hungry bite to it and the gauzy shirt she was wearing would be better suited to a summer's day.

Still, now was the time to open up the shop, and then just haul her stuff inside and unpack the basics—like vests and tea bags! She could risk moving the car later.

She was just fishing around in her shoulder bag for the great clump of keys which seemed to have got lost among all the clutter at the bottom, when she heard the sound of footsteps approaching.

Holly looked up sharply and her hair tumbled in copper-curled disarray all over her shoulders. She felt her mouth fall open in slow motion as she focussed on the man walking towards her, then blinked, as if her eyes were playing tricks on her. She blinked again. No, they weren't. Holly stared, then swallowed.

He was quite the most gorgeous man she had ever seen, and yet somehow he looked kind of *wrong* walking down the sleepy village street. Holly frowned. It wasn't just that he was tall, or tanned, or lean where it counted—though he was all of these, and more. Or that his broad shoulders and rugged frame spoke of a man you didn't mess with. Holly looked a little closer. His hair was dark—dark as muscovado sugar—and the ends were tipped with gold.

He wore jeans, but proper, workmanlike jeans—faded by constant use and hard work, not from stone-washing in a factory. And they weren't sprayed on so tightly that any movement looked an impossibility—with legs like *his* they wouldn't need to be.

With his thick cream sweater and battered sheepskin jacket, he looked vital and vibrant—like a Technicolor image superimposed on an old black-and-white film. More real than real. He made the drizzly grey of the day seem even more insignificant and Holly found that she couldn't drag her eyes away from him.

He came to a halt right in front of her, jeaned legs astride, returning her scrutiny with a mocking stare of his own.

Now she could see that his eyes were blue—bluer than the sea, even bluer than a summer's sky. A dreamer's eyes. An adventurer's eyes.

Holly felt that if she didn't speak she would do something unforgivable—like reach her hand out and touch the hard, tanned curve of his jaw. Just for the hell of it.

'Hello,' she smiled, thinking that if all the men in Woodhampton looked like this, then she was going to be very happy working here!

He stared back, at dark copper curls and white skin and green eyes, the colour of jealousy. For Luke it was like being stun-gunned—that was the only thing he could think of right then. Or hit, maybe. A physical blow might explain the sudden unbearable throbbing of his blood, the heated dilation of the veins in his face. He could feel his mouth roughen and dry and the beginning of an insistent ache in a certain part of his anatomy which filled him with sudden self-loathing.

The woman was a complete stranger—so how in hell had unwanted desire incapacitated him so completely and so mercilessly and so bloody *suddenly*?

Holly had to concentrate very hard to stop her knees from buckling, since her long legs seemed to have nothing to do with her all of a sudden. And why on earth was he *staring* at her like that?

'Hello,' she said again, only more coolly this time, because it wasn't very flattering to be ignored. 'Have we met before?'

His expression didn't change, but his voice was impatient. 'Don't play games. You know damned well we haven't.' He treated her to a parody of a smile. 'Or I think we would have remembered. Don't you?'

His voice was deep and dark, his accent impossible to define, and yet his words were mocking. Made her question into a meaningless little platitude. Yet he was right. She *would* have remembered. This was a man you would never forget. He would stamp his presence indelibly on your heart and mind and eyes.

Holly gave him a sideways look. 'Perhaps I would.' She shrugged quietly. 'I've certainly had better greetings in my life.'

'Oh, I bet you have, sweetheart,' he agreed softly, and managed to make the words sound like an insult. 'I *bet* you have.'

Suddenly Holly wished she were wearing some neat little boxy suit and a pair of tights, with shoes you could see your face in, instead of a faded pair of denims and a too-thin shirt. Maybe then he'd wipe that hungry, mean-looking expression off his face and show her a little respect. Though respect you had to earn, and she wasn't sure she'd care to earn anything from him...

'So what do you want?' she asked, not caring if it sounded abrupt. 'You must want *something*, the way you're staring at me like you've just seen a ghost—unless I have a smudge on my nose, or something?'

Staring at the pure lines of her lips, which were untouched by lipstick, Luke felt fingers of fantasy enmeshing him in their grasp. 'You haven't,' he told her huskily. 'And as to what I want, well, that rather depends—'

'On?'

He bit back the crude, unaccustomed sexual request he was tempted to make and channelled it instead into indignation, clipping out his words like bullets as he pointed to her Beetle. 'On whether that rust bucket of a car happens to belong to you, or not?'

'And if it does?' She tipped her head back and narrowed her eyes, and her hair swung in a copper curtain all the way down her back.

'If it does, then it's the worst piece of parking I've seen in my life!' he drawled.

Holly saw the light of combat sparking in the depth of unforgettable blue eyes and wondered what was causing this definite overreaction. Bad experience? 'Oh, dear. Have you got a thing about women drivers?' she asked him sweetly.

'Not at all. Just bad drivers.' His mouth flattened into a hard line. 'Though most women seem to need a space the size of an airstrip to park.'

Holly almost laughed until she saw that he meant it. She shook her head slowly. 'Heavens!' she murmured. 'I can't believe that anyone would come out with an outdated sexist remark like that, not when we're almost into the millennium—talk about a gross generalisation!'

Luke found himself mesmerised by her eyes. Too green, he thought suddenly. Too wide and too deep. For the first time in his life he understood the expression 'eyes you could drown in'. Tension caused his throat to tighten up. 'Really?' he drawled huskily. 'Not even if it happens to be true? That's usually how generalisations come into being.'

Holly's mouth twitched. Very clever; but not clever enough. She wasn't going to let him get away with that. 'You've done comparative research on male and female parking behaviour, have you?'

'I don't need to, sweetheart. I base my opinions on my own experience.'

'And your experience of women is extensive, no doubt?'

'Pretty much.' His gaze was cool as it flicked over her, and then suddenly not so cool. 'But you still haven't told me whether it's your car, or not?'

He knew damn well it was! Holly held her palms up in supplication. 'Okay, I admit it, Officer,' she told him mockingly, and then dangled the keys from her finger provocatively. 'The car is mine!'

It had been a long time since a woman had made fun of him quite so audaciously. 'Then might I suggest you *move* it?' he suggested softly.

Her eyes narrowed at the unfriendliness in his tone. 'Why the hell should I?'

'Because not only is it an eyesore—it's dangerous!'

It occurred to her briefly that if it had been anyone else talking to her in this way, then she would have asked them to show her a little courtesy. So why let *him* get away with it? Because he looked like her every fantasy come to life? Every other woman's fantasy, come to that.

A voice in her head told her that she was playing with fire, but she didn't listen to it, and afterwards she would cringe when she remembered what she said next. And the way she said it. 'Only if you ask me nicely,' she pouted.

Luke drew in a deep breath of outrage and desire, his mind dizzy with the scent of her, his eyes dazzled by the slim, pale column of her neck, the ringlets which floated down over her ripe, pointed breasts.

She looked like a student, he thought hungrily, with her well-worn denims and that gauzy-looking top, which was much too cold for winter weather and made the tips of her breasts thrust towards him. He forced himself to avert his eyes because he'd known plenty of women like this one. Foxy. Easy. Too easy. Women like this were put on this earth with no purpose other than to tempt.

And he was through with women like that.

He thought of Caroline, and swallowed down his guilt and his lust. 'Just do it, will you?' he told her dismissively. And he walked on without another look or glance—even though he could feel her eyes burning indignantly into his back.

Holly hadn't felt so mad for years, but then she couldn't ever remember being spoken to like that by a man. Not ever. The men she had met at college were 'in touch' with their feminine sides—strong on respect, weak on sex appeal. Not like him.

She stared at his retreating form and winced, wondering how she could have been so cloying and so *obvious*. Pouting at him like the school tease. But then sometimes you found yourself reacting in inexplicable ways to certain people—and she suspected that he was the type of man who provoked strong reactions.

Still. Men were a fact of life—even irascible ones. No, *especially* irascible ones! And she was a businesswoman now—she simply couldn't afford to let herself get uptight just because someone had got out of the wrong side of bed that morning. She watched him push open the door to the general store at the end of the street, telling herself that she was glad to see the back of him.

She unlocked the shop door and stepped over a stack of old mail and circulars. She hadn't been here since the summer, on one of the most beautiful, golden days of the year, when she had taken the lease on, and she found herself wondering what the shop would look like in this cold and meagre November light.

Inside it was so gloomy that Holly could barely see. She clicked on the light switch and then blinked while her eyes accustomed themselves to the glare thrown off by the naked lightbulb, and her heart fell. It obviously hadn't been touched since the day she had signed the lease.

The air wasn't just thick with dust—it was *clogged* with it, and cobwebs were looped from the ceiling like ghostly necklaces, giving the interior of the shop the appearance of an outdated horror movie. It might have been funny if it hadn't been her livelihood at stake.

Holly scowled, then coughed. Dust was the enemy of all fabrics, but it was death to the exquisite fabrics she tended to work with. So. What did she do first? Unpack the car? Make a cup of tea? Or make inroads into the neglect?

She half closed her eyes and tried to imagine just what the place would look like all decorated with big mirrors and fresh paint. Dramatic colours providing a rich foil for the snowy, showy gowns. But it was no good—for once her imagination stubbornly refused to work.

A dark shadow fell over her and Holly turned her head to see the man with the denim-blue eyes standing in the doorway. He stepped into the shop as if he had every right to.

He made the interior feel terribly claustrophobic. Holly found herself distracted by those endless legs, the dizzying width of his shoulders, and she felt a warm, unfamiliar tightening in her belly. He was, she noticed inconsequentially, carrying two cartons of milk, a box of chocolate biscuits and a newspaper. So—whoever he was—he certainly didn't have much in the way of domestic routine!

'Well, hello again,' said Holly, and smiled into the denim-coloured eyes.

'What in hell's name are you doing in *here*?'

'I'm admiring all the dust and cobwebs—what does it look like?'

'That isn't what I meant and you know it!' he growled. 'How did you get in here?'

Holly stared at him as if he'd gone completely mad. 'How do you think I got in? By picking the lock?'

He shrugged his massive shoulders as if to say that nothing would surprise him. 'Tell me.'

'I used my key, of course!'

'Your *key*?'

'Yes,' she defended, wondering if he always glared at people this much. She waved the offending item in front of him. 'My key! See!'

'And how did you get hold of a key?'

'I clutched it between my fingers and thumb, just like everyone else does!'

'Don't be facetious!'

'Well, what do you expect when you come over so heavy? How on earth do you think I got it? It's mine. On loan. I'm renting.'

'Renting?'

Her mouth twitched. 'Do you know—you have a terrible habit of repeating everything I say and making it into a question?'

'You're renting the shop?' he persisted in disbelief, as though she hadn't spoken. 'This shop?'

'That's right.'

'Why?'

Holly smiled at his belligerence. 'Well, you've barged in here as if you own the place, asking me questions as though I'm on the witness stand, so I suppose one more won't make any difference. Why do people usually rent a shop? Because they want to sell something, perhaps? Like me—I'm a dress designer.'

He nodded. 'Yes,' he agreed slowly, and an ironic smile touched the corners of his mouth. 'Yes, you look like a dress designer.'

Holly noted the disapproving look on his face and was glad she wasn't opening an escort agency! 'Is that supposed to be a compliment?'

'No.'

'I didn't think so. I fit the stereotype, do I?'

He shrugged. 'I guess you do.' His eyes flickered to the gauzy shirt, where the stark outline of her nipples bore testimony to the cold weather. 'You wear unsuitable clothes. You drive a hand-painted, beaten-up old car—I wasn't for a minute labouring under the illusion that you were a bank clerk!'

'Nothing wrong with bank clerks,' Holly defended staunchly.

'I didn't say there was,' came his soft reply. 'So tell me why you're renting this shop.'

'To sell my designs.'

He frowned as he tried to picture the insubstantial and outrageous garments in which emaciated models sashayed up the catwalk. He tried to imagine Caroline or any other woman he knew wearing one. And the only one who *could* get away with it was the leggy beauty standing in front of him. 'Think there'll be a market for them around here, do you?' he mocked. 'It's a pretty conservative kind of area.'

She ignored the sarcasm. 'I certainly hope so! There's always a market for bridal gowns—'

His dark eyebrows disappeared beneath the tawny hair. '*Bridal* gowns?'

'There you go again,' she murmured. 'Yes. Bridal gowns. You know—the long white frocks that women wear on what is supposed to be the happiest day of their lives.' She waited for him to say something about *his* wedding day, which was what people always *did* say. But he didn't. And Holly was both alarmed and astonished at the great sensation of relief which flooded through her at his lack of reaction. *He isn't married!* she found herself thinking with a feeling which was very close to elation, and then hoped she hadn't given anything away in her expression.

'You design *bridal gowns*?'

'You sound surprised.'

'Maybe that's because I am. You aren't exactly what most people have in mind when they think of wedding dresses.'

'Too young?' she guessed.

'There's that,' he agreed. 'And marriage is traditional...' his eyes glimmered '...which you ain't.'

'I can be. I know how to be.'

Interesting. 'And you'll be living—?'

'In the flat upstairs, of course.' She smiled in response to his frowned reaction to *that*, and wiped a dusty hand down the side of her jeans before extending her hand. 'I guess we'd better introduce ourselves. I'm Holly

Lovelace of Lovelace Brides.' She smiled disarmingly. 'Who are you?'

'Holly *Lovelace*?' He started to laugh.

'That's right.'

'Not your real name, right?'

'Wrong. I've got my birth certificate somewhere, if you'd like to check.'

He looked down at the hand she was still holding out, and shook it, her narrow fingers seeming to get lost within the grasp of his big, rough palm. 'I'm Luke Goodwin,' he said deliberately, and waited.

'Hello, Luke!'

There was another brief pause as he savoured a heady feeling of power. 'You haven't heard of me?'

'You're absolutely right. I haven't.'

'Well, I'm your new landlord.'

Holly was too busy blinking up at him to respond at first. Up this close he was even more divine. He had the kind of mouth that even the most hardened man-hater would have described as irresistible. She was just wondering what it would be like to be kissed by a mouth like that when his words seeped unwillingly into her consciousness.

'But you can't be my landlord!' she protested. Landlords were pallid and wore pinstriped suits, not faded jeans and a golden tan which she suspected might be all over.

He slanted a look at her from between sultry azure eyes. 'Oh? Says who?'

'Says me! You're not the person I signed the lease with!'

'And who did you sign the lease with?'

'I had to meet a man in Winchester—'

'Called?'

'Doug Something-or-Other...' Holly frowned as she recalled the smoothie who had tried plying her with gin and tonics in the middle of the day and sat leering at her thighs. His oily attitude had had a lot to do with the speed with which she had signed the lease. 'I know! Doug Reasdale, that was it.'

'Doug's the letting agent,' he informed her. 'He acted for my uncle.'

'Well, he certainly didn't mention that there was an absentee and highly hostile landlord!' snapped Holly.

'No longer absentee,' he amended thoughtfully. 'And Doug neglected to mention to *me* that he'd just rented out one of my properties to someone who doesn't even look old enough to vote!'

'I'm twenty-six, actually,' she corrected him tightly. She was getting fed up with people thinking she was just a kid. Maybe it was time she started wearing a little make-up, maybe even cut her hair...

'Twenty-six, huh?' He looked at the wild tangle of her curls and her wide-spaced green eyes. Bare lips that excited...invited... Right at that moment she looked like jail bait. 'Well, maybe you should try acting it,' he suggested softly.

Holly smirked. 'Really? That's neat, coming from you! You mean I should follow your shining example of adult behaviour and start throwing my weight around? I thought that dictatorships had gone out of fashion until I met you!'

'But clearly a very ineffective dictatorship in this case,' he observed, trying very hard not to laugh, 'since

I asked you to move your car, but it still seems to be taking up half the road!'

'You didn't *ask* me anything!' she fumed. 'You issued the kind of order that I haven't heard since I was at school!'

'Then you were obviously a very disobedient schoolgirl,' he murmured, before realising that the conversation was in danger of sliding helplessly into sexual innuendo and that he was in very great danger of responding to it.

Holly had never met a man she found as physically attractive as the one standing in front of her, and maybe his allure was responsible for what she did next. She tried to tell herself that it was purely an instinctive reaction to that suggestive velvet whisper, but, whatever the reason, she found herself slanting her eyes at him like a courtesan. 'Why?' she murmured provocatively, and put her hands on her hips. 'Have you got a thing about schoolgirls?'

Luke froze. When she leaned back like that it was easy to see that she wasn't wearing a bra, that her lush breasts were free and unfettered. He saw the way her lips were parted into a smile and he knew for certain that, if he tried to kiss her right then, she would melt into his arms in the way that so many women had done before. But no more. His mouth hardened.

'I'll tell you what I have a "thing" about,' he said carefully. 'And that's people who take on more than they're obviously capable of—'

'Meaning me?'

'Meaning you,' he agreed evenly, as he fought to keep his feelings under control. 'You clearly can't tell your left from your right, judging by your parking—so heaven only knows how you intend to run a thriving business! Or maybe that's why you enjoy flirting with me so outrageously. Maybe you suspect that you're destined to fail? Perhaps you like to have a little something to fall back on, huh? So that if your business goes bust, then the landlord might be lenient with you.'

Holly stared at him, first in horror, then in disbelief. Then with an irresistible desire to giggle. 'My God, you're actually being *serious*, aren't you? Are you really from planet Earth, or have aliens just dropped you here? Or do you honestly think that I'd leap into bed with you if I didn't have enough money to pay the rent?'

Luke knew that he had two choices. If he allowed her to think that he had actually *meant* that outrageous suggestion, then she would seriously underestimate his critical judgement—and Luke didn't like being underestimated by *anyone*. If she underestimated him then she wouldn't respect him either, and for some reason the thought of that disturbed him. Then he thought of Caroline, and swallowed. Maybe, under the circumstances, that would be the best of the two options.

Alternatively, if he laughed it off—then some of this rapidly building tension might dissolve...

He relaxed and let his blue eyes crinkle at the corners. It was a calculated move because he knew only too well the effect that particular look had. It worked on everyone—men, women, children, animals. It was a charm he had in abundance, but he had never used it quite as deliberately as he did right now. 'Don't be absurd,' he denied softly. 'It was just a joke.'

'Pretty poor taste joke,' commented Holly, but it was

impossible not to thaw when confronted by that melting blue gaze.

'Listen, why don't I help you unload your roof-rack so that you can move your car more easily?' He smiled at her properly then, and Holly honestly couldn't think of a single objection.

CHAPTER TWO

'UNLESS,' Luke queried, blue eyes narrowing, 'you have someone else to help you?'

Holly shook her head. 'Nope. Just me. All on my own.'

'Well, then. Show me what needs doing.'

She looked into his eyes, confused by this sudden softening of his attitude towards her. One minute he was Mr Mean, the next he was laying on the charm with a trowel, and—surprise, surprise—he was very good at *that*! 'What's the catch?'

'No catch.'

'Well, that's very sweet of you—' she began, but he shook his head firmly.

'No, not sweet,' he corrected. 'I am never *sweet*, Holly.'

'What, then?' She wrinkled her nose at him. 'Let's go on what we know about you already. Kind? Polite? Gentlemanly?'

He laughed, and even that felt like a brief betrayal, until he told himself that he was being stupid. Men could be friends with women, couldn't they? Or, if not actually *friends*, then friend*ly*. Just because you had a laugh and a joke with a woman, it didn't mean that the two of you automatically wanted to start tearing each other's clothes off.

'Let's just say that it wouldn't rest very easily on my

conscience if I walked away knowing that I had left you to deal with that outrageous amount of luggage. I'm kind of old-fashioned like that.'

Holly regarded him steadily, but her heart was beating fast. She wasn't used to men coming out with ruggedly masculine statements like that last one. 'You mean that I'm too much of a delicate female to be able to manoeuvre a couple of suitcases off the roof-rack?'

'Delicate?' Luke looked her over very thoroughly, telling himself that *she* had asked the question, and therefore he needed to give it careful consideration.

She was getting on for six feet—tall for a woman—with correspondingly long limbs. She had legs like a thoroughbred, he thought, then wished he hadn't—long and supple legs that seemed to go all the way up to her armpits. She was slim and narrow-hipped, but not skinny in the way that tall women very often could be. And her breasts were almost shocking in their fullness—they looked curiously and beautifully at odds with her boyish figure. 'No,' he growled. 'I wouldn't call you delicate.'

She wondered if he had noticed that she was blushing. Maybe not. He hadn't exactly been concentrating on her *face*, now, had he? There had been something almost *anatomical* in the way he had looked at her. If any other man had stared at her body quite so blatantly, she suspected that she would have asked them to leave. But she didn't feel a bit like asking Luke to leave. With Luke she just wanted him to carry on looking at her like that all day long.

'So do you want my help, or not?'

Holly swallowed, wishing that everything he said didn't sound like a loaded and very sexy question. And the decision was really very simple—if she wanted to be totally independent and self-sufficient then she should decline his offer and do it all herself.

But a *sensible* person wouldn't do that, would they? After all, she knew no one here, not a soul. Was she, the great risk-taker, really tying herself up in knots over a simple offer of assistance just because it happened to come from a man she found overwhelmingly attractive? Wasn't that a form of sexism in itself?

'Thanks very much! You can start bringing the stuff in from the car, if you like,' she told him, trying to sound brisk and workmanlike, 'while I go and see how habitable it is upstairs. I just hope it's more promising than down here.' But her voice didn't hold out much hope. 'Unless you happen to have been up there lately?'

He shook his head. 'I've never set foot inside the place before.'

Holly frowned. 'But I thought you said you were the landlord?'

'I did. And I am—but an extremely *new* landlord. It's a long story.' He shrugged, in answer to the questioning look in her eyes. In the dim winter light shining through the shop window he became acutely conscious of how pale her skin looked, how bright her green eyes. With the deep copper ringlets tumbling unfettered around her shoulders, she could have stepped straight out of a pre-Raphaelite painting, jeans or no jeans, and he suddenly felt icy with a foreboding of unknown source.

'And you didn't ask to see any credentials,' he accused suddenly. 'Basic rule of safety, number one.' His eyes glittered. 'And you broke it.'

'Do you have any on you?'

'Well, no,' he admitted reluctantly. 'But the lesson is surely that I could be absolutely anyone—'

'The impostor landlord?' She hammed it up. 'About to hurl me to the floor and have your wicked way with me?'

The air crackled with tension. 'That isn't funny,' he said heavily.

'No,' she agreed, and her throat seemed to constrict as their gazes clashed. 'It isn't.'

'In fact, it's a pretty dumb thing to do—to put yourself in such a vulnerable situation,' he growled.

Independent and self-sufficient—huh! She had fallen headlong at the first hurdle. 'Okay. Okay. Lesson received and understood.'

He was still frowning. 'You'd better give me the keys,' he instructed tersely. 'And I'll move your car when I've unloaded all the stuff.'

Holly hesitated. 'Er—you might find she's a little temperamental in cold weather—like all cars of that age.'

'I should have guessed!' His voice was tinged with both irritation and concern—though he didn't stop to ask himself why. How was she hoping to get a business up and running if she was *this* disorganised? 'Why the hell don't you buy yourself a decent car?' he drawled. 'Didn't it occur to you that you might need something more reliable?'

His sentiments were no different from her own, but it was one thing deciding that she needed a newer car for herself—quite another for a complete stranger to bossily interrogate her on why she hadn't bought one!

'Of course it *occurred* to me,' she agreed. 'But reliable usually means boring. And expensive. To get an interesting car that you can count on costs a lot more money than I'm prepared or able to spend at the moment.' She gave him a reassuring smile. 'But don't worry if she won't start first time. A little coaxing usually works wonders.'

That smile was so *cute*. He threw her a lazy look in response. 'And I'm a dab hand at coaxing the temperamental.'

'Just cars?' she quizzed, before she could stop herself. 'Or women?'

He held her gaze in mocking query. 'Do you always make assumptions about people?'

'Everyone does. You did about me. And was my assumption so wrong?'

'In this case, it was. I was talking about coaxing horses, actually—not the opposite sex.'

He had hooked his fingers into the loops of his jeans as he spoke, and he suddenly looked all man—all cowboy. Holly nodded and bit back a smile. It all made sense now. He had looked completely wrong strolling down a sleepy English village street, with his jeans and battered sheepskin and tough good looks. But she could picture him on horseback—legs astride, the muscle and the strength of the man and the animal combining in perfect harmony. It was a powerful and earthy image and she found that persistent fingers of awareness were prickling down her back. 'Really?' She swallowed. 'Round here?'

'No. Not round here. I've only just got back from Africa.' He read the question in her eyes. 'It's a long story.'

That might explain the tan. 'Another one? So when did you get back?'

He glanced down at the watch on his wrist—a tough-looking timepiece which suited him well. 'About twelve hours ago.'

'Then you must be jet-lagged?'

'Yeah, maybe I am.' Could he blame this troublesome tension on jet-lag, he wondered, or would that be fooling himself? He took the keys from her unprotesting fingers. 'You go on up and I'll start moving the stuff.'

Masterful, thought Holly wistfully, then immediately felt guilty as she found the staircase at the back of the shop, which led directly to the flat upstairs. Masterful men were very passé these days, surely?

The stair carpet was worn, and upstairs the accommodation was basic—in a much worse state than the shop below. Holly sniffed. It had the sour, dark tang of a place unlived in.

She glanced around, trying to remember what had caught her enthusiasm in the first place. There was an okay-sized sitting room, whose window overlooked the street, a small bedroom containing a narrow and unwelcoming-looking bed, a bathroom with the obligatory dripping tap, and a kitchen which would have looked better in a museum. So far, so bad.

But it was the main bedroom which had first attracted her, and Holly sighed now with contentment as she looked at it again. Dusty as the rest of the apartment, it nonetheless was square and spacious, with a correspondingly high ceiling, and would be absolutely perfect as a workroom.

She heard footsteps on the stairs and went out to the landing to see Luke, with a good deal of her belongings firmly clamped to his broad shoulders.

She rescued a tin-opener which was about to fall out of an overfull cardboard box. 'You shouldn't carry all that!' she remonstrated. 'You'll do yourself damage.'

He barely looked up as he put down two big suitcases and brushed away a lock of the dark, gold-tipped hair which had fallen onto his forehead. 'Nice of you to be so concerned,' he said wryly. 'But I'm not stupid. And I'm used to carrying heavy weights around the place.'

She watched unobserved while he took the stairs back down, three at a time. Yes, he was. A man didn't get muscles like that from sitting behind a desk. Holly had grown up in the city, and city men were what she knew best. And they tended to have the too-perfect symmetry gained from carefully programmed sessions in the gym. Whereas those muscles looked natural. She swallowed. Completely natural.

It wasn't until he had done the fourth and final load, and dumped her few mismatched saucepans in the kitchen, that Luke stood back, took a good look around him and scowled.

'The place is absolutely disgusting! It's filthy! I wouldn't put a dog in here! Didn't you demand that it be cleaned up before you took possession?'

'Obviously not!' she snapped back.

'*Why* not?'

Because she had been blinded by the sun and by ambition? Mellowed by the gin and tonic which Doug Reasdale had given her, and an urgent need to get on with her life? 'I was just pleased to get a shop of this size for the money,' she said defensively.

His voice was uncompromising. 'It's a dump!'

'And I assumed that's why it was so cheap—I understood that you took a property on as seen, and this was how I saw it.'

'And who told you that? Doug?'

'That's right. But I checked it out afterwards, and he was absolutely right.'

He laughed, but there was a steely glint in his eyes. 'Lazy bastard! I'll speak to him.'

'You don't have to do that,' she told him, with a shake of her head. 'Like I said—I didn't exactly insist.'

'He took advantage of you,' he argued.

No, but he'd have liked to have done, thought Holly, with a shudder.

'Sounds like you need a little brushing up on your negotiation techniques.' He frowned as he looked around, his mouth flattening with irritation. 'This place is uninhabitable!'

As if on cue, a rattle of wind chattered against the window-pane and raindrops spattered on the ledge. Luke threw another disparaging glance around the room. On closer inspection, there was a small puddle on the sill where the rain obviously leaked through on a regular basis.

'If I'd been around there is no way I would have let you move into a place when it was in this kind of state.'

'Well, there's no point saying that now because you *weren't* around,' she pointed out. 'Were you?'

'No.' God, no. But now he was.

Their eyes met again, and Luke tried to subdue the magnetic pull of sexual desire. It had happened before—this random and demanding longing—but never with quite this intensity. It was sex, pure and simple. And it meant nothing, not long term—he knew that. Its potency and its allure would be reduced by exposure and it was completely unconnected with the real business of living, and relationships.

He should get out of here. Now. Away from those witchy green eyes and those soft lips which looked as if they could bring untold pleasure to a man's body.

Yet some dumb protective instinct reared its interfering head, and when he spoke he sounded like a man who'd already made his mind up. 'You can't stay here when it's like this.'

'I don't have a choice,' said Holly quietly.

There was a pause.

'Oh, yes, you do,' came his soft contradiction.

Holly stared at him in confusion, convinced by the dark look on his face that he was going to tell her to go back where she came from—back where she belonged. But this wasn't the Wild West, and she was a perfectly legitimately paid-up leaseholder of this flat! She gave a little smile. 'Really? And what's that?'

Luke wondered if he had just taken leave of his senses. 'Well, you could always come up to the house and stay with me,' he offered.

She searched his face. 'You're kidding!'

'Why should I be? I feel responsible—'

'Why should *you* feel responsible?'

'Because it's bleak and cold in here, and because the property is mine and I have enough bedrooms to cope with an unexpected guest.'

'But I don't even know you!'

He laughed. 'There's no need to make me sound like Bluebeard! And what's that got to do with anything?

You must have shared flats with men when you were a student, didn't you?'

'Doesn't everyone?'

'So how well did you know *them*?

'That's different.'

'How is it different?'

The difference was that none of her fellow design students—for all their velvet clothes and pretty-boy faces and extravagant gestures and prodigious talent—had appealed to Holly in any way that could be thought of as sexual. She had shared flats with men of whom she could honestly say it wouldn't have bothered her if they had strutted around the place stark naked. Whereas Luke Goodwin...

She thought of soft beds and central heating, and couldn't deny that she was tempted, but Holly shook her head. 'No, honestly, it's very kind of you to offer, but I'll manage.'

'How?'

'I'm resourceful.'

'You'll need to be,' he gritted, his eyes going to the grey circle of damp on the ceiling. 'I'll have someone fix that tomorrow.'

He started to move slowly towards the door, and Holly realised that she was as reluctant for him to leave as he appeared to be. 'Would you like some tea? As a kind of thank-you for helping me bring my stuff up?' she added quickly. 'And you're the one with the milk!'

'And the biscuits!' He found himself almost purring in the green dazzle of her eyes. 'That would be good.' He nodded, ignoring the logic which told him that he would be far wiser to get out now, while the going was good. 'I left them downstairs. I'll go and fetch them.'

The room seemed empty once he had gone, and Holly filled the kettle and cleared a space in the sitting room, dusting off the small coffee-table and then throwing open the window to try and clear the air.

But the chill air which blasted onto her face didn't take the oddly insistent heat away from her cheeks. She found herself wondering what subtle combination of events and chemistry had combined to make her feel so attracted to a man she had known less than an hour.

But by the time Luke returned with the milk and biscuits she had composed herself so that her face carried no trace of her fantasies, and her hand was as steady as a rock as she poured out two mugs of tea and handed him one.

'Thanks.' He looked around him critically. 'It's cold in here, too.'

'The window's open,' she said awkwardly.

'Yeah, I'd noticed.'

'I'll shut it.' The room now seemed so cramped, and he seemed so big in it. Like a full-sized man in a doll's house—and surely it wasn't just the long legs and the broad shoulders. Some people had an indefinable quality—some kind of magnetism which drew you to them whether you wanted it or not, and Luke Goodwin certainly had it in spades.

She perched on the edge of one of the overstuffed armchairs. 'So what were you doing in Africa?'

He cupped the steaming mug between strong, brown hands and stared into it. 'I managed a game reserve.'

Holly tried hard not to look too impressed. 'You make it sound like you were running a kindergarten!'

'Do I?' he mocked, his blue eyes glinting.

'A bit.' She crossed her legs. 'Big change of scenery. Do you like it?'

'Give me time,' he remonstrated softly, thinking that, when he looked at those sinfully long legs, he felt more alive than he had any right to feel. And the scenery looked very good from where he was sitting. 'Like I said—I just got in late last night.'

Holly found that breath suddenly seemed in very short supply. 'And are you here for...good?'

'That depends on how well I settle here.' He shrugged, and he screwed his eyes up, as if he were looking into the sun. 'It's been a long time since I've lived in England.'

She thought that he didn't sound as though he was exactly bursting over with enthusiasm about it. 'So why the upheaval? The big change from savannah to rural England?'

He hesitated as he wondered how much to tell her. His inheritance had been unexpected, and he had sensed that for some men in his situation it could become a burden. He was Luke—just that—always had been. But people tended to judge you by what you owned, not by what you were; he'd met too many women who had dollar signs where their eyes should be.

Yet it wasn't as though he feared being desired for money alone. He had had members of the opposite sex eating out of his hand since he was eighteen years old. With nothing but a pair of old jeans, a tee shirt and a backpack to his name, he had always had any woman he'd ever wanted. And a few he hadn't, to boot. Even so, it was important to him that he had known Caroline before he had inherited his uncle's estate. And what difference would it make if Holly Lovelace knew about his life and his finances? He wasn't planning to make her part of it, was he?

'Because my uncle died suddenly, and I am his sole heir.' He watched her very carefully for a reaction.

Holly's eyes widened. 'That sounds awfully grand.'

'I guess it is.' He sipped his tea. 'It was certainly unexpected. One morning I woke up to discover that I was no longer just the manager of one of the most beautiful game reserves in Kenya, but the owner of an amazing Georgian house, land and property dotted around the place, including this shop.'

'From ranch hand to lord of all he surveys?'

'Well, not quite.'

'But a big inheritance?'

'Sizeable.'

'And you're a wealthy man now?'

'I guess I am.'

So he had it all, Holly realised, simultaneously accepting that he was way out of her league—as if she hadn't already known that. There certainly weren't many men like Luke Goodwin around. He had good looks, physical strength and that intangible quality of stillness and contemplation which you often found in people who had worked the land. And now money, too. He would be *quite a catch*.

She let her eyes flicker quickly to his left hand and then away again before he could see. He wore no ring, and no ring had been removed as far as she could tell, for there wasn't a white mark against the tan of his finger.

'You aren't married?' she asked.

Straight for the jugular, he thought. Luke was aware of disappointment washing in a cold stream over his skin. He shook his tawny head. 'No, I'm not married.' But still he didn't mention Caroline. He could barely think straight in the green spotlight of her eyes. 'And now it's your turn.'

She stared at him uncomprehendingly. 'My turn?'

'Life story.' He flipped open the packet of biscuits and offered her one.

Holly gave a short laugh as she took one and bit into it. 'You call *that* a life story? You filled in *your* life in about four sentences.'

'I don't need to know who your best friend was in fifth grade,' he observed, only it occurred to him that 'need' was rather a strong word to have used, under the circumstances. 'Just the bare bones. Like why a beautiful young woman should take on a shop like this, in the middle of nowhere? Why Woodhampton, and not Winchester? Or even London?'

'Isn't it obvious? Because, unless you work for yourself, you have very little artistic control over your designs. If you work for someone else they always want to inject *their* vision, and their ideas. I've done it since I left art school and I've had enough.'

'You're very fortunate to be able to set up on your own so young,' he observed. 'Who's your backer?' Some oily sugar-Daddy, he'd bet. An ageing roué who would run his short, stubby fingers proprietorially over those streamlined curves of hers. Luke shuddered with distaste. But if that was the case—then where was he now?

'I don't have a backer,' she told him. 'I'm on my own.'

He stared at her with interest as all sorts of unwanted ideas about how she had arranged her finances came creeping into his head. 'And how have you managed that?'

She heard the suspicion which coloured his words. 'Because I won a competition in a magazine. I designed a wedding dress and I won a big cheque.'

Luke nodded. So she had talent as well as beauty. 'That was very clever of you. Weren't you tempted just to blow it?'

'Never. I didn't want to fritter the money away. I wanted to chase my dream—and my dream was always to make wedding dresses.'

'Funny kind of dream,' he observed.

'Not really—my mother did the same. Maybe it runs in families.'

She remembered growing up—all the different homes she'd lived in and all the correspondingly different escorts of her mother's. But her mother had always sewn—and even when she'd no longer had to design dresses to earn money she had done it for pleasure, making exquisite miniatures for her daughter's dolls. It had been one of Holly's most enduring memories—her mother's long, artistic fingers neatly flying over the pristine sheen of soft satin and Belgian lace. The rhythmic pulling of the needle and thread had been oddly soothing. Up and down, up and down.

'And why here?' He interrupted her reverie. 'Why Woodhampton?'

'Because I wanted an old-fashioned Georgian building which was affordable. Somewhere with high ceilings and beautiful dimensions—the kind of place that would complement the dresses I make. City rents are prohibitive, and a modern box of a place wouldn't do any justice to my designs.'

He looked around him with a frown. 'So when are you planning to open?'

'As soon as possible.' There was a pause. 'I can't afford not to.'

'How soon?'

'As soon as I can get the place straight. Get some pre-Christmas publicity and be properly established by January—that's when brides start looking for dresses in earnest.' She looked around her, suddenly deflated as the enormity of what she had taken on hit her, trying and failing to imagine a girl standing on a box, with yards of pristine ivory tulle tumbling down to the floor around her while Holly tucked and pinned.

'It's going to take a lot of hard work,' he observed, watching her frown, wondering if she had any real idea of how much she had taken on.

Holly was only just beginning to realise how much. 'I'm not afraid of hard work,' she told him.

Luke came to a sudden decision. He had not employed Doug Reasdale; his uncle had. But the man clearly needed teaching a few of the basic skills of management—not to mention a little compassion. 'Neither am I. And I think I'd better help you to get everything fixed, don't you? It's going to take for ever if you do it on your own.'

Holly's heart thumped frantically beneath her breast. 'And why would you do that?'

'I should have thought that was fairly obvious. Because I have a moral obligation, as your landlord. The place should never have been rented out to you in this condition.' And that much, at least, was true. He told himself that his offer had absolutely nothing to do with the way her eyes flashed like emeralds, her lips curved like rubies when she smiled that disbelieving and grateful smile at him. 'So what do you say?'

She couldn't think of a thing. She felt like wrapping her arms tightly around his neck to thank him for his generosity, but the thought of how he might react to that made her feel slightly nervous. There was something about Luke Goodwin which didn't invite affection from women. Sex, maybe, but not affection. 'What can I say?' she managed eventually. 'Other than a big thank you?'

'Promise me that if you can't cope, then you'll call on me.'

'But I don't know where you live.'

'Come here,' he said softly. He gestured for her to join him by the window, where the yellow light was fast fading like a dying match in the winter sky. He pointed. 'See that house through the arched hedge?'

It was difficult not to—the place was a mansion by most people's standards! 'That's *yours*?' she asked.

'Yes, it is. So if it all gets too much, or if you change your mind, then just walk on right up to the door and knock. Any time.' Blue eyes fixed her with their piercing blaze. 'And you'll be quite safe there—I promise. Okay?'

'Okay,' Holly agreed slowly, though instinct told her that seeking help from a man like Luke might have its own particular drawbacks.

CHAPTER THREE

As soon as Luke got home, he phoned Doug Reasdale, his late uncle's letting agent—a man he had just about been able to tolerate down the echoed lines of a long-distance phone call from Africa. He suspected that this time around he might have a little difficulty hanging onto his temper.

'Doug? It's Luke Goodwin here.'

'*Luke!*' oozed Doug effusively. 'Well, what do you know? Hi, man—how's it going? Good to have you back!'

'After sixteen years away, you mean?' observed Luke rather drily. He had met Doug once, briefly, when he had flown over for his uncle's funeral earlier in the year. Luke and the agent were about the same age, which Doug had obviously taken as a sign of true male camaraderie since he had spent the afternoon being relentlessly chummy and drinking whisky like water.

'It's actually very good to *be* back,' Luke said, realising to his surprise that he meant it.

'So what can I do you for?' quizzed Doug. 'House okay?'

'The house is fine. Beautiful, in fact.' He paused. 'I'm not ringing about the house.'

'Oh?'

'Does the name Holly Lovelace ring a bell?'

There was a low whistling noise down the phone.

'Reddish hair and big green eyes? Legs that go on for ever? Breasts you could spend the rest of your life dreaming about? Just taken over the lease of the vacant shop?' laughed Doug raucously. '*Tell* me about her!'

Luke's skin chilled and he was filled with an uncharacteristic urge to do violence. 'Is it customary to speak about leaseholders in such an over-familiar manner?' he asked coldly.

Doug clearly did not have the most sensitive antennae in the world. 'Well, no,' he admitted breezily. 'Not usually. But then they don't usually look like Holly Lovelace.' His voice deepened. 'Mind you—not that I think she's much of a goer—'

'I'm sorry?' Luke spoke with all the iced disapproval and disbelief he could muster.

'Well, she's got that kind of wild and free look— know what I mean? Wears those floaty kind of dresses— but oddly enough she was as prim as a nun the day I took her to lunch.'

'You took her out to *lunch*?' Luke demanded incredulously.

'Sure. Can you blame me?'

Luke ignored the question. 'And do you do that with all prospective leaseholders?'

'Well, no, actually.' Doug gave a nervous laugh. 'But, like I said, she's not someone you'd forget in a hurry.'

Luke forced himself to concentrate on the matter in hand, and not on how much he was going to enjoy firing his land agent once he had found a suitable replacement. 'What do you think of the current condition of the property, Doug?'

Another nervous laugh. 'It's been empty for ages.'

'I'm not surprised, and that doesn't really answer my question—what do *you* think of the condition?'

'It's basic,' Doug admitted. 'But that's why she got it so cheap—'

'*Basic?* The place is a slum! The roof in the upstairs flat is leaking,' he said coldly. 'Were you aware?'

'I knew there—'

'The window-frames are ill-fitting and the furniture looks like it's been salvaged from the local dump,' interrupted Luke savagely. 'I want everything fixed that can be fixed, and replaced if it can't. And I want it done yesterday!'

'But that's going to cost you *money*!' objected Doug. 'A lot of money.'

'I'd managed to work that out for myself,' drawled Luke.

'And it's going to eat into your profit margins, Luke.'

Luke kept his voice low. 'I don't make profit on other people's misery or discomfort,' he said. 'And I don't want a woman staying in a flat that is cold and damp. If she gets cold or gets sick, then it isn't going to be on *my* conscience. Got that?'

'Er—got it,' said Doug, and began to chew on a fingernail.

'How soon can it be done?'

Doug thought of local decorators who owed him; carpenters who would be pleased to work for the new owner of Apson House. Maybe it was time to call in a few favours. And he suspected that his job might be on the line if he didn't come up with something sharpish. 'I can have it fixed in under a month!' he hazarded wildly.

'Not good enough!' Luke snapped.

'But good craftsmen get booked up ages in advance,' objected Doug.

'Then pay them enough so that they'll *un*book!'

'Er—right. Would a fortnight be okay?'

'Is that a definite?'

'I'll make sure it is,' promised Doug nervously.

'Just do that!' And Luke put the phone down roughly in its cradle.

Holly washed out the two mugs she and Luke had used, put them on the drainer to dry, then set about trying to make the place halfway habitable before all the thin afternoon light faded from the sky.

The 'hot' water was more tepid than hot, so she boiled up a kettle, added the water to plenty of disinfectant and cleaning solution in a bucket, and began to wipe down all the surfaces in the kitchen. Next she scrubbed the bathroom from top to bottom, until her fingers were sore and aching and she thought she'd better stop. Her hands were her livelihood and she had to look after them.

She sat back on her heels on the scruffy linoleum floor and wondered how many kettles of water it would take to fill the bath. Too many! she thought ruefully. She had better start boiling now, and make her bed up while she was waiting.

She gathered together clean sheets and pillowcases and took them into the bedroom, and was just about to make a start when she noticed a dark patch on the mattress and bent over to examine it. Closer inspection revealed that it was nothing more sinister than water from a tiny leak in the ceiling, but she couldn't possibly sleep on a damp mattress—which left the floor.

She bit her lip, trying not to feel pathetic, but she was close to tears and it was no one's fault but her own. Not only had she stupidly rented a flat which looked like a slum, but she had brought very little in the way of entertainment with her, and even the light was too poor to sew by. The only book in her possession was some depressing prize-winner she had been given as a present before she left, and a long Sunday evening yawned ahead of her. And now she couldn't even crash out at the earliest opportunity because the bed was uninhabitable!

So, did she start howling her eyes out and opt for sleeping on the floor? Or did she start acting like a modern, independent woman, and take Luke Goodwin up on his offer of a bed?

Without giving herself time to change her mind, she pulled on a sweater, bundled on a waterproof jacket, and set off to find him.

Luke was sitting at the desk in the first-floor study, working on some of his late uncle's papers, when a movement caught his attention, and he started with guilty pleasure, his eyes focussing in the gloomy light as he saw Holly walk through the leafy arch towards his house.

He watched her closely. With her long legs striding out in blue denim, she looked the epitome of the modern, determined woman. And so at odds with the fragility of her features, the wild copper confusion of the hair which the winter wind had whipped up in a red storm around her face.

He ran downstairs and pulled the front door open before she'd even had time to knock. He saw that she was white-faced with fatigue, and the dark smudges underneath the eyes matched the dusty marks which were painted on her cheeks like a clown. Again, that unwanted feeling of protectiveness kicked in like a mule. That and desire.

For a split second he felt the strongest urge to just shut the door in her face, telling himself that he was perfectly within his rights to do so. That he owed her nothing. But then her dark lashes shuddered down over the slanting emerald eyes and he found himself stepping back like a footman.

'Changed your mind about staying?' he asked softly, though he noticed that she carried no overnight bag.

'I had it changed for me,' she told him unsteadily. 'And you're right—it *is* a dump! There's no hot water, there's a big patch of damp on the mattress and springs sticking through it! And before you point anything else out, I admit I should have checked it out better—insisted it be cleaned out before my arrival, or something. *And* I came ill prepared. No radio, no television, and the only book I brought with me is buried at the bottom of a suitcase I daren't unpack because there's nowhere to put anything! Just don't make fun of me, Luke, not tonight—because I don't think I can cope with it.'

He heard the slight quaver in her voice and saw the way her mouth buckled into a purely instinctive little pout. He thought how irresistible she was, with her powerful brand of vulnerability coupled with that lazy-eyed sensuality. 'Come in,' he growled quietly, and held the door open for her. 'I have no intention of making fun of you. I'd much rather you came here than have you suffering in silence.'

'Would you? Honestly?'

'Yes,' he lied, as he felt his pulse drumming heavily against the thin skin around his temple. Irresistibly, he let his eyes drift over her. 'You look like you could use a hot tub—or maybe you'd prefer a drink first?'

'That's real fairy-godmother language.' She smiled at him, thankful that he hadn't seen fit to deliver another lecture. 'I'd like the hottest, deepest bath on offer!'

'A bath it is, then. Come upstairs with me.' His eyes glinted with humour. 'God—I *do* sound like Bluebeard, don't I?'

'Who *is* this Bluebeard?' she quizzed mischievously, her eyes sparking as she followed him upstairs, automatically running a slow finger along the gleaming bannister. 'Nice staircase.'

Nice house in general. It soon became obvious that no money had been spared in modernising the place. The paintwork was clean and sparkling and the floorboards had been polished to within an inch of their lives.

He led her to the biggest bathroom Holly had ever seen, with an elegant free-standing bath painted a deep cobalt blue, and enough bottles of scent and bath essence to start a *parfumerie*. He pulled open the door to an airing cupboard where soft piles of snowy towels lay stacked on shelves.

Holly looked round her with pleasure, feeling like Cinderella. 'Mmm! Sybaritic!'

'Did you bring anything to change into?' he asked abruptly.

'You mean—like pyjamas?'

He found that he couldn't look her in the eye; the thought of her in pyjamas—or, even worse, *not* in pyjamas—was distracting to say the least. Bizarrely, he felt the hot hardening of an erection begin to stir, and he forced himself to channel the desire into something less threatening—like irritation. 'I meant some different clothes—the ones you have on are filthy.'

Holly heard the undisguised disapproval in his voice and stared down at herself, at the dusty jeans and spattered sweater, the dirt beneath her broken fingernails. He was right—she looked like a tramp. She shook her head and damp tendrils snaked exotically around her face. 'No, I didn't.' She gave him a rueful look. 'It might have looked a little pushy if I'd turned up on your doorstep with a suitcase!'

It certainly wouldn't have been very beneficial to his blood pressure. 'I can loan you a dressing gown,' he told her evenly. 'And put everything else in the washing machine. It'll be clean and dry in a couple of hours. Leave it outside the door and I'll see to it. You can fetch your other clothes in the morning.'

'You're very kind,' said Holly, meaning it.

'Am I?' His voice was mocking, but then 'kind' wasn't an adjective he usually associated with himself. Certainly not where women were concerned. He watched as she shrugged out of her oilskin jacket and draped it over the back of a chair. 'It's all yours,' he told her, and decided to absent himself as quickly as possible—his mind was already working overtime as he imagined her wriggling her jeans off and sliding her panties down over those long, long legs. Always presuming she was wearing any... 'Take as long as you like.'

'I will,' she smiled, and shut the door behind him.

It was possibly the best bath of Holly's life. She

squirted jasmine and tuberose into the water and, when the bubbles had nearly reached the top, she climbed in and closed her eyes and tried to relax. She couldn't do *anything* about a damp mattress right now—so the most sensible thing would be to put it out of her mind altogether.

She had been in there for the best part of an hour, dreaming up a frothy white bridal petticoat inspired by the fragrant bubble bath, when there was a rapping on the door and she heard Luke's deep voice outside.

'You haven't fallen asleep, have you?'

She stirred in the water. Her flesh had deepened to rose-pink in the warmth, and the buds of her nipples instantly began tightening to the velvet caress of his voice. 'N-not yet, I haven't!' Shakily, she turned the tap on and flicked some cold water onto her burning skin.

'Then come and have something to drink. I've left you a robe outside.'

It was pure heaven to slide the soft white towelling robe on and knot it tightly around her narrow waist. She brushed her hair and left it, still damp and flapping around her shoulders, as she went in search of Luke.

He was sitting on the floor by a roaring fire in the first-floor drawing room, a tray of tea in front of him, half-read newspapers at his side. He watched as she came in, noticing how the pure white of the robe emphasised the firelight-red of her hair, while the soft fluffy material accentuated the carved delicacy of her bone structure. She looked a creature of contrasts, midway between angel and imp.

A pulse flickered at his temple and he felt the blood begin to pound in his head, but *he* had been the one who had invited her here. Was he crazy, or *what*? 'Would you like some tea?' he said evenly.

'Please.'

'How do you like it?'

'Just milk—no sugar.' She took the cup he handed her and sat in front of the fire, folding her long legs up beneath her and then carefully tucking the robe closely around her thighs until she saw him watching her, and stopped. She had meant to *cover* her legs, not draw attention to them.

Luke watched the flicker of amber and copper as the firelight danced across her face and wondered why he felt this random longing for her. Because of the apparent contradiction of her looks? Those sensual movements of the born siren—made all the more potent by that startled look of wide-eyed innocence she must have spent years perfecting?

His voice was a growl. 'Why don't you bring your tea through to the kitchen—I'm just about to make something to eat. I'm starving,' he lied. 'And you must be, too. Unless you brought provisions with you, which, judging by your general standards of preparation, I doubt.'

Holly felt too flustered by the way he had been looking at her to even bother acknowledging the criticism. Food was the very last thing on her mind, even though it had been hours since breakfast, when she'd eaten a banana on the run. But food would be a distraction, and Holly sorely needed something to distract her from those amazing blue eyes, and from the underlying tension which was crackling through the air like sparks from a newly lit bonfire. And besides, if they didn't eat, there was one hell of a long evening to get through...

'Starving,' she echoed dutifully. 'But surely there's no food if you arrived in the middle of the night?'

'I wasn't proposing anything fancy,' he drawled. 'But the freezer was filled in any case,' he explained. 'In time for my arrival.'

'How luxurious.'

'Yes,' he replied shortly.

Caroline again, of course, smooth and efficient. 'I know a company who will fill it for you,' she had told him briskly. 'With enough of the kind of food you like to see you through until I arrive.' She had playfully tapped the end of his nose with one of her professionally manicured nails. Caroline had smooth and beautiful hands, white and soft and unlined. 'Because we can't have you starving, can we, my darling?'

Luke found himself sneaking a glance at Holly's hands, as if to reassure himself of their unsuitability. *Her* nails were short, two were broken, two looked bitten and there were calluses on her palms.

The kitchen was downstairs, in the basement, and it looked as if it had been lifted from an illustration in a lifestyle magazine. It had been, as was the trend, 'sympathetically modernised'. There were light, carved wooden cupboards, and marble surfaces for chopping things, which even Holly—who could barely tell one end of a leek from another—could see were about as up-market as you could get. At the far end of the room was a fireplace piled with apple-wood logs, which glowed like amber, with two squashy-looking chairs on either side.

She sat down next to the fire and shook her damp hair out, watching while he began to boil up pasta and heat through a sauce.

'Like a beer?' he asked.

'Love one.'

He opened two bottles and handed her one, and she sipped it while he strained the pasta and stirred the sauce and pushed a bowl full of freshly grated Parmesan into the centre of the table.

'You look like a man who knows his way round a kitchen,' she observed slowly.

He shrugged. 'I'm used to fending for myself.'

'I thought people had lots of help in Africa?'

His smile was arcane. 'Some people do. I chose not to—just help with the cleaning, same as here. A woman named Margaret starts in the morning—I guess I'd better warn her that I have company.' He gave the sauce a final stir. 'I always think that, if you don't cook for yourself, then you lose touch with reality.' He looked up to where she sat, looking at him intently, and he thought that reality seemed a long way away at this precise moment.

Soon he had heaped two plates with pasta and sauce and they ate at the table in front of the fire.

Forcing himself to eat, Luke struggled to free himself from his rather obsessive study of the way the firelight warmed her skin tones into soft apricot and cream, casting around for something to say. Something which might make him forget that she was a very beautiful woman. 'So what were you doing before you came to Woodhampton?'

She shot him a half-amused glance. 'Just checking

that you haven't given refuge to some gun-toting maniac?'

'We could always talk about the weather, if you prefer,' he told her deliberately. 'But we have a whole evening to get through.'

So they did. Holly took a hasty sip of her beer. It was difficult to concentrate when those amazing blue eyes were fixed on her with such interest. 'After school I went to art school, where I studied textile and design.'

'And were you a model student?' he mocked.

Holly frowned. 'Actually, I *was*, now you come to mention it. And I get a little fed up with people thinking that, just because a person is *creative*, they're automatically a lazy slob—'

'I doubt whether a lazy slob would go to the trouble of starting up their own business,' he put in drily.

'No, they wouldn't.' Feeling slightly mollified, Holly put her beer bottle back down on the table. 'I got quite a good degree—'

'And are you being modest now?'

Her eyes threw him a challenge. 'Mmm! I'm trying—'

'Very trying,' he agreed, deadpan.

'After I left college I went to work for the same fashion house which had employed my mother, but I hated it.'

'Why?'

'Because I felt exactly like an employee, with little control over the entire design process—not really. I felt like I was working in a factory, and I didn't want to be. I wanted to feel creatively free. So I entered the competition.' A dreamy smile came over her face as she remembered. 'And won.'

'Tell me about it,' he said, aware that his voice was unusually indulgent—but that kind of sweet enthusiasm would have melted the hardest heart.

Holly finished a mouthful of tagliatelle and looked into his eyes. Such gorgeous eyes. 'It was organised by one of the glossy bridal magazines to celebrate twenty-five years in publishing.' She met his blank stare. 'You know the kind of thing.'

'Not really,' he demurred, and gave a sardonic shake of his golden-brown head. 'Don't forget I've been living in the wilds all these years—and bridal magazines are pretty thin on the ground!'

Holly got a sudden and disturbingly attractive image of Luke Goodwin wearing a morning suit. 'The idea was to create a wedding dress for the new century—'

'So, let me guess—you did something wild and untraditional?'

She shook her head slowly. 'No, I didn't, actually. Brides usually don't want to be too wild and wacky. Most conform. In fact, I based the dress on an idea that my mother had.' She saw his puzzled look. 'She was a dress designer, too,' she explained. 'She created this most wonderful wedding dress when I was little—I've seen pictures of it.'

'But if yours is almost the same as hers, isn't that called copying—even stealing?'

She shook her head. 'There's no such thing as originality in fashion—you must know that. What goes around comes around. My design was very similar to my mother's but it wasn't *exactly* the same. Unfortunately, Mum's dress was sold, and we never saw it again.'

Luke frowned. 'Why would you expect to?'

'Because she designed it for a very famous fashion house, and those types of garments don't usually disappear without trace. They're usually worth a lot of money.'

'But this one did?'

Holly nodded. 'Someone bought it in a sale. My mother was disappointed it was reduced in price, but not surprised—' Her face lit up with enthusiasm. 'It was a very unusual design, and only an exceptionally thin woman could have worn it. And that was that. Funnily enough, an older Irish woman who cleaned in the store where it was sold—she bought it. After that it disappeared into thin air.'

Luke was more interested in the things she *didn't* say than in the things she did. 'And where's your mother now?'

'Well, it's November, so she's probably in the Caribbean,' replied Holly flippantly. 'Either that, or on a cruise ship somewhere.'

The bitterness in her tone didn't escape him. 'And why isn't she here—helping her daughter get settled into her brand-new business venture?'

'Because her latest disgusting rich old husband probably won't let her,' grimaced Holly.

'Oh, it's like that, is it?' he queried softly.

She threw him a look, a nonchalant expression which had become second nature to her. At school she had quickly learnt that if you learned to mock yourself, then no one else would bother. 'Doesn't *everyone* have a mother who uses a man as a meal ticket?'

'You must hate it,' he observed slowly.

Holly shrugged. 'I'm used to it—she's used men all her life. But I'm not complaining—not really. Their money paid for my education, saw me through art school.'

'And wasn't there a father on the scene?'

'No, I never knew my father—' Holly met his curious stare with a proud uptilt to her chin, feeling oddly compelled to answer his questions. Maybe it was something to do with the penetrating clarity of his blue eyes. Or maybe it was just because he actually looked as though he *cared*.

She ran a finger down the cold beer bottle. 'And no, I'm afraid that it's nothing heroic like an early death—I mean it literally. My mother didn't know him either. According to her, he could have been one of two people and she didn't care for either of them—so she never bothered to tell either of them that she was pregnant.'

Luke expelled a slow breath of air. *'Hell,'* he said quietly, realising that he didn't have the monopoly on unconventional childhoods.

'I suppose I must be grateful that she saw fit to give birth to me.' Her gaze was unblinking. 'Have I shocked you?'

'A little,' he admitted. 'But that was part of your intention, wasn't it, Holly—to shock me?'

She looked at up at him, her eyes partially shaded by thick dark lashes. 'And why would I want to do that?'

'Because illegitimacy hasn't always been accepted the way it is now. When you were growing up, it was probably even a stigma—something to be ashamed of. Wasn't it?' he probed gently.

The memory of it was like a knife, twisting softly in

her belly. Little girls taunting her in the playground. The sense of always being different. 'Yes.'

Her reply was so quiet that he had to strain his ears to hear it. 'So maybe you got used to relating the facts as starkly as possible—to pre-empt that kind of reaction. And if *you* said the worst possible things about not having a father, then that way no one could hurt you. Or judge you.' He paused, and the piercing blue eyes were as direct as twin swords. 'Am I right?'

She put her fork down quickly. 'Yes, you're right.' He was very perceptive. *Too* perceptive. 'I don't know why I'm telling you all this,' she said. 'Just because you've been a Good Samaritan. I don't normally open up to people I've only just met, you know.'

He smiled through the ache that had haunted him since he had first laid eyes on her. 'Maybe it's *because* we're strangers. And because we've been thrown together in bizarre circumstances.'

'What's that got to do with anything?'

'Like people trapped in lifts, or stuck on the side of a mountain—that sense of isolation makes the rest of the world seem unimportant. You break rules.' He looked at her thoughtfully. 'Sometimes you make new ones in their place.'

Holly badly needed to distract herself—wasn't he *aware* that when he looked at her that way she just wanted him to kiss her? 'I may have told you things about *me*,' she corrected him. 'But it hasn't been very reciprocal. You've told me very little about *you*!'

'There's my inheritance,' he said blandly. 'You know about that.'

'Oh, *that*!' she scoffed. 'That's *boring*! I want to hear

about *real* life.' She tried an impersonation of his distinctive drawl. 'Life on the ranch!'

He laughed. It would be so easy to stay here, to bask in the firelight and the soft, green light of her eyes. Easy and dangerous...

'It's late and it'll keep,' he said, swallowing the last of his beer and wondering why it tasted so sour. 'And if I tell you about cheetah kills before bedtime—then you might have nightmares, mightn't you?'

'I suppose so!' She laughed nervously.

But then, Holly suspected that she might have trouble sleeping in any case. Because surely the thought of a big, virile man like Luke Goodwin sleeping in the same house would cause *any* normal woman to be restless.

Especially a woman whose green-eyed and naturally foxy appearance often gave people a totally misleading view of her true nature...

CHAPTER FOUR

DESPITE her reservations, Holly slept soundly and undisturbed in a beautiful high-ceilinged bedroom painted in palest blues and greys. It overlooked the rain-soaked lawn at the back of the house, which sloped down to a fruit orchard at the far end of the garden.

When she woke up it was almost nine, and she stretched luxuriously in the bed, rubbing her sleepy eyes as she threw back the duvet and padded over to the window.

The garden was like an illustration from a child's story book, and Holly could almost imagine the trees being able to speak, the fruits full of enchantment.

Her room had its own bathroom, a luxury she decided she would *never* take for granted! She showered and washed her hair again, put on Luke's white towelling gown, and was just thinking about going in search of her clothes when there was a rap on the door and she opened it to find him standing there, his eyes all shadowed, as though sleep had been at a premium.

His hair was still damp from the shower and he was dressed casually—still in a pair of faded blue denims with a thick, navy sweater pulled down low onto his hips.

'Hello, Holly,' he said softly, and just the sight of her stirred the memories of erotic dreams which had given him one of the worst nights in memory. 'Sleep well?'

She beamed at him with a sunny smile. 'Like a log!'

'Lucky you,' he commented drily, seeing the way her fingers fumbled to tighten the belt of her robe, or rather *his* robe, and he quickly held out her clean jeans, shirt and underwear. 'Thought you might need these. Washed and folded.'

She took the stack of neatly folded clothes from him, and looked down at them in surprise. 'I'm impressed,' she murmured.

Luke's eyes danced at her. 'Real men don't fold clothes, right? That's your stereotype?'

'I don't know enough game reserve managers-cum-lords of the manor to have formed a stereotype! But if ever times are hard—you could always find work in a laundry!'

She hugged the pile of clothes to her like a hot-water bottle, but the movement caused her black lace panties to dangle from the middle of the pile, and she realised that he must have folded *those*, too—as well as her jeans!'

'I'd better get dressed,' she said indistinctly.

'I'll have breakfast ready in ten minutes.'

'I don't generally eat breakfast.'

'I can tell.' Blue eyes roved over her narrow hips critically. 'Bad idea. The brain and the body need fuel after fasting overnight. You'll feel better for it. *Trust* me, Holly!'

Holly laughed as she shut the door on him. That was the oddest thing. She *did*! And, after the succession of doubtful escorts which her mother had trailed through her life, she didn't give her trust easily—certainly not to virtual strangers. Though when you'd shared a house with a man for the night, and he had washed and folded your underwear, then he hardly qualified as a stranger any more, did he?

She quickly put the clothes on, then went downstairs to find him.

He was standing in the kitchen, frying rashers of bacon on the Aga, and the aroma made her mouth water.

'That smells *wonderful*!' she confessed weakly.

He glanced up from flipping a rasher over in the pan.

'Sit down and have some juice,' he instructed, thinking that this was the first time he had ever cooked a woman breakfast without having had sex with her. He watched her intently reading the label of a marmalade jar. 'There's coffee in the pot—unless you'd rather have tea?'

She shook her head. The coffee smelt good, too. Far too good to refuse—hot and strong and black. 'Mmm. Bliss,' she told him, taking a sip.

'I make the best coffee in the world,' he said, with a not-so-modest shrug of his shoulders. 'Or so I'm told.'

'And there's your laundry skills. Tell me—is there no end to your talents?' she teased.

Well, there was something he'd been told he was *very* good at. There was a brief moment of silence while Luke bit back the temptation to look directly into her eyes and tell her exactly what it was...

'Have some toast,' he said abruptly as he put her food down in front of her.

It was the first time for as long as she could remember that Holly had sat down to a proper breakfast. She surveyed the plate piled with egg, bacon, mushrooms, tomatoes and beans, while Luke slipped in across the table opposite her.

'And where did all this food come from?' she wanted to know. 'Not the freezer?'

'No. While you were sleeping I went shopping—'

'You should have woken me,' she said automatically.

'What for? You looked like you needed the sleep.'

'I did.' Holly glanced around the kitchen as she finished a mouthful of bacon. Last night it had been dark, and she had been unable to properly appreciate the beauty of her surroundings. Through the French doors which opened out onto the garden she could see a winter-flowering blossom tree, its buds beginning to reveal the ice-pink petals which lay beneath.

It was so comfortable here, Holly thought. She leaned back in her chair and looked at him, trying to sound as though she minded the delay. 'And heaven knows how long it will take to get the shop looking habitable!'

'Two weeks, I've been told,' he offered drily. 'And that's going to be cutting it fine.'

'But I can't stay here for two weeks!'

Luke sipped his coffee, the cloud of steam obscuring the expression in his eyes. 'Have a problem with that, do you, Holly?'

'I'll get in your way—'

'No, you won't. I won't let you. I have a lock on my study door,' he grinned wolfishly.

Holly shrugged, the idea appealing more by the minute. 'It just seems a long time for me to impose on your hospitality—but if you're happy—'

'I don't know whether *happy* is the adjective I would have selected,' he observed drily. 'I had planned to spend the next couple of weeks sorting out my uncle's affairs—not entertaining a house guest.' Especially such a nubile house guest.

'Oh, but I won't need any entertaining!' she assured him. 'I've got masses to do myself. Paperwork and sewing and finding a florist I can work with. I'll keep out of your way. I promise.' It was no idle threat, either. Luke was an unsettling man, tempting and disturbing—and Holly needed that kind of distraction like a hole in the head right now.

He hoped she meant it. Lending her that bathrobe had been a bad idea. In fact, even *thinking* about that bathrobe was a bad idea. 'I've been on the phone to Doug again this morning. Who assured me that the structural repairs can be done inside forty-eight hours.' He glanced at his watch. 'Someone will be seeing to that roof right now.'

'Thank God for that!'

'Yeah,' he agreed blandly. 'Which just leaves decor. If you let me know your colour choices, I'll make sure that it gets done.'

Holly put her fork down and stared at him. 'But I thought that *I'd* be expected to decorate?'

Luke was keen not to come over as a completely soft touch. He told himself that he would behave in exactly the same way if the tenant happened to be a man. 'And so you would, if the condition of the place wasn't so disgusting—if it was just a question of cosmetics. But, since it needs more than a face-lift, I'll agree to decorate it to your specifications. How about fresh white paint everywhere? Sound okay?'

There was a pause. Holly pulled a face. 'Well, no. Now you come to mention it—not really.'

Denim-blue eyes narrowed. 'Oh?'

She pushed her plate aside, and leaned across the table towards him. 'I don't want to sound ungrateful, or anything, Luke—but what I envisaged as a colour scheme was something much more dramatic than that. Everyone else is doing white walls and big green plants in pots. But this is going to be the kind of bridal shop that no one will ever forget.'

He didn't react. 'Go on.'

'I wanted a deep, peacock-green wall.'

Luke noted her use of the singular. 'That's only one wall,' he commented.

Sharp of him. She drew in a deep breath, determined that he would be able to visualise the vibrant combinations of colours she had in mind. 'That's right—three walls and one window. I'd like another painted in that very rich, intense, almost royal purple—you know the shade.'

'And the final wall?' he queried, deadpan. 'What plans did you have for that—sky-blue pink?'

'Gold.' The same glossy gold which touched the tips of his hair.

'Gold?'

'Mmm.' Holly nodded her head enthusiastically. 'It's the perfect wedding colour—it symbolises the ring and it suggests pageantry and ceremony. And I want this shop to really stand out!'

He fleetingly wished that she wouldn't move with such a refreshing lack of inhibition when she got carried away like that. If only she'd wear a bra. Didn't she realise how ripe and how luscious such sudden movements could make her breasts appear? The hint of their succulent swell against the simple shirt she wore seemed positively indecent.

He swallowed down the erotic fantasies which were beginning to burgeon into life again. 'Stand out?' he quizzed mockingly, reflecting that it was a poor choice of phrase, given the circumstances. 'It will certainly do that!' He frowned. 'Though won't using specialist paints delay your opening—since I imagine that you'll have to buy the more unusual materials in London?'

Holly shook her head with a smile. 'Ah, but that's where you're wrong! There's a specialist paint shop right in Winchester—we need look no further than there!'

We.

Her easy use of the word caused Luke a moment of chilly disquiet, until he silently chided himself for his out-and-out arrogance. Was he now worried that Holly was getting possessive, or passionate, about him? When there had been *nothing* in his behaviour—not a word nor a gesture—which she could have interpreted or misinterpreted as some kind of come-on.

Holly saw the way his shoulders stiffened, and she could sense immediately what he was thinking. Her fingers crept up to cover her mouth apologetically. 'I'm sorry—I didn't mean to be presumptuous.'

He shook his head. 'You weren't being presumptuous. And we'll both go into Winchester to choose your paint.' After all, *he* was the one who was paying for them!

'But aren't you...?' She found that her words were tripping over themselves, as though they couldn't quite decide in what order to leave her mouth. 'Wouldn't you...?'

He looked into her widened green eyes with something approaching amusement. 'Wouldn't I what, Holly?'

'Wouldn't you rather be doing something else?'

He most certainly would.

Her words created such a shockingly graphic image in his mind that Luke briefly closed his eyes in despair. It was simply sexual attraction, he told himself over and over again, as if repetition would make it more believable. Nothing more than that—a combustive hormonal reaction which she had provoked in him, and which would fade as inevitably as the sunlight would fade from the afternoon sky. Was *she* aware of it, too? he wondered. Did it pulse and hum around *her*, too—the feeling almost palpable?

His mistake had been to take her into his house in the first place. To rush in playing the Good Samaritan, trying to fool himself into minimising the potency of the attraction he felt towards her—as if, by rationalising it, it would go away of its own accord.

Because it wasn't conveniently disappearing, and he somehow doubted that it would—unless you took sexual attraction through to its natural conclusion, which he had no intention of doing. For how could it disappear, if she continued to haunt him with those emerald eyes and that pale skin, and the careless cascade of coppery curls?

Maybe she was destined to always be one of those 'if only' women—if only he'd met her when he'd been in that sowing wild oats stage of his life. Holly Lovelace was enchantingly beautiful with her wild, artistic looks—great for a tempestuous affair, but...

The sooner she was set up in her newly decorated shop and out of his life, the better—and, just in case he was forgetting, he wasn't in the market for a lover.

'There's nothing else I'd rather be doing,' he lied. 'And besides, Margaret is coming in to clean the house this morning, so we'll leave for Winchester just as soon as you're ready.'

Winchester was crowded.

Luke looked at the throbbing crowds in disbelief. 'Where's the execution?'

'Sorry?'

'I mean, why else could all these people be here?'

'They're Christmas shoppers,' explained Holly, craning her neck to gaze up in awe at the cathedral.

'But it's only November!' he scowled.

'And some people buy their Christmas presents throughout the year. Apparently,' she added hastily, in case he thought that she was among them!

Luke stared at the looped ropes of fairy lights which twinkled in one shop window, surrounding the puffy cheeks of a beaming cardboard Santa. The same compilation tape of Christmas songs seemed to be blasting out of every shop they passed. He shook his head and thought longingly of the stark beauty of Africa. 'It's crazy—*crazy*—this whole commercial Christmas trip! A celebration of consumption and consumerism!'

Holly shrugged, pleased to hear his views echoing her own. 'I know. I keep planning to go into hibernation!'

They passed a florist's, where pots of fragrant winter

jasmine were stacked next to the gaudy crimson of the seasonal poinsettias. Luke saw a wreath—glossy green and spiky, and studded with berries the colour of blood. Ignoring the appreciative ogling of a young assistant through the window, he slowed down.

'I guess it's your birthday soon?' he hazarded.

Holly blinked. 'How did you know *that*?' she demanded, and then laughed as she looked down and spotted the holly wreath. *'Oh!'*

'Well, it's a Christmas name, isn't it?' He looked at her, a question in his eyes. 'Usually.'

'Yes, you're right. I was born on Christmas Eve.'

'"The night before Christmas?"' he quoted softly, until something in her eyes made him ask, 'But you don't enjoy your birthday?'

Maybe other men had always just asked the wrong questions in the past. Or maybe this man just asked the right ones. Whatever his gift, Holly found that she wanted to tell him things—personal things—in a way which was definitely *not* her usual style.

'No, I don't,' she told him slowly. 'Or, rather, I didn't—not when I was little. It's a difficult night of the year to get a babysitter—a fact that my mother never failed to remind me of. When I was older, she used to leave me while she went out, and in a way I preferred that. Less pressure—'

'How old?' he interrupted savagely.

Holly thought back. 'Ten. Eleven. But people weren't so paranoid about leaving children then,' she added hastily, as some innate loyalty to her mother made her want to defend her.

'And did you get presents?'

'Oh, yes. Huge presents sometimes—if the boyfriend was rich enough. Other years they were a little thin on the ground.'

He said something very soft beneath his breath.

Holly dodged a shopper who was steaming down the high street like a Sherman tank and sneaked a glance at Luke's hard profile. 'So how did you spend your Christmases in Africa?'

His mouth tightened as he found himself reluctant to *think* about it—let alone talk about it. Last Christmas he had spent with Caroline. She had flown in from Durban and had managed to create a traditional turkey dinner on his antiquated old stove. She had even brought linen napkins in her suitcase, and her gift to him had been fine crystal glasses, out of which they had drunk champagne, although his throat had been so dry with the heat that he would have preferred beer. She had raised her glass to him and, in that freeze-framed moment, had seemed to personify calm. An oasis in the hurly-burly of what his life had been up until that point. She had talked wistfully of the babies she longed to have, and everything had suddenly seemed to make perfect sense.

He'd remembered fragments of a conversation he had once had with an Indian friend, and these had drifted back to him as he'd stared into Caroline's serene face. It had been one of those East versus West debates. Dhan had said that it did not surprise him that the Western ideal of basing relationships on romantic love should be doomed to failure. Compatibility and respect were far more important in the long run. And Luke had agreed with him—every word.

Luke watched now as Holly excitedly browsed

through paint charts, impatiently scooping great handfuls of fiery curls away from her pale cheeks.

He wanted her, he thought guiltily. Far too much.

He cleared his throat and spoke to the assistant, who had spent the last ten minutes gazing at him mistily. 'I presume you have professional decorators you recommend?' he asked.

The assistant nodded and fluttered her lashes at him. 'Oh, yes, sir!'

He gave her his lazy smile. 'So how soon could I have a shop decorated?'

The assistant paused. Some people you could fob off. Others you wouldn't want to. Some people came into this shop with their symbols of wealth ostentatiously displayed. This man wore faded jeans and a sheepskin jacket and a pair of desert boots. There was no expensive watch gleaming discreetly on his wrist, and yet he exuded that certain something which spoke of power.

The assistant gave a smile she reserved solely for the really *hunky* customers. 'How soon do you *want* it decorated, sir?' she asked him pertly.

CHAPTER FIVE

'So—' LUKE handed Holly a cup of coffee and tried to inject a little enthusiasm into his voice. 'A week to go.'

'And counting.'

They looked at one another in silence over the breakfast table.

'It's been less...problematic having you here than I thought,' Luke said heavily. He had been down to the shop first thing, irritated to discover that for the first time in *his* experience, the building work was actually coming in on *time*!

'Well, it isn't quite over yet,' said Holly.

'No.'

The thought of moving out appalled her; she felt extremely comfortable where she was, thank you very much. And she liked Luke—she liked him a great deal.

Not that she had anything to be miserable about, not really. The business part of her—though still in a very embryonic state—was delighted that all the work on the shop was going according to schedule. It would be wonderful to hang a sign on the door saying 'Open'. To have all those dewy-eyed brides-to-be arriving and flicking through her sample swatches of Thai silk and duchesse satin.

But these past few days in Luke's company...

Holly sighed, recognising that somewhere along the way she had become completely captivated by him.

Whether or not he had intended for it to happen, she didn't know. She certainly hadn't *intended* to be held in thrall by those faded denim-blue eyes and the dark hair kissed with gold...

And when she thought about it logically, it wasn't really surprising that she was so reluctant to move out. There couldn't be many women who wouldn't enjoy sharing a house with a man like Luke Goodwin! A man with manners, who cooked, who read and who could make her laugh.

In fact, his only fault—apart from his unfair attraction to the opposite sex—was a distinct *bossiness*, and the idea that he was somehow always right.

He gave her a challenging look over the breakfast table. 'Right, Holly,' he said sternly. 'You might as well get your car looked at. You're not using it much at the moment. There's a Beetle dealer in Winchester—he can tell you what it's worth, if you really want to sell it.'

'I can't remember saying that I wanted to sell it,' she objected.

'Didn't you?' His eyes were baby-blue innocent. 'Well, it's up to you—but think of frosty mornings like yesterday, when it wouldn't start.'

When the car had glittered like a magnificent red and yellow jewel—but Holly's breath had been great white puffs of smoke, and her fingers had ended up blue and numb. And Luke had actually scowled, and got angry, and told her she was irresponsible, and asked how she was intending to cope if it broke down in the middle of a country lane at the dead of night.

'Okay,' she sighed. 'Let's go and see the car dealer.'

He drove her into the city, where she was quoted a

very healthy price which made her think seriously about selling. And while they were in town she went to see the signwriter whom she had persuaded to decorate the front of the shop in the most unforgettable and spectacular style before Saturday.

It was almost six as they drove along the back roads out of Winchester towards Woodhampton, and Luke glanced over at her in the dim light of the car.

'Fancy stopping off for supper on the way home?'

'I'd love to,' she whispered in delight, then could have kicked herself. How did she manage to come over like a sixteen-year-old being asked out on a first date!

Luke frowned in the semi-darkness. She confused the hell out of him; she blushed, she stumbled, she turned wide green eyes on him which made him feel guilty for wanting her. Which he did. Still. Frequently.

Sometimes she sounded as naive as a schoolgirl. An image which did not tally with the foxy way she had of looking at him sometimes. Or the way she looked herself... Today she was wearing dark velvet trousers which clung sinfully to those long legs of hers as she crossed one slim ankle over another. He tore his eyes away only just in time to narrowly miss bumping over a rock on the side of the road.

'Damn!'

'Don't swear, Luke,' she commented mildly.

Then cover up, he felt like saying, but resisted.

At the pub they settled down to eat plates of curry and half-pints of lager.

'That was good,' said Luke, wiping his mouth with a napkin and pushing the empty plate away. 'Reminds me of Sunday lunches out in Kenya.'

'Does it?' She stared at a piece of poppadom. 'And did you eat *these*?'

He grinned. 'Sometimes.'

'So was life very different out there?'

'Different to what?'

'Well...' she looked around the pub, glittering and gaudy with metallic streamers '...different to this.'

He looked at her. At the way her hair blazed like the sunsets he'd watched while drinking a beer in the hot dust at the end of the day. He thought about it. 'Yeah. Very different. The days are ruled by the seasons and the animals.'

'And was it a very big game reserve?'

He smiled then, a relaxed smile, thinking that she asked questions with the absorption of a child. 'There aren't really any little reserves, Holly! You need a plane to get around. I used to fly my little super-cub over the place—checking the herds and counting the game. Sometimes I'd get up early at six, and take the hot air balloon up—'

'Seriously?'

He smiled. 'Sure. It's the best time of all—very, very beautiful, and the wind is quite still. The animals don't even know you're there, and you can see cheetah kills or check if any damage has been done by the odd rogue elephant. If there were any injured animals I'd go back for them with a vehicle, and bring them back and tend to them.'

'And you loved the animals?' she quizzed softly.

'Not in the way you think.'

'And what way is that?'

'It's not like having a puppy running round the place;

not the same kind of thing at all. Man's relationship with wild animals tends to be based on mutual respect, but they aren't tame and they never will be.'

'So they don't love you unconditionally? I thought that was the thing which motivated people to work with animals.'

He shook his tawny head. 'Nope. If you're lucky, you can earn their trust—and that's a pretty good feeling.'

No wonder he looked so rugged and brown and strong. Holly stared at the strong lines of his jaw and again felt that stupid urge to trace her finger along its proud curve. 'I've never met a real-life adventurer before.'

'Hey!' he contradicted softly, with a shake of his head. 'It's just a job, Holly.'

'Not really,' she mused. 'It's hardly putting on your suit and getting on the 8:05 every morning with a rolled-up umbrella under your arm!' And it seemed such *physical* work, too. Most of the men she'd met in her life wouldn't have been able to punch their way out of a wet paper bag. Somehow she didn't picture Luke having any trouble. 'How about time off? What did you do then?'

He looked at her, imagined the vast African sun gilding her hair. 'Oh, I walked a lot—there are some beautiful rivers out there. Sometimes I camped out under the stars. I grew an orchard of oranges and lemons and had freshly squeezed juice for breakfast. Sometimes I'd get on a horse and just ride.'

'So it was solitary?'

'Sometimes.'

She opened her mouth to ask him about women, but something stopped her and she shut it again. She didn't want to know. Didn't want to lie in bed at night and torture herself—imagining those strong brown limbs tangled with someone other than *her*.

God, what was she *thinking*? She swallowed. That she'd like to go to bed with him—*that* was what she was thinking.

He narrowed his eyes. 'Why, Holly, you look awfully hot under the collar,' he commented on a murmur. 'Why ever's that?'

'Too many layers on,' she mumbled, and took a huge mouthful of lager.

But she might as well have been a nun for all the notice he took of her. In the same situation, any other man might have leapt on her, but, while only a fool would deny that *something* fizzled through the air between them, Luke behaved like a perfect gentleman. Holly felt protected and safe; safer than she could ever remember.

Just my luck, she thought gloomily that night, as she lay in bed reading what the competition was up to in *English Brides*. You find a man you can spin wild fantasies about and he treats you like a maiden aunt!

Still, at least there was plenty of work to keep herself occupied, while Luke sat in the study, frowning like mad over his legal documents, or driving out to a farm his uncle had owned on the edge of the county which he said was driving him nuts because no money had been invested in it for years.

'It will need a total rethink,' he prophesied grimly, pleased that he had managed to offload Doug Reasdale without too much unpleasantness.

'And is that what you're going to do in England?' asked Holly tentatively. 'Build on your inheritance?'

'I guess,' he mused. 'Maybe I'll make a fortune and then give it all away to someone who needs it more than me.'

There weren't *many* people who could have said that and made it believable, thought Holly—but Luke was one of them.

She had her dress samples sent down from London, and Luke gave her the use of a large ground-floor room to hang the wedding gowns up in. When they arrived she spent most of the day ironing them, and he brought her in a cup of coffee just as she was steaming the creases out of a silver taffeta gown with a huge skirt and a silver bodice encrusted with beads.

He stood looking at the elaborate creation for a moment, then frowned. 'Do you like that?' he asked her doubtfully.

Holly hid a smile. 'This? It isn't my particular favourite,' she admitted.

'Looks a bit like one of those dolls that some people use to cover up loo rolls,' he observed.

'They don't generally use pure silk-taffeta for those!' she laughed. She sat back on her heels to look up at him, then wished she hadn't. From here, it was all too easy to start fantasising about those endless legs...

She began to chatter brightly instead. 'This is a more traditional dress, because brides often come shopping with their mothers. And, no matter how way-out the bride might be, mothers do tend to like traditional dresses!'

'Do they?' he questioned thoughtfully. His eyes flicked over the other dresses on the rail. 'I'm surprised that hardly any of them are white—I thought that's what brides wore.'

It occurred to Holly that this was a man who knew very little about weddings. 'Brides have worn different colours throughout the ages—but, yes, you're right, white was the predominant colour for many years.'

'But not any more?'

'That's right.'

'Now they wear cream?'

'Ivory,' she corrected. 'Which suits most people's skin tones much better. White can be a difficult colour to carry off.'

'And its associations are obsolete?' he suggested drawlingly.

Holly looked at him. 'Meaning?'

Luke shrugged. 'Well, white is traditionally the colour of virgins, and most brides these days are no longer virgins. Are they?'

Afraid that she would start stuttering like a starter gun, Holly put the steamer down, took the coffee from him and carried it over to the window. 'Er, no. They're not.' It was time to change the subject. She really didn't feel up to discussing the modern decline of bridal virginity—not with Luke, anyway.

She realised that not once had he mentioned his own family—bar his uncle, who had left him this house, and that had been only fleetingly. He was an enigmatic man, that was the trouble. He kept his cards very close to his chest, and of course that made him all the more intriguing. Holly was so used to meeting men who told you their entire life story within the first five minutes of meeting them that she wasn't sure how to cope with a man who kept his own counsel!

She stood savouring the bitter, strong aroma of the coffee for a moment, before plucking up the courage to say, 'Are either of your parents still alive, Luke?'

'No,' he answered shortly.

She took another sip of her coffee, recognising that a barrier had come slamming down. Fair enough. Her own life had been unconventional and she knew that people prying only made her hackles rise in defence. She smiled at him instead. 'You know, you're absolutely right—you *do* make the best coffee in the world!'

Luke's mouth softened. So she wasn't overly inquisitive. The fact that she had correctly picked up the signals and retreated made him far less inclined to clam up about his past. And friendship was a two-way game—she'd told him plenty about herself. 'My mother was an opera singer,' he told her, going to stand beside her by the window.

It was not what she had imagined, not in a million years. She let out a low whistle. 'I'm impressed!'

But he shook his head as he stared into the middle distance. 'Don't be. She wasn't a soloist, more a jobbing singer. So she had all of the sacrifice and insecurity with none of the glory.' His smile held a sideways tilt of resignation. 'But still she carried on singing.'

'She must have loved it very much to continue,' commented Holly.

'Oh, there was ego involved, and certainly passion,' he commented wryly. 'Which are the two main motivating forces behind the arts.'

'Ego and passion? Hmm! Yet *another* generalisation from Mr Goodwin!' laughed Holly.

'Maybe,' he shrugged. 'But I think that artists generally have a better time than their unfortunate offspring.'

'You mean that they don't make good parents?' she asked tentatively, aware that the answer was suddenly terribly important to her. Because he thought of *her* as an artist? And if he damned their parenting skills in general, then surely he would also be damning her?

'I don't think they do make good parents, no. Try explaining to a five-year-old why Mummy has to go off for months on end on tour.' He shot her a swift look. 'Why the adulation of an audience means more than that of your small child.'

She glanced up at him. 'And did you have a father anywhere on the scene?'

'Oh, yes.' He watched the steam rise from his coffee. 'He used to care for me during my mother's absences, even turning a blind eye to her little dalliances.'

Holly's eyes widened. 'You mean she had...'

'Affairs?' he supplied acidly. 'I most certainly do. If there was one thing my beautiful, artistic mother excelled at, it was having affairs.'

'Heavens,' commented Holly uncertainly.

'They were necessary to that ego of hers again—to show that she was still a desirable woman.'

'I see.' The bitter disapproval in his voice was unmistakable and understandable. Holly put down her empty cup on the window sill and turned to face him. 'What happened to them? Your parents, I mean?'

There was a pause. His words were like lemon pips.

'My mother died of an infection abroad, when I was eight—'

'Oh, *Luke*,' said Holly, her heart going out to him. 'What a terrible thing to happen.'

He was caught in the sympathetic light from her eyes, and something in that emerald blaze started an aching deep within him, but he quashed it as ruthlessly as he would a fly. 'Yeah,' he agreed quietly, that one small word telling her more than anything just how bad it must have been.

She wanted to go and hug him, to take him tightly in her arms and enfold him, to soothe all that little-boy hurt away.

He saw the way she was looking at him, and it made him want to lose himself in the velvet softness of her lips, to melt and meld into the shuddering sweetness of her body. But he shook his head in denial, trying to get a handle on his senses.

'It *was* a terrible thing to happen,' he said quite calmly, as though these were words he had repeated many times. 'My father never really got over it. He loved her, you see—for all her capriciousness and her fickleness, her inability to accept reality. When she died it was as though a light had gone off inside him—'

'He gave up, you mean?'

'Not in the physical sense. He continued to care for me as best he could. A housekeeper cooked my meals and cleaned my clothes, and my father gave me what love he was capable of. Summer holidays were the worst—we lived in London, and the city used to feel like a cage during those long weeks. His brother began inviting me down here during the vacations—and the sense of freedom and space was a real eye-opener.'

Holly stared out of the window again, at the bare-branched beauty of the winter landscape. She imagined those same trees clothed in green, the summer flowers bursting into rainbow radiance. Yes, she thought, this place must have seemed like a paradise to a motherless little city boy. She turned back to him, her eyes full of questions. 'And?'

Luke looked at her with interest. Most people had usually overdosed on sadness by this stage in his story. Not that he had told it for a long time. Even Caroline had blithely told him that bad memories were best pushed away and forgotten. That cans of worms were best left unopened. He found himself wondering fleetingly whether she was right.

'My father died just after I finished school. It was as though he had been hanging on until he had seen through his parental responsibility. I was lined up to go to university—it was something my father wanted badly for me. Then, when he died, I suddenly thought, I don't have to *do* this any more—in fact, I don't have to do *anything* I don't want any more.'

'And that's when you went out to Africa?' Holly guessed. 'For even more of the space you had come to love here? And to escape the unhappy associations with England. And the past.'

'Intuitive of you,' he observed.

'It's one of the more positive sides of being artistic,' she told him archly. 'It isn't all *ego*, you know!'

'Did I offend you with my comments?' he drawled, noticing that she had failed to mention passion.

'The truth never offends me.' She was aware of him watching her closely. Too closely. Her long-limbed body seemed to suddenly lack co-ordination; her hand was shaking as she picked up the steamer once more and moved back towards the silver gown. 'I guess I'd better get back to work.'

'Yes.' But he remained rooted to the spot, transfixed by the sight of her. Today she was dressed in some filmy-looking skirt covered in a delicate floral print, which flowed all the way down to her slender ankles. The shirt she wore was white and loose and gauzy, and she had some sort of dark, tight vest beneath it, so it certainly wasn't indecent. But there was something about a woman in a diaphanous piece of clothing which would make any hot-blooded male's heart pound.

And Luke's was pounding now.

He swallowed, trying to ease the hot dryness in his mouth, the ache between his legs. He needed to get out of here. Away from here. Fast.

'I'm going out,' he told her abruptly.

'Oh?' said Holly pleasantly. 'Going somewhere nice?' she heard herself asking, as if she were his form teacher!

'Just out.' Damn her, and her curiosity. He had offered her house room for a couple of weeks and suddenly she was his keeper? 'I'll see you later,' he said tersely, and took himself off to telephone Caroline.

'Sure,' agreed Holly, in a casual tone which didn't quite come off. His abruptness hurt. Was he angry with himself for giving away too much? For opening up a heart she suspected had been ramparted for too many years? She picked up a needle and began to sew, and presently the comforting rhythm of the needle and thread made her feel calm once more.

Holly spent the next couple of days checking she had done everything that her guidebook to starting a new business told her to. She knew how important it was for her to establish strong links with all the other local companies associated with weddings. She needed to get to know caterers and car-hire companies, the managers of popular wedding venues and local florists. That way, they all helped one another.

She took her car into Winchester and discovered that the best florist in the city was the one who had been displaying the holly wreath which had caught Luke's eye that day when they'd braved the Christmas shoppers together.

The assistant who had ogled Luke so appreciatively went out to the back room to find the shop's owner, and Michelle McCormack appeared almost immediately.

She was a tiny dynamo of a woman, aged around thirty, with eyes the colour of expensive chocolate and glossy brown hair which was tied back in a dark green ribbon to match the green pinafore she wore. She was imaginative and enthusiastic, and she and Holly hit it off straight away. They went into the back of the shop to browse over the big book of wedding bouquets over cups of tea.

'I need plenty of fresh flowers for the opening on Saturday,' Holly explained as she peered at a photo which featured a stunning combination of cornflowers and sunflowers. 'For decorating the shop window—

that's as well as bouquets for the window. But naturally, this volume of blooms is a one-off.'

'After that, I could supply a mixture of silk flowers and fresh?' suggested Michelle. 'Fresh flowers should be saved for special occasions, because they don't last long and it won't set your beautiful dresses off if you have wilting petals in the shop window! Some occasions would obviously need fresh posies for the window.'

Holly nodded. 'All the key festivals, really. Brides get ideas at holiday times.'

'White lilies at Easter,' said Michelle dreamily. 'And scarlet silk peonies for Valentine's. Can I clash colours and break rules?'

'As long as you make them as well!' giggled Holly as she saw her dream begin to gather real substance. 'I want you to be as creative as I intend to be!'

Michelle gave Holly a penetrating stare just before she left, and said, 'So where's your hunk?'

It would have been pointless and rather pathetic to have expressed ignorance of whom she was talking about. Holly shrugged. 'Luke? I don't know—and anyway, he isn't *my* hunk.'

Michelle licked her lips exaggeratedly. 'Then can *I* have him, please?'

'You haven't even seen him!' protested Holly.

'No, but my assistant has—and I value her judgement on most things! Just tell me one thing—has she been exaggerating about his extraordinary beauty and sex appeal?'

Holly couldn't lie. 'Er, no,' she confessed. 'She hasn't.'

After seeing Michelle, Holly went in person to talk to

a reporter from the *Winchester Echo*, guessing that she would get better coverage if she laid on the charm offensive in person, rather than just telephoning.

The cub reporter was called Pete, and he was young and enthusiastic.

Holly gave him all the details while he scribbled them down.

'And you say you won a competition?'

'That's right. Sponsored by *Beautiful Brides*.'

'And the cheque was sufficient to get you started up in business?'

'Only just!'

'Interesting story,' he mused. He wrote something else down, then looked up. 'And where's this dress now? The winning design?'

'I have it packed away,' she told him. 'It's being featured in next March's issue of *Beautiful Brides*. I shall be unveiling it—if you'll excuse the pun!—on Saturday at the opening, and every person who visits the shop during the month of December will be entered into a draw to win the dress!'

Pete pursed his lips together and made a clicking sound with his teeth. 'Good publicity stunt,' he breathed, then smiled at her as he flicked his notebook shut and stood up. 'And it'll make a brilliant story!'

'I certainly hope so.'

'See you Saturday, then!'

On the way home, Holly couldn't resist going to peep at the shop, which was a flurry of activity. People were sawing wood and painting and knocking nails in walls. From the direction of the upstairs flat came the sound of a drill being used. She parked the car, and was standing outside for a moment, unsure of whether or not to go right inside, when a familiar figure came striding out of the shop, and predictably her heart leapt like a salmon.

He was dressed in a pair of faded jeans which matched his eyes and a fleecy blue-check shirt which made them look even bluer. His gold-tipped hair was sprinkled with sawdust that made Holly think of fairy dust, but his eyes were wary and reminded her that he'd been keeping his distance lately.

'Hello, Holly,' he said carefully. 'I thought you were going to stay away until everything was ready?'

'You sound as though you're warning me off!' she told him crossly.

Or himself, Luke thought grimly, before forcing a smile to hide behind. 'Well, I'd hardly do that, would I?' He forced his voice to sound placatory, but it wasn't easy. He had two more days of this to endure—just two more days and then his life would be Holly-free. He would be able to sleep nights. Eat a meal without having lustful thoughts about the morsels disappearing into that pink and delectable mouth of hers. He couldn't wait. 'When it's your shop.'

'*Your* shop, you mean,' she corrected sulkily, as she recalled her conversation with Michelle McCormack. He was the kind of man who made total strangers want to chat him up—so what chance did *she* have? Quite apart from the fact that his moods were so mercurial. One minute he seemed like her best buddy, while the next...

'If it's my shop then you have certainly made your mark on it,' he commented drily. 'Since I hadn't planned on green, gold and purple walls—or a bleached wood floor!'

Holly made herself sound grateful, and she *was* grateful. After all, there couldn't be many landlords who would decorate a shop exactly to the new leaseholder's specifications. If only he wouldn't be so spiky! 'It's lovely,' she said obediently, and pressed her nose up against the window.

'Well, it's not finished yet.' He looked down at her with a curious frown. 'What's up? I thought you'd be a lot more excited than this.'

'Oh.' Holly shrugged as she searched around for something to say. Something suitable. Rather than something along the lines of, I'm going to miss you, Luke Goodwin. I'm going to miss seeing that lazy smile which you give out so rarely, but when you do it's like the sun blinding you with its radiant power. 'I guess that the realisation of just what I've taken on has finally hit me.'

'Can't cope, huh?' he teased.

She slitted her eyes at him like a cat. 'Just watch me!'

He turned away—he had to, for fear that she would see him harden in front of her eyes. For God's sake—what was the matter with him? Getting erections like a schoolboy? It was sheer bloody instinct, this response. And a sheer bloody inconvenience, too. His voice was gritty as he spoke over his shoulder. 'Are you going back up to the house?'

'No, Luke—I'm planning to make myself a comfy bed of sawdust and sleep right here!'

He turned then, exasperation and humour making his mouth twist and curve in all directions. 'Any idea what you'd like to eat later?' Evenings were becoming increasingly difficult, but he found that he could cope with her a little better if they weren't on mutual territory.

Squashy sofas and large, comfortable beds within carrying distance were proving something of a distraction. 'We could always go to that pub again. Or find a restaurant, maybe?'

But Holly was reluctant. If they went out as a couple, it only served to remind her that they *weren't* actually a couple, much as she would have liked them to be. She shook her head. 'I'll probably just have some eggs and an early night. I've still got lots of paperwork to do—figures that need going over.'

'Everything adding up okay?'

She knew he found it fascinating that she could tot up a column of figures in her head. 'Just because I majored in art doesn't mean I'm a complete dough-brain when it comes to sums, you know!'

'I know! I know! Skip the lecture, Holly. I think you're brilliant in almost every way!'

'Almost?'

'If only you could cook!' he sighed, and gestured behind him with his thumb. 'Better get back in there—it's been years since I did any carpentry!'

Holly walked through the already dark village street towards the silhouetted arch of the yew bush which framed his beautiful house. Then she stood still for a moment, and just stared.

Saturday would be the first of December and the opening of her brand-new shop. She was an adult, a grown-up—on the start of something big. Something exciting.

Why, then, did the thought of Saturday and leaving Luke make her feel as miserable as when the tooth fairy forgot to visit?

CHAPTER SIX

AN OLD-FASHIONED bell chimed out as Luke pushed open the shop door and stepped inside.

Perched halfway up a stepladder, Holly halted in the middle of hanging a bunch of golden balloons from the ceiling and looked down expectantly at him. It was important to her what he thought. Everything about the day so far had been good—it was crisp and clear, with golden sunshine gilding the intense blue of the early December sky. And all the work had been finished bang on time.

Outside, painted in old gold on a deep green background, the shop sign bore the legend 'Lovelace Brides'. In the window itself, a faceless mannequin wore Holly's prize-winning dress. The ivory duchesse satin gleamed with all the milky lustre of moonlight, the soft, heavy material falling in perfect folds from the pleated waist. The stark simplicity of the style simply took the breath away. Or so the departing builders had told a pleased and bemused Holly—though she didn't have them marked down as wedding dress experts!

The mannequin was holding an exquisite bouquet designed by Michelle—a winter bouquet bright with glossy green foliage and scarlet berries, waxy white Christmas roses and sprigs of mistletoe.

In the background a CD played bridal music to add to the mood—at the moment it was trumpeting out the awesome majesty of 'Pomp and Circumstance'. And, all in all, Holly felt that there was little she could do to improve anything in the shop.

But Luke's opinion was somehow as important to Holly as all the other component parts which went to make up a success. He had put himself out on a limb by letting her choose the colour scheme, he had trusted her judgement—and she desperately wanted him to like it.

Luke looked around and took it all in very, very slowly. With the deep, rich colours she had chosen the effect could have been claustrophobic, but the high ceilings and elegant proportions of the building meant that it was exactly the opposite. Peacock, golden and purple. It was both ancient and modern—ageless and timeless. The huge mirrors on each wall which were a necessary feature of all bridal shops—since every angle of the bride had to be seen and scrutinised—reflected the colours and the space back and back again.

'Well, well, well,' said Luke, very softly.

'Do you like it?' she asked him quietly as she climbed down off the ladder and stood in front of him.

'I like it very much,' he replied. 'How about you?'

'I love it.'

'You left very early this morning.' He narrowed his eyes at her in question. 'With all your gear.'

'Well, I had a lot to do. And you were sleeping.'

'Oh?' There was a hint of teasing humour in the blue glint of his eyes. 'Did you come in and check up on me, then, Holly?'

'I—stuck my head round the door.' Holly picked up a silver balloon and began to tie it to another, wondering whether he would notice that her fingers were trembling with the memory.

It had been a daunting and magnificent sight—Luke's bronzed and muscular body sprawled carelessly out over most of a double bed. He had been covered by a duvet, true, but some of his chest had been bare and Holly's eye had been drawn with fascination to the riot of gold-tipped hair which grew there. The soft feathers of the goose down quilt had moulded themselves closely to his shape—defining each muscular leg as it shifted restlessly, causing Holly to leave the room more hurriedly than she had intended.

'Well, I didn't hear you,' he observed softly. He always slept in the raw, and now he found that his pulses were leaping with unbearable excitement at the thought of Holly watching him while he lay sleeping. 'You should have woken me.'

She had been tempted—oh, yes! For one brief, mad moment of fantasy she had actually contemplated stepping out of her warm and cosy pyjamas and climbing in naked beside him, wrapping her soft skin against the hardened contours of his body. In the fantasy which followed he said nothing, just pulled her into his arms and began to kiss her very thoroughly. And that was as far as she had got before fleeing the room as sanity had seeped back in.

Luke walked up and down the shop, past the flowing silks and satins of the dress rail full of samples. He paused for a moment beside the pale frothy haze of bridal veils, with their pearled or glittery tiaras. There were shoes too, in different styles, lined up in neat lines, like rows of ivory satin soldiers. While right in the corner lay tiny drifts of minuscule bras and panties in finest silks and Belgian lace.

'Underwear?' he asked her, in surprise.

Holly flushed a horrid, unbecoming shade of magenta. 'There's no need to look so shocked!' she complained.

He shook his head, the corners of his mouth lifting with amusement. 'I'm not shocked,' he told her. 'Merely curious. Fascinated, actually—as to why you're flogging knickers in a bridal shop!'

Holly sighed. 'You men can be so dense sometimes! Because the bride-to-be is under enough stress as it is. What she wants is to *simplify* her life—and you can do that by saving her time. You sell as much as possible of what she wants to wear on the big day under one roof. And bridal underwear is a little bit specialised.'

'Oh?'

'It must be the very best—the finest silks, the purest lace—'

'The flimsiest?' he suggested with an ironic smile, as he impudently dangled a cream lace tanga from his index finger.

Holly's eyes swam as the image of him holding the wisp of lace imprinted itself onto her mind. It looked— and she felt her heart race like fury—looked as if he had just slid that outrageous little garment off. Off *her*, perhaps? Oh-oh! There was that lethal wishful thinking again! She couldn't look him in the face, let alone the eye, so instead she bent to pick up an imaginary speck of dust from the softly gleaming floorboards.

'The house seems very bare without you,' he said suddenly.

Holly swallowed down the lump of emotion which

had risen in her throat and aimed for humour. 'And very quiet, I imagine?'

Dark eyebrows were elevated. 'Well, there *is* that,' he admitted, with a smile.

He stood looking at her; he could have stood there looking at her all day. 'You look fantastic, Holly,' he said.

'Do I?' Holly searched helplessly for another speck of dust. She was wearing a daring thigh-high tunic made of thin layers of embroidered cream voile, with sheer floaty sleeves gathered tightly at the wrist. It was one of her own designs, which was what people would expect, and could *almost* be a wedding dress—if the bride had absolutely no qualms about showing acres of leg! 'Honestly?'

'Honestly. I didn't realise you had legs.' He let his eyes linger on them. Bad mistake. Luke quelled the heat which was threatening to rise.

'You, um…you look very…very nice yourself,' said Holly tamely, because she thought that 'sensational' might be a little too strong an adjective! She wasn't used to seeing him dressed up—in fact, she realised that this was the first time she had seen him in anything other than faded denims.

He usually looked much more like a ranch hand than a man of some means, but today was the closest he had got to that particular image, in a shirt of delphinium silk and dark navy trousers. Yet he didn't look a bit like a stuffed shirt, which a lot of men did if they weren't used to wearing smart clothes. Luke just looked sexy. Unbelievably sexy. 'Very nice,' she finished.

'Why, thank you,' he answered drily, but he found that he was absurdly flattered by her halting compliment.

The darkening of his eyes was immensely flattering, but Holly found that it was making her feel light-headed, and she couldn't think straight. Her voice sounded faint. 'I-I'd better go and open some wine.'

'I'll do it.' He followed her out to the small, newly fitted kitchen at the back of the shop and took the corkscrew she handed him. 'What time are they arriving?'

'Soon.' But not soon enough, thought Holly with a swift glance at her watch. Much more time alone with Luke and she would surely do something unforgivable, like hurling herself into his arms and asking him to kiss her. Every bit of her!

She tipped crisps and peanuts into bowls and lined up the glasses she had hired for the day, while Luke extracted corks from wine bottles like an expert. They worked together in companionable silence, and Holly wasn't sure whether to be pleased or not when she heard the clanging of the doorbell as the first of her invited guests arrived.

It was Michelle McCormack, the florist. She was dressed in apple-green and had brought two girlfriends with her. 'Candy and Mary are both getting married in the summer,' she told Holly excitedly. 'So they're going to be your first two customers!'

'Please don't feel under any pressure,' Holly told them, with a smile.

'Now that's not the right marketing approach!' scolded Michelle, but Holly shook her head.

'On the contrary—I'm confident that with one look— they'll be hooked!'

'Well, why don't we put it to the test?' suggested Candy with a giggle, and she and Mary went off to gaze longingly at the wedding dresses.

'Who'd like some wine?' asked a deep voice behind them, and Holly watched as Michelle turned round and was momentarily transfixed by the sight of Luke Goodwin, resplendent in the soft silk shirt, his blue eyes glittering like a sun-kissed sea.

'Me, too,' whispered Michelle, goggle-eyed.

'Me, too—what?' asked Holly, blinking with confusion.

'One look and *I'm* hooked!'

From Luke's faint smile, Holly guessed that he must have heard, but Michelle didn't appear to mind—or maybe it had been her intention that he heard!

Holly introduced them. 'Luke, this is Michelle McCormack, who is responsible for all the beautiful flowers you can see. Michelle, this is Luke Goodwin—he owns the shop.'

'You *own* it?' Michelle's eyes widened into saucers as she took a glass of white wine from him. 'Holly didn't tell me you were rich as well as beautiful!'

'I don't remember saying he was beautiful, either!' said Holly crossly.

'Didn't you?' queried Luke, with a teasing smile. 'Oh, Holly—now I *am* disappointed!'

'Why don't we find a quiet corner together, Luke?' suggested Michelle. 'And then you can tell me your life story.'

Luke smiled. Women like Michelle he could cope with. Charming. Flirtatious. A bit over-the-top, maybe. But ultimately safe. There were no secrets or mysteries lurking behind Michelle McComack's dark eyes. What you saw was what you got. 'Love to,' he replied easily.

Holly tried not to feel indignant or jealous or miffed—not when she knew that she had no right to feel anything other than gratitude towards Luke. Thanks to him, she had a shop which would not have looked out of place in one of London's most exclusive streets.

The bell rang once more and the place began to fill up. Holly had sent an invitation to the local vicar, and, much to her astonishment, he turned up on a motorbike! He had collar-length blond hair, a face of almost cherubic innocence, and looked far too young to be legally entrusted with the task of performing marriages!

'Hi, Holly, I'm Charles Cape,' he told her, and held out his hand. 'Pleased to meet you.'

'Thanks for coming,' smiled Holly, who had thought he would toss the invitation into the nearest bin.

But he shook his head. 'No—thanks for inviting me.' He grinned. 'Don't look so surprised that I'm here! Apart from wanting to meet you, since you're new to the village, we're both in the business of making marriage more attractive to the general public, aren't we?'

'I suppose we are,' she agreed thoughtfully.

Holly changed the music to an old-fashioned Christmas tape and began to refill everyone's glasses, and soon the shop took on a party-like atmosphere, particularly when a few people plucked up courage and began to walk in off the street.

'*She* doesn't look like she's in the market for a wedding dress!' whispered one of Michelle's friends to Holly, as a well-padded woman of about eighty plonked herself down on one of the window seats and began to glug contentedly at a glass of wine.

'No, but she might have granddaughters who will be,' said Holly, as she moved a bowl of peanuts away from the satin shoes.

Pete Thomas, the reporter from the *Winchester Echo*, had turned up with a photographer in tow.

'We want to emphasise the wedding dress competition,' he told Holly. 'It's a good angle—and it's different. When are you planning to make the draw?'

'On January the First,' said Holly. 'First day of the New Year. New beginnings, and all that. We won't be open—but I'll announce the winner in the window.' She glanced across the room to where Luke was still sitting, chatting to Michelle, only they had now been joined by Michelle's two friends.

For two brides-to-be, they were certainly paying a lot of interest to whatever Luke was saying, were Holly's rather caustic thoughts. But she ignored the nagging feeling of jealousy and went round, topping everyone's glasses up, until the shop was buzzing with chatter.

People began to filter away just before three, when some of the light had already begun to fade from the sky.

Michelle stood up to go, swayed on her high heels and giggled as she put her hand onto Luke's shoulder to steady herself.

'Whoops! Too much wine on an empty stomach. I need sustenance! How about you, Luke? A big, strong man like you could probably do with a plate of food, right?'

He shrugged and gave a regretful smile. 'Perhaps

some other time. I promised Holly I'd help her tidy away,' he demurred smoothly, meeting a pair of pleased but bewildered emerald eyes over Michelle's head.

Michelle shot Holly another envious look. 'A boss who tidies up? Where have I been going wrong for all these years?' She smiled. 'Well, you know where I am, Luke. If you're ever in Winchester and you fancy some company.'

'I'll be sure to bear that in mind.' He smiled again.

Holly stood at the door, saying goodbye to those who were leaving, though part of her was distracted, wondering whether women came on to Luke like that on a regular basis. He must have an address book like an encyclopedia, she found herself thinking wistfully. No wonder he never talked about women—he'd probably lost count!

'Bye, darling!' trilled Michelle, giving Holly the benefit of a rather glassy smile.

'They loved your flowers,' Holly told her softly.

'I loved your boss,' retorted Michelle. 'Is he free, do you know?'

Holly resisted the urge to tell her no—that if Luke Goodwin was lined up for anyone, then it was her. But that would be the act of a child, not a woman. She nodded, and copper ringlets dangled around her face like burnished corkscrews as she quickly turned her head to check that he wasn't listening. 'Well, he hasn't talked about a particular woman since I've been here—and he's definitely not married—so I think it's fairly safe to say he isn't in love.'

'So he's all mine?' Michelle queried, with a delighted grin.

'Well...' Holly smiled as Michelle planted a wine-laden kiss of farewell on her cheek. 'That's rather up to him, isn't it?'

'Mmm,' said Michelle. 'I'm metaphorically licking my lips at the thought of it!'

Everyone bar Luke had left by four, by which time the faint silver blink of stars had begun to pepper the indigo sky.

Holly looked around. What had happened to her beautiful shop? On every available surface were empty and half-empty wine glasses, bowls containing the remaining crumbs of crisps and peanuts, and lying on the wooden floor were two fading white roses which someone had obviously plucked out of one of Michelle's flower arrangements.

'Why the sour face?' came a deep voice from behind her. 'I thought it went very well.'

'It did. It went brilliantly.' She drew a breath, then flapped her hands around. 'It's just that it all looks such a mess!'

He threw her a disbelieving look. 'Can this be the same woman who, days ago, was about to inhabit a building which resembled a corporation tip?'

'Yes, I was. But that's the whole point,' she argued firmly. 'Once a place looks beautiful, you want to try like mad to keep it that way.'

He walked towards the kitchen at the back.

'Where are you going?' asked Holly curiously.

'To find a tray for the empty glasses. Come on—I'll help you clear up.'

CHAPTER SEVEN

LUKE washed all the glasses and dishes while Holly rearranged flowers, shoes and dresses, and by six the shop was looking pristine once more.

'Now watch this,' said Holly, switching off the main light and pointing to her window display. She had dressed the window to dazzle both during the day and by night, and the effect was exactly what she had been aiming for.

A single spotlight illuminated the prize-winning gown, turning the heavy satin into a buttery gold, while the moonlight added a contrasting silvery sheen all of its own.

For a moment he was silent. 'It's absolutely spectacular,' he told her quietly, and Holly's heart leapt with pleasure as she heard his unequivocal praise. 'Quite stunning.'

'Would you...?' Her words disappeared into the air; she was terrified he would misinterpret them.

In the shadowy half-light his gaze was quizzical. 'Would I what?'

The words spilled out like grain from a sack. 'Would you like to come upstairs and see what they've done to the flat?'

He didn't hesitate, even though the voice of his conscience, the voice of his sanity, told him that he should have done. 'Love to,' he answered.

'After all—you were the one who paid for its decoration!' She wondered why she was tripping over herself to justify the invitation, which was pretty ridiculous when you thought about it. After all, she had shared his house without incident—she was hardly inviting him upstairs in order to start leaping on him!

Luke saw that she was trembling, and frowned. 'Have you had anything to drink?'

She shook her head. 'No, not even a sip. I wanted to keep a clear head, and I was so busy filling up everybody *else's* glasses that I wouldn't have had time to drink my own with any degree of enjoyment!'

'Then how about we open some champagne? To celebrate properly?'

'That would be lovely—but there isn't any, I'm afraid. My budget didn't run to champagne, but perhaps the off-licence might be open?'

Luke laughed, went into the kitchen, and returned—carrying a frosted, foil-topped bottle. 'No, but this very soon will be!' He saw her look of bafflement. 'I brought it with me when I arrived,' he told her softly. 'Didn't you notice? No. Come to think of it, you were too excited to notice anything—'

Not quite true, thought Holly guiltily. She had noticed how wonderful he looked.

'So why don't you take me upstairs now?'

Holly was glad of the half-light, grateful that it would provide some camouflage for the mass of confusions which must have flitted across her face. When he said things like that, he could sound very provocative... She grabbed two glasses and a spare bag of peanuts.

'Come—this way,' she said unsteadily, and the blood pounded like thunder to all her pulse-points.

Upstairs, too, Luke had given her the complete freedom to decorate the flat in the colours of her choice. The leaks were no more, and there was fresh plaster on the ceilings. Luke followed her from room to room and Holly noticed how clean everything smelt—of fresh paint and new wood.

The sitting room was painted a sunny yellow, graduating into deep tangerine in the kitchen. By contrast, the bedroom was blue, although Holly didn't linger there and she noticed that Luke stuck his head round the door only briefly. The tiny bathroom was made to look double its size by the judicious use of mirrors on every wall and Holly was particularly proud of it.

Luke made all the right murmuring sounds of approval, then opened the champagne, and they drank it in the sitting room, in front of the coal-effect gas fire, whose flames flickered convincingly up the chimney.

Sitting on the rug opposite him, Holly drank half a glass of champagne, feeling the alcohol take effect almost immediately, her limbs starting to unfurl as the tensions of the day slowly seeped out of her body.

Luke watched her obsessively, though he was doing his best not to, and wondered just why he had allowed a situation such as the one he now found himself in to develop. Was he merely being protective towards her? Or was he arrogant enough to imagine himself immune to that colt-like beauty of hers?

Holly felt that she ought to say something formal. Something which would remind her that, however kind he was, and however friendly, he remained her landlord—and that he had never shown the remotest sign of wishing to change that relationship. And from today that relationship would change irrevocably, whether she wanted it to or not. Because she would no longer be living with him and that would automatically create a distance between them.

She cleared her throat. 'Thank you for everything you've done for me, Luke. I mean that. Today was a big success—I *hope*!—and I could never have pulled it off if I'd had to handle everything on my own. I probably wouldn't have opened until late summer—and spent most of my capital beforehand. So thanks.'

'It was my pleasure—and I mean *that*.' There was a pause while he considered the wisdom of his next words, but something more powerful than reason made him say them anyway. 'I'm going to miss you, Holly.'

'Will you?' She turned to him with pleasure and surprise.

'Of course I will. You're very good company.'

Holly gave a slightly woozy smile. 'So are you. And I'll miss you, too.'

'Do you suppose we're what's known as a mutual admiration society?' He laughed, and his blue eyes crinkled at the corners.

'I suppose we are,' said Holly breathlessly. He was looking at her in a way that made her heart patter erratically, her skin prickle with heat and excitement. It was as though her body had shifted into a gear she didn't recognise.

He lifted up the bottle. 'Here—have some more champagne.'

'Do you really think I should?'

'Oh, I really do,' he teased, remorselessly slamming the door shut on his doubts.

'Okay, then.' She held her glass out languidly while he topped it up in a cascade of creamy foam, shifting her legs comfortably as she sipped it. Though the oddest thing about champagne was that the more you drank, the thirstier you got. Holly put her head back and sighed dreamily. Everything was too good to be true. Her shop was going to be a success—she just *knew* it was—and sitting opposite her was the most gorgeous man she had ever met. She was floating on a sea of happiness and champagne bubbles.

Luke wished that she wouldn't sit like that. Well, part of him did. The other part of him wanted to replay every movement she had made in slow motion. The tiny cream overskirt had ridden right the way up her legs, and it was proving an extremely distracting sight. He cast around for a safe topic, something which would lead his thoughts away from the milky-white heaven of her thighs. 'So does this feel like home yet?' he asked.

The words were blurted out before she could stop them. 'It does with you here.'

Luke's eyes glinted dangerously. Wasn't she aware that when she said something as silkily as that, with those big green eyes widening up at him like a cat's, he wanted to capture that rosebud mouth of hers and to spend the rest of the night kissing it?

Go, said a voice in his head. Go, now. Before something happens. Before it's too late.

But, for the first time since his teens, desire took precedence over wisdom. His throat felt as though it had been constricted by a vice. Every word a victory. 'Oh?' he asked unsteadily.

Holly shrugged, drained her glass and put it down on the fireplace. 'I've kind of got used to having you around, I suppose. And these last few days...' She hesitated, aware that, if she was totally honest with him, she might come over as weak. And pathetic.

'These last few days....what?' he prompted.

'Well, they've been easy. Relaxed. Civilised.'

'Civilised?' he laughed.

'Sure.' She nodded passionately, too tempted by the clear blue light in his eyes not to lay her feelings bare. 'When I was a student I lived in houses which were too cold and too crowded, and when I was a child I lived in lots of different houses. Houses where I was a stranger—tolerated simply because whoever owned the house really only wanted my mother. I never felt I fitted in—not anywhere. I used to have dreams about proper houses with proper fires, where people made proper meals and ate them sitting at proper tables. Storybook houses that I never really believed in. Except...' and her voice went very quiet '...that yours was exactly like that.'

There was silence while he thought about the import of what she had just told him. Did she not realise just how potent was the power of her vulnerability? The enormous compliment she had just paid him? She was an enigma with the face and the body of a sorceress and the trusting vulnerability of a little girl. So which was the real Holly Lovelace?

Had he been weak to come up here, or merely foolish? Luke wondered if she could see the tussle on his face. Wondered whether she was deliberately tucking her legs up beneath her like that, so that the movement not only emphasised their length, but also drew attention to the pert thrust of her breasts. His hands felt shaky, his mouth as dry as tinder and, all the while, there was the slow, painful build-up of desire.

He diverted his thoughts by focussing on her words instead of her body. 'Then yours is an upbringing I can identify with,' he told her. 'Only mine was the more institutionalised version of solitary confinement.'

Her hand stilled over the peanuts. 'Tell me.'

The women he had known had not wanted to hear sad stories about dispossessed little boys—they'd wanted hard, strong bodies and hands that knew exactly how best to please them. He shook his head, aware of the dangers in baring a soul which necessity had clothed in secrecy many years before.

'Everyone knows what British boarding-schools are like,' he said dismissively.

'Not unless they've been to one, they don't. And I haven't. So I don't. Tell me, Luke!'

He shrugged. 'It's a system which works well on many levels,' he conceded levelly. 'So it isn't necessarily *bad*—just *different*.'

Holly smiled. 'It's okay—you don't have to defend the status quo to me, you know.'

She was chipping away with her persistence, each soft word exposing the hard, cold core of pain he had hidden away for so long.

'So which particular aspect would you like me to reveal to you?' he demanded. 'The isolation? The lack of physical warmth? The total lack of time to just sit and think? The disgusting food? The freezing dormitories?

The even more freezing early-morning showers which followed the equally freezing cross-country runs?'

'You must have been pretty fit,' she observed slowly, and cast him a long look from beneath lashes which could not quite obscure the glittering of her eyes.

Luke started. Of all the things she *could* have said... He had expected and been dreading the kind of cloying sympathy which most women seemed so comfortable with. Not a light, teasing kind of comment delivered with a little glint in her eye which made the slow pulsing of his desire escalate into an insistent pounding.

This was a game he was familiar with...

He bent his legs, just in case his exquisite hardness would be revealed to damn him. He needed to get out of here fast, but first he needed to kill that desire stone dead. And the only way he could think of doing that was by getting Holly and her long, long legs out of his line of vision.

'How about some coffee?' he suggested throatily, as his vocal cords joined in with his body's conspiracy by telling her how much he wanted her.

Coffee? Holly was both startled and disappointed. She wanted much more than coffee. She wanted *him*. And she wanted him badly—just as she had done from the moment she had first set eyes on him. When she had experienced an attraction towards him which had started with a thunderbolt and just continued to grow.

She had thought that he felt something for her, too— if not exactly the same in terms of intensity, then something very similar. Or had she simply been imagining that raw gleam of hunger which sometimes illuminated his eyes with a deep blue radiance? The easy companionship they had shared during her time at his house? Easy enough for her to think that there might be something more than just friendship...

Shakily, and trying to use as much grace as possible—which wasn't easy, given the length of her skirt—Holly rose to her feet and stood looking down at him.

'Coffee it is, then,' she said quietly, but still she didn't move, and there was a question in her eyes.

During his life, Luke had faced the very real adversities of hunger and pain and physical danger—and yet now he found himself in a situation far more threatening. He had a will of steel, forged by need in the long, lonely hours of his childhood, and yet that will now seemed to have deserted him.

He put his hand out towards her, and looked at it with bemused detachment, as if that hand were not under his control any more. It alighted on the slender curve of her ankle, and he felt the tiny shudder which thrilled her flesh as he made that first contact.

Slowly, lingeringly, he let his hand move upwards, so that it encircled her calf, and that calf suddenly seemed like the most erotic zone he had ever encountered. He let his middle finger trickle along the silken swell, in a way that made his body shudder as he imagined the natural path for that finger to now travel...

Holly didn't dare move, didn't dare speak, some instinct telling her that to do either would be to break this bewitching spell he had cast on her. His hand felt like the centre of a furnace. Or maybe his touch had transformed *her* into a furnace—for she could feel a fire beginning to blaze at the fork of her legs, the honeyed wetness which followed doing nothing to quench the remorseless heat building up inside her.

Luke's hand reached her knee. Never had he felt such an erotic contrast between bone and velvet-soft skin. He felt for the fleshy pocket behind the knee itself and sighed with pleasure. Using his thumb, he circled the skin there, round and round, over and over, until he felt it tremble helplessly beneath his touch. His hand crept inexorably upwards; he knew where he wanted to touch her most and, from the give-away little sag of her knees, he knew that she wanted it, too.

He knelt before her then, tightening his arms around her bottom, burying his face in the softness of her belly through the filmy voile of her dress. He felt her sway, and pulled her down so that she was kneeling, too, their eyes almost on a level, her expression one of breathless curiosity as she waited to see what he would do next.

Her eyes had never looked greener—luminous and bright as leaves which had just been rained on—nor more inviting. He saw her lips pucker helplessly, noted that the lush, dark lashes were in danger of fluttering to a close.

'I want to kiss you,' he told her, in a voice which sounded as heavy and as sweet as syrup.

'Then kiss me,' she managed drowsily, half despairing of her passivity.

'God, yes...' He would have kissed her anyway, invitation or not, for it would have been impossible to resist those lips. He lowered his mouth slowly... brushing it against hers with the merest whisper of contact...and Holly felt her lips part immediately.

Steadying himself with a hand now buried in the rippling copper ropes of her hair, Luke deepened the kiss with his tongue and felt her meet it, matching his own passion and need, and yet inciting it further...demanding more...

Fireworks threatened to explode inside his head and in his aching groin, and he thought how intoxicating this kiss was...

Intoxicating...

The word began to batter relentlessly at his conscience like rain lashing against a window, and Luke felt his body freeze with rejection, his lips stilling against hers.

For this was the act of a fool. This woman was like a glass of champagne: the sudden high, the slaking of a sensual thirst and then—what? The dry mouth, the headache and the regret of a hangover—that was what.

He was not in the market for any woman—but particularly not one who was everything he most feared and despised in a woman. With her fey, enchanting beauty, and all the restless inner energy of the creative personality, she was the kind of woman who was bad news. Very bad news indeed.

He plucked his mouth away from hers, and something in his attitude must have unnerved her, for he saw the sudden whitening of her face and the way that her eyes had grown leaf-dark and startled.

And, even then, that treacherous protective instinct which she alone seemed to inspire in him reared its interfering head once more, and he reached out automatically to steady her, afraid that she might simply crumple to a heap in front of him.

'Luke—what on earth is the *matter*?' she demanded, as she unseeingly let him gently propel her back towards the sofa, where she slumped down like a puppet whose strings had just been cut. 'What are you *doing*?'

'I'm doing what I should have done about ten minutes ago,' he told her grimly. 'I'm leaving!'

'But why? I don't understand!'

'And you don't need to understand,' he gritted, his mouth hardening into an ugly line as he thought of how close he had come to...to... 'Forget it ever happened, Holly, because it meant *nothing*! It was an aberration, that's all.'

'An "aberration"?' she challenged, then wished she hadn't because the look he threw her in response was insulting. 'What a *horrible* word!'

'Like me to explain it to you?' he queried, with silky condescension.

'I think I can just about work it out for myself, thank you!'

With the grace of a natural predator, he rose to his feet and came to stand over her, and Holly found that the trembling simply would not leave her. From her position on the sofa, Holly thought that his towering height made him look impossibly intimidating.

And distant.

Their eyes met, and in hers remained a query he could not ignore.

'That wasn't in my general scheme of things,' he told her brutally, in answer to the unasked question.

'You mean that *kiss*?' she demanded, her voice incredulous. Why was he making her feel like some night club stripper over a simple *kiss*? 'Is that all?'

'*All?* Kisses like that generally lead on to something else, but I'm sure you don't need me to tell you that.'

His eyes were wintry. 'But maybe that's why you invited me up here? To "christen" the new flat in the way you like best?'

'You flatter yourself,' she observed furiously.

He shook his head. 'I don't think so.' A muscle began to work in his cheek as she frantically pulled at the hemline of her dress. 'Or are you denying that we've had the hots for each other since the moment we first met?'

So she *hadn't* been imagining it! 'No, I'm not denying it!' she told him, as she sat up straight and looked at him, her voice softening as she said, 'It isn't a crime!'

'No, it's just sex,' he told her. 'And that's *all* it is, Holly!'

'*Sex?*' she demanded. '*Sex?* What an insulting thing to say!'

He made an impatient movement with his hands. 'Call it chemistry, then—or mutual attraction. Whatever words you want to use if the truth offends you.' His voice dropped to a throaty whisper. 'And it's powerful, this feeling—I don't deny that. Potent as hell itself—but nebulous. Insubstantial. It peaks and then it wanes and leaves all kinds of havoc and destruction in its wake.'

Anger laced her voice with sarcasm. 'Aren't you overstating your case a little?'

He shook his tawny head. 'Am I? I don't think so, Holly. All I know is that I've had a fortnight of torture, of watching you move with that unconscious grace you have. Of imagining you undressing in the room down the hall from me. I've had to contend with the sight of you drifting around in one of *my* robes, knowing that you're buck-naked underneath, and I've had to stay sane and control my baser impulses. And it's been hard.'

Or, rather, *I've* been hard, he thought ruefully. Bad choice of word, Luke. 'But now that you're safely settled in your new home, our paths need hardly cross. And I think that's for the best.'

Best for *whom?* she almost yelled, but suspected she already knew the answer to that one. There was just one question she needed to ask him. 'Why, Luke?' And then she plucked up courage to add, 'When we both want to.'

But he shook his head, steeling himself against that plaintive little appeal. 'Why spend time going over it—when the outcome will remain the same? My reasons are both simple and complex and you don't need to know them.'

'Well, that's bloody *insulting* to me!' she stormed.

He raised his eyebrows. It was the only time he had ever heard her swear, and the zeal with which she did it only reinforced all his prejudices. The shutters came crashing down and he clicked out of emotion and into formality. Old habits died hard...

'Thank you for inviting me to your opening,' he finished politely. 'And I wish you every good fortune in your new endeavour. Goodnight, Holly.'

Still sitting collapsed on the sofa, her long legs sprawled in front of her, made Holly feel at a definite disadvantage, but she was damned if she was going to stumble to her feet to show him out. She would be bound to fall flat on her face, or something equally humiliating.

She gave him an unfriendly smile, his kindness to her forgotten in the face of sexual frustration and the accompanying rejection and bewilderment. 'Thanks for everything, Luke,' she told him insincerely. 'But you'll forgive me if I don't show you out.'

CHAPTER EIGHT

IT WAS just very fortunate that starting a new business meant that there were always a hundred and one things to think about, and to do—and for that Holly was extremely grateful. At least it meant that she didn't allow her mind to get stuck on that frustrating loop which wanted to know just why Luke Goodwin had:

a) Kissed her (and more)
b) Then acted as though she had some kind of infectious disease; and
c) Had disappeared conclusively from her life in the days following the opening of her shop.

She supposed that she could have picked up the telephone, or even gone round to his house, to ask the great man in person—but she had her pride. Luke wasn't a man she could imagine being railroaded into anything, and she certainly wasn't going to march round to beg him to make love to her!

So she forced herself to be sensible, filed all these unanswered questions away under 'Waste of Time', and resolutely refused to dwell on them further. Even though she missed him. Missed him like mad.

She had a few long, sleepless nights asking herself what had gone wrong, and why. Then she came to the conclusion that, since she wasn't going to get any answers, then there wasn't much point asking the questions. It was a useful safety mechanism.

Then she happened to bump into Luke's cleaning lady, Margaret, in the general store.

Margaret smiled encouragingly at her, and Holly plucked up courage to ask, very casually, 'How's Luke?'

'I wouldn't know, dear,' Margaret replied, with the repressed excitement of someone who knew that the person who had asked the question was hanging onto every word. 'He's gone away!'

Holly nearly dropped her organic wholemeal loaf on the floor. *'Gone?'* she echoed in horror. 'Gone *where*?'

'He didn't say, dear. Just upped and left the day after your shop opened, I think it was.'

'And is he coming back?' asked Holly, her heart feeling like a leaden weight in her chest.

Margaret shrugged. 'I expect so. He hasn't taken much—apart from his passport.'

'His *passport*?' repeated Holly, like a parrot.

'That's right.'

'But you don't know where he's gone?'

''Fraid I don't dear.' A mischievous gleam entered Margaret's rheumy eyes. 'Shall I say you was asking?'

'Er, no,' said Holly quickly. She flashed her most beseeching smile. 'I'd rather you didn't, Margaret.'

The article about Lovelace Brides had appeared in the *Winchester Echo* and captured the public's imagination. The people of Hampshire loved the story of Holly winning a wedding dress competition and opening a bridal shop—and then offering the same wedding dress as the prize in *another* competition!

It had proved so popular that it had been picked up

by the national press, including one of the broadsheets as well as three tabloids. In a week where news was scant, journalists and photographers were dispatched to Woodhampton, where Holly posed standing next to the dress, trying like mad to pin a happy-go-lucky smile to her lips.

It was fabulous publicity for her, and she knew that she *should* feel overjoyed—it was just very annoying to feel so deflated. Especially over a man she had foolishly imagined had shared her feelings.

Which only went to prove that her imagination was best left to dreaming up wedding dresses, and not romantic scenarios with would-be suitors.

Lured by the competition, brides-to-be flocked into the shop in what became an unusually busy December. It was traditionally a slack month—too many parties and too much preparation for Christmas leaving brides with little enthusiasm for buying their wedding dresses. With the added inches from too much merry-making, they tended to leave that until the New Year.

As the steady stream of customers filed into the shop, Holly soon realised that she was going to have to recruit more outworkers than she had originally anticipated. She needed workers who were good enough to sew her intricate designs and close enough for her to be able to keep an eye on them. She scribbled out an advertisement and put it in the *Echo*.

On a dull Monday morning, a couple of weeks before Christmas, Holly was rearranging her window display when she saw a woman standing waiting on the pavement outside, trying to catch her attention.

'Are you open?' mouthed the woman, pointing exaggeratedly at her watch.

'Not until ten!' Holly mouthed back, then wondered why she was sounding so inflexible. It was her business, and she could open when she liked! With a final twist of fern, which Michelle had concocted into a huge, old-fashioned bouquet with white silk roses, Holly jumped down out of the window and went to unlock the door.

'Come in,' she smiled.

'You're not supposed to be open until ten, are you?' murmured the woman, but she stepped into the shop anyway and looked around. She was wearing dark corduroy trousers, a green padded jacket and wellington boots. She wore the traditional country clothes well—they suited her clear skin and her neat, butter-coloured hair. She was trim, with tiny wrists and tiny ankles—the sign, or so Holly had been told by her mother, of a true lady.

'You're only ten minutes off, and the shop is still very new,' said Holly with a smile. 'I need to build up a reputation, and it wouldn't do mine much good if I forced you to stand outside in the cold, instead of bringing you in here and letting you browse around. I'm presuming that you *are* a bride-to-be?'

'I most certainly am!' giggled the woman. It was an attractive, infectious laugh, but a little girlish, too. And maybe just a tad inappropriate for someone pushing thirty, Holly thought. Until she reminded herself sternly that she was here to make wedding dresses, not value judgements! Still, she would bet, with a giggle like that, that this woman would go for flounces and frills and a bouquet as big as the Blackwall Tunnel!

'When,' asked Holly immediately, 'is the wedding?'

The woman pursed her lips together in a smile. 'Well, we haven't quite decided yet—you know what men are for making a commitment! My fiancé came over without me—to get everything ready,' she added with a coy shrug.

'But you're not planning a sudden Valentine wedding, are you?' asked Holly quickly. 'Because if you are, we'll have to get a move on.'

The woman shook her head. 'Oh, no! My fiancé and I haven't actually discussed a date—but I want to be sure that, when we do, I'll be ready to go!'

Keen, thought Holly with a smile. But, there again, so many brides were—and it would be a little disappointing if they weren't! 'Then we'd better introduce ourselves,' she said. 'I'm Holly Lovelace—owner and designer.'

'Caroline,' said the blonde, holding her hand out. 'Caroline Casey. I'm afraid that I'm a novice at all this—what do I do now?'

'You take a look at all those sample gowns hanging over there on the rail, and decide which ones you like the look of. Then you try them on, see which suits and whether you want any modifications made, and then I can have it made to measure.'

'And do they all have price tags?'

Holly nodded. 'Yes, they do.' Not all shops carried prices on their gowns, but it had been a conscious decision of hers to do so, because nothing was worse than falling madly in love with a wedding dress, only to discover that it was much more than you could afford. Holly knew that brides rarely looked too closely at a gown which was financially out of their reach. 'But if you're on a budget and particularly like a certain design, then we can sometimes have it made up in a less expensive fabric.'

'Oh, no!' Caroline laughed delicately, showing teeth which were straight and white and even—teeth which told of a lifetime's good nutrition, of sunshine and milk and no sweets to cause cavities. 'Money's certainly no object.' She paused and gave Holly a helpless little shrug. 'My fiancé has just come into a very large inheritance!'

Blinking away a brief but distracting feeling of *déjà vu*, Holly managed to smile, even though she thought the woman sounded more than a little smug. 'Good for him! And for you!' she added robustly, supposing that it was difficult to talk about a large inheritance *without* sounding smug. 'Nice to be in love,' she said wistfully. 'And it's probably even nicer if he's rich into the bargain!'

'Oh, I'd never have agreed to marry him if he hadn't come into money,' said Caroline, smiling and shaking her head when she saw the look of horror on Holly's face. 'Oh, no! I don't mean that I'm marrying him *just* for the money—although I have to agree, it helps! It's just that money brings with it responsibilities. And, more importantly, stability. And my fiancé was pretty wild before he inherited!' She wrinkled up her pretty nose. '*Very* wild!'

The mind boggled. 'In what way?' asked Holly curiously.

'In every way.' Caroline shrugged. 'The original rolling stone!'

Holly smiled, feeling a sneaking sympathy for the man. She suspected that the pretty but determined Caroline Casey would keep her errant fiancé on a very short rein indeed! 'Listen—why don't I make us some coffee and leave you to browse through the dresses at your leisure?'

'That's very sweet of you.'

When Holly came back with coffee, it was *her* turn to feel smug, since the woman had done exactly as she'd predicted and picked out the most frothy, fairy-princess dress on the rail! It had a low, flounced neck, a jewel-encrusted bodice, nipped waist and a skirt wide enough to hide a family of six beneath its voluminous silk folds.

Holly didn't just design dresses that she was passionate about—she also designed dresses to sell. You had to if you were a businesswoman, or so her favourite tutor had told her at college. And frothy, traditional dresses *did* sell—no doubt about it, there was always a market for them.

Caroline experimentally held the dress up in front of her. 'Do you like it?'

'Your waist is going to look like Scarlett O'Hara's in that,' promised Holly truthfully.

Caroline clutched the dress to her. 'I've dreamed of a wedding dress like this one ever since I was a little girl!'

'Well, that's what tends to happen.' Holly smiled. 'Just so long as you aren't marrying a man who wants you to elope in a short red dress on the back of his motorbike!'

Caroline frowned. 'I think that's what most men *would* like, if the truth were known. Men don't like a lot of fuss, do they?'

Holly had learnt to agree with the customer—up to a point. 'Generally speaking, no.'

'But I'm a great believer in tradition,' said Caroline firmly.

'But not tradition simply for the sake of it, surely?' the imp in Holly argued back.

Caroline fixed her with a look of mild amusement. 'Most certainly I do. Tradition is the bedrock of society—the fabric that binds us together and links us with our past. Now...' she ran her finger along a ruffle of lace on one of the sleeves '...can I go and try this on?'

'Please do,' said Holly. 'The changing room is over here. What shoe size are you?'

'Only four.' Caroline gave a little wriggle of her shoulders as she projected a dainty foot forward like a ballet dancer. 'I'm only little, I'm afraid.'

'Then take these shoes with you—and call me if you need me,' said Holly gently, and drew back the velvet curtain to the changing room. She found herself wondering why Caroline had no one with her. Brides rarely came looking for gowns alone—they generally brought their mother or a best friend. Someone close enough to be brutally honest when asked the universal question, Does my bottom look big in this?

While Caroline was in the changing room, Holly hunted around for more accessories—veil and headdress—which she thought might go well with the dress.

And when Caroline reappeared, looking a little self-conscious in all her finery, Holly experienced the familiar feeling of awe and wonder at how a wedding dress could transform a woman into a goddess. Women *stood* differently in a wedding dress. *Walked* differently.

'That ivory silk does wonders for your complexion,' she told her admiringly.

Caroline twirled in front of the floor-to-ceiling mirror. 'Does it? It's beautiful,' she said breathlessly. 'I feel just like a fairy princess!'

'It's much too big around the waist. Here—let me take it in a bit.' Pins on her wristband, Holly crouched down and adjusted the waist and then the hem.

While she was making her alterations, Holly chatted and listened. Women opened up to their dressmakers, and Caroline was no exception. By the end of the fitting, Holly was left with the impression that Caroline was a pleasant and competent woman, but grindingly dull and conventional!

It was getting on for lunch-time when the bride-to-be came out of the changing room, an ordinary woman once more in her cords and sweater. Holly looked up from the ivory silk and smiled at her. 'So what made you choose my little shop in Woodhampton for your wedding dress?'

'Nothing more inspiring than geography, I'm afraid.' Caroline found a compact inside her handbag, and, peering into the mirror, began to pat the shine off her neat little nose. 'I'm going to be living here, you see.'

'Oh? Whereabouts?'

'In Woodhampton itself.' Caroline's voice became injected with pride. 'There's a rather nice Georgian house in the village,' she confided. 'Apson House. I expect you know it.'

For a moment Holly's heart missed a beat while the world stopped turning. Either that or she would wake up in a moment. She felt all the blood draining from her face, and wondered whether she had a corresponding colour loss. 'Yes, I know it,' she replied, in a muffled voice which seemed to come from a different pair of lungs than hers. Then forced herself to ask the question, as if she didn't already know the answer, 'And wh-who's your fiancé?'

Caroline frowned, antennae alerted by the fine beads of sweat sheening Holly's brow. 'It's Luke,' she said precisely, her pale grey gaze piercing. 'Luke Goodwin. Do you know him?'

Holly was experiencing sensations she had only ever read about. Head like cotton wool. Legs like jelly. Stomach turned to water. She was terribly afraid that she might faint. And meanwhile the unbelievable fact was hammering into her brain. *Luke Goodwin was engaged to be married to the grindingly dull Caroline Casey!*

Luke Goodwin was a no-good *deceiving bastard*!

'Do you know him?' repeated Caroline ominously, sounding as if she were counsel for the prosecution, and Holly were on the witness stand.

Well, she couldn't lie. Margaret, Luke's cleaner, knew that she had been staying up at the house while the shop was being renovated, and so did everyone else in the village. 'Yes, I know him,' she answered steadily.

Caroline looked at her wordlessly, her eyebrows raised in expectation.

'You see, I was...I was staying up at Apson House—'

'You were *what*?' came the disbelieving snap.

'Just for a couple of weeks—'

'A couple of *weeks*?' Caroline's eyes were spitting fire. 'Perhaps you'd care to explain?'

Holly swallowed. 'This shop and the flat above it were

in the most dreadful state when I arrived, and Luke kind of came to the rescue. He had to sack the agent and there was nowhere habitable for me to stay—that's why he put me up.'

'And why would he do that?' Caroline asked, in a voice of quiet menace.

'Because he owns the freehold of this building—but you probably knew that already.'

Caroline's mouth had thinned into a sarcastic line. 'I'm afraid that my knowledge of Luke's life in England is somewhat patchy—certainly when compared to yours. You must fill me in, Holly. Just how *well* do you actually know Luke?'

Holly stared at her. The inference was clear. 'What do you mean, exactly?'

'I'll tell you *exactly* what I mean!' Caroline put her head forward, like a tortoise emerging from its shell and blinked rapidly at Holly. 'Luke is a man with certain, shall we say...appetites? And he's a little old-fashioned at heart. You know, one of those men who marry a woman because they love and respect her, but who will avail themselves of an attractive substitute should the need arise—if you'll forgive the pun,' she finished maliciously. 'So did he?'

Holly's throat was so tight she could scarcely breathe, let alone speak, but somehow she forced the words out. 'Did he what?'

'Did he sleep with you?'

Only in her tortured and exquisite dreams. 'How dare you ask me that?'

There was a pause. Caroline looked her straight in the eye. 'I'll ask you again, Holly. I'm a very understanding woman, you know, and sex has nothing to do with respect—especially where Luke is concerned. Did you sleep with him?'

Thoughts buzzed into Holly's mind like sandflies, but the most disturbing dominated all the others. She could hear Caroline saying it defiantly, almost proudly: 'Oh, I'd never have agreed to marry him if he hadn't come into money.'

She met Caroline's gaze without blushing. Guided solely by instinct coloured with a gut feeling of pure *indignation*, Holly realised that with her next words she could wreck her reputation. But she had gambled everything else—why not her reputation? 'I stayed in his house for days,' she replied, with slow deliberation. 'And you know Luke. What do you think?'

'I'll tell you what I think! I think you're deluding yourself if you think you stand any chance with him.' Caroline gave her a smile which was almost sympathetic. 'Because Luke was always rather bored by any woman who was such an easy lay!'

CHAPTER NINE

AFTER Caroline had flounced out of the shop, telling Holly exactly what she could do with her wedding dress, Holly went through to the kitchen at the back and sat down, her hands trembling, her nerves shot to pieces by what Luke's fiancée—Luke's *fiancée*!—had just told her, and by the enormity of what she had done in retaliation.

Luke was engaged to be married.

That was the one fact which overrode every other thought. Crucial.

But even more crucial was the fact that he had deceived her. He had lied by omission. He had allowed an easy companionship to develop, and had ignited the flames of sexual desire when he could have effectively doused them completely by telling her the simple truth.

That he was engaged to be married.

Holly buried her head in her hands as she thought about him and found that she wanted to weep—she who never wept. Who as a child had constantly kept the non-committal smile expected of her, even when her life had been torn up by the roots, time and time again.

It was bad enough that he had lied. Bad enough that he had chosen to commit himself to someone who, yes, Holly could see, had all the attributes of a good wife. Caroline was intelligent enough. Neat, organised, attractive, and determined but, *oh*...how could a man like

Luke—*Luke*—be contemplating spending the rest of his life with her?

Because even worse than the pain of his deceit was the pain of knowing why he had pushed her away, and why he had stayed out of her life in the days since that frustrating encounter. For he wasn't hers, and he never would be. Holly had finally met a man she would change her life for, but he belonged to somebody else.

But businesswomen couldn't hurl themselves to the ground and drum their feet in anger and frustration, which was what she *felt* like doing! There wasn't even a packet of biscuits to defiantly plough her way through—not that she really wanted to start comfort eating at *this* stage in her life.

Instead, she spent the afternoon sewing her first full order—a gown for a Christmas wedding, with a full white taffeta skirt and a buttoned bodice in deep forest-green velvet. The tiny bridesmaids' dresses had the pattern reversed, with velvet skirts and taffeta bodices, and Michelle was going to make mistletoe and holly coronets.

She was undisturbed for the most part, with just two customers wandering in. Young women who said that they wanted to browse. They also wanted to enter the free draw for the prize-winning dress, which Holly suspected was their main reason for coming into the shop!

They filled out their cards respectively, and dropped them into the slightly garish red satin box which Holly had provided.

'When's it being drawn?' asked one.

'New Year's Day,' answered Holly with a faint smile.

'At the stroke of midnight?' asked the other hopefully.

'Like Cinderella, you mean?' Holly smiled properly then. Your emotional world could collapse around you, and yet romance never seemed to die. Thank heavens. 'Why not?' She shrugged.

The rest of the afternoon dragged like Christmas Eve to a child. At four o'clock she was longing to shut up shop and go upstairs. There were accounts which needed to be sorted out and she could put the finishing touches to the green velvet wedding dress in comfort. Enough to keep her busy for the rest of the evening, anyway. That was if she could resist the temptation to crawl beneath the duvet and just wish that the world would go away.

She was just tucking a frilly blue garter to the back of a drawer when the shop bell rang and she looked up, her words dying on her lips when she saw who it was.

Her first thought was that it didn't really look like Luke at all, since he was wearing an unfamiliar deep blue suit and a silk tie of palest blue. A *tie*! *Luke!* She would never have imagined him wearing such fine wool and silk, though it came as no surprise to see how well the formal clothes fitted his rugged frame. But the impeccably cut outfit had the effect of distancing him, making him look like some cool and devastating stranger.

Luke quietly closed the door behind him and then locked it, and something about his face and the rigid set of his shoulders made Holly run her tongue over her lips and say nervously, 'What do you think you're doing?'

'What does it look like? I'm locking the door.'

'But we're still open!' she objected, her pulse picking up speed like a racehorse. 'You can't do that.'

'Oh, can't I?' He turned round then, and the shadowed

fury which darkened his features made Holly freeze with apprehension.

'Just watch me, sweetheart,' he drawled, and he began to walk towards her.

Holly correctly read the menace and determination in that walk, and some mad, unthinking part of her wanted to run away from him. She found herself looking frantically from side to side, as though a trapdoor would suddenly appear and she would be able to make her escape.

Luke could see her anxiety, but he felt not a jot of pity for her, only the anger which had burned through his veins all afternoon and which was threatening to consume him.

He was directly in front of her now, and Holly saw that he was controlling his breathing only with great difficulty.

'What are you doing here?' she whispered, her voice sounding like a husky croak.

It was the wrong thing to say. His mouth curved into a thin parody of a smile which chilled her.

'You know damn well what I'm doing here.'

'I d-don't.'

He drew a breath as though he were taking in poison. 'What exactly did you tell Caroline?'

'You mean your fiancée?' she bit back.

'Answer me, you little bitch!'

The insult first rocked her, then filled her with the fury to fight him back.

'I told her the truth!'

'You're lying, Holly.' He was itching to grab her by the shoulders, to haul her up against his chest and extract every raw, painful word of what she had actually told Caroline. And then?

'You weren't there,' she pointed out.

'I didn't need to be.'

'Well, then.' She shrugged. 'It's her word against mine—whatever she's told you.'

Her audacity momentarily stunned him. 'I'll tell you what she *told* me, sweetheart. That you and I apparently slept together.' He gave a cold, empty laugh. 'Strange, that—the earth can't have moved for either of us, since I don't actually remember doing it.'

Doing it. Holly felt the hot rush of excitement and prayed for it to pass. She shook her head in an effort to distract herself. 'I didn't *tell* her that I slept with you,' she contradicted. 'That was her accusation.' Her lashes lowered by a fraction to partially conceal her eyes, but she was certain that he had read the longing there. 'An accusation which she found impossible not to believe was true.'

'Particularly as you refused to deny it?' he suggested, with icy calm.

Holly shrugged. 'There was no point in denying it. Since *Caroline*—' she spat the word out, appalled at herself for doing so and yet unable to prevent the anger which was still distorting her voice '—had already made her mind up. And she seemed to find it unbelievable that you and I had managed to remain under one roof for a fortnight without having sex!'

He found it pretty unbelievable himself, come to think of it, but that was beside the point. 'What right do you think you have to start meddling in my life?' he demanded. 'How *dare* you let Caroline believe that we had been intimate?'

Holly had had enough. He was acting as if there had been nothing between them—as if the camaraderie which had grown up between them had not existed! 'But we *were* intimate! You know we were!'

His mouth twisted. 'I'm sorry? Have we been existing in parallel universes, or is there something I have missed? Just *when* are we supposed to have been intimate?'

She felt as if she was floundering in a dark, cold pool of misunderstanding. She remembered the touch of his hand on her ankle, the way she had drawn in a breath and looked down at him. Their gazes had locked the instant before they'd kissed, and something momentous had happened—surely he wasn't going to deny *that*?

'You *touched* me!' she protested throatily. 'You know you did!'

'I touched you?' he echoed in disbelief. 'And you think that gives you carte blanche to try to take control of my life by implying that there had been so much more than that? What right do you have to do that, Holly?'

She shook her head distractedly, copper curls spilling like corkscrews over her shoulders. 'But there are other kinds of intimacies, too—the little, unspoken ones. We grew close when I stayed with you, Luke—you know we did! You even admitted it! If you'd been honest with me *then*, and told me about Caroline, there would have been a completely different atmosphere between us! An atmosphere which would not have given rise to that kiss.' She drew a deep shuddering breath. 'So why *didn't* you tell me, Luke? Just answer me that?'

He gave an arrogant smile. 'You didn't ask.' But that wasn't the full story, and he knew it. He hadn't wanted to tell her, hadn't wanted to say the words out loud because that would have meant acknowledging reality, and it had been sweet indeed to pretend that reality didn't exist. It had been wonderful having Holly around. He had been enjoying the warmth of her company, and that was a fact. Enjoying the easy atmosphere coupled with the excitement of knowing that he couldn't have her...

'I can't believe you didn't even *mention* a girlfriend!'

His eyes glittered in legitimate challenge. 'Well, maybe you should have asked me.'

'That's not fair and you know it!' she objected hotly.

'Isn't it?' His eyes were azure spotlights which fixed her in their glare. 'Then let's just say that I didn't want to stray into the dangerous waters of the deeply personal.'

'But you told me all about your mother—and you can't get more personal than that!'

'That's different!' he snarled, remembering her gentle questions, the careless way she had shrugged at his reluctance to answer, so that—perversely—he had wanted to tell her. And then the way that it had all seemed to come pouring out of him, like the bursting of a dam. Disturbing. And especially disturbing for a man like Luke who had grown up with no one to confide in, who had convinced himself that it was better like that. That feelings should be locked out of sight and out of harm's way. When you were the only motherless boy in an English boarding-school, it was easier like that...

Holly gave a bitter laugh as she saw the shuttered look which had given him the face of a dark, beautiful statue.

'I used to wonder why you hadn't jumped on me like most men try to—'

'Did that disappoint you, then?' he enquired silkily. 'Do you like being jumped on, Holly?'

She ignored the crude taunt. 'I *thought* it was because you were a gentleman and that you respected me, but now I see I couldn't have been more wrong! You're a bastard, Luke Goodwin—to make a promise to one woman, and then to flirt like crazy with another!'

A pulse began to flicker ominously in his cheek. 'If I had flirted like crazy, then you would have known all about it, sweetheart,' he ground out. 'And the bottom line is that we kissed. Nothing more. Like you said yourself at the time, as I recall.' His mouth twisted with agonised desire. 'Though, quite frankly, if you wear skirts as short as the one you had on that day then—'

'Then I can expect men to lose all control?' she put in. 'Is that what you were about to say, Luke? That I was asking for it?'

'But I *didn't* lose control, did I?' he retorted. 'I stopped at a kiss, though God knows how, since you weren't just asking for it, Holly, you were simply *begging* for it—'

That did it! 'You *bastard*!' There was a loud crack as her palm connected with his cheek, and they both looked at one another, aware that an unbreachable line had just been crossed.

Luke felt desire and anger bubbling up in a heady cocktail inside him as he slowly rubbed his reddening cheek. 'So that's the way you want it, is it, sweetheart?'

Holly looked at him, powerless to resist the primitive emotions which were swirling so powerfully in the air around them. 'Luke...' she began, but he shook his head, and something in his eyes silenced her words, though he could do nothing to still the shuddering of her breath.

He moved to within a step away, his mouth a grim, forbidding line, the blue eyes dark as sapphires. 'Why did you let her think that I'd slept with you, Holly? Why did you let Caroline believe a lie like that?'

She pushed the feelings of guilt away. *He* was the one guilty of deceit. 'Haven't you stopped to ask just *why* she believed me? There doesn't seem much hope for a relationship if your fiancée is so willing to think that you'd be unfaithful at the first opportunity. Or maybe in the past you have been? Maybe she's judging you on past experience?'

'You think that of me?'

She heard the outrage and the surprise in his voice and shrugged. 'I don't know,' she told him tiredly. Her head was spinning so much she didn't seem to know anything any more.

'Well, I'd hate to disappoint you, sweetheart,' he drawled. 'So let me be the bastard of your dreams instead...'

She should have anticipated what was coming next from the heat which burned in the depths of his eyes, and the husky note which had deepened his voice to rich, dark velvet. But she had thought that he might be restrained by the fact that they were standing in the middle of the shop, for all the world to see, reflected three times over by the vast mirrors which lined the walls, with the chandelier spilling golden nuggets of light onto their heads.

'Luke—' she whispered again, but he pulled her into his arms and roughly, brutally, almost punishingly began to kiss her. 'Luke, no!'

This was wrong. She knew it was wrong for lots and lots of reasons—so why was she allowing herself to be swept along by the power of his kiss? 'Stop it,' she beseeched in a whisper against the softness of his lips, but it was a meaningless entreaty and they both knew it. 'Stop it, Luke.'

'Make me,' he whispered back, following his words with a provocative little lick at the roof of her mouth, and Holly swayed in his arms, laced her fingers into the thick, gold-tipped richness of his hair as she had wanted to for so long that it seemed a lifetime of wanting. 'Go on—*make* me...'

Very deliberately, he moved his hands from her narrow back and splayed them proprietorially over her buttocks, bringing her right against him. Then he slowly began to circle his hips in the most blatantly provocative way, letting her feel the hard, butting ridge of his desire.

She felt him, and jerked with a spasm of shock and excitement. 'Luke...' said Holly weakly, as his lips continued their relentless onslaught, overloading her senses until she could barely think at all, let alone think straight.

'What?' Moving one hand from her bottom, he allowed his fingers to trickle with agonising slowness up towards her breasts, and he heard her long sigh of surrender even as he felt her body melt against him. He opened his eyes and saw their reflection in one of the huge mirrors, their bodies glued together—and it turned him on unbearably.

She was wearing a long, flowing velvet skirt in richest

burgundy and a floaty white chiffon shirt. With it she wore a matching burgundy bodice which fitted as closely as a glove, with lots of tiny, velvet-covered buttons all the way down the front. Her hair flowed like a river of copper curls down her back, caught back from her face by two tortoiseshell combs. With her white skin and emerald eyes, he thought that she looked as if she had stepped out of a painting from another century.

'Luke, please...' she pleaded, without knowing what it was she was asking him for.

He gave a low laugh tinged with passion and power. He had her right where he wanted her. 'What?' he whispered again, and Holly was too befuddled to hear the mocking tone which coloured his voice.

Luke turned his attention to the bodice, snapping open first one button and then another, making a small groan of frustration beneath his breath as he saw just how many buttons there were. This was going to take for ever and he didn't want to wait. He wanted to tear the clothes from her body, to reveal those lush, creamy breasts and then to take them in his mouth and suckle them. Bite them and tease them until her head was thrown back and through dry lips she would be demanding that he take her, take away the remorseless aching.

'God, your breasts are beautiful,' he breathed, as another button flew open.

'*O-oh.*' She stumbled, as his thumb brushed over the velvet, tantalising the nub which was thrusting against the thick material.

'Don't you ever wear a bra?' he wanted to know, his excitement rocketing as his fingers realised that there was no scrap of silk or lace to restrain them....

'Never,' she managed weakly. Her fingers seemed to have a mind of their own as they moved possessively over his broad back, moving beneath his jacket and wantonly caressing the warm flesh through the silken shirt.

'Don't you know how much it turns men on?' he managed, finding that he wanted to outrageously demand that she always wore one in future. Unless she was with *him*... He pulled his mouth away from hers then, fighting for sanity through the mists of his desire. He would have to take her upstairs right now, because if he didn't...

A sudden banging at the door was like having a bucket of iced water hurled over her, and Holly found herself swaying in Luke's arms, blinking up at him in confusion.

'W-what's that?'

Luke had razor-sharp reflexes which had been honed over years of working in the reserve, and he had swiftly rebuttoned Holly's bodice and straightened it almost before she realised what was happening.

'You have a customer,' he mocked her darkly. 'Remember? This is a shop.'

And Holly looked towards the door in dismay, where a stocky young woman stood looking in. Her eyes flickered towards Luke's face for some kind of reassurance, but none was forthcoming. His features displayed all the disgust she might have expected from a man she had almost let make love to her in public. Oh, *Lord*, what had she *done*?

'Hadn't you better let her in?' asked Luke, his voice as distant as the wind.

And Holly went to unlock the door.

CHAPTER TEN

HOLLY'S first thought was that the young woman who stood outside didn't look a bit like a bride-to-be. Not just because she was plump—although plump brides tended to buy their dresses in the safe, anonymous atmosphere of the department store rather than specialist shops. Or because she wore no glittering engagement ring—lots of women chose not to wear *those*. Caroline had not worn one, she remembered, wincing.

No, it was the woman's general expression of harassment—she looked flustered and out of breath, and carried none of the satisfied glow of a woman about to choose her wedding dress.

'Are you sure you're open?' she asked, as Holly pulled the door open, her soft cheeks growing pink. And Holly found herself blushing too, as she wondered just how much of that passionate little bout with Luke the woman had witnessed. And speaking of Luke...

She glanced over her shoulder. Why was he still standing exactly where she had left him, like a dark, immovable force? Their eyes met—his still angry and glittering with frustration, while Holly felt totally compromised by that outrageously effective demonstration of his sexual skills. He had ruthlessly manipulated her, almost...almost... She glared at him but still he didn't budge.

'Yes, of course we're open,' smiled Holly brightly. 'Do come in.'

'Thanks.' The woman stepped into the shop and looked around, but again and again her attention kept coming back to the spotlit dress in the window.

Close up, Holly could see her plumpness couldn't detract from the most beautiful pair of dark blue eyes she had ever seen, with lashes so long you could have hung your washing from them. Her skin was all berries and cream, and she had a thick head of glossy black hair caught back in an old-fashioned chignon.

'I'm Holly Lovelace,' said Holly, holding out her hand.

The woman smiled and an irrepressible dimple appeared in her right cheek. 'Is that your real name?'

Holly nodded. 'It really is!'

'I'm Ursula O'Neil. Pleased to meet you.'

'And I'm Luke Goodwin,' came a silky dark voice from behind them.

Ursula turned round and beamed. 'Hello,' she said shyly.

'What sort of thing are you looking for?' asked Holly, glowering at Luke.

'Well, it's a bit difficult to explain...'

Holly asked her stock question for dithering brides. 'How do you see yourself on your wedding day?'

The woman shook her head. 'Oh, no! I'm not getting married. It's a bit of a funny old story...'

Glad to be distracted from Luke's brooding figure, and intrigued by the woman's hesitation, Holly gestured towards the velvet sofa. 'Look, why don't you sit down,' she suggested 'and tell me all about it?'

The woman looked across the shop at Luke. 'I don't want to disturb anything—'

'You aren't disturbing anything—*honestly*,' interjected Holly quickly—much *too* quickly, really. 'Luke was just going, weren't you, Luke?'

He gave her a bland smile as their eyes met. 'Actually no.' He smiled. 'I think I'll stay.'

Holly threw him a warning look. She wanted him *out*. *Now!* For how could she concentrate on anything when he was standing there like some dark, avenging angel, with that arrogant half-smile serving as a constant reminder of what they had been doing just a few moments ago?

'But the customer might prefer to speak to me in private,' she said icily.

Luke turned a hundred-watt smile on the woman and Holly knew immediately that she wouldn't stand a chance in hell of resisting him. 'You don't mind, do you, Ursula?'

Obediently the woman shook her head at him, melting under the impact of that mega-watt dazzle. 'No, I don't mind at all.' She settled herself on the velvet sofa, but her attention remained focussed on the window and she laced her fingers together nervously, before taking a deep breath. 'That dress you have in the window...'

Holly looked at her encouragingly as her words tailed off. 'Yes?'

'Is it...is it a very old dress?'

Holly looked at her in surprise. 'No, it isn't.'

'How old?'

'Well, I made it earlier this year.'

'*You* made it?'

Holly blinked. 'Yes, I did.'

'I see.' Ursula's face crumpled with disappointment and she began digging around in her handbag, eventually extracting a scrunched up tissue and loudly blowing her nose.

'Is something wrong?' asked Holly gently.

Ursula shook her head. 'No, nothing's wrong. It's just that I saw a picture of it in the newspaper, and I thought...I thought...'

'What did you think?' interposed Holly quietly.

'It looks exactly the same as a wedding dress my mother bought,' Ursula gulped, like a woman about to burst into tears. 'But of course it can't be!'

'No, it can't be.' Holly paused, then frowned as the facts began to piece themselves together in her mind like a jigsaw. 'This dress that your mother bought—when was that exactly? Can you remember?'

Ursula shrugged her fleshy shoulders. 'It'd be over twenty years ago now.' Her voice softened. 'It was in a sale at the big London store she worked in. She queued all night in the rain to buy it. It was for me, and for my sister—we were each to wear it when we got married...'

'And what happened to it?'

Ursula lifted her head proudly and looked Holly straight in the eye. 'My father died, and we had no money.' Her voice faltered. 'So she sold it. She put an advert in the paper. She had to. It broke my mother's heart to see it go.' She shrugged, her voice wobbling a little. 'But what use is a fine dress in the cupboard when there's no food on the table?'

'No use at all,' said Luke slowly, and they both turned round to look at him, as though they had forgotten he was there. But Luke, it seemed, had all the answers. 'Your mother bought the original dress, you see, Ursula.'

'Yes, of *course* she did!' breathed Holly slowly.

'I'm sorry?' Ursula looked at them both in confusion. 'I don't understand what it is you're saying.'

'That dress you see in the window, yes, *I* designed and made it,' explained Holly. 'But I based the design on one of my mother's original sketches—because she was a dress designer, too, and it was one of her favourite gowns. And *your* mother must have bought *my* mother's dress! Now do you see?'

'Heavens!' said Ursula.

Holly smiled. 'So, although the two dresses aren't exactly the same, they're very, very similar.'

Ursula stood up and moved closer to the window to look at the dress, her eyes as wide as saucers, like a child taken to the ballet for the very first time. 'Yes, they are,' she agreed. 'Very similar. Dear me, it's unbelievable!' She was silent for a moment as she stared at the soft satin. 'The dress used to hang in the wardrobe in our bedroom and we were allowed to look at it and touch it, but only through the plastic. Except on our birthdays, when she used to take it out of its covering and we were allowed a proper look at it. Oh, how we loved that dress!'

'And did your mother never even try it on?' asked Holly. 'Just to see what it looked like?'

Ursula shook her head. 'It was a tiny dress, and she was a big woman.' She glanced down at her generous curves with a rueful expression. 'Like me. She used to say that she wouldn't even be able to squeeze her fingers into the sleeves! But it would fit my sister, and she's getting married soon. It may not be the original, but it's the next best thing. That's why I came here today.' She pulled a purse from her bag as if she were about to start bartering down at the market and gave Holly a huge smile. 'To buy it.'

Holly didn't know what to say. Or rather she did, but she wasn't sure how best to phrase it without sounding cruel or hurtful.

'How much is it, please?' asked Ursula.

Holly shook her head. 'But I'm afraid it isn't for sale.'

Ursula frowned. 'I don't understand. It's in the window—'

'Yes, I know it is. But didn't you read the whole article? It's a bit of a stunt. I've only just opened the shop, and I'm offering the wedding dress as the prize in a draw. So, although you can't buy it, you're very welcome to enter into the draw to win it.'

Ursula bit her lip. 'But what if I don't win?'

'Well, if your sister desperately wants that particular design, then I can have one made up—but she won't be able to wear it until March.'

'March?' queried Ursula. 'But Amber is getting married in February! How come?'

Holly sighed. 'Because the bridal magazine who sponsored the competition are doing a whole big feature on the dress in the March edition—and part of the deal was that, if I sold it, then it could not be worn until after that edition has hit the shelves. They want the feature to have maximum impact, you see.'

'That would be a pretty difficult rule to enforce,' Luke reflected.

Holly frowned at him. 'Yes, I know it would! But it

would be pretty churlish not to abide by the competition rules, wouldn't it? Especially as their prize money financed my business in the first place!'

His eyes were thoughtful as they rested on Holly. 'You mean you'll abide by the spirit of the law as opposed to the letter?'

'That's exactly what I mean!'

Ursula gave a resigned shrug. 'Oh, well, then. I guess I'll put my name in the hat with the rest of them and say a prayer or two! It would be great to have the dress, even if Amber won't be able to wear it.'

'Do you have no idea who your mother sold the original to?' Luke asked.

Ursula shook her head. 'No idea at all. Mum kept it all pretty hush-hush. Selling off your possessions because you were short of money wasn't something you shouted from the rooftops—not where I came from, anyway.'

'And where's that?' queried Luke.

'South London. I live on the opposite side of town, these days.'

Luke nodded. 'And how are you getting back there tonight?'

Ursula shook her head. 'I'm not. I've booked in at The Bell. I don't like these country roads at night.'

'I don't blame you,' he said.

'Here.' Holly handed her one of the entry forms and Ursula filled in her name and address, then dropped it into the red satin box.

Afterwards she shook hands with both of them. 'It's been great meeting you both! And thank you for your help,' she said. 'Even if I don't win, it was interesting to learn a bit more of the dress's history.'

'I'll tell my mother when I next see her,' promised Holly. 'She usually turns up in England for Christmas!'

'I'd like to tell mine,' said Ursula with a sad smile. 'But she died a long time ago.'

'I'm so sorry,' said Holly. On an impulse, she picked up one of her cards from the counter and thrust it into Ursula's hand. 'If you ever need a wedding dress, then you know where I am.'

Ursula smiled. 'Thanks—but I'm hoping I might win that one!'

Holly hoped so, too—though she couldn't see what use it would be if she did. The prize-winning dress would never fit Ursula, and her sister would be getting married before it could legitimately be worn...

There was silence in the shop once she had gone, and it took every bit of Holly's courage to turn to Luke and say, 'Is that everything? Only I don't want to keep you.'

'Everything?' He laughed, but it was an angry, bitter kind of laugh, as though Ursula leaving the shop had negated any need for him to be pleasant to her. 'Sweetheart, I haven't even started yet. We may have just been treated to a touching story, but nothing has changed. Think back to what we were doing before Ursula arrived, Holly.'

Her cheeks flamed, even as her heart began to pick up speed. That was the *last* thing she wanted to do. 'Luke, I really think it's best if you go.'

'I'm sure you do. And we must always do what's best for Holly Lovelace, mustn't we?' A muscle began to work convulsively in his cheek. 'But damn the rest of the world, isn't that right?'

'I don't know what you're talking about.' She made to turn away but he wouldn't let her, grabbing her by the arm, and even that rough contact made her blood sing.

'Don't you?' He was staring deeply into her eyes, and Holly seemed paralysed, rooted to the ground, mesmerised by the magic of that dark denim-blue gaze.

'N-no.'

'Oh, I think you do, Holly. Be honest now.'

'I don't.' He was still holding tightly onto her arm, his expression a mixture of disdain and desire, and yet still she remained fixed to the spot. 'Let me go,' she protested ineffectually.

'No.' He tipped his gold-brushed head to one side and gave her a long, considering look. 'See what it feels like when someone takes control? You should do—after all, you're the ultimate control freak, aren't you, Holly? You decided that you wanted me, didn't you? You wanted me real *bad* and you weren't going to let anything as inconvenient as a fiancée in your way. That, presumably, is why you told her that we'd been sleeping together—'

'Luke, don't—'

'Don't what?' He raised his eyebrows mockingly. 'Don't tell the truth? But why ever not, Holly? Does the truth make you feel uncomfortable? And it is the truth, isn't it, Holly? *Isn't* it?'

'Y-yes,' she admitted brokenly. 'Partly.'

He nodded. 'Yes, I know what you mean—and it *is* only part of the truth, because of course we *haven't* slept together, have we, Holly? Not yet.'

His words sent shivers down her spine. 'That wasn't what I meant. Luke—'

'After all,' he interrupted remorselessly, 'you've got what you want now, haven't you? Caroline is off the scene. You made damn sure of that—'

'Caroline has *gone*?'

His mouth shaped itself into a cruel curve. 'Yes, she's *gone*!' he mimicked ruthlessly. 'Of course she's gone! Or did you imagine that she would hang around hoping that we could all have a cosy little threesome?'

'Don't be so disgusting!' she snapped.

'Oh, I can get a lot more disgusting than that, sweetheart!' he vowed, and Holly wondered how his pitiless words had managed to produce the tantalising excitement which was currently tiptoeing its way up her spine.

'But you probably like it that way, don't you?' he persisted. 'Isn't that what you got up to at art school? Threesomes? Perversions are all the rage, surely—and it would be so incredibly *bourgeois* not to join in, don't you think?'

'I don't have to stay here and listen to this!' she snapped, making to pull away from him, but he caught her other arm to pull her against his chest. His mouth descended on hers and all his anger and frustration and pent-up desire exploded in a fever of need which only matched hers.

One touch and she was lost.

She knew it and he knew it, and there didn't seem to be a damned thing she could do to stop it.

'Now kill the lights,' he growled.

And like a willing puppet she did as he told her.

CHAPTER ELEVEN

The darkness clothed them like black velvet. Holly stood immobile by the light switch, knowing that it was not too late to change her mind, but then she heard Luke behind her, felt his warm breath on her neck and realised that she had no resistance left.

He slowly turned her round to him, his shape becoming a pale blur before her as her eyes began to gradually accustom themselves to the gloom of the room. He imprisoned her face in the warm cradle of his hand and she held her breath in fearful longing as she waited for him to speak. And when he did, the last of her foolish dreams crumbled like dust around her.

'You owe me, Holly,' he told her grimly. 'You owe me this.'

Her heart jerked with a judder of pain, but at that moment she vowed that he would never know the hurt he had caused her. And all the hurt to come...

'In lieu of rent?' she questioned smartly.

His mouth hardened. 'No.'

'Or for decorating the shop so nicely, perhaps?'

He laughed, but it was the bitterest laugh she had ever heard. 'Trying to shock me into leaving, are you? Well, it won't work, sweetheart. You decided to play this game, Holly—but maybe the stakes were higher than you imagined.'

'Luke—'

'No,' he whispered against her ear, and that deep velvet voice tugged relentlessly at her heartstrings even as she tried to steel herself against his words. 'You told Caroline what you pretty damned well pleased. You led her to believe we'd slept together and now she's gone. Well, you can't play God with people's lives and expect to get away with it. So now it's time to pay your dues, Holly, and I've come to collect.'

As he spoke he began to caress her, his hand moving expertly down the side of her body, sculpting the curves there as though he were fashioning her from damp clay, and Holly felt a shiver of longing ripple over her skin as despair sharpened her hunger instead of blunting it. She had waited her whole life to feel this kind of response to a man—so why in God's name did that man have to be Luke Goodwin?

All those books she had read, the paintings she had seen, every statue and film depicting the supposedly mindless passion which accompanied the act of love—hadn't she sometimes wondered whether it was a conspiracy and it was a figment of everyone's imagination?

But now she had discovered the power of desire for herself, and Luke was bringing it to life in her. Breathing passion and fire into her blood with his touch, until it blazed from every pore. 'Oh, Luke,' she sighed brokenly, as his fingers brushed negligently over the swell of her breasts. *'Oh!'*

'Come over here,' he said softly, taking her hand and leading her towards the back of the shop.

She couldn't bear to resist him. At that moment if he told her to walk naked into the street she honestly thought she might give it serious consideration. 'W-where?'

'Here.'

Here? Oh, my God, he was taking her into one of the changing rooms, where a bolt of silk dupion lay stacked on one side, like a giant ivory cylinder. The light was dim, but she saw his eyes glitter at the sight of the material, and he tugged at one end of the bolt, rolling it out so that it covered the entire floor of the cubicle in a great creamy, silken carpet. 'A bed for my beauty,' he mocked.

Holly's heart was thundering, her mouth so dry with excitement that she could barely articulate a word, let alone a sentence. 'We c-could always go upstairs?'

He swept a slow, possessive hand through the unruly tumble of her hair. 'I know we could,' he agreed softly. 'But I don't want to. Upstairs is yours, but this is no one's. I want to take you here, on this sumptuous covering in this anonymous room where no one has ever made love before, nor ever shall again. I want to see the apricot tones of your soft skin contrasted against the pale sheen of silk. I want to finish what I should have finished earlier...'

He began to swiftly unbutton her burgundy velvet bodice, and, even as her heart pulsed beneath his touch, she forced herself to close her mind to the matter-of-fact cruelty of his words—and of one word in particular.

Finish.

He wanted to finish what he had started earlier. He made her sound like an itch he needed to scratch.

She would have this one glorious initiation and then it would be over. Logic told her that she was crazy, that if she walked out now he would not force himself on her, nor beg. But her senses overrode all logic. She could not refuse him, nor would refuse him. She had dreamed too long of this moment to deny it now. Her body trembled as he discarded the waistcoat and turned his attention next to her white chiffon shirt.

His face was shadowed but the tension showed in the tight set of his jaw as he surveyed the dark-tipped globes which thrust towards him through the pale, gauzy material. 'Oh, God, yes,' he breathed, like a man bewitched. *'Yes.'*

Her breathing was shallow, and rapid as a hunted animal's, and yet he had scarcely touched her. Her cheeks were burning as she stood before him like a willing victim, not knowing what to do or what to say next.

Luke frowned. This was not how he had imagined it. He wanted fire from her, not fear. He wanted her to fight him, not accept him. This would be a glorious battle before it became a victory. 'Take your shirt off,' he told her unsteadily. 'Do it very, very *slowly…*'

Holly let out a long, low sigh. So this was what he wanted, was it? This was what would turn him on. And if he wanted her to play the vamp—then vamp she would be.

She lifted her chin proudly, feeling the heavy sway of curls falling down her back, then unhurriedly let one finger slowly circle the button of her shirt, as though the button itself were an erogenous zone. She heard him suck in a breath as she popped it open, and then another, another…until her breasts sprang free and then, to her surprise, he leaned forward to bury his head in them, holding her tightly by the waist for a moment, before letting his tongue and his lips taste each heavy and sensitive mound.

'Oh!' gasped Holly, her head falling back helplessly, her hands blindly seeking the thick, gold-tipped hair to balance herself as she swayed, saturated with desire, feeling his tongue wet and warm against her nipple.

'Is that good?' he demanded thickly.

It was heaven. She made an indistinct sound of assent as his teeth lightly scraped against the rosy tips which puckered and strained for his lips.

He fell to his knees before her, but she soon realised that it was no gesture of homage, merely a way that he could unbutton her velvet skirt with a speedy accuracy which spoke of lots of practice. It pooled with a whisper to the floor around her ankles, so that she was left wearing nothing but the unbuttoned chiffon shirt, minuscule white panties and a pair of knee-high black leather boots.

'My God!' he groaned. 'Holly!'

Vamps were verbal. 'What is it?' she whispered provocatively.

'This is like every fantasy I've ever had, condensed into one!' he groaned.

Vamps incited too. 'Just you wait,' she promised, wildly wondering whether she would be able to follow through.

'Lie down,' he urged her. 'Lie down just like that.'

She knew what to do. She lay on her back on the ivory satin, with her hands pillowed behind her head, her knees bent, and looked straight up into his face. Even through the gloom she could sense the sexual promise in the searing glance which he sent jackknifing through her.

Her heart pounded as she watched him drop his suit jacket to the floor, his hands unsteadily beginning to unbutton his shirt. Oh, God—she needed something to distract her from the moment of truth when Luke Goodwin would stand before her proud and naked.

'W-what do you want me to do?' she murmured, through lips which felt bee-stung swollen.

He stilled momentarily, and she saw the sudden twisting of his mouth. 'Straight sex bore you, does it?' he drawled, and she was certain that she could sense *disappointment* in his voice. Or was it contempt? He stood looking over her, and for one mad, terrible moment she thought he was about to change his mind and walk out.

But he didn't.

'Play with your breasts, baby,' he breathed shakily. 'Touch them, Holly. Pretend they're *my* hands. Go on...touch them.'

She had seen a dirty movie once. Someone at college had smuggled it into the film club for a joke, and Holly and three others had left halfway through. But she remembered how the buxom women had performed. The way they'd writhed their hips in exaggerated circles, moaning as they palpated their huge breasts as if they were kneading dough. And that was presumably what turned men on. Even so, she couldn't look him in the face as she did it.

She closed her eyes and began to run her hands experimentally over herself. It felt strange and wicked and oddly good, though nothing like as good as when *his* hands had been upon her. She risked raising her eyelashes by a centimetre, and through the shade of her lashes she could see Luke ripping his tie off and hurling it to the floor.

Next she heard the rasp of a zip and saw a grim look of determination on his face as he struggled to free himself—kicking first his trousers off and then his boxer shorts. And then...

Holly swallowed and screwed her eyes tightly shut. The only adult males she had ever seen in the nude before had been in a life class, and they hadn't been... hadn't been...

Dear Lord, she thought as she allowed her lashes to flutter up by a fraction, and fear skittered over her skin. If that was masculine arousal, then it was pretty daunting.

'Are you peeping, Holly?' he questioned silkily. 'Don't peep, sweetheart—open your eyes properly and take a good look at me.'

Running a nervous tongue over parchment lips, she did as he suggested.

'What's the matter?' he whispered. 'Afraid that this—' and he touched himself with a total, almost arrogant lack of self-consciousness '—will prove too much for you, Holly? Don't think you can take it?' He reached out his hand and without warning skimmed his finger down over the centre of her panties, wet with wanting now, the way they had never been before. She shuddered with pleasure as his finger came away moist from the cotton, and as he slowly licked the tip of it he gave a smile of desire and satisfaction.

'Oh, I think you can take me, Holly. You're so ripe and ready for me, sweetheart, and I haven't even started.'

He dropped to the ground over her, his knees to either side of her hips so that she was confronted with the sight of his manhood pushing a hard, tight column against his belly, and she gave a little moan of wonder. Forgetting everything, she raised her hand falteringly, then let it fall, but he captured it with his, raised it to his mouth and kissed it, his eyes never leaving her face.

'If you want to touch me, sweetheart—then I'm all yours.'

Curiosity made her reach out, her fingertips lightly skating down the broad, silken shaft.

He bore it for no more than a few seconds before his hand came down again, but this time it halted hers with steely insistence. 'Don't,' he said tersely.

'You don't like it?'

'You know damned well I do,' he ground out painfully, as he sucked in a deep breath of control.

'Then why stop?'

'No games, Holly.' His laugh was hollow. 'No games—okay? No pretence. This is going to be so good. *So* good. We both know that. Because you want me, baby—you want me real bad.'

What she had wanted was for him to kiss her. She wanted him to kiss her now. Oh, she wanted this, too— but a kiss was what she longed for.

And maybe he sensed it, for he lowered his head to hers. But the kiss was not sweet, or tender—it did nothing for her emotions but everything for her senses, making desire accelerate so rapidly that she felt she was spinning in a dark vortex where Luke was the only thing that mattered. He kissed her until she had no breath left in her body and every last trace of resistance had flown. With that kiss he claimed her and made her his.

Eventually he wonderingly raised his head, and carefully brushed a lock of hair from her face. 'Are you on the pill?'

She shook her head and began to blush, thanking heaven that the darkness meant he wouldn't be able to see. For heaven's sake, she had been touching him just about as intimately as a woman *could* touch a man—so why was the mention of contraception making her suddenly go all coy? Was she hurt that his words had been so prosaic, lacking the tenderness she had been longing to hear?

He took a condom from his pocket and slid it on, then moved back over her again, taking some of his weight on his elbows, and she shivered with anticipation as she felt the hard, warm weight of him. The feel of crisp, hair-roughened skin. Experimentally, she scraped her fingernails over the rock-hard globes of his buttocks, and felt him jerk beneath her touch with pleasure.

Luke looked down at her, revelling in the feel of her softness beneath him. He had longed for this moment since he had first seen her standing in all her colt-like beauty outside the shop, her face framed by the flames of her hair. She had been a fever in his blood ever since, and he wondered if only this would cure him of his obsession.

He trickled a leisurely finger over her peaking nipple, then bent and took the rosy nub into the warm, moist cavern of his mouth.

'Oh!' Holly's eyes shivered to a close as she felt his tongue slicking against her.

She felt his hand on the flat of her belly, circling its palm over the heat which radiated from her skin, and she felt her hips rise up to meet his, demanding more, *more*—as if instinct was controlling her and she no longer had dominance over her own body. She tried to pull his hand down to where the ache was becoming unbearable, but he wouldn't let her.

He laughed unsteadily. '*Yes!* You're greedy, Holly,' he whispered against her ear. 'I knew you would be. Wild, artistic, temperamental—seeking out every new sensation you can, is that it?'

Blindly she nodded her head, not knowing what she was agreeing to, only that if he didn't do something soon to ease this terrible wanting she would explode.

'Please, Luke...' she beseeched him. 'Oh, please!'

At *last*! This was where he had wanted her, soft and naked and writhing beneath him, begging him to bring her to fulfilment. That in itself should have been victory enough, and yet Luke was suddenly aware of a void...of this not being enough.

'Please,' she pleaded again.

His mouth hardened as he felt her impatience. She wanted satisfaction, and she wanted it quickly. 'You heartless little bitch,' he whispered, the sight of her naked against the luxurious folds of creamy silk exciting him to fever-pitch. 'I'm just a body to you, aren't I, Holly? A hot, slick machine designed to bring you pleasure.' But he drew in a deep breath until he had himself under control once more.

'W-what?' she stumbled, trying in vain to surface from this enchantment.

'Nothing.' He let his hand drift downwards, a featherlight flick to where she was taut and molten, and she gasped. 'God, you're responsive,' he murmured, disbelief growing on his face as he realised how close to the edge she was. He flicked again, then circled, around and around, and felt her arch beneath him, her body stretched with unbearable tightness until the spasms began and he could feel her pulsing beneath his finger, while she clung to him, making little cries of pleasure into his ear.

Her eyes flickered open as the sensations began to fade, and she looked at him in bewilderment. 'W-what happened?'

'What *happened*? You had just about the quickest orgasm on record, sweetheart, that's what happened.'

She gave him a befuddled gaze. 'But I...I don't understand.'

His laugh was as cold as his body was hot and longing to thrust into her moist heat. 'Oh, come on—baby—I think we're both a little too experienced to fall for that one, don't you? Though it's a pretty good line to take, I give you that.'

She stared up at him in confusion, as if he were speaking to her in a foreign language. 'Line? What line?'

'Do you imply that to all your lovers?' he whispered. 'That you've never had an orgasm before? Does it flatter them? Swell their egos—and maybe something else, besides?' He gave a throaty laugh. 'Well, there's no need to invent things on my account, Holly, and I certainly don't need any encouragement to incite me. Feel for yourself.' And he took her hand, guided it to him, folded her fingers around the great throbbing width of him.

'Luke,' she said again, only this time it was halfway between a gasp and a sob.

'I want to savour this,' he murmured, as he began to position himself above her. 'Every sweet moment. Every stroke I make and every cry you utter. I'm going to imprint myself on your soul, my angel, give you so much pleasure that you will recoil in disgust if any other man ever tries to touch you.'

But for all his brutal words, he experienced a sense of wonder as he thrust deeply into her, and Holly felt a swift, piercing spasm before her muscles clenched and then exquisitely unclenched to accommodate him.

'God, you're so tight,' he whispered, and kissed her. Tighter than he'd ever known. Or was it simply that he was more excited than he had ever been in his life? He found that he was trembling, that he could hardly bear to stop kissing her. He began to move slowly inside her. 'I'm going to make you come again,' he promised. 'Would you like that?'

Mutely, she nodded, and hooked her hand around his neck, bringing his head down to hers and opening her mouth to his. This time the kiss was sweet, but perhaps it was made all the sweeter by the communion of flesh, those great strokes which filled her, heated her, sent her hurtling towards that place again.

His resolve was steely until he felt her nearing the brink, and only then did he allow himself to relax into it. He had never been harder or fuller or closer, but he kept drawing back and drawing back, until he felt her suck in a great breath, waited until she had started to shudder beneath him, and only then did he let go, his last fleeting thought being that it had never been as good as this before. Never. His grip on her tightened. 'Love me, Holly,' he breathed shakily. 'Oh, love me!' And his universe dissolved.

As consciousness returned, so did sensation. Holly became aware of the silky fabric which lay rucked up beneath her naked flesh, and of the wetness between her legs.

Luke felt it, too, and raised his head. 'I think the condom may have burst,' he told her ruefully, realising that, stupidly, he didn't care. He kissed her bare shoulder and slid his hand down between her legs, but his fingers came away oddly sticky...

He rolled off her and snapped on the cubicle light, then stared down in disbelief at the tell-tale scarlet stain which had flowered over the creamy silk, his eyes widening with horror as he realised the full implications.

'Blood,' he breathed. *'Blood.'* He turned to her with disbelief written in his eyes, and, before he could hide it, pride. A primitive, unimaginable pride. 'Holly. Holly, sweetheart—you're a...'

But the tender words had come too late. 'Yes, I'm a virgin!' she spat back at him. 'Surprised?'

'Surprised? I'm absolutely bloody flabbergasted,' he admitted in a dazed voice, until he realised from the look on her face that it was entirely the *wrong* thing to say. 'Holly, sweetheart—come here—'

'Get *away* from me!' she told him furiously, and she pushed him away and jumped to her feet. He snaked his hand out and tried to capture her ankle, but she shook him off, hurriedly pulled her shirt back on and then wiped the thin scarlet film of blood from her thighs with her discarded panties.

'Holly—'

'Don't you "Holly" me!' she declared furiously, and pointed at the stained fabric. 'Why don't you take the evidence of my virginity and wave it triumphantly out of the window?' she raged. 'That's what they used to do in the barbaric old days, isn't it? Well—that should suit you right down to the ground!'

'Listen to me—'

'I won't listen to another word you say, Luke Goodwin! And you can take your smug, outdated hypocrisy somewhere else! How *dare* you think you can suddenly elevate me from tramp to Madonna—just because I happened to have an intact hymen!' She drew in a deep, shuddering breath, but not before she had seen his shocked expression. *Good!* Then she'd shock him some more! 'We've both had what we want, so now you can go! I'm sorry I lied to your fiancée about sleeping with you—but, if you want to know the truth, at the time I thought she wasn't good enough for you. Now I think you're probably a match made in heaven! It may not be too late, Luke—so why don't you go crawling back to Africa and find her?'

'I'm not going anywhere until we've talked this over sensibly. I've told you—it's over with Caroline. She's gone back.'

But his words brought her no joy. 'And I told you that I don't *care*—and nothing will ever change that fact!'

He should have looked ridiculous, sitting naked among the sheening undulations of the ruffled silk, but, oddly enough, he looked divine. 'Holly.' His voice was soft. 'Not to talk about this is crazy.'

Holly closed her heart and glowered. 'It's too *late*!

There's nothing left to say. I've paid my *dues*,' she told him deliberately, and saw him flinch. 'So get out. Out of my shop and out of my life! And don't come back! I *mean* it, Luke!'

He could see she did. He could also see that nothing he said right now would help. If he tried to gentle her, then he would be accused of patronising her. If he tried to love her he would be the sex-crazed taker of her innocence. This might be the hardest thing he had ever had to do, but...

Rising to his feet, Luke began to reach down for his clothes while Holly, with folded arms and trembling lips, stood and watched him.

She meant every word she'd said, but that didn't stop her from having to bite back bitter tears as he silently began to pull on his trousers, ready to leave her.

CHAPTER TWELVE

THE mammoth Christmas tree twinkled merrily in the sumptuous dining room of the Grantchester hotel, and Holly pushed her barely touched plate of lobster away.

'Have another glass of champagne, darling!'

'I don't want another glass of champagne, thank you,' answered Holly moodily, slapping her hand over the crystal flute before her mother could tip any more wine into it.

'It might put you in a better mood,' said her mother carefully. She'd never known her compliant Holly be so grumpy!

'It might also give me a splitting headache,' objected Holly. 'And I've got to drive back to Woodhampton.'

'Darling, *not* tonight—it's New Year's Eve,' protested her mother, although not, Holly noticed, terribly convincingly.

But who could blame her?

Since Holly had arrived to spend Christmas with her mother and husband number four at one of London's most luxurious hotels, she was aware that she had been like a bear with a sore head. Oh, she had gone through all the motions of seasonal celebration, but she knew that she hadn't put up a very convincing performance.

Her mother lit a cigarette. 'Are you going to a New Year party, then, darling?'

Holly shook her head, and flapped her hand to dispel

some of the fog. 'Nope. But I promised that the draw for the wedding dress would take place on the stroke of midnight!'

'Huh!' scoffed her mother. 'Who's going to be there to see it? Who will know if you draw it tomorrow morning instead? That way you can stay on and party here, with us!'

'*I'll* know,' said Holly firmly. 'And besides, I don't want to spoil your fun, Mum,' she added truthfully.

Holly's mother looked guilty as she refilled her glass. 'Darling, I know I haven't been a good mother—'

Holly sighed. It was getting to that melancholy stage of the lunch. 'You did your best, Mum,' she said placatingly. 'That's all anyone can do. You're you, and I'm me.' She sniffed miserably. 'And I just happened to make the mistake of falling in love with the biggest rat this side of the Atlantic!'

'This is this *Luke*, is it? The man you won't tell me anything about other than his name and the fact that he might be a member of the rodent family?'

'That's right,' said Holly, staring gloomily into her empty glass.

'It is rather irritating, darling,' objected her mother prettily. 'You've never shown interest in a single man in your *life*, and now you have done and you won't tell me anything about him!'

'That's because there's nothing to tell, other than he's left and probably gone back to Africa! He's past tense!' she snarled. 'History!'

Her mother lifted her shoulders expressively. *'Men,'* she colluded darkly. 'They're all the same!' She batted her eyelashes as she saw the squat, toad-like shape of husband number four approaching across the restaurant, and hissed, 'But they keep you in comfort as you get older, dear! Just remember that!'

Holly shuddered as she rose to her feet. She would rather stay single, thank you very much, than rely on some odious creep to support her!

Half an hour later, she was driving fast out of London towards Woodhampton in her Beetle. The garage that Luke had recommended had telephoned to renew their offer, and it seemed like an indecent amount of money for the gaudy car. 'Beetles are *big* right now!' the salesman had informed her.

But while the sensible side of her urged her to take the money and run...well, there was another side which couldn't bear to part with the car. God knew, she hadn't got Luke—was she going to lose everything else that was dear to her?

All the way back, her thoughts threatened to drive her crazy. However brutish Luke had been, the unchangeable fact was that she missed him more each day, and the longer he was out of her life, the greater the temptation to justify his behaviour.

All right, he hadn't told her about Caroline—but his behaviour had been exemplary while she'd been staying with him. Yes, they had been close—but their closeness had been no more sinister than warmth and affection. He hadn't laid a finger on her in the whole two weeks, and that must have taken some self-control since she had spent the entire time giving him the green light.

And afterwards, in her flat after the party—he hadn't exactly been guilty of a capital crime *there* either, had he? What had he done? Touched her ankle and *kissed* her. Big deal! It had been a *party*, for heaven's sake, and, like her mother said, people always kissed people they shouldn't at parties. Why, it was how her mother had found most of her boyfriends and all of her husbands!

Woodhampton High Street was deserted, but loud disco music was blaring from the fairy-lit interior of the Bell Inn, and Holly remembered that they were having a New Year party. She thought she'd probably pass on that…

She parked outside Lovelace Brides and couldn't resist turning her head to look up at Apson House, hope flickering in her heart despite all her best attempts to stem it. But the house was in complete darkness, with not a flicker of light anywhere to be seen.

So he wasn't back and he obviously had no intention of coming back. He had missed Africa and had probably managed to change Caroline's mind, and no doubt they were busy planning a romantic, open-air wedding out there right now.

She fished around in her bag for her keys, her eyes automatically flickering to the window, where the prize dress was spotlit, then back to her handbag again.

She stilled.

Narrowing her eyes, she turned and looked back towards the window. Everything looked exactly the same as when she had left it, and yet it was *not* the same.

For it was *her* dress in the window, and yet it was *not* her dress.

Fingers shaking, she managed to get the door open, and stepped into the half-light of the interior, where the spotlight focussed so brightly on the wedding dress gave out the only illumination.

Holly walked forward, slowly as a sleepwalker, until she was just feet away from the gown, and then her hands began to tremble. She reached forward to touch it, and the difference became evident in a moment. Her mother's gown was made of far costlier material than hers, the stitching on it exquisitely fine. Holly's wedding gown was a beautiful dress, but her mother's was an heirloom.

'Like it?' came a deep voice from the shadows.

It should have given her a fright, but it didn't—it was a voice she had grown to love and which she recognised immediately. She didn't even turn round, but then maybe that was because she could sense he was moving across the shop towards her, and she didn't speak until he was right behind her.

'Where did you find it?' she asked dully.

'Long story.'

She did turn round then, and she could do absolutely nothing to stop the great rush of emotion which washed over her. She'd missed him, she realised, more than she had any right to miss him.

She met his gaze. 'No need to ask how you got in.'

He shrugged. 'The landlord always has a spare key.' He looked at her face closely for some kind of reaction. 'Surprised to see me?'

She thought about it. 'I'm not sure.'

He thought that her voice contained neither warmth, nor chill—just a matter-of-factness which was oddly emotionless. She sounded like a tired teacher at the end of term.

She frowned. 'Have you lost weight?'

'Yeah.' His voice was wry. 'Haven't had a lot of appetite recently.'

Me neither, she thought, but, 'Oh,' was all she said. She wanted to ask what *his* reason was, but that might sound as if she was concerned about his welfare, and she wasn't. Because she still hadn't forgiven him.

He threw her a conciliatory look. 'Do you want to know about the dress?'

She wasn't going to make this easy for him. 'I'd rather know the truth about you and Caroline.'

He nodded. 'I thought you might say something like that. Can we go and sit down somewhere more comfortable while I tell you?'

'Where did you have in mind?' she asked nastily. 'The changing room?'

Luke resisted the temptation to say, If you like, and shook his tawny head instead. 'Upstairs?'

'I thought you didn't like my flat!' she snapped.

He had come prepared for a fight, but even so it was the hardest thing in the world to just tiptoe round her raw feelings like this, when all he wanted to do was to scoop her up in his arms and kiss the breath out of her.

'I like your flat very much, Holly,' he told her equably. 'But if you'd prefer we could talk somewhere else. How about the quiet, intimate atmosphere of The Bell?'

Her mouth began to twitch, but she wouldn't laugh, she *wouldn't*. 'Come on, then,' she said ungraciously, and stomped loudly up the stairs, like a child sent early to bed, while he followed her.

The flat was warm. 'Have you turned the heating on?' she demanded suspiciously.

'Guilty.'

'But why? I might not have been back at least until the day after tomorrow. The shop won't open on New Year's Day.'

'I know. But I also knew that you'd be back tonight—'

'How could you know *that*, for heaven's sake?'

'Because that's when you said the draw would take place.'

Holly nodded, pleased that he had remembered and pleased that he had taken her at her word. But if he had *really* taken her at her word, then he wouldn't be here, would he? Not when she had told him that she never wanted to see him again.

She sat down on the sofa and looked at him, steeling herself against the denim-blue eyes, the tawny head, the irresistible mouth.

'I guess it would be an unfair advantage of me to sit down beside you?'

'Yes, it would—and it's a little late in the day for old-fashioned courtesy,' she scolded, despairing of herself as she added, 'You can sit right up at the other end as long as you don't move.'

He did, stretching his long legs out in front of him before turning to look at her. 'And I guess you want an explanation of my behaviour?'

'Damn right I do!'

His eyes narrowed. 'And then perhaps you'll explain to me why you let me take your virginity in the most inglorious fashion imaginable?'

'Because I "owed" you?' she mocked.

He winced. 'You know that I would never have said that if I'd had any idea that—'

'That I wasn't the strumpet you had me down as?'

Luke sighed. 'Sweetheart, you are an enigmatic woman.' His mouth softened as he tried to put it into words. 'There's just something about you. You have the kind of eyes...the kind of lips...a certain way of looking...'

'Just what exactly are you trying to say, Luke?'

'That you look like someone who's been around the block several times over!' Seeing her perplexed look, he elaborated. 'It didn't occur to me that you weren't sexually experienced!'

'Because I'm twenty-six?'

'No.' He shook his head. 'It's nothing to do with your age. Just the way you looked at me the first time you met me—well...' he shrugged '...without wishing to sound arrogant—'

'Oh, cut the false modesty, Luke, *please*!'

'You looked like you just wanted me to drag you off to the nearest bed and ravish you all night long.'

'It's a look you recognise well, is it?' she asked sarcastically.

'Well, women *have* come on to me like that before,' he admitted.

'And you always take them up on it, I suppose?'

'Well, no—I don't! That's the whole point!'

'What, never?' she queried, in disbelief.

'Not for years, no. Not that instant wham-bam-thank-you-ma'am thing, anyway.'

'That must be some small comfort for Caroline.

Remember Caroline, Luke? The fiancée whom you conveniently forgot to mention?'

'I was coming to that.'

'I can't imagine that there's anything you could tell me about Caroline which would make your behaviour forgivable.'

'Are you going to let me try?'

She shrugged, knowing she was going to say yes and feeling weak because of it—but how could she get through the rest of her life not knowing the truth? 'I suppose so.'

He stared at his hands, at the jagged scar down the side of one thumb. He'd nearly lost the digit, and remembered the pain he had felt at the time—but that was nothing compared to the agonising ache inside him now. 'I've known Caroline for a long time,' he began. 'Years and years. She was a teacher at the nearest school to my ranch and we used to meet at various socials.'

'How nice for you both! Was it love at first sight?'

'Not at all. She used to heartily disapprove of my lifestyle and I never thought of her in that way. I used to look on her as a friend.'

'So what happened to change her mind? Your undoubted prowess in bed—or maybe I should say on bolts of pure silk?'

At least he had saved his trump card for exactly this moment; he just prayed that he hadn't destroyed all her faith in him, because if he had she would never believe him... He drew a deep breath. 'Actually, I've never slept with Caroline. Never.'

'You've never slept with me either,' she put in pointedly.

It was not the reaction he had wanted—it sounded so unforgiving, and it started him thinking about things he hadn't planned to think about. Not yet...

Sexual tension crackled through the air as their gazes locked with erotic memories. 'Okay—let me phrase that a little differently. I've never had sex with Caroline,' he told her baldly. 'Ever.'

She stared at the wall unseeingly. 'I'm not sure that I believe you.'

'Yes, I thought you'd say that. But it's true, Holly. I haven't.'

Hope stirred with a flicker in her heart, but she kept every trace of it from her voice. 'Why not?'

He hesitated. He had never been disloyal to a woman in his life, and he certainly wasn't going to start being disloyal to Caroline now, but these past weeks he had been left wondering whether some minor brainstorm might have afflicted him this past year. 'Because she thought that not having sex until we'd made some kind of commitment would make me respect her more. That's how some women think.'

Oh, God—so what did that say about *her*?

'Holly, let me try to explain to you. Do you want me to?'

A small voice. 'Yes.'

He forced himself to concentrate on the past; it was the only way he could stop himself from taking her into his arms and just holding her until all the hurt had left her beautiful face. 'I once told you that my life has been chequered. That I've been rootless and wandering for a long time, and working on a game reserve allowed me to carry on living that life legitimately. A kind of paid-up nomad. Do you understand?'

She nodded. 'I think so.'

'Until earlier this year, when I looked around at what I had, and it just didn't seem enough any more—'

'You mean, money-wise?'

He shook his head. 'No, not money-wise. I'm talking fundamentals. I asked myself did I want to still be doing what I was doing when I was sixty, and the answer was a very loud no.'

'And then you inherited?'

'Then I inherited,' he echoed. 'And my relationship with Caroline changed.' He saw the way she pursed her lips. 'Oh, I know what you're thinking, and I agree—that Caroline would never have agreed to marry if I hadn't inherited. I knew that.'

'You *knew* that?' she asked, outraged. 'That she was a gold-digger?'

He smiled at the old-fashioned term. 'Life isn't as simple as that, Holly. Caroline wouldn't have been interested in marrying a ranch manager who slept out under the stars. She wanted stability and she *offered* stability, and for a while there I thought that's what I wanted, too. And my inheritance gave *me* the stability that I'd been lacking up until then.

'We talked of marriage—I *didn't* propose, and I bought her no ring—we talked of marriage in an abstract way. The way people used to talk about marriage—as an institutional framework in which to bring up children, and I certainly didn't want to miss out on having children. Neither did she.

'But there was no romantic love—that's one of the

reasons I convinced myself it might work. No great passion—but we got along together pretty well. Nothing was definite, but I had to come over to sort out my uncle's affairs, and we decided to use that space to think it over. To decide whether that was what we both really wanted.'

'And Caroline certainly decided that the answer was "yes", didn't she?' demanded Holly.

'Yes, she did. But I had done exactly the opposite. I had started to feel uneasy about the cold-bloodedness of such an arrangement. And I had seen you and it was like a thunderbolt that knocked me right off balance. I fought it because I thought it was simply romantic love, a love which would fade.' He sighed.

'And then you came to stay with me, and I realised that it wasn't going to fade. That this was it. Love. The real thing—and all-consuming. The only thing that mattered any more. I'd denied it and fought it all my life, but now it had finally happened—and how!'

She looked at him in confusion. 'But why? Why fight it?'

'Because I was pretty short on female role models when I was growing up, Holly,' he told her urgently, and it was as though he had lifted a veil from before her eyes. 'There were none at boarding-school, unless you counted the matron, and no one did. My mother was the only one I had, and she died before I had time to get to know the real woman she was, because as a child your perception is distorted by dependence.

'And after she died, I saw her through my father's eyes—as feckless and beautiful. Because he was besotted with her and yet he resented feeling that way. She made a fool of him over and over again, and yet he never stopped loving her. And I was determined that the same fate would never befall me.' He saw the slope of her shoulders relax, and began to let himself cling onto a grain of hope.

'You had the same kind of bewitching beauty as she did, and it terrified me. It terrified me enough to realise that I couldn't possibly marry Caroline, not when I felt that way about someone else. So I flew back to Africa, to tell her.'

So *that* was where he had gone! 'Only she wasn't there,' she realised wonderingly. 'Caroline had unexpectedly brought herself over here and was busy choosing a surprise wedding dress.'

'I came back to fireworks. When I found out you'd let Caroline believe we'd slept together, I was almost *exultant*—'

'*Exultant?*'

'Of course.' He shrugged. 'It meant that I could now cast you in the role of the bad fairy—allowing me to keep my prejudices alive. It meant that I could have you...' his mouth curved into a sexy line '...in the truest sense of the word—and afterwards I would be free of my obsession for you.'

'But it didn't work like that?'

He shook his head. 'No, it didn't—not with you, sweetheart. You had ensnared and captivated me, and then I made the most catastrophic discovery of all—that you were completely innocent. It blew my mind.'

'I thought you liked that,' she argued, as she remembered that almost *smug* look of pride which had darkened his features.

He gave a slow smile. 'Well, of course I *liked* it—'
'But?'
'It wasn't a question of not *liking* it, just that I felt so bad about my attitude towards you. I would have been more gentle if I'd known. More loving...much more loving.' He looked at her properly then, a question burning in the dazzling blue fire of his eyes. 'Why was I the first?' he asked her bluntly. 'Did someone put you off men, sweetheart? Are you hiding some kind of heartbreak?'

She shook her head. 'No heartbreak, no. In fact, there was nothing before you. Nothing at all, not in the way of feelings. I'd never been in love before, and sex without love just wasn't an option for me.' She sighed. 'You see, we're all victims of circumstance to some extent, Luke—and I had grown up seeing my mother use men. I saw relationships as a bartering mechanism—sex for money, if we're being honest.' And they *were* being honest, she realised, both of them, more honest than she'd ever been before. But how honest dared she be?

'Tell me,' he urged, and she heard vulnerability there, and realised in that moment that this big, strong, adventuring man needed her reassurance just as much as she needed his.

'I never felt for anyone the love I felt for you,' she said simply.

'Felt?'

She smiled. 'Feel. Present tense. And future tense.'

'Future perfect tense?' He grinned as he took hold of her hand and pulled her towards him. 'Please come here right now, because I think I'll die if I don't kiss you soon.'

'Oh, Luke,' she sighed dreamily, and went straight into his arms.

His features softened. 'Now look at me and listen, Holly Lovelace,' he said sternly. 'I love you—'

'Luke—'

'And I was wrong to think that I could make reality go away by pretending it didn't exist. I should have done things differently, but, oh, sweetheart—I guess that deep down I didn't want to run the risk of losing you.'

She nodded, remembering that she had been his for the taking at Apson House. But he hadn't taken. 'And Caroline?' she asked slowly.

'Is justifiably furious, but not heartbroken—'

'She must be! *I* would be!'

'She wasn't in love with me, Holly,' he said gently. 'Not ever. It was a transaction of the head, not the heart—and I'm not just saying that to make you, or me, feel better. It's true.' He hesitated. 'Caroline craves security over everything else, it's the one thing she hasn't got—'

'She hasn't got you any more.'

'But I was never hers to have, not really.' He looked into her eyes and she read so many things in his. Love. Regret. Hope. Trust.

'Would you mind if I bought her a house?' he asked softly.

'Of course I don't mind.' Holly traced the outline of his lips with her finger. 'Do you think she'll accept it?'

'I'll ask her—she can only say no.'

Holly couldn't imagine anyone saying no to Luke, but then he started kissing her, and it wasn't until some time later that she got a chance to ask, 'So how did you find my mother's dress?'

'It wasn't easy,' he admitted. 'But I was determined to do it.' His eyes had never looked bluer as they read the question in hers. 'As some kind of peace-offering, I guess, because I felt so bad about everything. After you kicked me out, I went back to the house to change, and I started thinking about Ursula—'

Holly blinked. He certainly was a man of surprises. 'Why?'

'I wondered if maybe she knew more about your mother's dress than she realised.' He swept a hand back through the thick, gold-tipped hair. 'I knew she was staying at The Bell that night, so I went to see her and found out which local newspaper *her* mother had advertised the dress in. Luckily it still existed. So then I travelled down to London to see the editor.'

'What on earth for?'

'Well, I thought it would make a good Christmas story. To find out if the person who had bought it still read that newspaper. The editor agreed to run a piece on it, to see what it would turn up.'

'And what happened?' asked Holly, fascinated now.

'The woman who bought it contacted me and told me the whole story. She had been let down. She bought the dress for a wedding which never took place—because the man she was in love with was married to someone else. He'd spun her the oldest story in the book and abandoned her when she was just a couple of weeks pregnant.'

'Oh, *no*,' said Holly, and bit down painfully on her lip.

'She grew to hate the dress, but she could never bear to get rid of it because it was so beautiful. Later, she thought about selling it once or twice, but no one offered her anywhere near its true worth.'

'So what did you do?' breathed Holly.

'I met with her and offered to buy the dress from her—'

'For a lot of money?'

'For what it would be worth today.'

Holly gave a low whistle. 'That's a hell of a lot of money.'

His eyes were very blue. 'Small compensation for the hurt she had suffered.'

'And she agreed?'

'She was delighted—her only proviso was that there should be no publicity, and I could understand that. So, I'm giving you back the dress, Holly.'

'And the catch?'

'No catch.' He shook his head. 'It's yours—to do what you want with.'

She looked down into her hands for a moment, and when she lifted her head again her green eyes were very bright. 'I think I'd quite like to wear it,' she told him softly. 'In church.'

Luke smiled. 'That's what I was hoping you'd say.'

Michelle McCormack was feeling flustered as she repositioned a dark green leaf. 'Holly, will you please hurry *up*?' she scolded. 'Everyone is there. The vicar is there. Luke is there. Much more time and I'm sure that some of your arty friends are going to kidnap him—I overheard one girl say quite shamelessly that she'd love to sculpt him!'

'I'll bet she did,' agreed Holly calmly. 'And she probably has no intention of using marble!'

'Holly!' Michelle's voice softened. 'You look wonderful. Just wonderful.'

'Do I?' Holly stared at herself in the mirror. It seemed strange to be preparing for *her* wedding, in *her* shop. She was the first bride to wear her mother's dress and it looked perfect. 'It doesn't look dated at all, does it?'

'Not at all—and you're the most beautiful bride I've ever seen,' said Michelle honestly.

'You look pretty nifty in that outrageous hat yourself!'

Holding Holly's bouquet, Michelle came up behind her to look in the mirror, and the two of them silently observed the stunning impact of the thick, ivory satin and the delicate pleating at the waist. In Holly's hair was a coronet of copper roses and dark, glossy green leaves which echoed her bouquet.

Luke had chosen the flowers, much to Michelle's amusement and envy. 'I've never met a man who chose his bride's flowers before,' she sighed. 'But he insisted. The roses were to match your hair, he said; the leaves your eyes.'

'Shame they don't do any green flowers,' smiled Holly serenely.

Michelle briefly switched from soft romantic mode to frustrated florist. 'Well, as it's an Easter wedding, I was *hoping* for something like lilies, or pansies—'

Holly's voice softened to a smoky whisper. 'But that's traditional, and Luke's not traditional, Michelle—*you* know that.'

'Luke's just gorgeous—beginning and end of story—and you're a very lucky woman.' Michelle shot her friend a glance. 'You are *okay*, aren't you, Holly?'

'Mmm?'

'I mean—you seem awfully *distracted*—you have done all week! You're not having any second thoughts, are you?'

Holly giggled as she shook her head, the copper curls contained today beneath the fragrant circlet of roses. 'Not a single one,' she said firmly. 'Why?'

Michelle frowned. 'You just seem *different*, that's all. There's a kind of *bloom* about you, and—' her brown eyes narrowed assessingly '—that dress looks a little small around the waistband—'

Holly burst out laughing. 'Why don't you just come right out and ask me?' she teased. 'It isn't a secret you know, not really.'

'You're *pregnant*?' breathed Michelle.

'Yes, I am.'

Michelle's eyes were like saucers. 'But what about your *shop*? What's going to happen to it?'

Holly shrugged her shoulders, a dreamy smile curving her lips. 'Oh, the shop no longer seems like my be-all and end-all. It was the freedom to design and make my own wedding dresses that I craved—and, fortunately, that fits in very nicely with motherhood. Luke says...' she sighed with pleasure '...that I can have someone in to run the shop if I want. Maybe even start a co-operative to help young, talented designers who don't have the good fortune to win competitions. Several of the girls I was at college with have already expressed a *huge* interest about coming to live here!'

'Surprising, that,' offered Michelle drily. 'Maybe they think they'll end up marrying millionaires, too!'

'Luke isn't a millionaire, not really,' said Holly firmly. 'Lots of his inheritance is in assets—'

'I know. It's a hard life!' teased Michelle. 'But you are a *lucky*, *lucky* woman, Holly Lovelace!'

'I'd have married him if he'd still been that man sleeping out under the stars,' said Holly truthfully.

'I know you would, dummy.' Michelle's voice was soft. 'I meant lucky that you're carrying his child.'

Holly turned, as pleased and surprised by the intimacy of the old-fashioned term as by her friend's response to her news. 'That's not the reaction you expect if the bride waddles down the aisle.'

Michelle looked at Holly's tall, slim figure and shook her head. '*Waddle?* Do me a favour, Holly—at twenty-eight weeks you'll probably have the same kind of figure that most of us have, and we're *not* pregnant!'

'Why lucky, then?' asked Holly curiously.

'Oh, because you've found Luke, and he's found you, and quite honestly it's restored my faith in men to see him look at you the way he does when he thinks no one is watching.' She sniffed, then glared. 'There I go again! Much more emotion and I'll start blubbing—and I can't afford to let my mascara run. Have you *seen* Luke's best man?'

'Well, of course I've seen him! His name's Will, and he's very nice.'

'I know,' sighed Michelle. 'He just wasn't what I expected. Terribly English, isn't he—in a way that Luke isn't?'

'They were at school together,' explained Holly. ''I'll introduce you afterwards, if you like.'

'Mmm! Yes, *please*!' Michelle made a final adjustment to her outrageous hat. 'Oh, and my friend Mary said to wish you all the best, and to be sure and tell you that she's over the moon at winning the wedding dress.'

'Good. Should be perfect for a summer wedding.' Holly smiled with satisfaction. 'So everybody's happy.' She held out her hand for her bouquet. A moment's quiet reflection, and she felt ready.

'Come on, Michelle,' she said softly. 'Let's go.'

The organist was coping admirably with some African music which Luke had had sent over. It was livelier than the usual offering at an English country wedding, and already the congregation were getting into the swing of things. A couple of people had even been noticed swaying their shoulders!

Holly's mother had left husband number four sipping champagne cocktails back at the hotel. Men never really appreciated a wedding in the way that a woman did! He would only cramp her style, and she intended to bask in the reflected glory of the wedding dress that *she* had designed all those years ago. She sighed. If only she had known then what she knew now...

She sat next to Ursula O'Neil, who had been surprised and delighted to be invited to the wedding. But, as Holly had explained, if it hadn't been for Ursula, then she would never have got the dress back. Ursula's sister Amber had also been invited, but had declined. She had called her own wedding off at the last minute, and said she couldn't face seeing the inside of a church for the time being.

Caroline had been invited but, as expected, had declined. She had sent them six very ugly place-mats and explained that she would be far too busy furnishing her brand-new house to attend.

At the altar Luke sat next to Will, just enjoying the music and the sight of sunlight streaming cobalt, scarlet, jade and saffron through the stained glass windows. He felt...well, he felt just great. He would even go so far as to say that he was the happiest man on earth. He didn't know what the future held; no one did. Whether their baby would be born here, or in Africa. But Holly was flexible and so was he. Nothing seemed to matter any more, now that they had found one another.

The lively music stilled, and then began to play the traditional notes of the 'Wedding March', and Luke, together with the rest of the congregation, slowly rose to his feet.

He didn't know whether he was supposed to or not, but Holly was in the same building and therefore he just couldn't resist turning round to look at her.

She took the slow, careful steps of every bride—the pure, clear light from the windows turning the buttery satin of her dress into a soft kaleidoscope of colour. The understated beauty of the copper roses only emphasised her exquisite colouring. God, how he loved her.

Holly saw him watching her and smiled back, a look of pure happiness.

Luke's heart thundered as their gazes held for a private, infinitesimal moment, and he knew that everything was going to be just perfect.

He had come home at last.

Kate Walker was born in Nottinghamshire but as she grew up in Yorkshire she has always felt that her roots were there. She met her husband at university and she originally worked as a children's librarian but after the birth of her son she returned to her old childhood love of writing. When she's not working, she divides her time between her family, their three cats, and her interests of embroidery, antiques, film and theatre, and, of course, reading.

Don't miss the next intense and engaging story by Kate Walker:
BOUND BY BLACKMAIL
On sale May 2005, in Modern Romance™!

NO HOLDING BACK
by
Kate Walker

CHAPTER ONE

SAFFRON pushed open the office door and sighed with relief when she saw that the room beyond was empty. Having come this far, she didn't want to be put off by the sight of Owen's elegant secretary, and she didn't know what explanation she could have given that would have persuaded Stella not to buzz through to her employer to let him know that she was there. Everything would be spoiled if he had any warning of her presence.

And she didn't want to risk the possibility that she might lose the impetus that had driven her so far, the wonderful, liberating rush of anger that had pushed away any thought of doubt or hesitation. She had nurtured that feeling ever since last night, since the moment it had become obvious that Owen was not going to turn up. Then, her mood had been so bad that simply recalling it now brought a red haze of fury up before her eyes, pushing her into action as, without bothering to knock, she flung open the door and marched into the office beyond.

'You'll know why I'm here!'

The man seated at the desk had his dark head bent, his attention directed at some notes that he was making on a pad in front of him, but Saffron barely spared him a glance. She wouldn't have been able to see him too clearly anyway, that mist of anger blurring her vision so that he was just a dark, indecipherable shape. Her fingers shaking with the intensity of her feelings, she tugged at the buttons on her coat, vaguely aware of the fact that, surprised by her appearance, he had glanced up sharply.

'You promised me a special night out—'

Her voice wasn't pitched the way she had wanted it to be, pent up emotions making it too high and tight.

'"A special night for a special girl", you said! I waited for you for over three hours—'

That was better. Now she sounded more confident, stronger altogether, the sort of woman people would take notice of.

'But you couldn't even be bothered to phone—to explain. Well, that's your hard luck!'

She certainly had his attention now. His stillness, the way he sat upright, his hand still gripping the pen, told her that. But she couldn't look him straight in the face or she would lose her nerve. The last button on her coat came undone and she drew a deep, gasping breath.

'I just thought I'd let you know that *this* is what you turned down—'

As she spoke, she flung open the trenchcoat, revealing the skimpy scarlet silk basque, laced up the front in black, the matching provocatively small panties and the delicate, lacy web of a suspender belt that supported the sheerest of stockings on her long, slender legs which tapered down to bright scarlet leather sandals, their spiky heels giving her five feet eight a further impressive three inches.

In the stunned silence that followed her dramatic gesture, Saffron finally found that her eyes would focus at last, and she turned a half defiant, half teasing look on the man at the desk. Only to recoil in shocked horror as her eyes met the contemptuous, coolly assessing stare of a pair of light grey eyes—eyes that in their silvery paleness bore no resemblance to the bright blue gaze she had expected to see.

This wasn't Owen! She had never even seen this man before in her life!

Frozen into panic-stricken immobility, Saffron could only watch, transfixed, her own brown eyes wide and shocked, as that narrow-eyed gaze slid slowly, deliberately downwards from her hotly burning cheeks. They lingered appreciatively on the amount of creamy flesh, the soft curves of her breasts exposed and enhanced by the ridiculous slivers of material, and on her dark hair, falling in wanton disarray around the pale skin of her shoulders.

'Very nice,' he said at last, his voice a smooth drawl, making Saffron think wildly of rich, dark honey oozing slowly over gravel. 'Very nice, indeed. But, believe me, if I *had* been offered something so very tempting, then in no circumstances would I have been fool enough to turn it down.'

The mocking humour that threaded through that low, attractive voice was blended together with a warmly sensual note of appreciation, breaking into the trance-like state that had held Saffron frozen.

'Why, you—!' Words failed her, shock and disbelief forming a knot in her throat that threatened to choke her.

'Oh, come on, honey—' His smile was as slow and provocative as his voice. 'If you don't want the customers to be interested then you shouldn't display the goods quite so attractively.'

'Display— customers!' Saffron exploded as the insulting implications of that taunt sank in. 'I don't want you—'

'No?' The amusement in the single syllable stung more than any harsher comment might have.

'No! You're—you're not who I meant—you're the wrong man entirely!'

'Is that so? Well, I hate to disagree with you, but from where I'm sitting I'm the *right* man—and you—'

Those silvery eyes moved over her again, seeming to

burn where they rested, so that Saffron's pale skin glowed in fiery embarrassment.

'You're exactly what I've been looking for—so if you'll just tell me your terms, I'm sure we'll be able to come to some arrangement.'

'Terms!' Saffron spluttered, unable to believe that this was happening to her. 'We will do no such thing! We—'

She broke off on a terrified gasp as the man dropped his pen on to the desk and straightened, as if about to get to his feet. The tiny movement shattered what little remained of her self-control, and whirling in panic she headed for the door, running as fast as she could towards the lift.

'Wait! Please—'

The lift doors were just closing as Saffron reached them, but luckily her strangled squawk of near-panic caught the ears of the solitary female occupant, who reacted swiftly, obligingly pressing a firm finger on the 'Door Hold' button, halting them in their tracks. A couple of seconds later, with a metallic rattle, they jerked apart once more, allowing her to step inside.

'Thanks!'

It came out on a choked gasp as, not daring to look behind her, she hurried into the compartment, huddling into the far corner and giving a deep sigh of relief as the doors slid closed again and the lift started to move smoothly downwards. If that man had followed her, then surely she'd got away from him now.

'In a hurry?' The other woman, someone she vaguely remembered from Richards' last Christmas party, enquired smilingly.

'You could say that!' Saffron's response was wry, her voice still shaking in a way that she prayed her companion would believe to be the result of her dash along the corridor and so not ask any awkward questions.

'And those heels aren't made to run in—'

'They most definitely are not!' she returned feelingly.

How she wished she could kick them off—her feet were killing her! But she was sure that if she did she would never get the damn things back on again. She had borrowed them from her friend and workmate Kate and, as well as being much higher than anything she normally wore, they were a very tight fit indeed—Kate being built on a much smaller scale than her tall, fine-boned friend.

Saffron pushed a disturbed hand through the tumbled mane of her shining dark brown hair, holding her coat closely fastened with the other, her lips twisting slightly as she recalled the way Kate had described the offending footwear, the words repeating inside her head with a worrying significance.

'They're real tart's shoes,' her friend had said, laughter lifting her voice. But now, remembering, Saffron felt no trace of her earlier amusement. If that was how that man might describe what she was wearing on her feet—then what words would he use to describe *her*?

'Are you all right?' Her companion had noticed her involuntary shudder, and was studying her more closely.

'As a matter of fact, I think I'm going down with flu,' Saffron improvised hastily. 'That's why I'm going home.'

She prayed that the explanation would cover any other betraying reactions she might be showing. She knew that her cheeks were brightly flushed, and that probably her brown eyes were overbright and glittering with reaction to the shock she had just had. The way she was clutching her coat to her must also look peculiar, to say the least, particularly in this well-heated building. That thought had her instinctively tightening her grip on the black trenchcoat. She had reacted automatically, not thinking straight enough to check that all the buttons were fastened, the belt securely tied. If it should gape open, this woman would get the shock of her life.

'Bed's probably the best place for you, then.'

Somehow Saffron managed a vague murmur that might have been agreement, her mind too busy with other, more troublesome matters. Thinking straight! She hadn't been thinking at all, just reacting. All that had been in her head had been the need to get out of there fast, to hide her embarrassment, get away from those coolly mocking eyes, that hateful voice.

It was all Owen's fault, she told herself furiously. If he hadn't stood her up last night, then none of this would have happened. The bad temper that his neglect had sparked off in her had burned all through the night, not at all improved by a restless, unsatisfactory attempt at sleep. The fact that as the morning progressed it had become obvious that Owen wasn't even going to bother to ring up and explain had been positively the last straw, finally causing the simmering volcano of fury inside her to boil up and spill over like red-hot lava.

'I'm not going to put up with this, Kate!' she had declared at last, slamming the phone down on yet another caller whom she had hoped might just be Owen, offering a very belated excuse for his non-appearance, but in fact had turned out to be an assistant at the laundry with a thoroughly mundane enquiry about the number of napkins and tablecloths they had sent in their usual Monday morning bundle of linen. 'He's just taking me for granted, and I won't stand for it.'

'Perhaps he was ill,' Kate had suggested, her tone soothing.

But Saffron had refused to allow herself to be placated.

'How ill do you have to be before you're incapable of using a phone?'

'My, you *have* got your knickers in a twist, haven't you?' Kate teased, studying her friend's indignant face with a touch of amused curiosity. 'This isn't just about being stood up, is it? There's more to it than that. I know you—and I haven't seen you this worked up in a long time.'

'I don't like being taken for granted,' Saffron muttered, not meeting Kate's eyes. She wished the other girl didn't know her quite so well—well enough to put her finger on an uncomfortable spot in her feelings.

'And—?' Kate prompted laughingly, but then the flush of embarrassment that had shaded Saffron's cheeks was replaced by a stronger, hotter colour, that could only be the result of deep embarrassment. 'Saffy!' she exclaimed in frank disbelief. 'You didn't!'

'Didn't what?'

'Don't stall me! You know perfectly well what I mean. You've been fretting over things for weeks, trying to make your mind up. So, confess—had you finally decided that last night was to have been *the* night?'

'I don't want to just drift any more, Kate. I'm ready for some sort of commitment. I want a future—I have been seeing him for over six months.'

'But I never thought you saw him in the light of a grand passion. Poor Owen.' Kate laughed. 'All these months he's been begging you to go to bed with him and getting nowhere, and when you finally decide to let him have his wicked way he doesn't even turn up. No wonder you're hopping mad.'

'You should have seen me last night,' Saffron put in, a touch of rueful amusement mingling with the quiver of anger in her words. 'There I was, all done up like a dog's dinner—little black dress, perfume, stockings and suspenders—the works. I even bought new underwear.' The shake in her voice grew more pronounced.

'Oh, Saffy—'

'It was pure silk!'

Her anger was growing again, fighting against the tenuous grip she had on it. She had felt such a fool, sitting there, dressed up, made-up—keyed up—waiting for a man who didn't come.

Kate's whistle was long and low. 'The sacrificial lamb! It's a pity Owen doesn't know just what he missed! You'll have to find some way of getting that home to him.'

That was when the idea came to her, Saffron reflected as the lift by-passed the second floor. Her anger wouldn't be appeased unless she did something about the way Owen had treated her, and Kate's remark had given her the perfect way to show him how she felt.

'Well, here we are.'

The voice of her companion broke into her thoughts, bringing her back to the present with an abruptness that, combined with the jerky movement of the lift as it came to a halt, almost knocked her off-balance, so that she fell back against the wall.

'Are you OK?'

'Fine—'

It was impossible to concentrate on what she was saying, all her attention directed towards the lift doors as they started to open. Was that man still upstairs in the office, or had he followed her? And if so, having missed the lift, had he come down the staircase after her?

She could just imagine those long legs—for such an impressive torso had to be matched by an equally powerful lower half—taking the stairs two or more at a time, matching or possibly even outstripping the speed of the lift in which she had travelled. So, was he, even now, prowling around the hall, waiting for her? The thought sent a shiver of apprehension sliding down her spine.

A hasty, cautious inspection of the reception area reassured her on that point—temporarily, at least. He wasn't anywhere in sight, but that didn't mean that he wasn't on his way down. He might appear at any moment, so she had better not take any risks. The sooner she was out of here the better.

'How will you get home?'

'I've got my car—'

Saffron was hurrying across the well-worn floor as she spoke, pulling open the door in a rush. A cold wind, touched with a hint of rain, sneaked around her as she stepped outside, making her shiver uncomfortably, painfully aware of how little she had on under the protective layer of the coat. That thought brought a rush of burning colour to her cheeks, something that clearly worried the other woman.

'Are you sure you're fit to drive? Perhaps I should ring upstairs for someone—'

'No!' If he thought she was still in the building, heaven alone knew how he might react. She couldn't face him again; couldn't look him in the eye. 'I'll be all right— honest—it's not very far—'

'Well, if you're positive…'

She still sounded unconvinced, and Saffron had to fight hard not to scream at her in panic as, through the large plate glass doors, she saw the other lift open and a tall, masculine figure appear in the hall, looking round him a way that made her think unnervingly of a hunting tiger. She could almost imagine him scenting the air, breathing in the trace of her perfume…

'I have to go—'

Reacting purely instinctively, she kicked off the crippling shoes—she would buy Kate another pair—and turned to run towards the spot where her car was parked. The wind seemed to have found every opening in her coat, sliding in at the neck, whipping around her hem, revealing far more than was comfortable to her already precarious peace of mind, but she was oblivious to the cold and discomfort of her bare feet on the tarmac, reaching her small Fiat with a sigh of relief.

It was as she slid into the driving-seat and pushed her wild, wind-blown dark hair back from her face that she saw the other car, the one that, blinded by her anger, she hadn't noticed on her arrival at the factory. Sleek and powerful, and gleamingly expensive, its paintwork was a shining light grey, almost silver, reminding her disturbingly of the eyes of the man in the managing director's office—eyes that had looked at her with such contempt at first. But then that expression had swiftly changed to something much more worrying.

The car was in the MD's private space too, she now realised, struggling with the shake in her hand that made it difficult to insert her key in the ignition. It was parked in the spot that had previously been reserved solely for the use of Owen's late father—a space which must now, by rights, belong to Owen himself. Which, logic told her, bringing with it a wave of nausea, meant that there was only one person it could belong to—and that made matters all the worse.

Perhaps if she had been more aware of her surroundings on her arrival, if she'd been thinking straighter, she would have noticed it then, and its elegantly alien presence might have made her pause to reconsider her plan of action. But the truth was that she had been blind to everything but that plan. In fact, she had actively encouraged her anger on the journey here, feeding the flames, so that she hadn't even noticed that Owen's car wasn't even in the car park at all.

She hadn't even paused to look around her, Saffron reflected, sighing with relief as the slightly untrustworthy engine caught, and she let the brake out with nervous haste, not even glancing behind to see if her pursuer had come out of the building. She only wanted to get out of here without any further confrontation with the owner of that sleek, powerful vehicle, she told herself. Her stomach twisted into tight, painful knots of apprehension as every sense became tensely alert, ears straining for the shout she expected as she headed for the exit; unwillingly she contrasted her speedy departure, like a dog with its tail between its legs, with her confident, even cocky arrival such a short time earlier.

Then, fired up with determination and anger, she had barely allowed herself time to park the car before she was out of it and striding towards the main entrance, her brisk, forceful movements mirroring the state of her thoughts.

'Hey!'

The shout cut into her thoughts, sounding clearly even above the noise of the engine, and the car swerved dangerously as her hands clenched on the wheel. A swift, nervous glance in the rearview mirror confirmed her instinctive fear, her stomach twisting painfully as she saw the way that letting her mind wander had slowed her responses, stilling her foot on the accelerator. Alerted by the sound of the engine, her pursuer had come out of the building and was heading purposefully across the car park towards her.

'Wait! I want to—'

The rest of his words were drowned in the roar of the car as, heedless of safety or concern for her elderly vehicle, she rammed her right foot down to the floor. She knew very well what he wanted—he had made that only too plain—and she had no intention of waiting around to endure any more of his blatantly lecherous remarks.

It was just as she swung out of the car park and on to the main road that she glanced back one last time and saw the way he had halted, bending to pick up something from the ground.

Kate's shoes, she reflected ruefully, wondering if, as in the Cinderella story, he thought he might use them as evidence to track her down. The problem was, though, that *he* was no sort of Prince Charming—quite the opposite—and if he did turn out to be who she suspected then she would need more than just a fairy godmother to get her out of a *very* sticky situation.

CHAPTER TWO

'FOR God's sake, Saffron—how many times do I have to apologise?'

Owen pushed impatient hands through his hair—hair that was not quite as dark as that of the man in the MD's office, Saffron noted inconsequentially. His had been black as a raven's wing where Owen's was just a deep brown. That should have warned her, but she'd been too angry to think straight, and after all she had been expecting Owen to be there—hadn't anticipated the possibility of anyone else being in the office.

'Saffy, are you listening? I said I'm sorry.'

He didn't *sound* penitent, Saffron reflected privately. If anything, he was quite the opposite—almost aggressive, in fact.

'We had a date, Owen. I bought a new dress—'

The words dried in her throat as the thought of just what else she'd bought slid into her mind, bringing with it an all too vivid picture of the scarlet wisps of silk that she had pushed firmly to the bottom of the washing-basket. She doubted that she could ever wear them again when just the thought of putting them on awoke uncomfortable memories of the scene in the office, the sensual amusement in that appalling man's voice. In fact, she didn't know what had possessed her to buy them in the first place. They were a million miles away from the sort of thing she normally chose.

'I waited for hours.'

'I *know*.' Owen sounded positively snappish now. 'But

I promised you dinner at Le Figaro and—' an airy wave of his hand indicated their elegant surroundings '—I'm keeping my promise.'

'Twenty-four hours late!'

Saffron couldn't bite back the retort. Owen was the one who had stood her up, and yet he was behaving as if *she* was the offender. If he'd kept the date as arranged, she would never have gone to his office in a temper and made such a spectacle of herself.

'Saff, you know how important this takeover is to me! I couldn't keep our date yesterday because the big man turned up without warning.'

'The big man?'

Saffron fought hard to keep her voice under control, but the rising tide of colour in her cheeks was a different matter. Try as she might, she couldn't avoid the logical connection that her mind was making between Owen's words and the hateful character she had encountered in the MD's office. She had suspected this, had known that there wasn't really a hope that she could be wrong, but to hear it confirmed by Owen was almost more than she could cope with right now.

'Niall Forrester himself. Oh, come on, Saff! Where have you been for the past month? Niall Forrester owns Forrester Leisure, and Forrester Leisure—'

'Is considering buying Richards' Rockets—I know *that*.'

She knew only too well that Owen, whose interests lay in a very different direction, had been delighted when the huge international corporation had shown an interest in the small, rather rundown family business that he had inherited from his father six months before.

'After all, you've talked about nothing else all month.'

She found it impossible to erase the tartness from her

voice, but, well-launched on his major preoccupation, Owen seemed oblivious to the sharpness of her tone.

'So, you'll understand that when Niall Forrester himself rang to say he was coming up to Kirkham to look at the factory I just had to be there to meet him—and take him out to dinner in the evening. He kept me busy, I can tell you. He wanted to know everything there was to know—I didn't have time to think—'

Or to ring and explain, Saffron reflected with a touch of asperity. But at the forefront of her mind was a more pressing worry.

'And this Niall Forrester—the "big man"—'

The description fitted. Even sitting down, he had looked decidedly impressive, and the width of the straight, powerful shoulders under the immaculately fitted navy suit had been evidence of a formidable physique that, if she had had her wits about her, she should have known could not possibly have belonged to Owen.

'Where is he now?'

'Back in London, I expect. He said he'd seen all he wanted to see at the factory.'

Hastily Saffron tried to convert the choking sensation that had assailed her into an innocuous cough. Niall Forrester had seen everything he wanted and more! But at least it seemed that she could relax about one thing. Obviously, whatever his feelings about her appearance in the MD's office, Forrester had said nothing about it to Owen. Of course, he wouldn't know her name, but he could have asked the receptionist. If he'd described her, Beth would have known who he meant. The colour flooding her cheeks deepened hotly at the thought of just how he might have described her.

'You're not exactly chatty, Saff!' Owen sounded decidedly peeved. 'Is this because you haven't forgiven me for last night? You're not going to sulk all evening, are you?'

'I'm not sulking!'

Saffron was indignant. Clearly Owen thought that he had apologised, but to her mind it seemed that what he'd really done was bring home to her the way that she came in second place in his life, after his business interests. From being angry about the way he had stood her up, she was now forced to wonder whether in fact his non-appearance last night had been a lucky escape in some ways. After the decision about their relationship that she had come to, only so recently, it was disturbing, to say the least, to find that her attitude towards him had shifted ground.

In fact, ever since Owen had appeared at her flat, she had been seeing him in a very different light. It was more than just annoyance at the way he had stood her up, though obviously that had a lot to do with it. Suddenly almost everything he said seemed to irritate her.

'I've—just got something on my mind. I'd planned on working on the accounts this evening. Things are really getting a bit tight, and—'

'Oh, they'll keep until tomorrow. After all, a tiny business like yours can't have many real problems—nothing compared to the white elephant of a factory my father left me lumbered with. I mean—who wants to buy fireworks nowadays?'

Once more he was launched on his own concerns. Listening to him, Saffron had to bite down hard on her lower lip in order to keep back an angry response. Owen had always had a tendency to be like this, but somehow tonight it seemed much more infuriating than usual. Was she just feeling unsettled after the disturbing meeting at the factory that morning, or did it go deeper than that?

At that moment her thought processes stopped dead, because in the second that she had looked away, needing to distract herself from Owen's soliloquy and the urge to tell him to shut up, her attention had been drawn to a flurry of activity at the entrance to the restaurant and then, unbelievingly, inexorably, to the tall figure of the man who had just come in.

She recognised him immediately. There was no mistaking that jet-black gleaming hair, the straight, firm shoulders, the arrogant, upright carriage that had impressed her even when he was sitting down. Seen on his feet like this, that dark, sleek head towering inches above the head waiter—who, recognising intuitively the innate self-assurance and air of power that only a great deal of money could buy, was buzzing around him like a bee around an open honey-pot—he was even more imposing, a forceful, vital figure of a man who would always be noticed the moment he walked into a room. Even through the haze of shock that clouded her brain she was well aware of the fact that hers weren't the only pair of female eyes that had noted his arrival—noted it and lingered in frank appreciation.

'Forrester!'

Dimly, with a sense of terrible inevitability, she heard Owen's exclamation confirm her earlier fears, depriving her of any possible weakly lingering hope that she might have been mistaken about the identity of the man in the managing director's office.

'But I thought he'd gone back to London.' Her voice was an uncomfortable croak as she struggled to believe that this was actually happening, that he could be here—now. If he saw them—saw her—

'So did I. Something must have kept him. Hey, Forrester! Niall!'

To Saffron's horror, Owen was out of his seat, waving a hand to attract the other man's attention.

'I'll ask him to join us—you should meet him. Forrester—over here!'

'Owen!' Saffron whispered through clenched teeth, but it was too late. Owen's actions had drawn Niall Forrester's gaze, those unforgettable light grey eyes narrowing slightly as they focused on his face from across the room.

He was not at all pleased at being accosted in this way, Saffron realised, seeing with a twist of apprehension the way that his dark brows drew together sharply, indicating an annoyed response that had her shrinking down in her chair, fearful of that cold-eyed scrutiny being turned on her too. Perhaps he would ignore Owen, take a table at the far side of the room.

'Over here!' Owen tried again, beckoning ostentatiously, in the same moment that Saffron realised just how ridiculous she was being, hiding away like this, as if she was some small, hunted animal.

With an angry reproof to herself, she straightened up again, and then immediately wished she hadn't as the slight movement caught Niall Forrester's attention, and with a sinking heart she saw his expression change swiftly. Even from this distance she could see the fierce, almost predatory gleam of triumph that lit up those pale eyes, turning them to silver and making all the nerves in the pit of her stomach twist into tight, painful knots of panic. It was all that she could do to remain in her seat, only suppressing the urge to push back her chair and run with a supreme effort.

But he was coming towards them now, his stride as determined and purposeful as his expression, and with a bitter sense of despair she knew that there was no way she could avoid the confrontation that was approaching as swiftly and inexorably as the darkness that was gathering outside. If she *did* run, she had no doubt that he would come after her, would catch up with her without any difficulty. And that that would result in a scene even worse than the one she now anticipated with such dread, she acknowledged miserably, wiping suddenly damp palms nervously on her napkin, convinced that the diners at the next table must hear how heavily her heart was pounding.

'Richards. Good evening—'

The sound of that smooth, attractive voice was like a blow to Saffron's head, the single phrase reverberating over and over in her disturbed thoughts. She had only heard perhaps ninety-five or a hundred words in those deep, slightly husky tones, and yet she felt as if every note of it, every shaded inflexion was etched into her brain in red-hot strokes.

'Would you like to join us?' Owen was totally oblivious to Saffron's discomfiture. 'It's no fun dining alone.'

'Thank you—I'd appreciate that.'

The smoothness of Niall Forrester's tone made Saffron blink hard in shock. Had she been seeing things a moment earlier? Or had her own nervousness made her misinterpret his expression? Certainly, there was no sign of the cold-eyed look she had seen on his face; now he was all affable approachability, oozing social ease from every pore.

'I'd anticipated a solitary meal, so some company would be welcome.'

The words were directed at Owen, but Saffron had caught the swift flicker of a glance in her direction, a look that left her in no doubt that he was only too well aware of her presence.

He *was* even more impressive standing up. She had

tried to convince herself that the image she had created of him in her mind had been exaggerated, blown up out of all proportion by her own feelings about their meeting, but now she had to admit that, if anything, she had erred on the side of moderation. He had changed his clothes, but the dark suit he now wore was every bit as sleek and expensive as the first one, its superbly tailored lines clinging to a lean but strongly muscled frame, and under the fine material his waist and hips had the slimness of an athlete, showing that he kept himself very fit. Standing beside Owen like this, he made the other man, who was a good six feet in his socks, look slight and underweight. And those eyes! Saffron kept her own gaze firmly fixed on her plate for fear of meeting the silver intensity of Niall Forrester's scrutiny.

'Won't you introduce me to your charming companion?'

Hastily Saffron tried to impose some control over her expression as Owen, belatedly recalling her presence at the table, turned in her direction.

'Of course—this is Saffron Ruane. Saffy, this is Niall Forrester. I told you about his interest in Dad's factory.'

'I remember.'

She managed a small, tight smile, feeling as if her face might actually crack if she tried any more, and, because courtesy demanded it, she held out her hand in greeting. It was taken in a warm, firm grasp that folded around her fingers, enclosing them in a way that in any other person would have inspired confidence and trust. To her consternation, this time it had exactly the opposite effect. She felt as if a live electric wire had coiled around her fingers, sending burning shockwaves pulsing across her palm and along every nerve in her arm so that it was all she could do not to snatch her hand away again with a cry of distress.

And in the moment that his broad, strong hand closed over hers she found herself looking into those clear, steel-grey eyes, her gaze held transfixed, held with such magnetic force that for a second or two she felt physically dizzy and actually swayed slightly in her seat, knowing that if she had been standing her legs would have given way beneath her and she would have fallen to the floor.

'Miss Ruane—' A slight inclination of his dark head acknowledged her, nothing about his expression or demeanour giving any indication that he recognised her. 'I hope you don't think that I'm intruding?'

The act of polite concern, nothing more, was near-perfect, almost too much so, and if she hadn't been so excruciatingly aware of the circumstances of their previous meeting, Saffron knew that she wouldn't have been able to fault it.

'Not at all—' What else could she say? 'Won't you sit down?'

Saffron took the opportunity to remove her hand from his with a rush of relief, turning the movement into a gesture towards the empty chair opposite in order to cover the rather abrupt way in which she snatched her fingers away, unable to bear his touch any longer.

Or was she worrying unnecessarily? she couldn't help but wonder, as Niall seated himself. After all, he had only seen her for a very few minutes in the office—and she very much doubted that, for the most of them, his attention had been concentrated on her *face*! The memory of just what *had* held his interest had her reaching for her glass and taking a hasty gulp of her wine, hoping that its cool sharpness would halt the rush of colour to her cheeks, and she was grateful for the appearance of the waiter at

Niall's side, providing a welcome distraction from her betraying response.

She might have known that Niall Forrester would attract such prompt and almost obsequious service, she reflected wryly, seeing the waiter's overly polite concern. He was the sort of man who emanated an aura of power and control—and he looked as if he would tip generously, she added with a touch of cynicism, recalling just how long she and Owen had had to wait before anyone came to take *their* order.

'I'll pass on the starter, then we'll all be at the same stage.' Clearly, Niall had noted their almost empty plates. 'And bring another bottle of wine.'

'Oh, but—'

Saffron had been about to protest that Owen was driving, and that she had no head for anything other than a couple of glasses, but even as she spoke Niall forestalled her, lifting their original bottle of wine from its ice-bucket and refilling their half-empty glasses.

'Thank you,' she was obliged to murmur, struggling against an impulse to lift her glass and fling its expensive contents in his face.

'Not at all,' he responded smoothly. 'In fact, I'd like you to consider yourselves my guests tonight—my thanks for a most interesting day at the factory.'

Was she being unduly sensitive? Saffron couldn't help wondering. Or *had* there been a worrying emphasis on that 'interesting', turning it into something that made her shift uncomfortably in her seat?

'It was my pleasure.'

Owen tried to match the other man's easy assurance but only managed to sound oily and insincere, and the way he had to lean forward as he spoke in order to make his presence felt made Saffron aware of the way that, while his remarks had *seemed* to have been aimed at them both, Niall had concentrated that silvery gaze on her face alone, making her feel like the selected victim, deliberately singled out by a ruthless predator.

'I must admit that I'm surprised to see you here tonight.' She forced the words out, determined not to let him see how much he worried her. 'I thought you'd be over halfway back to London by now.'

'That was my original intention, but I changed my mind and decided to stay overnight—do some sightseeing.'

'Sightseeing? In Kirkham?' Saffron didn't bother to hide her scepticism.

'Oh, you'd be surprised,' Niall returned, with a smile that made every nerve in her body tense uneasily. It wasn't humour that lit those pale eyes from within, but a hint of taunting triumph, that made her think worryingly of a hunting cat sitting patiently outside a mousehole, waiting for the unwary rodent to venture out. 'For a sleepy little Northern town, this place has some unexpected attractions...'

That silvery gaze slid deliberately to her face, and Saffron's breath caught in her throat as she saw that the mocking glint had brightened but not warmed those light eyes, so that they glittered with the brilliance of ice in the sun.

'Wouldn't you agree, Miss Ruane?'

As he spoke he looked straight into her eyes, that smile making a mockery of her earlier foolish hope that perhaps he hadn't recognised her. He was playing with her, well aware of her discomfort; he was enjoying watching her squirm.

'Oh, Saffy isn't a local girl,' Owen put in cheerfully. 'She only came to live in Kirkham a couple of years ago.'

'That's a pity.' The cool grey eyes never left Saffron's

troubled brown ones. 'I had rather hoped that you might be able to show me around.'

His tone was dangerously soft, worryingly gentle, making Saffron think uncomfortably of the cat she had compared him to earlier—the soft fur of its paws concealing the powerful, tearing claws.

'I was sure that you were the sort of girl who knows the best places to go for a special night out.'

A special night out. This time there was no mistaking the subtle deepening of his drawling tones on those words, forcing her to recall how she had used them herself only a few hours before. And the implication behind what he had said was painfully clear too, to anyone who had seen the insultingly knowing smile on his face when he had spoken of customers and terms. She could have little doubt as to what sort of nights out were in his disgusting mind.

'On the contrary,' she returned sharply. 'I'm very much a stay-at-home, Mr Forrester. Not at all a clubs-and-pubs sort of woman.'

'That wasn't exactly what I had in mind,' he disconcerted her by saying.

'Well, if it's night-life you want—' Owen put in, anxious, Saffron knew, to give a plug to the night-club he hoped to buy a half-share in.

'Not really.' Niall barely spared him a glance. 'Look, Richards, is that a friend of yours?' A nod of his dark head indicated a table on the other side of the room, where a man Saffron vaguely recognised was waving to gain Owen's attention. 'Hadn't you better see what he wants?'

He didn't even watch Owen leave, instead concentrating all his attention on Saffron, continuing the conversation as if the interruption had never happened.

'I can assure you that I wouldn't think of hiding you

away in some smoky, dimly lit club. A beauty such as yours should be seen in the full light of day.'

Saffron's soft mouth parted on a gasp of astonishment, both at the arrogance of his dismissal of Owen and at the outrageous compliment.

'Are you trying to flirt with me, Mr Forrester?'

His smile was a challenge, the intent gaze of those steely eyes seeming to draw her to him like some irresistible magnet, holding her transfixed, unable to look away.

'On the contrary—flirting is a frivolous occupation, meant only light-heartedly. I am deadly serious—'

That voice would charm the birds out of the trees, Saffron thought hazily. Low and huskily sensual, it was pitched so as to make her feel as if she was the only woman in the room—in the world—and his words were for her alone. And it was working!

In spite of her determination to resist, fired by the knowledge of the low opinion he really had of her, it seemed as if her surroundings, the buzz of conversation from the other diners, had all faded from her awareness, blending into a multi-coloured blur, so that all she was aware of was a pair of hypnotic grey eyes and a silkily seductive voice.

'You must know that you are an exceptionally lovely woman—such dark hair and eyes, and a face like a Madonna.'

'Oh, really!' With an effort Saffron struggled to break free of the hypnotic hold he had on her. 'Now you're exaggerating!'

She felt desperately out of her depth. It was as if she had been floating lazily on a sunlit sea and had suddenly realised that the shore was much further away than she had thought, with the current growing ominously rougher.

The concentration of his gaze, the intensity of that huskily seductive voice, were more suited to the intimacy of a bedroom than this public place. As her mind made the connection between the man before her and the thought of the sensual surroundings of a bedroom her thoughts reeled, the image working on them like some powerfully intoxicating cocktail.

'I never exaggerate.'

Niall Forrester dismissed her protest with the same casual indifference he might have used to flick away a fly that had come too near his face, and the gleam that lit deep in his eyes told her that he was well aware of her struggle to break away from the hold he seemed to have on her. That hold was as delicate as a spider's web and yet as powerful as if she were actually confined by steel cables. The rational part of her mind was screaming at her that all she had to do was look away, look at someone else, but she found it impossible to move.

'And in your case I have no need to. Though I have to admit...'

A tiny flicker of his eyes, downwards over the simple navy dress she wore, and a slight deepening of that smile, curling his mouth up at the corners, acted as a danger signal, warning Saffron that she wouldn't like what was to come.

'That that particular shade of blue you're wearing is not perhaps the most flattering to someone of your dramatic colouring. I would have thought that something warmer—perhaps red...'

He caught the flare of apprehension in her eyes and the smile grew, becoming tauntingly triumphant as Saffron's start of shock betrayed her awareness of the direction in which he was heading.

'Scarlet, possibly.' He drew the first word out so that

it was a softly sensual sound on his tongue, almost a caress in itself. 'Yes, I can see you in scarlet—something in silk—'

'Oh, *please*!' Saffron put in hastily, loading her tone with sarcasm. She'd had enough of this cat-and-mouse act; it was time to fight back. 'You have to be joking! I only ever wore scarlet silk once—never again!'

She gave a carefully delicate shudder of distaste, dark brown eyes meeting silver, hers burning with defiance, her chin lifting challengingly.

'It was a dreadful mistake—one I have no intention of repeating—*ever*.'

The deliberate emphasis on the final word was like a verbal throwing down of a gauntlet in front of Niall, an attempt to throw him off-balance, but to Saffron's annoyance he didn't react in the way she had anticipated. If anything, her challenge seemed to have amused rather than disconcerted him, and that smile grew in a way that she found positively hateful.

'I can't believe that. I can picture you in scarlet—'

The gleam in those pale eyes told her just *how* he was picturing her, and it took all Saffron's self-control not to react to the almost lascivious pleasure that was so clearly stamped on the hard-boned features before her. Her fingers itched to lash out and wipe it from his face and she had to clamp them together tightly in her lap in order not to give in to the impulse.

'And, in my opinion, it wouldn't be any sort of a mistake at all.'

'Really?' Using every ounce of acting ability she possessed, Saffron injected the word with an icy hauteur. 'Well, I'm afraid that you're never likely to see me in any such thing.'

After this, she wouldn't be able to bear to wear the

scarlet silk underwear ever again. She would sooner die! Even just to see it would remind her unbearably of the look in his eyes, that hateful smile, his voice...

'So, we'll just have to agree to differ on this.'

She knew that by defying him like this she was risking his anger, possibly even the fact that he might call her bluff and tell Owen everything, but she couldn't stop herself. She had to stand up to him, give as good as she got.

For a carefully timed moment he kept her hanging, waiting for his response, then, just at the point where she thought that she would scream if he didn't say something, he lifted his broad shoulders in a nonchalant shrug.

'So we will,' he said easily, adding in a tone so soft that only she could hear, 'For now.'

At that moment the waiter appeared with their meal, Owen returning to the table at the same time, and Saffron welcomed the interruption thankfully as a chance to gather her thoughts and try to cling on to the shattered remains of her composure. She knew exactly what Niall Forrester was up to. He had made it only too plain that he appreciated—and enjoyed—the possibilities of some rather nasty emotional blackmail, was well aware of how uncomfortable she would be at the prospect of Owen finding out about the fact that they had already met—and in what circumstances!

The problem was that he couldn't be more wrong. In the same second that she had considered the possibility of Niall telling Owen everything, she had realised just how little it worried her. All through the evening—in fact, ever since Owen had stood her up—she had had second, and third—even fourth thoughts about their relationship, and now she knew that there no longer was a relationship to worry about. She didn't care if Owen found out—and yet she still felt threatened. And that was what really worried her.

Earlier she had thought of Niall Forrester as a cat sitting outside a mousehole, and now she could be in no doubt as to just who was his prey. This particular sleek, dark-coated feline clearly had all the patience in the world when it came to hunting, and he wanted her to know that he was prepared to play a waiting game, showing no sign of pouncing until she put herself in a position of weakness by venturing too far outside the safety of her hiding place.

The problem was that she didn't know quite what she was hiding from. It wasn't any threat of exposure to Owen, however embarrassing that might be, instead it was something much more specific to Niall himself. Simply by existing, by awakening this unwilling, unwelcome response in her, he seemed to threaten her security, her peace of mind. It was as if she were one of the fireworks produced in Owen's factory, and someone had placed a lighted match to her own personal fuse. That fuse was burning worryingly swiftly, and she had the frightening feeling that in a very short space of time something was going to blow up right in her face.

CHAPTER THREE

'SAFFRON is an unusual name—though I suspect that you're more than tired of people commenting on it.'

'Oh, well, it was my aunt who suggested it. It came from a favourite song of hers.' Saffron was determined not to let him see how exactly he had hit upon the truth. 'And by the time they'd named five other daughters my parents had run out of names that they liked.'

To his credit, Niall didn't even blink, which was surprising. Many people were so accustomed to the idea of small families that the thought of six children—and all of the same sex—had them reeling back in astonishment. Owen had almost had to pick himself up off the floor when she had told him.

'Saffy's the youngest of this ridiculously huge family.' Owen had grown tired of being kept out of the conversation. 'Seven women! It's no wonder her father buried himself in his books.' Reaching for the wine-bottle, he refilled his glass.

'Don't you think you'd better go easy?' Saffron put in hastily, and was subjected to a look of such withering scorn that the protest died on her lips.

'Lighten up, Saff! No one likes a killjoy.'

Owen's retort was accompanied by a swift, expressive glance in Niall Forrester's direction. It was a look of pure conspiracy, man to man, of banding together in the face of female constraint in a way that made her prickle with irritation.

'But you're driving me home.'

'I'll be fine—'

And her concern was dismissed, so that unless she persisted, creating a nasty little scene in front of the interestedly watchful Niall, she had no option but to remain uncomfortably silent.

Perhaps in the past she might have shrugged off Owen's behaviour, possibly even telling herself that she might have over-reacted. But tonight she found that his rudeness had her boiling inside, anger searing through her like a red-hot tide so that she had to bite her lip hard in order not to tell him exactly what she thought of him. In fact, looking at his smiling self-absorbed face as he returned once more to his favourite subject of the proposed takeover, she was forced to wonder what she had ever seen in him.

Could she really have ever considered sleeping with this man? But hadn't that been exactly what she had planned on doing—last night, at least? Barely twenty-four hours ago, she realised, surreptitiously consulting the slim gold watch on her wrist, she had been so sure about everything. Now, she no longer knew what she felt. It all seemed to have happened since Niall Forrester had come into her life.

'I'm sorry—' Niall's sharp eyes had caught the tiny movement as she checked the time. 'We're boring you.'

'Not at all.' She hoped that her cool tones would communicate that nothing he could do would trouble her in the least. 'I appreciate that you have plenty to talk to Owen about. After all, it's his company that you're going to buy.'

'Possibly.' The single word held a suggestion of doubt, a reminder that all was not yet certain. 'If I decide I want it...'

Because she was already on edge, that, 'If...I want it' seemed to catch of Saffron's raw nerves.

'Is that really what life's about—getting what you want?'

'Isn't it?' He questioned coolly. 'I think if you asked the majority of people they'd say that most of their days are spent dreaming of something they want—trying to obtain it. I'm not unusual in that—only in that perhaps I know more clearly than most what I do want, and that when I see what I want, I go for it. I make sure nothing stands in the way of my getting it.'

The way he looked straight into her eyes as he spoke, a curl at the corner of his mouth, made Saffron think uncomfortably of his words that morning. 'You're exactly what I've been looking for—'

'And what if, when you've got your hands on whatever it is, it turns out not to be so desirable after all?'

His smile mocked her indignation, almost as if he knew the thoughts that were in her mind. 'Oh, then I'd just turn and walk away.'

'No backward glances?'

'Looking back is just a waste of time. If you want to make any progress, the only way is forward.'

She wished he would look away from her, turn the silvery force of those pale eyes on someone else. They might have started out talking about Owen's company and, ostensibly, to anyone not in the know, it might appear that they were still discussing just that, but Saffron was hypersensitive to the dangerous undercurrents in the atmosphere around her, uncomfortably aware of the other possible interpretation of Niall's words.

'And does that apply to emotional matters as well as business deals?'

She felt she didn't need to ask the question, already anticipating what the answer would be.

'So far I've never encountered anything that I couldn't resist or leave behind with no regrets.'

'Anything or anyone?'

Niall's only response was a slight inclination of his dark head, but a worrying gleam in those silvery eyes made her decide that it would be much safer to move the talk back on to the original topic.

'And do you think you'll want Richards' Rockets?'

As she had hoped, the question brought Owen back into the conversation and she was able to withdraw, sit back and watch as once more the two men became absorbed in their discussion.

The problem was that she didn't experience the relief she had hoped for. Only moments before she had wanted Niall Forrester to turn his attention elsewhere and leave her in peace, but now that he had, perversely, she felt irritated by the ease with which he seemed able to dismiss her from his thoughts. The chocolate torte which the waiter had brought her, together with another bottle of wine, now seemed much too rich for her taste, and she laid her spoon down, painfully aware of the fact that there was really nothing wrong with the sweet, only with her mood.

She couldn't stop her gaze from lingering on the man opposite, on the sculpted planes of his face, shadowed softly in the flickering candlelight, on the jet darkness of his hair, the unexpected softness of his mouth. Her eyes followed every gesture of his hands as he ate, talked, poured the wine. Those pale grey eyes of his were turned away from her now, but in her mind she could see them in all the changeable moods that, even after such a short acquaintance, she could recognise—the cold, steely glitter that could turn so swiftly to the warm glow of polished silver, or darken with something she couldn't—or didn't dare—put a name to.

'Is there something wrong with your food?'

'What?'

Niall's voice had been soft and low, but even so the sound of it jolted Saffron from the sensual trance that had held her. It was as if the gentle warmth of the candleflames had spread throughout the room, growing in intensity, heating the blood in her veins so that she felt as if she was adrift on a golden, glowing tide, the sight and sounds of the other diners fading to a blur on the edges of her consciousness, every nerve, every sense centring on Niall Forrester, like a compass needle drawn irresistibly to the North.

'I'll send it back if it's not right—'

'Oh, no—no, it's fine.'

I'll send it back, she noted resentfully. Niall Forrester had well and truly taken over the evening.

'It's just—that I haven't as much appetite as I thought.'

For food only, a rogue part of her mind commented. Other appetites were not so easily appeased. In fact, with those silvery eyes on her once more, the way he was leaning towards her bringing him so close that she caught the scent of some musky cologne he wore, she felt as if every inch of her skin was newly sensitised, and a previously unknown sensation was uncoiling in the pit of her stomach, as if some sensuous snake-like creature had been sleeping heavily but was now starting to awake...

'Eyes too big for my stomach!' she managed on a shaky laugh.

'Then perhaps we should think about leaving.'

Was she being unduly sensitive? Saffron wondered. Or was it just his physical position, the concentration of his attention on her, that seemed to make that 'we' exclude Owen, who, having tackled a large portion of his favourite Black Forest gateau, was now draining the last of his wine?

'Yes,' he said on a sigh of satisfaction. 'Better be going. Waiter!'

'Let me—' Once more Niall took charge, catching the waiter's eye with an ease that made the other man's waving hand look gauche and unsophisticated. In fact, it was rather over the top, even for Owen, Saffron reflected, her attention caught suddenly.

'Most gracious of you—'

It was the first couple of words, with the hint of slurring, that alerted her, making her turn a concerned frown on him, to see his flushed face and overbright eyes. Her fears were confirmed as Owen got to his feet unsteadily, swaying and clutching at the table for support.

'Owen—you're drunk!'

'Not at all!' He gave a foolish grin. 'Just a bit mellow.'

'But you're not fit to drive!' She thought despairingly of the long journey home, the lack of buses, the prohibitive cost of a taxi.

'Perhaps I could help?'

Did this man have ears like a bat? Her conversation with Owen had been conducted in a furious whisper, while he was occupied with the waiter and his credit card, but he was still very much aware of what was happening.

'I have my car here—I could take you both home.'

'But—didn't you—?'

Anticipating her question, Niall shook his dark head. 'I'm well under the limit—you'll be perfectly safe.'

And, looking into those clear grey eyes Saffron knew that he spoke the absolute truth. He had been decidedly abstemious, she recalled. If only Owen had been equally restrained!

'I can drive!' Owen protested.

'I don't think so!' Niall's voice was warm with humour, and he moved swiftly to support the other man as he lurched clumsily away from the table. 'Come on, mate—this way—'

Owen was more intoxicated than Saffron had first realised, and in the first flurry of activity involved in getting him out of the restaurant, across the courtyard and into Niall's car—the same sleek, grey vehicle that she had seen in the factory car park—she had little time to think of anything beyond a strong sense of gratitude for Niall's calm, helpful presence.

She doubted that she would have been able to cope without him, without his physical strength to support Owen's unsteady progress, the amused but firm tact with which he distracted the other man from his determination to drive home, and the final intuitive sensitivity he showed in personally supervising Owen's delivery into the care of his disapproving mother, enabling Saffron to remain in the car and out of sight. She was well aware of just what Mrs Richards would think if she knew of her presence.

'At last!' Niall exclaimed, sliding back into the driving-seat and pushing both hands through his hair with a sigh of relief. 'I thought we'd never get rid of him.'

'Thanks for seeing him to the door for me. If Ma Richards had realised I was with him she'd have blamed me for the state he's in.'

'She wouldn't believe him capable of getting that way by himself?' Niall slanted a quizzical glance in her direction as he turned the key in the ignition, bringing the powerful engine to swift, purring life.

'Her precious Owen?' Saffron assumed an expression

of exaggerated horror. 'Not on your life! He can do no wrong—except for the fact that he's seeing me. Mrs Richards has never really liked me—she doesn't think I'm quite good enough for her only child. As a matter of fact,' she added, impelled by scrupulous honesty, 'he's never really been quite so silly before.'

'No?' Niall sounded unconvinced and dismissively uninterested. 'Where to now? Where do you live—Saffron?'

But Saffron's sudden silence was not because she hadn't heard his question. Instead she had been struck by something in his tone, something distinctly cagey and with a dark note that made her nerves twist in sudden apprehension. As the sleek car pulled away from the kerb she heard again in her thoughts that expressive, 'At last!' and found herself looking back at the evening with fresh eyes, seeing belatedly how Niall had kept Owen's attention, picturing him chatting easily, summoning the waiter, ordering wine—refilling the other man's glass...

Suddenly she was sitting upright in her seat, her body taut with indignation, rejection, and something very close to fear.

'It was you!'

Niall didn't try to deny the accusation. He didn't even bother to ask exactly what she meant, but simply turned and gave her a swift, unrevealing smile before apparently concentrating his attention on the road ahead.

'It was you! *You* got Owen drunk quite deliberately! You poured him all that wine—'

'No one forced him to drink it,' Niall put in, his carefully reasonable tone only incensing her further. 'I didn't exactly pour the damn stuff down his throat.'

'You might just as well have done! Owen doesn't get presented with that sort of vintage every day of his life—certainly not in such quantities! And you know perfectly well that he wouldn't have wanted to offend you by refusing.'

'I'd have thought better of him if he had,' Niall commented drily, but Saffron wasn't listening. Her mind had gone into overdrive, whirling frantically as she tried to see just what this meant to her—because she was suddenly uncomfortably certain that Niall Forrester hadn't got Owen drunk just for his own twisted amusement.

'You knew that I was concerned! I said that I needed Owen to drive me home, and yet you continued to ply him with wine—'

But he had accepted her own refusal to drink any more with perfect equanimity.

'Why—?' she began, her strangled tone revealing that she already suspected what his answer was going to be, and didn't like it at all. 'Why?'

Niall turned another of those mocking, knowing smiles on her, his face half-shadowed and eerie in the light of the streetlamps.

'Oh, come on, Saffron,' he reproved gently. 'You don't need to ask that. You know exactly what I had planned. I had to get Owen out of the way because I wanted to be alone with you. But of course you knew that, because, after all, it was just what you wanted too.'

'I wanted—' Saffron choked on the words in her haste to get out an indignant refutal. 'I wanted no such thing!'

'Oh, but you did, sweetheart. I'm not blind. I could see it—read it in your face. It was there in the way you couldn't take your eyes off me, the way you tried to play it oh, so cool and failed miserably—the way you snapped when I spoke to you but sulked when I turned my attention away.'

'You arrogant pig!'

The knowledge that she was using her anger as a defence against his accusations made her tone even more aggressive than she had intended. The problem was that she couldn't deny the facts—but it was the interpretation he had put on them that was so infuriating.

Or was it? When her own mind played traitor, flinging at her a series of sensual images, reminding her of the effect Niall had had on her, that sensation of something awakening deep inside, she was forced to doubt her own conviction. Was that what he had seen in her face? She was grateful for the shadows that hid the rush of hot colour into her face at the thought.

'It wasn't like that,' she muttered, shifting uncomfortably in her seat.

'No? Seemed that way to me. Enough to make me want to test out the theory, anyway. And as young Mr Richards was something of an obstacle to that I—provided him with an excuse to leave us alone at the earliest possible opportunity. I think he enjoyed the experience, and there won't be too much embarrassment on his part.'

'On his part!' Saffron exploded. 'Owen wasn't the only one who was manipulated! How the hell do you think *I* feel? What about *my* embarrassment? Or don't my feelings count for anything in all this?'

For a long, intent second Niall took his eyes off the road and subjected her furious face to a sharply assessing scrutiny that made her skin crawl in response.

'On the contrary, it was your feelings I was considering.'

'My feelings! You decide that you know what I want, without so much as consulting me, deliberately get my boyfriend drunk so that I end up alone with you, whether I like it or not, and then you have the nerve to say you were *considering my feelings*! Consideration doesn't come into it! Pure, arrogant selfishness is more like it!'

'Oh, come on, honey!' Niall wasn't in the least bit rattled by her outburst. 'You know I made things easier for you. It would have been *embarrassing*, to say the least—' with silky deliberation he emphasised the word she had flung at him so angrily '—to have had to say to your boyfriend, "Look, I know I came with you, but I'm leaving with someone else." Don't you think?'

As Saffron's mouth actually gaped in shock, the knowledge of the fact that she no longer wanted to continue seeing Owen depriving her of the ability to form any angry retort, he continued smoothly, 'Especially if he'd paid for your dinner—so I took care of that too.'

'And you think that for the price of one meal you've *bought* me! That isn't so much Old Man as positively barbaric! What are you? Some sort of primitive Neanderthal?'

'At the moment, what I am is hopelessly lost,' Niall stunned her by replying. 'How about getting down off your high-horse and giving me directions?'

'Directions?' Thoroughly confused by the change of subject, and bewildered by the teasing note that had suddenly appeared in his voice, Saffron could only stare blankly. 'To where?'

'To your home, of course.' The patient resignation that shaded his tone riled her further. 'I did say I would drive you back, so if you'll just tell me which road—'

No! The word screamed inside Saffron's head, cutting through the whirl of confusion and anger like a cold metal blade, so that suddenly she could think again, her short-circuited brain-cells beginning to make connections—and the link she could see between her own comment about buying her for the cost of a dinner and his insulting, 'If you'll just tell me your terms…' of earlier that day, made her blood boil.

'I'm not going anywhere with you! Stop the car! Damn you—I said stop!'

CHAPTER FOUR

For a terrifying moment she thought he wasn't going to do as she said, and just as she was nerving herself for desperate action—though quite what, she had no idea—Niall shrugged indifferently, and, with a swift glance in the mirror, steered the powerful car to a safe position at the kerb.

It had barely come to a halt when Saffron wrenched at the door, only to find that, to her intense frustration, the handle remained stubbornly immovable, resisting all her efforts.

'Open this!' she flung at Niall, brown eyes flashing fire.

'Calm down. Can't we talk about this like rational human beings?' His tone was one that a vet might use to soothe a highly-strung horse, but it had exactly the opposite effect on her.

'There's nothing to talk about! I'm not going anywhere with you, so open this door!'

'It's locked, and it's going to stay locked until you're prepared to discuss things like a reasonable—'

'There is nothing to discuss! And how you dare use the word *reasonable* in the context of what you've done—'

'What have I done?' Niall's immovable calm was infuriating. 'No—tell me,' he went on at her angrily wordless exclamation. 'Just what is it that has so offended you? I've made it obvious that I find you attractive—so much so that I wanted to spend some time alone with you—is there anything wrong with that?'

Put that way, it sounded perfectly reasonable, Saffron

had to admit, though it ignored the high-handed way he had behaved.

'Oh, perhaps I should have *asked* if you felt the same way, but usually my instincts on such things are pretty reliable. If I apologise, will that help matters? I *am* sorry if I behaved like a—what did you call it?—a primitive Neanderthal. I didn't plan on using caveman tactics.'

When he paused, obviously waiting for some response, Saffron could only manage an incomprehensible murmur, a sound halfway between a growl of rejection and a mumbled acceptance of his apology. What he had said was all very well, but it didn't do anything to ease nerves made tight with suspicion or erase the memory of the way he had treated her in the MD's office that morning. But when his mouth quirked up at the corners like that, his eyes glinting with humour in the light of the streetlamp, his whole face changed, that smile making his expression much more appealing—dangerously so for her peace of mind.

'So now will you let me drive you home?'

Still not fully convinced, Saffron regarded him in mutinous silence, so that he sighed his exasperation, raking an impatient hand through the sleek darkness of his hair.

'You're determined not to make this easy for me.'

'Then why don't you just let me get out and make my own way home?'

She had little hope that he would give in that easily, and of course he didn't.

'At this time of night? You must be joking.'

'I'm perfectly capable of looking after myself.' She wouldn't let herself think of the fact that the buses stopped at ten and she doubted if she had enough cash in her purse for a taxi-fare.

'I'm sure you are. You seem lke one very independent lady to me.'

Saffron wasn't quite sure why that comment stung so sharply. Possibly it had something to do with the sardonic emphasis he gave it, seeming to communicate the fact that her independence was not a characteristic that appealed. What she liked even less was the way he shook his head, adamantly rejecting her hopeful suggestion.

'I'll give you a choice,' he said. 'Either you give me directions to your home now—' That disturbing smile resurfaced at the sight of Saffron's suspicious expression.

'Or—?' she prompted stubbornly, refusing to let herself be swayed by the softening effect it had on his hard-featured face.

'Or I'll take you back to my hotel and we'll talk it out there,' he finished blithely.

Which, of course, left her with no choice at all, as he knew only too well. The prospect of being on Niall's own territory, so to speak—which smacked very much of putting her head at least into the lion's den if not actually into the lion's mouth—was not one she relished at all.

'All right, then—'

Her voice revealed her reluctance, but she had been left with no alternative. There was only one comfort to be drawn from all this, she reflected as she gave the first set of directions. She'd be willing to bet that Niall hadn't bargained for her living so far out of town. He had probably thought that she had a flat in Kirkham itself, and so would not be anticipating the long drive through the centre and out the other side.

If she had expected any complaint when he realised what was happening, she was disappointed. Apart from her instructions, the drive was continued in complete silence, Niall only revealing his feelings when she directed him on to the York road and told him to follow it for a couple of miles by another of those swift, sidelong glances, this one touched with faint suspicion. Meeting it head-on, Saffron smiled back at him with blithe innocence.

'You wanted to drive me home,' she said sweetly. 'Surely you're not having second thoughts?'

'Not at all—after all, the idea was to spend some time on my own with you.'

Which was guaranteed to drive all sense of triumph from her mind, bringing her up sharply against the fact that, now that they had left the lights of the town behind them, the road was very dark and deserted and she was in the company of a man who had propositioned her in no uncertain terms that morning. Hastily Saffron abandoned a half-formed plan of sending Niall the long way round, opting instead for the quicker route through the village. The satisfaction she might have obtained from giving him an unnecessarily long journey didn't outweigh the more practical concern of ensuring she got home safely.

'Turn right here—'

As she spoke she lifted her hand, meaning simply to indicate the correct direction, but the movement made her fingers brush against the hard strength of his arm beneath the fine material of his suit jacket. Immediately she felt as if she had touched a live electric wire, a shock of several hundred volts shooting through her hand and making her snatch it back hastily, shrinking down into her seat.

At first she thought that Niall hadn't noticed her reaction, but once he had negotiated the sharp turn and they were travelling along the straight road again he said quietly, 'There's no need to panic—I'm not an axe-murderer.'

'I never thought you were!' Saffron retorted, and then, to cover the revealing quaver in her voice, added with what she hoped was a convincing display of airy insouciance, 'And I'm not worried!'

'Then you should be,' Niall returned sharply, metaphorically snatching the rug from under her feet. 'Do you make a habit of getting into cars with men you don't know?'

'No, I do not make a "habit" of it!'

Strangely, it was the undercurrent of anger in his voice that made her feel better about the situation. She was profoundly relieved to find that he had put her nervous response down to fear. If he had known the real way she was feeling—with every nerve seemingly heightened, quiveringly aware of the lean power of his body so close to hers, of that faintly musky scent tantalising her nostrils, setting up a twisting, disturbing response deep inside her—his reaction might have been very different.

'And may I remind you that—one—you didn't exactly give me much choice about coming with you, and—two—when I got into the car, Owen was with me.'

'A great deal of help he'd have been if you'd needed him,' Niall returned drily.

'And whose fault was that?'

'Saffron—I did not pour the damn wine down his throat. I simply provided the opportunity for him to drink it if he chose. He could have stopped me at any time—he only had to refuse—to say no...'

His pause was perfectly timed, just long enough to alert her to the fact that something more was to follow, something significant enough to have her sitting tensely upright, her eyes on his shadowed face.

'As do you.'

'I wasn't aware of the fact that I'd said yes to anything!' Saffron snapped, and was thoroughly disconcerted to hear the soft, warm sound of his laughter.

'Oh, Saffron, you didn't have to *say* that. Everything about you—every look, every bit of body language—has already said it for you.'

Which was guaranteed to drive every ounce of fight from her in the same way that a blow to her chest would have left her breathless and gasping for air. But even through the reeling sense of confusion she registered, with a small flare of pleasure, just how attractive her name sounded when he spoke it in that warm, amused voice that turned the syllables into something close to a sensual caress, making her feel that she had never heard it before in her life. How much more caressing would it sound if it was whispered in more intimate surroundings, when that low, husky voice murmured words of love?

'So, where do we go from here?'

'Nowhere!'

Dragged from the sensual little dream into which her wanton thoughts had taken her, Saffron snapped out the word in an instinctively defensive response, and was shocked into total alertness, her heart pounding, as Niall suddenly swung the car to the side of the road and slammed on the brakes. With the sound of the engine shut off the country lane seemed very silent, and threateningly dark and deserted, the man beside her very big and powerful.

'Wh-what are you doing? Why have we stopped?'

'You tell me.' The look Niall turned on her was worryingly enigmatic, just a flash of those silvery eyes in the moonlight, revealing nothing. 'You're the navigator—I'm the one who doesn't know my way around.'

'You—!'

Saffron almost choked on her exclamation of disbelief.

'I doubt if you've ever been unsure of where you're going in your entire life. You must have been born knowing exactly which path you were going to follow—'

No, not follow—which path he would *take*, she amended privately. Niall was one of life's takers, never a follower.

'But not now. Well, sweetheart?' That rich voice had softened even more, whispering over her sensitised nerves. 'Why *have* we stopped?'

'Because you—'

Even in the darkness she could sense the smile that curled the corners of his mouth and knew that his amusement was at her expense. Slowly the haze of confusion receded and a degree of logical thinking returned as she looked around her with new clarity, seeing just ahead of them the crossroads with its three possible choices of route. Where do we go from here?

'Oh!' Once more she was grateful that the shadows hid the fiery colour in her cheeks as she realised her mistake.

But it seemed that Niall could sense that too, was intuitively aware of her embarrassment and the thoughts that had created it.

'Oh, Saffron—what *were* you thinking? Did you really imagine that seduction was what I had in mind? That I'd stopped the car in order to have my wicked way with you? I'm thirty-two, sweetheart...'

The amusement in his voice had deepened into something so dangerously close to laughter that it was threatening to her self-control.

'A little too old to be making out in cars. But, of course, you're not—'

'I'm twenty-five!'

Tension made her voice tight. If he was going to

pounce, why didn't he do it? At least then she would have something to react against.

But pouncing seemed to be the last thing on Niall's mind. Far from being a fiercely predatory jungle cat, now he seemed instead like a sleepily satisfied tiger, one that was content to lie back lazily and watch his potential prey thrash itself into a frenzy of fear, without any inclination to hunt. So, had she read all the signals wrong? Had she misinterpreted what was in fact just a simple offer of help? But how could anyone misinterpret, 'If you tell me your terms...' and the way he had got Owen drunk?

'And I'm not your sweetheart!'

Privately she cursed the shake in her voice, knowing it would not go unnoticed—and of course it didn't.

'What's wrong, honey?'

The soft voice was deceptively solicitous, and as he spoke he leaned even closer, so that Saffron had to close her eyes against the sensual assault created by the mixture of that subtle aftershave with the clean male scent of his body. He was so near that she could almost feel the heat of his skin through the barrier of their clothes.

'Are you disappointed that the only reason I stopped was that I didn't know which way to go—to reach your house, I mean?'

It was a snake-charmer's voice, Saffron thought desperately, one that would hypnotise and control even the most dangerous of reptiles, and the mocking humour behind the deliberate double meaning only added to her feeling of losing control. As if in response to that voice, her own private serpent of need was waking once more deep inside her, stretching, uncoiling...

He was so close that he was almost touching her, and yet not quite. He was so near and yet so far, and she was so intensely physically aware of the latent power of that lean, male body that it came as a sudden shock to realise that, apart from that disturbing handshake, he had never really touched her. It didn't seem like that. Instead, she felt so sensitive to every move he made, to the soft sound of his breathing, the strong beat of his heart, that it was as if he actually held her imprisoned in a confining grip, as if his voice and eyes had been fine metal strands that had spun an unbreakable web to hold her.

'*Are* you disappointed? Because I'll tell you a secret—so am I. It seems a terrible pity to waste such a perfect opportunity—'

Through ears sensitised by the fact that she couldn't see, Saffron heard Niall's indrawn breath, soft as a caress, and sensed almost physically the movement of his gaze down to her lips. But she didn't dare to open her eyes, knowing that if she did so she would not be able to resist the growing need to reach out and touch him, to feel the warm strength of the real man beneath those sophisticated clothes, and a faint whimper of protest escaped her.

'A terrible pity!'

The sudden change in his tone alerted her, her eyes flying open, her body poised for flight, as he flung his safety-belt aside and gathered her into his arms, his mouth coming down on her.

His gentleness was totally unexpected. If he had been forceful, demanding, if his kiss had had anything of the blatant sensuality of his tone, then she would have panicked and resisted, fighting hard to be free. But this was so unlike the tiger's pounce that she had anticipated. This was a slow seduction of her senses, a softly enticing awakening that seemed to draw her soul from her body, making her head swim and every inch of her skin start to glow as if the cool light of the moon had suddenly changed, bathing her instead in the heat of a midday sun.

The problem was that her nerves were already awake, needing no gentle encouragement to rouse the passionate fires that were smouldering within her, and before she knew quite what was happening she was responding fiercely, kissing him back with a strength and an intensity that she would never have believed herself capable of. The reaction along every inch of her body and inside her head felt like the eruption of a volcano or the shattering of a meteor falling from the heavens, the touch of Niall's hands leaving a fiery trail like that of a shooting star blazing across the sky.

The last time she had seen such an explosive display of light and brilliance had been years ago when, during a family bonfire display, one of her sisters had accidentally dropped a burning sparkler into the box of fireworks and everything had been set alight at once. But these pyrotechnics were only in her mind, flaring and sparking with a dazzling intensity that made her feel as if *she* was a keg of gunpowder to which Niall had held a lighted torch.

She didn't know how much time had passed before Niall drew back, lifting his head and looking into her eyes, his own expression unseen and unreadable in the darkness. His sigh was a sensuous sound, one of pleasure and contentment, and yet communicated only too clearly the hunger that had not been appeased but stimulated by their closeness, their passionate caresses, so that she knew without a word being spoken that his appetite had been sharpened rather than dulled by the taste he had had of what he wanted.

For a long, silent moment he held her gaze, his pale eyes gleaming in the moonlight, making her think fearfully of the hunting jungle cat to which she had likened him earlier. Then, his movements slow and almost dreamy, he trailed the backs of his fingers down the side of her cheek before lifting the same hand and pushing it roughly through the smooth blackness of his hair.

'Like I said, sweetheart,' he said, in a voice that was low and slightly hoarse, as if his throat was suddenly painfully dry, 'where do we go from here?'

Her senses were still reeling, her pulse throbbing, her body humming like a violin string that had been plucked, but through it all, like a cold, sneaking trickle of icy water, ran the sense of danger that simply being with this man created, the need to act for her own self-preservation shining a cold, rational light into the muddied pool of her thoughts.

'Straight on at the crossroads and take the first turning on the left—it's the fourth house down.'

She refused to let herself be disturbed by the way his head snapped back, his hands dropping from her arms. She could sense the mental distance he had put between them almost as strongly as if it had been a physical one— which in another moment it was, as Niall moved back into the driver's seat, twisting the key in the ignition and revving the engine with an unnecessary violence that spoke more clearly than words of his state of mind.

'First on the left?' he said, and she could only nod in painful silence, the cold harshness of his tone striking her like a physical blow.

Only now, as her body reacted to the loss of his physical warmth, did the chilling sense of losing something very important begin to creep over her, making her feel miserably bereft and unhappy. Without the brilliant explosions of delight his touch had triggered off in her mind, her spirits sank to a despondent low, her eyes unfocused as she stared unseeingly out at the darkened countryside.

But those explosions had been just illusions, as transient and pointless as the momentary brilliance of a firework display that lit up the sky for a few seconds and just as quickly burned itself out. Niall had made it only too plain that he was attracted to her—but that was all. She was something he had wanted and, as he had said, if he wanted something he went for it—and when he tired of it he walked away without a backward glance. She would do well to remember that.

'This the one?'

'Yes—'

Her fingers were already on the handle, waiting for him to release the lock on the door, as he drew the car up by the kerb. Niall studied her cottage in silence for a moment.

'I never expected you to live in a place like this—it looks like a doll's house.'

'It is tiny.' Saffron was relieved to find that her voice was reasonably even and relaxed. 'But that's the way I like it—at least it's all my own; I don't have to share with anyone.'

As soon as the words were out she bit down hard on her lower lip, cursing herself for giving away that vital fact. Luckily, at that moment the handle moved and the door swung open.

'I won't keep you any longer,' she said hastily, trying to sound as casual as possible. 'Thanks for the lift—will you be able to find your way back to town?'

'Oh, I'm sure I can remember the route,' Niall murmured drily. 'Your instructions were clear enough.'

'Well, goodnight...' Saffron decided that discretion was the better part of valour, that it was wisest to ignore that double-edged remark. 'And thanks again.'

She was out of the car and straightening up when Niall moved, leaning across the seat towards her.

'No chance of a cup of coffee?'

Just for a second the appeal of his voice, that smile,

almost weakened her, but common sense murmured a hasty warning and she shook her head.

'No—it's late, and I have a job to go to in the morning.'

'Then, what about—?'

'Niall,' she said, emboldened by the fact that it would take him far longer to get out of the car and come round to her than it would for her to run to her house and slam the door against him if it was necessary, 'what part of "no" did you not understand?'

That, and the coolness of her tone, got through to him, and she saw a dark scowl cross his face.

'The word I understand perfectly,' he declared harshly. 'What I can't get my head round is why you're using it when you don't really mean it.'

Then, as she gasped in shock and fury at the arrogance of his words, he shrugged his broad shoulders dismissively and shook his dark head.

'But you did, and so I'll just have to accept that you obviously don't know your own mind as well as I do mine. All right, Saffron—I can wait. Off you go to your little doll's house and your lonely bed. You never know—perhaps you'll dream of me.'

'Never!' Saffron couldn't believe what she was hearing. 'I could never dream of you—and if I did, believe me, it would be a nightmare!'

His smile was like something out of that nightmare, cold and hard and totally humourless, a travesty of the gesture of warmth it was supposed to be.

'Which just proves my point. Forgive me if I don't believe you, sweet Saffron—one of these days I'll show you exactly why.'

'Not if I see you first!' Saffron declared, slamming the door with a violence that gave her intense satisfaction.

But that was as far as her courage went. Not daring to

look at his face to see how he had taken her response, for fear that she might discover that he was actually getting out of the car, she headed for her cottage as quickly as her legs would carry her, wrenching the door open and dashing inside, leaning back against the solid wood with a sigh of relief only after she had secured the lock and pushed the two strong bolts home.

Even then, with solid wood between herself and any intruder, she found that her heart was racing painfully, setting a pulse throbbing in her throat so that she could hardly breathe. It was only when she heard the car's powerful engine roar and the tyres squeal as he drove away that she finally managed to make her way into her tiny living-room, where she sank down on the settee, weak with reaction, her legs unable to support her any more.

CHAPTER FIVE

'WELL, come on.' Kate's voice was tinged with barely-controlled impatience. 'Put me out of my misery!'

'Mmm?'

Saffron lifted her head, frowning her confusion. She had been trying to work on the weekly laundry list, but if the truth was told she hadn't been able to read a word on the page, the image of a sleek, dark head and pale, steely eyes dancing before her instead.

'What do you want to know?'

'What do I—?' Kate rolled her eyes expressively. 'Isn't it obvious? Just what happened between you and Owen yesterday?'

'Owen?'

'Yes, Owen—the man to whom you were going to give your all just twenty-four hours ago. Was he impressed by the scarlet siren outfit?'

The laughter in Kate's voice grated over Saffron's tightly strung nerves, and abruptly she turned away, shuffling through the papers in an attempt to hide the burning colour she knew was rising in her face.

'He wasn't there,' she said abruptly, praying that Kate would ask no further questions, but the other girl was not so easily deterred.

'But you saw him last night? And?' she prompted at Saffron's silent nod.

'And he had a bit too much to drink. As a matter of fact, he got decidedly tipsy.'

'Owen!' Kate exclaimed in mock horror. 'Mrs

Richards' perfect son! So, of course that meant you had no chance to talk things over—or take any action?'

Once more those exaggeratedly raised blonde eyebrows left Saffron in no doubt as to just what action her friend meant.

'That's not a consideration any more.'

That was one definite decision she had reached last night, as she had tossed and turned restlessly until just before dawn when she had finally fallen into a shallow and unrefreshing sleep.

'I think perhaps I'm not the commitment type after all.'

'Why ever not? How can you have changed so completely in just twenty-four hours?'

Which was just the question that had kept Saffron awake late into the night, though not quite in the context in which Kate had meant it. Just how could she, who had always believed in taking things very steadily where relationships were concerned, have found herself responding to Niall Forrester's kisses with such—such enthusiasm? Her mind flinched away from the more accurate word—passion.

Looking back at the girl who had been in Niall's arms, she couldn't recognise herself in the uninhibited, wanton creature she had become, and in the cold light of day she had been forced to admit that her reaction to him later, her forceful rejection of any further overtures on his part, had really been a form of panic at the thought of how she could have changed so much, so quickly, and as a result she had run away from the man who had been the cause of that change.

'I—' she began, but was interrupted by the ringing of the doorbell downstairs.

'I'll go!'

Kate disappeared down the steps that led to the door

into the street, leaving Saffron breathing a silent prayer of gratitude for her escape. She didn't know how she would have answered Kate's question if she had had to.

'Well, now, look at this!' Her friend reappeared in the doorway, a rather smug smile on her face. 'Owen must be feeling very guilty about last night.'

'Those are for me?'

Saffron held out her arms to receive the bouquet of roses, her expression bewildered.

'This isn't at all like Owen. But they are gorgeous.'

'Beautiful! And there's a card—what does it say?'

'Hang on—let me open it! It's—Oh!'

The pleasure faded swiftly from Saffron's face, her heart lurching painfully as she saw the words inscribed on the white card in strong black letters—handwriting that was nothing like Owen's small, precise neatness.

'What is it?'

Curiosity overcoming her, Kate peered over Saffron's shoulder and read the inscription out loud.

'"As soon as I saw these, I thought of you. N. F." Not Owen, then?'

Of course not Owen. Saffron knew that she should have realised that from the first. Owen had never bought her flowers in all the time they had been together.

But she should have known. For one thing, the colour of the glorious flowers should have given her a clue. They were the same rich, glowing scarlet as the silk basque and suspender belt Kate had described as the siren's outfit.

'Who's N. F.?'

She had known that the question must come, and was partially prepared for it.

'Niall Forrester.' To her relief, she was able to say the name without revealing the way her nerves twisted into tight, painful knots at the thought of him. 'A business acquaintance of Owen's. We had dinner with him last night.'

'Was that when Owen blotted his copybook by getting drunk?'

Saffron bit back a groan of despair as she looked into her friend's green eyes, bright with interest, behind which she could almost hear the other girl's brain ticking over, adding two and two together...

'So he wasn't fit to drive...?'

'And, yes, Mr Forrester gave me a lift home—but don't read anything into that,' she added hastily as the gleam in her friend's eyes brightened. 'It was just a polite gesture, nothing more.'

'So why is he sending you flowers?'

'I don't know.'

And that was the honest truth. After the way she had left him last night, the anger she had seen in his face, the cold dismissal in the words he had flung at her, she would have thought that Niall was more likely to want to put her out of his mind for good. But then a memory slid into her mind, the echo of that coolly drawling voice saying, 'I can wait...'

But how had he known to send flowers here instead of to the cottage? How had he found out where she worked? The thought of him asking questions, probing into her life, made a sensation like the trail of icy wet footprints slide slowly down her spine.

'I suppose—'

She wasn't at all sure how she would have gone on if she hadn't been rescued once more by the sound of the bell.

'Now who's this?'

'Let me see to the door while you put those flowers in water,' Kate said obligingly. She was part-way down the stairs when her curiosity got too much to bear. 'And what's he like, this Niall Forrester?'

'Oh, you know—' Saffron aimed for airy insouciance '—a real businessman.' She raised her voice to carry down the stairwell. 'Smooth as silk and oily with it, with nothing to recommend him but his money—boring as hell. *Ow*!'

She broke off on a cry of pain as a sharp thorn caught her thumb through the cellophane wrapping and pricked it savagely. If she had been superstitious, Saffron thought wryly, watching the bright red bead of blood on the tip of her injured finger, she might actually believe that the tiny wound was an act of fate—punishment for lying through her teeth in her description of Niall. But she had had to squash Kate's curiosity once and for all.

As she put her thumb to her mouth to soothe the sharp sting she heard her friend's footsteps mounting the stairs again.

'Who was it?' she asked around her injured finger, and just had time to take in her friend's expression, the look of barely subdued excitement combined with a hint of concern, before her eyes went to the tall, dark figure of the man who stood behind Kate. An uncontrollable groan of reaction escaped her.

'It's Mr Forrester,' Kate announced, the look in her eyes finishing her statement with the unspoken comment, And he's *not* boring! without a word having to be spoken.

For a couple of uncomfortable seconds the room actually seemed to swing round Saffron, making her take a step backwards to lean against the desk for support. Her mind buzzed with questions, wondering frantically just how Niall had found out where she worked and, even more disturbing, just how much of her foolish, unthinking comment he had heard. The door had been closed, but she had raised her voice quite considerably to make sure that it carried far enough to reach Kate.

'Good morning, Saffron.'

Niall's voice was cool and easy, no hint of any strong emotion rufling its smooth surface.

'You got the roses, I see.'

Saffron managed a vague murmur that sounded like agreement, astonishment depriving her of the ability to speak. This wasn't Niall Forrester! At least, he wasn't the man she had had dinner with last night or—her breath caught painfully in her chest—the one she had encountered in the MD's office yesterday morning. The sleek, expensive suit had gone, to be replaced by a well-worn leather jacket, white heavy cotton shirt and a pair of denim jeans so tight and clinging they were positively X-rated. With his black hair blown on to his forehead by the same wind that had brought a glow of colour into his cheeks, he looked vitally alive and potently male, the aura of success and money that surrounded him, even in the very casual clothes, enhancing his undeniable, forceful physical attraction.

As on the previous night, Saffron found herself thinking unnervingly of the similarities between Niall and a wild jungle cat. His sleek appearance was belied by a hint of wildness, an untameable quality that she knew some women would find totally irresistible. Certainly Kate was impressed, if the sparkle in her wide green eyes and the way she could hardly take them off him was anything to go by.

'I hope you like them.'

'I—'

With an effort Saffron clasped her mouth shut on the enthusiastic response that had almost escaped her. Only a few moments before, she had been wondering just why

Niall would send her flowers, but of course the answer was obvious. 'When I see what I want, I go for it—' Clearly he hadn't taken her refusal of last night as seriously meant. Just what did she have to do to convince him? She had no desire to end up as just one of those things he ultimately walked away from without a backward glance.

'The flowers? They were all right.'

It was a struggle to ignore the way Kate's eyebrows flew upwards in an expression of frank amazement at her swift about-turn from her earlier enthusiasm, and she had to look away hastily, praying that Niall hadn't seen the other girl's reaction.

'But, really, red roses are such a cliché, don't you think?'

Niall's smile was a slow, dangerous curling of his sensuous mouth, one that matched the steel-grey ice of his eyes in its lack of warmth.

'Ah, but then I wasn't thinking of any supposed symbolic meaning that tradition has given them. It was something else that attracted me. Didn't you read my note?'

The grey eyes were suddenly smoky, worryingly so, as his voice softened enticingly, and they drew her gaze once more, holding it in the same mesmeric spell that he had managed to weave around her the night before.

'I'll just sort these out—'

With superb tact, Kate picked up a sheaf of papers from the desk and left the room, heading for the kitchen below, but neither Saffron nor Niall saw her go.

'When I saw them, I knew I had to buy them for you...'

Reaching out, he took the bouquet from Saffron's unresisting grasp and with a neat, efficient movement drew a single perfect bloom from the bunch.

'I knew how wonderful they would look against your skin.'

The rose brushed her cheek softly, its velvety petals sliding over her skin in a delicate caress that sent a shiver of sensual awareness sliding down her spine. His smile showing his recognition of her response, Niall let the flower trail gently downwards over the pale blue linen of her suit, the white blouse, coming to rest at the point of the deep V-neck, its rich colour startling against her pale skin.

'As they do...' His voice had dropped to a husky whisper.

For a moment Saffron shut her eyes, swallowing hard. Her mind screamed a furious rejection of the suggestive position of the scarlet flower, resting just at the point where her breasts curved softly. But her lids flew open again at the realisation that her temporary blindness only intensified the sensual enticement created by the combination of that low, caressing voice, the delicate touch of the rose's petals and its heady, musky perfume.

Her heart was racing, her mouth dry, and she knew that, under the light pressure of the delicate flower, her breasts rose and fell jerkily with her quickened breathing.

'Yes, well—'

With an abrupt movement she snatched the rose away, refusing to let herself feel any guilt or regret when her rough action snapped the thin stem, breaking it, so that she was left with only the blossom in her hand.

'Roses really aren't my favourite flower.'

In a disdainful gesture she dropped the broken flowerhead into the wastepaper bin and moved to seat herself in the swivel chair behind her desk. She felt happier with the solid wood between them, though her composure was severely threatened by the way that Niall immediately took several steps forward, the movement bringing him to stand opposite her, his imposing height emphasised by her position in the chair, so that he seemed to be towering over her. She refused to let herself feel threatened.

'Well, perhaps you'll be more pleased to see these—'

She hadn't noticed the carrier bag in his hand, but as soon as he deposited it on the polished wood of her desk she knew just what it must contain.

'The shoes—how thoughtful.' Her tone dripped a deliberate honeyed sweetness that only a blind fool would take as being sincere. 'Kate will be so pleased to get them back—'

'Kate?'

To her annoyance he didn't look in the least disconcerted. There was even a touch of amusement in the single word, a faint curl at the corners of his mouth.

'You didn't really think they were mine, did you? They wouldn't exactly go with what I'm wearing—'

It wasn't just the shoes that she wanted him to know were not hers, but the image of the woman who had worn them. She knew that the picture she presented now, with her dark hair pinned up in a neat coil at the nape of her neck, wearing the severely tailored suit and blouse, was one of controlled, businesslike efficiency, light-years away from the scarlet-clad siren he had first set eyes on.

'Hardly.' Disconcertingly, the laughter was more pronounced now. 'But then you wouldn't be the first woman to conceal her true self under a carefully restrained exterior.'

The smile grew, becoming a wicked grin that was mirrored in the glinting grey eyes.

'I learned very early on not to judge a woman's character by her clothes but by what she wears beneath them.'

'And I suppose that you've tested out that theory on innumerable occasions?'

'Hardly innumerable—that would be totally irresponsible. But, yes, I've evidence to support the premise.'

'Well, in my case, I'm afraid your theory doesn't hold water—though I suppose you would say that makes me the exception that proves the rule.'

She was going to regret provoking him. She knew that as she saw the wicked glint in his eye brighten perceptibly.

'On the contrary. With you, I'm forced to wonder just what makes you so determined to deny your true self by—'

'Don't you really mean that I'm denying you?' Saffron snapped acidly.

Infuriatingly, her barbed dart seemed to bounce ineffectually off his thick skin.

'Not at all. I've told you—I'm perfectly prepared to wait until you come to your senses.'

'Then you'll wait till hell freezes over!'

'Oh, I don't think so—'

Too bemused by Niall's smooth-toned arrogance to think of a suitably crushing retort, Saffron was infinitely relieved when their conversation was interrupted at just that moment by the shrill summons of the phone. She was even happier to discover that the identity of the caller meant that she had to call for Kate, who reappeared swiftly, hurrying to answer.

The slight pause had given her the opportunity to collect her thoughts, restore some degree of composure.

'So, tell me, Mr Forrester—' Deliberately she emphasised the formality of her use of his surname, hoping it would distance her from him mentally as well as her position behind the desk did physically. 'What can we do for you?'

Her glance in the direction of her friend made it plain that Kate was included in the question every bit as much as herself, that 'we' having been used as meaningfully as the 'Mr Forrester', as was the gesture she now made towards the other girl, who had now finished her conversation and was replacing the receiver.

'I'm sorry—this is my partner, Kate Macallinden. She runs A Movable Feast with me.'

'Miss Macallinden—' Kate was treated to the sort of smile that, if it had been an electric light, would have had to be measured in megawatts, and Saffron saw her friend actually step back in reaction to its stunning brilliance.

'Kate, this is Niall Forrester. His company is taking over Richards' Rockets.'

The sudden recollection of that silkily emphasised 'possibly' on the previous night made her stumble over her words. He had never put any such qualifying terms on his insolent declaration that she was exactly what he had been looking for.

'Now—how can we help you?'

'That really rather depends on exactly what sort of services you're willing to provide,' Niall returned smoothly, and, having floored her with the deliberate double meaning, he went on with a smile, 'But, after last night, I think we can dispense with the formality of surnames, don't you?'

Which was guaranteed to make Kate even more curious, Saffron reflected furiously, refusing even to look at her friend, knowing only too well the intrigued message her expressive eyes would be telegraphing—wanting to know just what Niall had meant by 'after last night'.

'A Movable Feast is a catering company—'

Furious with herself for having fallen into his trap, she launched into her business speech, deciding that her professional persona was the best one to hide behind at this particular moment. At least it kept the topic of conversation to strictly impersonal matters—though Niall seemed capable of twisting anything round to mean something else entirely!

'We can provide food for any sort of function, formal or informal—a child's birthday party—a twenty-first—a picnic at the races—even—' she couldn't stop the hopeful note from creeping into her voice '—business lunches or meals for staff attending conferences.'

Perhaps he *was* looking for someone to offer to take on a contract for staff meals at Richards' Rockets. With something like that under her belt, she wouldn't need to worry about money quite so much.

'You just name the occasion and we'll do the rest. We provide sample menus for you to choose from—all the china and cutlery—'

Niall looked slightly bemused at her enthusiasm.

'I didn't realise you were quite such a forceful businesswoman.'

'Why—did you think that I was merely a decorative accessory to Owen?' Anger sparked at the thought. 'Just an attractive adornment, the traditional requirement of a successful businessman, a bimbo without a brain in my head?'

The mocking question implied by the way one dark eyebrow drifted slowly upwards stopped her dead in midtirade. After all, their first meeting was hardly likely to have given him any other impression.

'You hardly gave me a chance to come to any conclusion—you were so damn determined I should talk to

Richards,' he retorted. 'But, if I do decide to spend some time in Kirkham, perhaps I might be able to use your company.'

'Our rates are very competitive.' Saffron made no attempt to hide her keenness. 'And I'm sure you'll find that, although we're only a small establishment, we can match the very best. What exactly was it that you had in mind?'

'A special night with a special lady?' Niall murmured, with a wicked smile that made her heart lurch painfully. 'Perhaps we could discuss the details over lunch?'

'Lunch?'

Saffron schooled her face into something that approximated polite disappointment. If he really planned to use their services, it would be a terrible mistake to alienate him completely, but after that dig there was no way she would consider eating with him.

'I think I'm busy—another client—'

'Not for lunch.' Either Kate was blithely unaware of Saffron's attempt to wriggle out of the invitation or she was determined to ignore it. 'Mr Robinson won't be here until after two.'

'Then, lunch it is.' Niall was swift to seize on the opportunity she had given him. 'I'll collect you at twelve-thirty.'

And before she had time to protest, or think of a possible excuse, he had strolled from the room and could be heard running lightly down the stairs. If she had been alone, Saffron would have screamed or stamped her foot in rage at the way he had outmanoeuvred her, but she had to be content with screwing up a piece of paper and flinging it furiously into the bin.

Kate, however, felt no such restraint.

'Wow!' she exclaimed dramatically. 'Now I see why Owen's in the doghouse!'

'Don't be silly!' Saffron snapped. 'Niall Forrester has nothing to do with it.'

The look her friend turned on her was frankly sceptical.

'Oh, doesn't he?' she said. 'Well, that's not the way it appears to me.'

'It's just a business lunch, Kate. After all, we desperately need his custom.'

But, even as she spoke them, Saffron had to admit that, coming from anyone else, she wouldn't have found her words at all convincing. And, to judge by Kate's smile, neither did she.

CHAPTER SIX

'So, WHEN exactly are you planning this special meal?'

The only way to play this, Saffron had decided, was absolutely straight, pretending that those words meant nothing to her other than the possibility of some much-needed business.

'I'm not sure.'

Niall shrugged broad shoulders under the crisp cotton of his shirt. For the first time that year the wintry weather had improved slightly, finally becoming more like May, and he had discarded the leather jacket as they sat outside the riverside pub he had driven her to, slinging it over the back of his chair and lounging back to enjoy the warmth of the sun.

'I told you, I haven't thought of the details yet.'

'Well, perhaps you'd like to think about them now.'

It was a struggle to be strictly businesslike. She had to force herself to ignore the way the sunlight caught on the glossy blackness of his hair, highlighting its sheen, the way it made those pale eyes gleam like burnished silver, cool against the warm tinge of his skin. Those long legs in the worn denim were stretched out in front of him, dangerously close to her own slim ones, and she moved rather pointedly, earning herself a swift, dark frown.

'Did you want to entertain at home or—'

Her throat closed suddenly at the thought of the implications of Niall 'entertaining' at home, and she reached hastily for her glass of mineral water, swallowing hard to ease the constriction.

'Eat your lunch,' Niall commanded brusquely. 'We can talk about that later.'

'But I *need* to know what you want!'

'Do you?'

The words fell sharply into the silence that had descended as soon as—too late—she realised just what a mistake her own comment had been.

'Do you really want to know, Saffron?' Niall questioned softly, dangerously. 'Because I'll tell you if you like—but you'd better be very sure that that is what you want.'

'Niall!'

It was a croaked protest, too feeble to have any effect. He was determined; she knew that from the set of his features, the sudden smokiness of those formerly clear grey eyes.

'I want *you*, Saffron.'

The words were silkily intent, pitched to reach her ears only, and, as on the previous night, it was suddenly as if they were no longer in a public place, but enclosed in an intimate bubble, shut off from the rest of the world.

'I want you so much that I've gone completely off my head. You're driving me crazy, Saffron—'

'Oh, come on!' she managed shakily. 'You're exaggerating!'

'I told you, I never exaggerate,' he shot back. 'And if you don't believe me you can ring my secretary. Ask her about the meetings she's had to postpone—the appointments she's had to rearrange—the schedule she's probably still struggling to readjust—no doubt cursing me to hell and back as she does it.'

'But why?' Saffron stammered, and earned herself a look of laughing reproach.

'Think about it,' he murmured, holding her shocked,

wide-eyed gaze with hypnotic ease once more. 'My secretary thinks I've blown several fuses; my deputy manager will probably never speak to me again; I may have lost a valuable contract, and there's an important meeting I should be at right this minute. But I didn't even consider them when I decided what to do today. I'm where I want to be right now, with the person I want to—'

'Niall,' Saffron interjected hastily, 'you can't—'

'Why can't I?'

'But your company—those people—that contract—'

A nonchalant wave of his hand dismissed her concerns and the needs of his job as totally unimportant.

'They'll always be there, and if not I can replace them. Since you walked into my life yesterday...'

Was it really only the previous day? Saffron wondered shakily. She felt as if she had lived through several lifetimes since then. Barely thirty hours had passed, and yet she knew that she could never take the scattered jigsaw pieces of her life and put them back together in such a way that they would form exactly the same picture as before. That image of her existence was shattered and gone forever.

'...I've only been able to think of one thing—you. Your eyes, your hair, your face—'

His own eyes darkened even more, becoming almost black, with only the tiniest rim of silver at the edges.

'Your body—'

'Please!'

Fiery colour rushed into Saffron's cheeks. It seemed somehow indecent to be sitting like this, in this quiet, sunlit garden, with the subdued chatter of the other people all around them blending with the ripple of the river in the background, hearing words that would be far better suited to the privacy of a bedroom.

'Naturally, I'm flattered—who wouldn't be?—but I can't really believe that a man like you, who holds the reins of a huge corporation in his hands—on whose shoulders rests the responsibility for thousands of jobs—would let those reins drop—would neglect everything—just because—because—' She faltered, unable to complete the sentence.

'Because of you?' he finished for her. 'Believe it. I had planned to go back to London as soon as I'd finished with Richards. I *should* have gone back then, but after you appeared so dramatically in my office yesterday morning I couldn't get you out of my mind. I couldn't leave Kirkham without finding out more about you. The receptionist told me your name, and about your relationship with Owen; Owen's mother told me he was at Le Figaro, so I knew there was a good chance you would be too.'

Owen's mother had told him! So his appearance at the restaurant had not been the appalling coincidence she had believed it to be. And this morning—

'How did you find out where I worked?'

Niall's lips curled in a worrying smile, and once more Saffron felt the same icy footprints creeping down her spine that she had experienced earlier at the thought of him asking questions. She was beginning to feel like a frightened rabbit, running from a very determined and skilful hunter. 'When I see what I want, I go for it.' But when he had got what he wanted and had tired of it, by his own admission, that was when he coldly walked away.

'Mrs Richards again. She gave me the information when I rang this morning to see how her son was faring after last night's indulgence—'

'You rang Owen?' Saffron couldn't disguise her surprise. 'Isn't that a touch hypocritical? I mean, it's rather like some thuggish mugger phoning the hospital to ask about the progress of his latest victim.'

'His mama appreciated my concern. And, yes,' Niall added, deliberately emphasising the dark irony that threaded through his voice, 'he's fine—if a little hungover.'

'I never doubted that he would be.' Saffron refused to let herself be pushed into feeling guilty that she hadn't been the one to enquire about Owen's condition, that it hadn't even crossed her mind.

'And on my way through the town centre I passed a flower shop,' Niall went on, as if her interjection had never happened. 'Those roses were in the window, and as soon as I saw them, naturally I thought of you.'

'Naturally,' Saffron echoed sardonically, refusing to let herself dwell on just what his thoughts would have been.

'I'm sorry you didn't care for them—you must let me know what you prefer so that the next time—'

Saffron couldn't let him go on.

'There isn't going to be a next time. What do I have to do to convince you of that? I told you last night—'

'I know what you *said* last night, but I also know that I don't believe it. I held you in my arms, remember?'

Remember! Could she ever forget it? Once more, Saffron reached for her glass, wanting to ease the sudden heat in her body that had nothing to do with the mild warmth of the sun, but almost immediately reconsidered, setting it down again without taking a sip at the realisation that there was no way she would be able to swallow. She was sure that the water would catch on the tight knot of feelings in her throat, choking her.

'I kissed you. I felt your response. I saw it in your eyes—as I can see it now—'

And before Saffron had time to think, to register just

what he had said, he was on his feet and moving round the white-painted wrought-iron table, pulling her to her feet, clasping her tight against his powerful body with one arm while his other hand slid under her chin, lifting her face to his as his mouth swooped downwards.

If his words had been indecent, then his kiss was practically pornographic in its deliberate sensuality. It made Saffron's blood sweep hotly through her veins, her legs giving way beneath her so that she leaned limply against Niall, supported only by his strength. Her soul seemed to be drawn from her body, her head spinning wildly as if she was delirious, and the coiled serpent in the pit of her stomach lifted its head in an act of sharp need.

It was several moments before she became aware of anything other than Niall, the hard power of his body, the warmth of his skin and its intensely personal, musky scent, and only when she was released, blinking hard as if she had been dazzled by a sudden bright light, did she come back to a realisation of just where she was and the interested stares of the other diners.

'Niall!' she whispered in angry reproach. 'People are watching!'

'Let them watch.'

His shrug was a gesture of supreme indifference, and with total composure he simply returned to his seat, refusing to acknowledge the openly fascinated stares of the people around them.

'It's all right for you!' Hastily Saffron sat down too, making sure her back was to their audience. 'You don't have to live here, with these people! Kirkham is a small place—'

'They're just envious.' Niall dismissed her concern. 'And I was right, wasn't I? You did want me to kiss you—it was written all over your face.'

Did he know her better than she knew herself? He must do, because what he had said he'd seen in her face was something she hadn't known she wanted until he had taken her in his arms. Only then had she realised that she needed his kiss so much that she felt she would have died if he hadn't kissed her.

'Just tell me one thing—can Owen make you feel like that?'

'Owen—'

The burning colour left Saffron's face, leaving her looking pale and strained at the thought of what she had almost revealed. She might have come to the conclusion that there was no future for her relationship with Owen, but she could just imagine what interpretation Niall would put on that decision if she let him know about it.

'What about Owen?' She had trouble getting the words out, struggling with the uncomfortable twisting of the nerves in her stomach.

'What about him?' Niall was clearly not pleased with the mention of the other man's name, even though he had been the first to use it.

'*Will* you buy Richards'?'

'I told you—I haven't made my mind up yet.'

Privately, Saffron took leave to doubt any such thing. All she had seen of Niall Forrester left her in no doubt at all that he was a man who made up his mind far more quickly than most.

'There are one or two—considerations—to be taken into account.'

'Considerations?' Saffron echoed hollowly, her thoughts growing even more uncomfortable. 'Is this an attempt to blackmail me into your bed?'

'Blackmail?'

Either Niall was a far better actor than she had realised,

or that was genuine confusion that showed in his eyes, making Saffron suddenly a prey to strong second thoughts about her outburst. 'Blackmail?' Niall repeated, and she knew there was no backing down now.

'If I don't sleep with you, then you won't buy Owen's company, is that it? Because, if it is, then you couldn't be more wrong. I don't care if Owen doesn't get the price he wants for the factory, or if he never gets that damn night-club he's been hankering after! So if you think you can use that as a hold over me—'

The words died in her throat as she saw the way Niall's eyes narrowed, the cynical twist to his mouth.

'Dear me, what a vivid imagination you have,' he drawled with sardonic mockery. 'Did you really think I'd stoop so low? I've never had to force any woman into my bed in my life—or use blackmail, which, after all, is the psychological equivalent. And, even if I did, I would never bother to bring Richards into this. You see, I've known right from the start that he wasn't the man for you.'

'What do you mean? You don't know anything about me—'

'Oh, come on, Saffron! Any fool can see that a man who'd turn down an invitation like the one you offered me—' the dark smokiness of his eyes told her only too clearly that he was thinking of the scene in the MD's office '—hasn't enough red blood in his veins to handle a real woman.'

'How do you know that he did?'

'Oh, I know.' His voice was rich with loathsome conviction, a dark triumph that seared over her hypersensitive nerves. 'I know frustration when I see it, and you were burning up with it. He turned you down flat—

either that or he wasn't even offered what you were offering me.'

'I wasn't—' Saffron began, but he ignored her, continuing with silky ruthlessness.

'Was that it, sweetheart? Did you change your mind?'

'Once I'd set eyes on you?'

God, the man was arrogant beyond belief! She'd give anything to knock him down a peg or two—or three!

'You really have got the biggest ego of any man I ever met! Did you honestly believe that because I met you then suddenly I'd forget all about Owen—?'

Her voice failed her embarrassingly as a ruthless conscience brought her hard up against some harsh facts. Because wasn't it actually strictly true? Didn't Niall's arrogant claim have some real foundation in fact?

And, all the more worrying, what had happened to her own conviction that she was ready for commitment? She had told Kate that that was what had been in her mind, had used it to justify her decision to sleep with Owen—but had that just been sex, pure and simple, all along? Was she, in Niall's crudely blunt terminology, so burningly frustrated by her celibate state that she would turn to any man—to Owen—or—?

Or Niall. The thought slid unwanted into her mind, shocking her like a slap in the face, reminding her of her powerful response to him, her intense physical awareness of his presence. Just to look at him sent a blazing heat rushing through her veins, and when he touched her she fizzed like a firecracker. No, she couldn't be so shallow! Violently she shook her head to drive the disturbing thought from her mind.

'No?' Niall questioned, seeing the betraying movement. 'Is that, no, you didn't change your mind, or no, Owen wasn't offered what I was?'

'I never offered *anything* to you! I thought you were Owen!'

Too late, she realised how bad that sounded, following on from her earlier declaration that she didn't give a damn about Owen. Still, what did it matter? she thought bitterly. Niall obviously thought she was cheap and mercenary enough to sell herself to the highest bidder, and, after the way they had first met, could she really blame him?

'So why didn't you repeat your offer to Owen? Oh, I know you haven't.' Niall went on when Saffron glared at him furiously. 'He complained about how—unforthcoming—you were.'

'He did *what*?'
Saffron couldn't believe what she was hearing.
'You actually discussed me with him—!'

'On the contrary—I never said a word. Owen, however, seemed to think I'd want to know all about you.'

And he obviously had been quite open about some very intimate details too! She couldn't believe that she had ever considered any form of commitment to the louse. And as for Niall Forrester—he might claim that he hadn't said anything, but he was clearly prepared to use what he had heard against her!

Suddenly she couldn't bear to remain in his company a moment longer. Pushing back her chair with an ugly scraping noise, she got to her feet in a rush.

'I'd like to get back—I do have an appointment!' she added fiercely when Niall looked pointedly at his watch.

'Fine!' He stood up too, raising his hands in a defensive gesture against her fury, the impact of which was belied by the laughter in those silvery eyes. 'Don't take it out on me just because your boyfriend can't be trusted to be discreet!'

'Discreet is not the word!' Saffron flung at him from

between clenched teeth as he turned towards the exit. 'And you didn't have to listen—I've never heard of anything so bloody ungentlemanly and—!'

'Oh, didn't you know?' Niall drawled tauntingly when her anger left her lost for words. 'There weren't exactly too many gentlemen around in Neanderthal times. Which reminds me—'

Abruptly he came to an unexpected halt, but, driven by blind fury, Saffron marched straight past him.

'I said I wanted to get back to work!' she threw over her shoulder, heading for the spot where his car was parked. 'So would you mind getting a move on?'

For one awful moment she thought that her shrewish tone would drive him finally to lose his temper. The sensual mouth compressed to a thin, hard line, his eyes narrowing dangerously, so that she flinched inside, anticipating the coming explosion. But then somehow he seemed to rein in the violence that was simmering inside him as he moved to open the car door for her.

But, once inside the sleek vehicle, he showed no sign of being prepared to start the engine.

'I'm going to be late!'

Niall's response was a second, even more pointed glance at the clock on the dashboard, which showed only too clearly that they had over twenty-five minutes in which to make a journey that had taken no more than ten on the way out.

'I have something to say, and we're not going anywhere until you listen,' he stated, in a tone which brooked no further argument.

CHAPTER SEVEN

SAFFRON'S breath hissed between her teeth in a sound that she hoped was more expressive of her earlier impatience than the sudden twinge of fearful apprehension that gripped her at the way he spoke.

'You really seem to make a habit of this—' she began, then broke off abruptly as he made a sound that was a blend of exasperation and a genuine snort of laughter.

'Only because you drive me to it! It seems to be the only way I can get you to listen to a word I say.'

'That's because I don't want to hear—'

'Oh, yes you do,' he interrupted firmly. 'Because I want to apologise.'

'You—'

Saffron knew she was gaping foolishly, but she just couldn't stop herself. She didn't believe she had heard right. Had Niall really said *apologise*?

'For what?' she asked suspiciously, and to her complete consternation his laughter grew into a genuine grin, that devastating smile lighting his face in a way that made her heart thud dangerously in her chest, making her breathing fast and uneven.

'Don't you ever let up? All right,' he went on hurriedly, when she glared at him threateningly, 'I wanted to say that I'm sorry if I behaved badly last night. Believe it or not, that was one of the reasons I asked you to have lunch with me—so that I could apologise for behaving like a— what was it you called me?—a barbaric Neanderthal?'

'Primitive,' Saffron managed shakily, weakened by that

smile. She didn't believe for one moment that Niall actually meant his apology—the big man himself saying he was sorry? No way!

'Yeah, well. I think barbaric was in there somewhere too. You were right, though, I shouldn't have manipulated you like that—or got Owen drunk. I never meant to ride roughshod all over you. From now on I'll always give you the choice—all right?'

'All right.' Saffron nodded shakily, her brain reeling in shock at the sudden change in his behaviour. He had actually sounded sincere, his apology apparently genuine. Whatever had happened to the arrogant, lordly Niall Forrester?

'Forgiven?' he asked softly.

'Apology accepted,' Saffron muttered, not prepared to go quite that far. 'Forgiven' sounded like conceding too much, meeting him more than halfway.

She was startled by Niall's response. His unexpected laughter had a warm, friendly sound that went straight to her heart, easing the angry discomfort that the thought of Owen's behaviour had left behind.

'Still fighting?' he murmured teasingly. 'What is it about me, Saffron, that strikes such sparks off you? You're like one of Owen's damn rockets—light the blue touchpaper and stand well back—you're on an exceptionally short fuse!'

'*I* am?' Saffron exclaimed disbelievingly. That description sounded as if it could be applied far more accurately to Niall himself. 'Ever since I first met you I've felt as if I was in the middle of some huge, uncontrolled firework display, with rockets exploding all over the place and Catherine Wheels whirling—firecrackers sending sparks up into the sky.'

'Really?' Niall's tone was rich with dark satisfaction.

'Well, at least you're prepared to admit that I'm having some effect on you.'

'I didn't say I liked it!' Saffron retorted hastily, realising how much she had given away.

She had been too easily swayed by that smile, his laughter, she told herself. He might have apologised, but only for manipulating her into his car and for getting Owen drunk—not for anything else.'

'But you do—don't you?'

It was that snake-charmer's voice again, slow and softly seductive, coiling round her senses like warm smoke, and his eyes held hers captive. She was incapable of looking away in spite of the urgent commands from her brain. Her throat was suddenly parched and she swallowed nervously, her tongue coming out to moisten painfully dry lips. As it did so, she saw the silvery gaze drop downwards to follow the small revealing movement, and her stomach clenched on a painful spasm of response.

'Don't fight me on this, Saffron,' Niall urged huskily. 'Not any more—because, quite frankly, I won't believe you, and it all seems such a waste of energy.'

'I—' Saffron tried to protest, but he laid a gentle finger over her lips to silence her.

'You admit that since we met there have been fireworks between us, and I know you respond to me physically— most people would be glad enough to start from there—'

'A few kisses!' Saffron protested against his restraining finger, and immediately wished that she hadn't because the feel of the warmth of his skin against her lips, the slightly salty taste of it, sent shockwaves of response shooting along her nerves like tiny, brilliant explosions in a chain reaction that built up to a force of nuclear intensity, so that instinctively she closed her eyes against her reaction, terrified of what she might reveal to his watchful gaze.

'A few kisses...' she heard Niall repeat, his voice a sensual caress in itself. 'That is one hell of an understatement, lady. And those kisses were only the start—let me show you—'

She hadn't the strength to move away—and even if she had found it, she knew she couldn't have found the will to use it. 'Don't fight me,' he had said, and suddenly she didn't know why she had been fighting, or even what she was struggling against.

She *wanted* his kisses, wanted the excitement they lit up inside her. Fireworks, Niall had called it, but it was more than that. It was fireworks and rockets and, above all, like setting a torch to a hot, blazing bonfire that had been standing, already carefully laid, just waiting for one tiny spark to set it flaring. Niall, it seemed, had the necessary match, and all he had to do was touch it to the bone-dry tinder and suddenly she was totally alight, all hesitancy, all reticence melting away in the heat of the need blazing up inside her.

When his lips touched hers she gave a small, wordless moan of delight, her fingers moving up of their own volition to link together under the silky black hair at the nape of his neck, drawing his face down to hers and holding him a willing prisoner. Her body was crushed against his, the hardness of his chest against the soft warmth of her breasts, and she could feel the fierce racing of his heart that echoed her own heightened response, making her writhe in aching frustration.

Niall laughed softly and slid his fingers down her cheek, down over the path that he had traced with the delicate petals of the rose, and down, and down... And this time he didn't allow the silk of her blouse to hinder him, but slipped the tiny buttons from their fastenings with practised ease, sliding warm, strong fingers in to push aside the lacy barrier of her underwear and capture one satiny breast in a tantalisingly gentle grip.

'You see,' he whispered in her ear, his breath warm against her cheek, his thumb moving teasingly over the roused nipple as she murmured a yearning response. 'I knew from the start that it could be like this—and, believe me, sweetheart, this is just the beginning.'

Just the beginning! Saffron felt that her head was swimming, as if she was in the grip of some heated fever that had resulted in burning delirium. If this was only the beginning, then she didn't know how she was going to cope with what was to come—because it *would* come; she knew that without a doubt. It was as inevitable as a summer forest-fire raging through a drought-dry forest—raw, primitively powerful, and totally devastating, shrivelling everything in its path and completely unstoppable. There was no further thought of fight in her mind. One day she would be Niall's—the only question was when and how.

At long last Niall drew away, his sigh reluctant, his hands going to smooth his ruffled hair back into place, to fasten the buttons on his shirt, and even though the gestures seemed to speak of a cool collectedness that indicated an unemotional lack of involvement, Saffron was pleased to see a faint tremor in those strong fingers that revealed the way he wasn't quite as composed as he would like her to believe. As for herself, she was a shattered wreck, limp as a wrung-out cloth, her bones seeming to have melted in the heat of their shared passion, but with the writhing, aching serpent of need deep inside her totally unassuaged and furiously demanding more.

'Look what an effect you have on me!' Niall's laugh was wry and self-deprecating. 'Not only do my workmates think I've gone out of my mind, but I'm as hot as any adolescent on his first date. I said I was too old for making out in cars, but, believe me—' his eyes darkened and his voice became a deep, husky growl '—you'd tempt any man.'

Looking deep into her face once more, he abandoned all pretence at restoring order to his appearance, and bent towards her. But this time his lips had barely brushed hers before, with a groan, he jerked himself upright again.

'Oh, God! This isn't the time or the place. Saffron—'

But Niall's talk of time had drawn Saffron's eyes once more to the clock, an exclamation of shock escaping her as she registered what it said.

'It certainly isn't! Niall, it's almost two—my appointment!'

'Is it really so important?'

'It's vital! I need that contract or A Movable Feast will go under! Niall, please—'

But he was already moving, ramming the key into the ignition and setting the powerful engine roaring as he fastened his seatbelt.

'The mirror—' he said sharply, swinging out on to the road.

'What?' Saffron frowned her confusion.

'Look at yourself in the mirror.'

As soon as she did so, Saffron saw only too clearly just what he meant. She was in no fit state to meet a prospective client, or anyone else for that matter. Her dark hair was like a bird's nest, her lipstick was smudged, her brown eyes were overbright above burning cheeks, and, worst of all, her blouse gaped widely where his urgent hands had tugged it open, exposing the tops of her breasts, and the delicate flesh was marked with red patches from his fierce kisses, his urgent caresses.

With a shocked exclamation, she set about repairing the damage, fastening buttons with frantic haste, tugging a comb through the tangled ebony waves of her hair. She had barely completed the task when Niall, who had ignored all speed-limits on the journey, drew the car up outside her work premises.

'Will I do?' she asked, still breathless from the speed of the necessary readjustment.

Eyes that were a surprisingly cool grey, showing none of the reaction that had darkened them earlier, skimmed over her in a swift, assessing glance.

'You'll do,' he assured her. 'Even Owen's mama couldn't find fault.'

'Oh, I doubt that.' Saffron laughed. 'I'd never be right for her—I'd swear she thinks I'm after her precious son's inehritance. Niall—I have to go—'

'One minute—'

His hand around her arm was firm, holding her with a grip that was so hard it was bordering on painful, and she felt she would bruise where his strong fingers had fastened on her wrist.

'Owen will have to go.' It was an order, not a statement. 'I don't share my women with anyone.'

If only he knew that Owen was no longer a consideration, and hadn't been ever since Niall himself had exploded into her life. But she wasn't going to tell him that, not now, possibly not ever.

'My *women*', was the phrase he had used, and suddenly all her fears came back in a worrying rush.

What was she doing? She had thought that she wanted commitment, the security of a loving marriage like the one her parents and sisters enjoyed, instead she had become entangled with a man she scarcely knew, a man who spoke no words of love but only desire, a man who had openly declared that when he saw what he wanted he went for it without hesitation.

And he wanted her. The shiver of excitement that shot through her at the thought told her that, for now, that was enough.

'Saffron—' There was a warning note in Niall's voice. He hadn't liked her silence. His hand came under her chin, lifting her face up to his.

'Yes!' Desperate to be gone, Saffron would have agreed to anything. 'Now will you please let me go—?'

'Just one more thing,' Niall said, his voice huskily intent. 'I really have to get back to London—sort things out—for a couple of days, at least. There'll be hell to pay if I don't. You do understand?'

This time she could only nod, using her silence to hide her private disappointment at the way that, having, in his opinion, wooed and won her, he could now turn his attention to more pressing matters.

'But I'll be back.' Niall's eyes darkened suddenly, and he pressed warm, soft lips against her cheek. 'I promise,' he whispered, his breath feathering her ear. 'Just as soon as I can get away—I'll be back.'

His words and the gentleness of that kiss eased the ache of disappointment. The intensity of that whispered promise was all that she could have asked for.

Niall's fingertips touched her cheek where his lips had rested a moment before, and in a gesture of infinite tenderness he tucked a stray lock of dark hair behind her ear.

'Think about me,' he murmured, his eyes holding hers.

'Think about me,' Saffron's thoughts echoed dazedly a few moments later when, standing on the pavement outside her office, she watched the powerful car accelerate down the road and turn the corner out of sight. Think about him! She doubted that she'd be able to think about anything else.

CHAPTER EIGHT

SAFFRON studied her reflection in the mirror and frowned at the look of nervousness in the brown eyes staring back at her, the tension in her face echoed by the apprehension twisting her stomach.

It was ten days since she had last seen Niall; two weeks in total since the day he had exploded into her life and turned it upside-down. Since he had returned to London he had been in contact by phone, and had paid one flying visit en route to somewhere else. He had stayed just long enough to take her out to dinner, and had literally left her on the doorstep on their return to her cottage.

'I shouldn't be here, sweetheart,' he had told her. 'In fact, I should be anywhere but here, but I couldn't let another day go by without seeing you.'

There had been a fire at one of their factories, he had said. Arson was suspected, or, at the very least, negligence, and the reputation of the company was at stake. There were other people he could send, who could deputise for him, but he preferred to handle it himself. He had been sure that she would understand.

She did—of course she did—but all the same she still cursed the way that fate seemed to have conspired against her, to keep Niall working and far away from her just at this point in their relationship. His absence gave her too much time to think, to worry about the effect he had had on her, to consider her own behaviour and wonder over and over just what she was doing.

Kate had been characteristically blunt in her response to the situation in which Saffron found herself.

'So whatever happened to, I'm ready for commitment?' she had demanded. 'Are you trying to tell me that Mr White Tornado Forrester is now offering hearts and flowers, wedding-bells and happy-ever-afters when you've only known him for twenty-four hours? Because, quite frankly, he didn't strike me as that kind of man.'

'No,' Saffron had admitted reluctantly. 'I don't think anything could be further from his mind.'

Or from her own, when she was with him; that was the trouble. With Owen she had been looking for security—a future. With Niall, the present was all that mattered, and she was incapable of looking beyond it.

'I think the problem was that I was suffering from post New Year blues. You know, Christmas at home, all those sisters and their husbands—and the new babies—'

Kate, whose only family consisted of a mother who was currently backpacking around Australia with a man fifteen years her junior, smiled rueful sympathy. 'Everyone asking when you were going to join the happy throng—?'

'I thought there had to be more to life than struggling with a business that's dying on its feet.'

'And you thought that sleeping with Owen would provide that?'

Saffron couldn't help laughing at the sceptical expression on her friend's face. 'My relationship with him was another part of my life that seemed to be going nowhere. I thought it just needed a push—some extra input on my behalf. I didn't realise that that, too, was something that was dying on its feet.'

'Owen didn't take too kindly to being given the push?'

'He was furious—called me every name under the sun.

I'm just grateful I didn't tell him about Niall. I didn't even say there was someone else.'

It was all too new, too fragile. She still couldn't believe it was happening.

'I don't know how he would have reacted if I had. But I didn't want him to think I'd just broken up with him because of Niall.'

She didn't want Niall to think that either. The memory of that arrogant, 'Owen will have to go,' still rankled, provoking a sense of defiant rebellion. She hadn't just been following Niall's orders.

'Owen and I had come to the end of our particular road—the relationship wasn't giving me what I needed, no matter how much I put into it. That was really brought home to me the night he stood me up.'

'The night you were all ready to do your sacrificial lamb act?'

Saffron nodded slowly, suddenly becoming aware of just how appropriate Kate's words were.

'I didn't decide to sleep with Owen because I just couldn't help myself—because it was what I *wanted*—but because of the restlessness I was feeling.'

That restlessness that had driven her to want to improve their relationship somehow—*anyhow*.

'But it shouldn't be like that. If you are to give yourself to someone it should be because you can't do anything else, because you feel that you'd die if you don't.' As she now felt with Niall. 'I was just kidding myself,' she added ruefully.

'So, what now? I mean, if that was the end of winter blues, then what are you suffering from now? Belated spring fever? Early midsummer madness?'

'I don't know, Kate, and to tell you the truth, I don't

really care. When I'm with Niall he makes me feel so very different. He excites me, he—'

'You're in love!'

Kate's laughing comment pulled Saffron up short, forcing her to look at herself and her behaviour with a cool clarity of thought that hadn't been possible since she had first encountered Niall.

Was she in love? No, it wasn't possible, not after such a short time. After all, she had only known Niall— what?—two weeks? And in that time she had spent perhaps twenty-four hours in total in his company. She couldn't know him in that time, let alone feel anything deep for him. No, she wasn't in love, but he had knocked her flying—mentally that was. She hadn't been able to get her feet back on solid ground since.

'Don't be silly, Kate!' Her voice wasn't quite as steady as she might have wished. In order to bring herself firmly down to earth, she went on, 'And now we'd better talk about some rather more practical matters—like how we're going to hold A Movable Feast together, for one.'

'Is it really dying on its feet?' Kate asked in some concern.

'Not far off it—the patient's condition is critical, I should say. Apart from Mr Robinson's contract for the bowls club, and a couple of children's birthday parties, we've nothing on our books. We desperately need some more customers, Kate. If we don't get them, we're going to go out of business—'

The sound of the doorbell interrupted Saffron's memories, bringing her back to the present with a rush, with the realisation that while she had brooded Niall's car had pulled up outside, and now the man himself was on her doorstep.

Her heart suddenly set up a new and disturbingly rapid

pattern, bringing a rush of colour to her cheeks and making her breathing uneven as she checked her appearance in the mirror again, smoothing down the cream-coloured sweatshirt that she wore with sand-toned Lycra leggings, and pushing a wandering dark strand of hair back into the thick braid that hung down past her shoulders before hurrying to open the door.

'Hi!' Niall dropped a brief kiss on her forehead before strolling into the house as if he was the one who actually owned it. 'I got here earlier than I expected—traffic on the motorway wasn't half as bad as I'd anticipated. Missed me?'

Had she missed him? Saffron knew that she hadn't realised just how much until he was standing there before her, his height and strength seeming to dwarf the tiny proportions of her minuscule peach-and-green-painted living-room. Like her, he was casually dressed, in the supple leather jacket he had worn when he had taken her out to lunch, with a pale green T-shirt and darker green jeans. Everything about him seemed so much bigger and more forceful, even his colouring more dramatic than she remembered, and her heart suddenly seemed to stop at the thought that this strong, devastatingly attractive man—this wonderful specimen of potently concentrated masculinity—had actually travelled all the way from London just to see *her*.

'Hey!' Niall's quiet voice drew her attention. 'You don't look exactly pleased to see me. Is something wrong?'

'Wrong? No, it's just—' The truth broke from her before she had a chance to consider the wisdom or otherwise of revealing it. 'I wasn't really sure that you'd come.'

'And why wouldn't I? I said I would, didn't I?'

'Yes, but—'

'And I never say anything I don't mean—you would do well to remember that.'

His words were laced with an ominous undercurrent that made Saffron shiver faintly, her mood changing abruptly as she was forced to recall his adamant declaration about being able to walk away from anything. She could be in no doubt that he had meant that too.

She had told Kate that she didn't care about the possible consequences of a relationship with him—but was that strictly true? Was she really capable of handling a situation that offered her nothing more than the here and now?

'I'm sorry—' she began, but then Niall's mouth curled into a slow, enticing smile, driving all thought of what she had been about to say from her mind as he held out his hand.

'Come here,' he said softly, and without being quite aware of having moved she was suddenly in his arms and being held up against the hard strength of his body, his warmth reaching her even through her clothes, his scent all around her, as she was kissed with such ruthless efficiency that within seconds her head was spinning deliriously.

'Now do you believe me?' he demanded, and she could only nod silently, her heart singing with happiness, too full to allow her to speak.

All she had ever wanted was right here, beside her, as he let her know with his kisses, his touch, the husky murmur of need that broke from him, that *she* was what he wanted, and that when he had told her so he had meant every word he said.

When Niall moved, taking her with him to the settee and sinking down on it, she was unable to resist, a puppet obeying his every masterful tug on her strings, and she knew that if he was to loosen his grip then, like that puppet with its strings cut, she would collapse in a limp heap on the floor, unable to support herself.

Her mouth opened under his, the provocative teasing of his tongue adding fuel to the fire of passion that flared inside her as she returned his kiss with deliberate provocation, clinging to the muscular strength of his arms and letting her head loll back against the hard support of his shoulder. She was trembling with desire, every nerve alive with excitement as his hands moved lower, sliding under the soft cream cotton of her sweatshirt, the sensation of the warmth of his hard fingers on her skin making her sigh against his mouth and try to strain even closer. Niall wasn't immune to passion either, and she felt the shudder that ran through his long body before, with a harsh groan, he wrenched his mouth from hers, breaking the kiss, and pushed her slightly away from him.

'Niall!' It was a cry of reproach, her voice uneven, her breathing ragged. Why had he stopped? Didn't he know how much she wanted him? Couldn't he feel it in every inch of her slender frame?

'Hold on, sweetheart,' he said in a tone that was rough and thick. 'Don't you think that before we take things further we ought at least to know a little more about each other than just names and occupations?'

'"Before we take things further!" You're very sure of yourself—' Saffron couldn't hide her reaction to Niall's casual confidence.

'And why not?' he returned easily. 'I'm not stupid—or blind. It isn't a matter of *if*, Saffron; the only question is when—and you know that as well as I do.'

There was no way she could deny the truth of his blunt statement. She knew what Niall wanted from her—wasn't it just what she wanted from him? Surely the aching disappointment she had felt at the abrupt cessation of his lovemaking told her that?

'I just don't want to be taken for granted—'

'Oh, Saffron, I could never do that—you're not the sort of lady anyone could take for granted in any way. But if it seemed that way, I'm sorry.' His smile was cajoling, enticing. 'And to prove it, I have a present for you.'

'A present?' Saffron's mood lifted swiftly.

The sound of Niall's laughter as her expression brightened was like balm to her heart, easing the faintly bruised sensation of a moment before.

'What is it?'

The tissue-wrapped package was slim and soft, and when she tore it open it was to find the most beautiful silk scarf she had ever seen, fine and cobweb-delicate. It was shaded only in bronze and gold tones, without a trace of the gaudy scarlet that held such disturbing implications for her, and she was able to accept it without restraint and with no disturbance to her volatile mental equanimity.

'It's gorgeous!' she almost danced to the mirror to fasten it loosely about her throat. 'Perfect! What do you think?' she asked, spinning round to face him.

His eyes, burning like molten silver, gave her her answer without words, and she knew without any hope of salvation that if he held out his arms to her once more she would go straight into them without thought or hesitation. If he said, Come to bed, her response would be just the same, she realised, and the revelation made her close her eyes in confusion, breaking the spell that held them both.

'Let's go for a walk,' Niall said abruptly, the words sounding strangely stiff and tight, as if he had forced them from a painfully dry throat. 'It's a beautiful day, and I've been stuck in offices or the car almost all the time for the past ten days—I could do with some air.'

'We'll go down by the river, if you like,' she said as lightly as she could, leading the way through the kitchen and out into her pocket handkerchief-sized garden, at the bottom of which ran a pathway down to the riverbank.

'Perfect.'

Niall paused for a moment to draw in a deep breath of the clean, fresh air, warmed by the afternoon sun.

'London is no place to be in the spring.'

'You surprise me—'

Saffron spoke quickly to cover her own spontaneous and very sensual reaction. With the sunlight gleaming on his jet-black hair, his jacket now discarded and slung over one shoulder so that she could see how the soft cotton of his T-shirt clung to the strong lines of his shoulders and chest, emphasising the lean maleness of his shape, it was all she could do not to reach for him and kiss him with fierce and inviting passion.

'I thought you were a city man through and through.'

Niall shook his dark head firmly, causing a lock of black hair to fall forward on to his forehead, and Saffron's fingers itched to touch it, feel its silky softness under their tips as she brushed it gently backwards into the rest of the shining mane.

'Not me; not by choice. When you get to know me better you'll see that that's only one side of me.'

When she got to know him better! The words had a wonderfully hopeful sound inside her head, but then, almost immediately, harsh realism brushed aside her happy delusion, dismissing such thoughts as just idle dreams. Niall was with her now because it suited him to be there. He wanted her—the look in his eyes as she had turned from the mirror had left her in no doubt about that—but only for now. She would be wise not to allow herself to hope for any more.

'London's where my offices are—where the contacts, the influences are—but it's no place to live full-time. I've always had a dream of a home in the country somewhere—like yours.'

'But it would hardly be anything like my tiny place. How did you describe it—a doll's house? It suits me fine, but you'd want something more than a little shoebox of a cottage.'

'It wasn't exactly what I had in mind.' Niall's tone was dry. 'But one of these days I'm going to start a hunt for something that is.'

'So what's stopping you?' Because obviously he couldn't want it *enough*. The man who had declared that when he saw what he wanted he went for it wouldn't let just anything hold him back.

Niall's broad shoulders lifted in an offhand shrug.

'The time has never been quite right—and it always seemed a little greedy when I already have a perfectly adequate home in the city. If I had a family, it would be different.'

'So you haven't ruled out the idea of marriage and children?'

The impulsive question escaped before she had time to consider the wisdom of asking it, and she regretted speaking as Niall turned to her, his eyes steely cold and indifferent, all emotion blanked out.

'One day, maybe,' he said, his tone warning her not to press the matter further, so that she was surprised when he added, 'But that's something of a problem when you're as rich as I am. People tend to see you only in terms of figures on a bank statement, and in my experience women find the idea of a large income more of a turn-on than any physical attraction.'

Saffron turned wide, startled brown eyes on his face, shocked by the dark cynicism in his voice, the way his expression had suddenly become distant and remote.

'You can't really think that someone would only want you because of your money!' Was this what was behind his determination to stay in control, his ability to walk away without a backward look?

'It happens,' he drawled laconicaly. 'I've been there—'

'Has there never been anyone you felt mattered more than that? Someone you—'

'Loved?' Niall supplied when she hesitated. 'Whatever love is. There was someone once—her name was Jayne—but I made the mistake of introducing her to my brother.'

'What happened?'

'She decided to marry him instead of me.'

'Oh, God!' The starkness of the declaration, the flatness of his tone, shocked Saffron. 'I'm sorry—that must have hurt terribly.'

Once more that dismissive lift of his shoulders expressed his indifference to any extreme feeling.

'As a matter of fact, it was how little it bothered me that was worrying. It made me realise that what I'd thought was a great passion was in fact no such thing. Anyway, there's no harm done. It's past—over—'

'No looking back,' Saffron couldn't stop herself from murmuring, her voice low, but Niall caught the soft words.

'Exactly. Besides—' his laugh was careless, disturbing in its indifference '—Jayne makes a great sister-in-law—far better than she would have done a wife.'

The next moment he had turned away from her, his action and the way he stared out across the river—running high because of the recent rain—communicating without words the fact that the topic was now closed and that he would not welcome any attempt to reopen it.

'Is this the same river as the one beside the pub where we had lunch?'

'That's right.' It was safer to follow his lead and not risk any argument. 'It runs all the way from here into York and right through the city.'

'I've never been to York—is it as beautiful as they say?'

'It's wonderful—one of my favourite places! It's such a mixture of the old and new—I think you'd love it. Perhaps—'

She broke off hastily, belatedly seeing the danger in saying that perhaps they could visit the city together. To do that was to assume that they had some degree of a future together, but Niall wasn't the sort of man you could make such assumptions about.

'I'd like to go there some time.' Niall's smile told her that he had watched her face and interpreted only too accurately just what had been going through her mind. 'After all, it looks as if I'll be up in Yorkshire for a while—a couple of months at least—while I sort things out at Richards.'

'A couple of months—'

'It's all I can spare. After all, Richards' Rockets is hardly a major concern.'

'You are going to buy the factory, then?'

She couldn't iron out the jerky note in her voice. How much time could he spare for her? She had told herself that she wouldn't ask for a future, but a couple of months seemed like no time at all.

'Why? Don't you think I should?' He had caught the

hesitant note, but attributed it to some totally different explanation.

'I—I'm not sure.'

If she had wanted to make sure that he stayed in Kirkham she would have done better to be more enthusiastic, but somehow she was incapable of speaking anything but the exact truth. She also had the uneasy feeling that, if she didn't, Niall would know.

'I mean—there's nothing wrong with the company, except perhaps that it's a little old-fashioned.'

'I had noticed.'

'Owen's father wasn't well for the last year or more of his life. He rather let things go...'

'And how.' Niall's mouth twisted cynically. 'And his son didn't bother to make much effort either. The whole place needs a bomb putting under it.'

'It's not exactly Owen's cup of tea—his interests lie elsewhere.'

'In a night-club called the Safari, to be precise.'

'You know?'

'He has mentioned it.' Niall stopped abruptly, spinning her round to face him. 'Come on, Saffron, what exactly are you trying to say?'

In the sunlight, his grey eyes gleamed like the blade of a well-sharpened knife, and Saffron suddenly felt uncomfortably like some small, vulnerable insect impaled on its point.

'It's just—I wonder if your money might not be better spent elsewhere. I mean— Owen—'

'Owen's trying to bump up the price to well over the odds—asking for far more than the place is worth in order to get his share of the night-club and still make a profit? Is that it?'

'I—yes.'

Saffron felt vaguely foolish. Of course he'd known all along; he wouldn't be in the position he was now, with a reputation for being something of a genius in the business world, without the sort of clear-minded acumen that could match Owen a thousand times over.

'I just wanted you to know—'

'Which I appreciate, but what concerns me more is your personal relationship with Mr Richards.'

If those light eyes had been bright before, now they were practically translucent.

'Are you checking up on me—making sure that I obeyed orders?' she parried with a sudden flare of defiance.

'Do I need to?' he returned, his tone implying little doubt that she would have done exactly as he said. 'And it wasn't an order. I suggested—'

'Oh, it was a suggestion, was it? I'm sorry—I don't know you well enough to tell the difference.'

'My secretary could enlighten you.' Niall was completely unabashed. 'So, what have you done about Richards?'

For a second she was sorely tempted to tell him that she had done nothing at all, but then she rethought hastily. After all, he would find out for himself soon enough.

'I don't have a personal relationship with Owen any more—but that's not because of you.' She wouldn't give him the satisfaction of thinking that he commanded and she jumped. 'I realised that we weren't going anywhere— and I wanted more out of life than that. I didn't say anything about us,' she added, not sure how he would take that.

But Niall simply nodded. 'We'll leave it that way, then. There's no need for anyone to know our business. Small towns can become a hotbed of gossip.'

'I learned that fast enough when I moved here.' Saffron laughed. 'My efforts to set up A Movable Feast were the subject of an interest that's only just beginning to settle down. They'll be talking enough anyway if you take over Richards,' she added wryly. 'They're reluctant to accept anyone new around here. You'll have to work hard on public relations—coming from London, particularly.'

'You seem to have managed to.'

'Oh, well, I'm hardly from the *South*. Lincolnshire is at least north of Watford—and I did have Kate and Owen to help me settle in. It helped having the backing of the son of the area's major employer.'

'So why did you move away from home in the first place?'

'Why does anyone? Independence—proving yourself—and I wanted to assert my individuality. I suppose I felt that more than most, being the baby of such a large family.'

'All those sisters,' Niall murmured smilingly.

'I like being part of a big family! I know it's not exactly fashionable nowadays, but—'

'Hey!' Niall caught hold of the hand with which she was gesticulating furiously. 'Don't be so damn prickly! You really are defensive about your family, aren't you? Did I say anything critical?'

'No...' Saffron admitted. 'But people usually do. I'm sorry—I just thought—'

'You mean, you didn't think,' he reproved. 'Do you usually overreact like this?'

'You don't know the half of it! All my life I've been teased about my family. When I was at school there were so many whispered comments, or laughter behind my back—'

'I'm not laughing. So, tell me. What other skeletons do

you have lurking in your cupboards? You have five sisters—and, personally, I think that if they're all as lovely as you, then there couldn't be too many of them. What else?'

'My father...' Saffron murmured, the edgy, defensive feeling partly soothed by his casual compliment. But, even so, the words wouldn't come.

'Richards said something about him being an intellectual—absorbed in his books. Ruane? The only man I know by that name is the one who writes on the derivation of placenames.'

The sharp grey eyes caught Saffron's uneasy movement.

'Is he some relation to Turner Ruane?'

'Not some relation.' Saffron was surprised that Niall had heard of her father, let alone was aware of his obscure field of work. 'He *is* Turner Ruane.'

'But he must be—'

'Positively ancient,' Saffron cut in sharply. 'Old enough to be anyone else's grandfather—or even great-grandfather. I've heard them all before. And, yes, he was nearly fifty when I was born—Mum was forty-three—'

She broke off in consternation as Niall threw back his head and laughed.

'Is that all? Saffron, you had me worried that there was some terrible dark secret in your family.'

'My schoolfriends thought there was.' Saffron wasn't used to this sort of response. 'They couldn't get their heads round the fact that my parents were still—had still been—'

'Making love?' Niall supplied, when embarrassment overcame her. 'At that incredibly advanced age!'

The mockery in his voice was aimed at those so-called friends, she realised, not at her or her family.

'Why do adolescents think that they're the only ones who know about sex? I would have been proud to think that my parents still cared about each other—and you must have been very much a wanted child.'

'That's not how Agnes Richards sees it. She was frankly aghast. She sees my father as some weird, otherworldly nutty professor, shut away in his ivory tower, with no sense of reality, making no practical contribution to things.'

'And a factory that produces fireworks is *practical*?' The mockery was sharper now.

'Oh, well, that was an embarrassment to her—she only tolerated it when it was keeping her in the manner to which she'd grown accustomed. That was why she wasn't keen on my part in Owen's life. I think she thought he'd use their money to support my business—one that was rapidly failing around me.'

'Is that a fact, or just what Ma Richards would think?'

There was an odd note in Niall's voice, and the arm he had slung around her shoulders felt tense suddenly.

'Both,' Saffron admitted. 'I'm afraid that the market for freelance caterers isn't exactly huge. What I need is a very wealthy benefactor—someone to bail me out and put the whole thing on a sound footing.'

'Me?'

Niall had come to a halt again and was staring out at the river once more. After a moment he took his arm from her shoulders and bent down to pick up a large, flat pebble, aiming carefully before sending it skimming across the smooth, gleaming surface.

'Would you like me as your benefactor?'

If only! Saffron couldn't help thinking. It would solve her financial problems at a stroke. But then reality intervened, with the recollection of his cynical comment about the emotional consequences of being a rich man. His question had seemed almost *too* casual.

'Are you trying to buy up the whole of Kirkham?'

It didn't sound quite as it had inside her head; the teasing note she had aimed for came out with a flirtatious inflexion that made it seem as if she was trying to probe deeper rather than refute his suggestion.

'Would you think it would be worth my while?' To her relief, he matched her teasing. 'Would I get a good return on my investment?'

He had turned to face her again, eyes narrowed against the sun, and her heart lurched sharply on a wave of intense physical awareness.

'Oh, I don't see why not!' It was suddenly an effort to speak, with her heart beating high up in her throat so that she felt breathless and light-headed. 'Play your cards right and you could have anything you wanted.'

'Could I?'

Everything had changed. The lightness of his voice was suddenly not echoed by the flare of sensuality in his eyes, the incandescent blaze of primitive desire that was somehow shocking in contrast to his carefully civilised tone.

The second stone he had picked up to throw after the first fell from his loosened grip, to land unheeded on the grass as his other hand reached out to draw her close, the strength of his arm coming round her, holding her like a steel band, as hard fingers under her chin tilted her face up towards his.

'Could I really, Saffron? Could I have *anything* at all?'

The last words were murmured against her mouth, his lips barely brushing hers, but it was as if the delicate touch was a blazing brand, scorching right to her deepest soul, marking her out as his and drawing from her a moan of response and yearning as fiery need raged through every cell in her body.

'Anything!' she choked, pressing swift, feverish kisses on the lean planes of his cheeks, feeling the roughness of the day's growth of beard against her sensitive skin, inhaling the scent of his body. 'You know you don't have to ask!'

The thought of a future, of more time with Niall, no longer concerned her. All that mattered was here and now. And here was in Niall's arms, held so close that she could feel the rapid, uneven beat of his heart, could tangle her fingers in the sunwarmed silk of his hair. Now was being kissed until her senses reeled, until her bones became as soft and pliant as warm wax and she melted against him, waiting only to be moulded as he wanted, so that she made no protest when his hands slid under the soft cotton of her top, drifting upwards with agonisingly delicate deliberateness to the taut sensitivity of her breasts.

'I think we know all we need to know about each other,' Niall muttered, his voice thick and rough. 'This is enough—'

He kissed her again, making a deep sound of pleasure low in his throat as she let her hands wander over the tight muscles of his back and shoulders, slipping her fingers in at the neck to feel the satin warmth of his skin. But then abruptly his mood changed.

'Oh, God!' Niall's raw-toned exclamation slashed through the sensual haze that enclosed her, dragging her back to a painful awareness of reality. 'No—not here—not the first time. Saffron—honey—'

He stopped her when she would have kissed him once more, his breathing ragged and uneven.

'Saffron!' Niall's laughter was low and sensual, with a slightly shaken edge to it. 'Are you really such a wild and wanton creature that you'd let me take you here and now, on the grass, where anyone could see? But, of course, I should have expected it...'

At last, cold reality penetrated the burning haze of Saffron's thoughts. She knew what was in his mind. He was thinking of their first meeting, of the scarlet basque and tiny lacy suspender belt—those flirtatious, provocative garments that had given him quite the wrong impression of her.

Or had they? Because the trouble was that she knew that if he hadn't stopped when he had, if he had pushed a little more, pressed her just the tiniest bit harder, if he *had* wanted to make love to her right here and now, on the soft grass of the riverbank, then she would not have been able to stop him.

'Come on—'

Niall slid an arm around her waist and pulled her so close that the muscular length of his leg was against her slender limb from hip to knee, his hand resting with warm intimacy under the curve of her breast. The immediate and electric rush of warmth through her body once again told her a disturbing truth. The problem with the way she felt about this man was not whether she could become the sensual woman he believed her to be, but whether, having once given the passion he woke in her free rein, she could ever find a way to get it back under control again.

CHAPTER NINE

MUCH later, Saffron found herself wondering how she had ever got home. At times the short journey had seemed to drag on forever, each step covering only the tiniest space, at others it had been as if they were part of a film that was being played at the wrong speed, every action jerky and unnatural, the countryside flashing past at an alarming rate. Sometimes it had seemed that her legs would not support her, and that only the strength of Niall's arm was keeping her upright, moving her inexorably in the direction he wanted her to go.

And then, at last—or did she mean too soon?—they were at the gate to the cottage garden, and she didn't know whether she was on her head or her heels emotionally.

'We're here,' she managed inanely.

'Yes,' Niall said, 'we're here.'

His tone made his words much more than a statement of fact, and suddenly all her confidence deserted her, replaced by a churning sense of panic deep in her stomach, so that she practically raced up the path and into the kitchen.

'I'll make some coffee.' She spoke rapidly to cover her nervousness. 'I'm sure you could do with a drink.'

'No.'

The single, flat syllable came starkly, completely destroying what little remained of her composure, and she couldn't help but be aware of the way that Niall's silvery eyes watched her pointless, jittery movements around the room, as a collector might watch a rare butterfly he had trapped in a jam jar, beating its wings against the sides.

'Well, then, something to eat. Let me make you some—'

'I'm not hungry,' Niall cut in harshly.

When she stopped dead in the middle of the room, her wide, soft brown eyes going to his face, seeing the determination, the raw need stamped on its strong-boned features, he took a single step towards her, reaching out one strong hand and catching hold of her own nerveless fingers, drawing her gently but inexorably towards him.

'At least, not for food,' he murmured, and his eyes were no longer silver-light, but dark and smoky, his voice husky with a desire that she knew could not be communicated in words, but which coiled around her taut body, warming and loosening the tightly-strung nerves, melting her resistance, sending electrically charged impulses through pleasure spots she hadn't known existed.

'Do you want to eat?' Niall asked, and she shook her head slowly.

'No...'

And with that single syllable it was decided. There was no going back. But Saffron knew that was now the furthest thing from her mind. The only way she could think of was forward, forward into the unknown of this relationship. She closed her eyes and took a deep breath as Niall's lips came down on hers, sealing their unspoken agreement with a kiss that seared right to her heart, branding her as his, now and for whatever future they might share.

It started gently, the touch of his mouth light and surprisingly delicate, but in the space of a heartbeat it was as if that brief contact had fuelled a blazing, roaring conflagration. 'Light the blue touchpaper and stand well back,' Niall had said, describing the sparks that flew between them, but in the moment that their lips met Saffron knew that the fuse that had been lit at their first meeting had now burned away completely. The resulting explosion, inside her head and in every cell of her body, made her feel as if her blood had turned to liquid fire, melting her bones, so that she sagged against Niall and would have fallen if his arms hadn't come round her, sweeping her off her feet and carrying her out of the kitchen and towards the stairs.

In her room, he lowered her gently on to the bed, his hands coming up to cup her face as he looked deep into her eyes.

'You won't regret this,' he told her softly. 'I promise—'

'No—' Hastily Saffron placed a finger against his mouth, silencing him. 'No promises.'

She didn't need him to say anything to convince her that this was right; couldn't bear him to make any promises he couldn't keep. All that mattered was here and now, in this room, in her arms…

'Kiss me—'

Reaching up, she drew him down to her, her lips replacing her finger, communicating the gnawing, aching need that could never be assuaged by words, and with a sound that was half a sigh, half a groan deep in his throat, he came down on to the bed beside her, pulling her close to him with an urgency that spoke of the struggle he had had to keep his feelings under control.

Saffron welcomed that urgency with a tiny cry of delight. The time for hesitation, for restraint, for thought was past; now she wanted only to feel, to be taken out of herself and into a world where nothing existed beyond their two bodies and the glorious, mind-blowing sensations they could create between them.

'Is this what you want?' Niall whispered as he eased her sweatshirt from her, swiftly unclasping the front fastening of her bra and lowering his head to press his hot mouth against her breasts. 'And this—?'

She could only respond with a choked, incoherent sound of pleasure, lifting shaking hands to tangle in the jet darkness of his hair. She was incapable of words, only knew that she had never known sensation like this, a pleasure so sharp it was like a shaft of pain. She had never known what it felt like to be so desired, so wonderfully wanton, so supremely, totally female.

Her thoughts shattered, her fingers clenching in the black, silky strands, as Niall's mouth found one nipple and closed over it, tugging softly. It seemed as if the serpent of need that she had felt was now wide awake and desperately hungry, stretching its gleaming body and swaying restlessly, driven by purely primitive desire.

'Oh, Niall—Niall!'

His name was a restless, desperate litany on her lips, her voice coming and going unevenly as Niall's lips scorched a burning trail from one breast to the other, subjecting the second one to the same savage pleasure and reducing her to a mindless, shuddering state of blind delight.

'You're beautiful,' he muttered thickly against her sensitised skin, the warm, featherlight caress of his words making her arch her back in uninhibited response. 'I've wanted this since the moment I first saw you in that ridiculously provocative outfit—'

It was exactly what she hadn't wanted him to say. She didn't want him to think of that woman, the woman who wasn't really her.

'Niall...' Her voice was just a whisper, so that he had to bring his dark head down close to her lips to catch it. 'I—I'm not very good at this—'

His laughter was low and soft, his mouth curving warmly.

'Oh, Saffron, sweetheart, you don't have to worry—this isn't some sort of test. It will be fine—trust me. Just relax—'

And she did trust him—completely. In that moment she would have given him her soul if he had asked for it. Because it seemed that Niall, with his burning kisses, his fiendishly knowledgeable touch, that seemed to know exactly where to caress her in order to appease one hunger and awaken another in the same shattering moment, was the man she had been created for. This was so right, it had to have been written into the script of her life from the moment she had been born. It was as inevitable and necessary to life itself as every breath she drew into her body.

Impatient now, fingers clumsy with need, they found buttons, fastenings, until their clothes fell discarded to the floor. The silence of the early evening was broken by Saffron's small sharp cries of pleasure as Niall's kisses and caresses woke responses that were even stronger and more demanding than before.

'Yes—oh, yes—'

The word beat at her brain like the wild, uneven pulsing of her heart, and under her cheek she heard it echoed in the ragged breathing that told of Niall's loosening grip on his control as those tormenting hands moved lower, touching the very core of her, so that he knew without a word having to be spoken that she was open to him, the crescendo of passion reaching its peak as the hard, muscular length of his body moved over hers.

Helplessly she clung to him, her fingers digging into the silken warmth of his skin, into the powerful strength beneath it. Niall's groan of pleasure as their bodies became one mingled with her own cry of shocked delight before the sound was crushed back into her throat by the pressure of his lips on hers.

'I knew it could be like this,' he muttered against her lips. 'Now you see why I had to act, why I had to separate you from Richards. Would he ever be able to do this to you?'

Hot fingers scorched a trail over the sensitised tip of one aching breast and Saffron cried aloud at the exquisite pleasure he was inflicting on her.

'Could he make you respond like this? Could he make you beg for his kisses—his touch?'

'No—' It was a moan of torment and delight that escaped her. 'No—never—never—'

'Of course not. He never knew you—but I did. I knew you could be like this—that together—'

He broke off on a sharp gasp as beneath him she moved with intuitive eroticism, needing to feel him deeper within her as she reached for the culmination that she knew was now so close—so close...

But when it came she was totally unprepared for the intensity of it, for the explosions that went off inside her, the rockets that soared upwards in a stream of multicoloured sparks in her mind. From somewhere she heard a voice, gasping Niall's name, almost sobbing in reaction, and was shocked to realise that it was her own, and that as the white-hot blaze of ecstasy slowly subsided to the shuddering, sweat-slicked exhaustion of repletion, she had no idea what she had said, having lost all control of her tongue as well as her body.

But Niall seemed to need no words as his breathing

gradually slowed to a comfortable pace and he curled strong arms around her, drawing her into the warmth of his body and holding her there, safe and secure and totally at peace, until relaxation drifted into deep and totally restful sleep, with her head pillowed on his chest, her dark hair spread out across his shoulder.

She had no idea how long they lay like that, legs tangled together, his arms still holding her. She only knew that at some point she was wakened by the warm, enticing touch of his wandering hands, the soft caress of his fingers arousing that yearning need in her slowly and surely, until she was once more reaching for him, clinging to him, wanting to feel the deep, fulfilment of his lovemaking all over again.

When she finally surfaced fully enough to become aware of her surroundings, it was to find that night had closed in on them while they lay oblivious to its approach, and that now her small bedroom was in darkness, only the weak rays of the half-moon coming in through the uncurtained window giving enough light by which to see. As Saffron stirred tentatively Niall's arm tightened about her waist, and he lifted his head slightly to whisper in her ear.

'Now I *am* hungry. Starving, in fact. What about you?'

As if in answer to his question, her stomach growled a protest at being left empty for so long, and she felt rather than saw the smile that curled his wide mouth, the laughter that shook his strong body.

'Enough said. Do you have any food in this doll's house of yours?'

'Plenty. Enough even to feed an outsize brute like you several square meals.' Indignation coloured her tone, causing Niall to lever himself up, supported on one elbow, and look down into her moonlit face.

'It seems I've put my foot in it somewhere, without meaning to. So, tell me, sweetheart, why so huffy?'

That soft-toned 'sweetheart' almost defeated her, all the more so because it was accompanied by a lazy, sleepy smile, those silver eyes gleaming warmly under heavy lids.

'I wish you wouldn't refer to my home so disparagingly! I realise that it must seem microscopic to you when compared to what you're used to, but I love it! It may only be two up, two down, but it's all mine—and after years of no privacy, of sharing with one or more sisters, that means a lot, I can tell you.'

'All right, I'm sorry!'

The defensive gesture Niall made with his hands, lifting them up before his face as if to protect himself from her furious glare, was belied by the laughter in his eyes.

'I won't speak ill of the place ever again—it's a little palace! It wasn't meant to sound disparaging,' he went on, sobering abruptly. 'And I certainly never intended to compare it to my place in London—'

'No, I don't suppose you did.'

Saffron didn't want him to talk about his home or London. To do so seemed too much like a bitter reminder that he had a life that was completely separate from this time spent with her, a life to which he would eventually return, leaving her behind.

'Now—what about a meal?' Hastily she turned the conversation on to less worrying topics. 'What would you like to eat?'

'Don't go to any trouble.'

Niall stretched lazily, rolling over on to his back and freeing her from the sensual imprisonment of the warm weight of his body.

'Just something light—' a grin surfaced, wickedly teasing, like the glinting glance he slanted in her direction '—so that I can get my strength back…'

'Right—' Saffron flung back the covers and swung her legs out of bed. 'Would you like a shower?'

'If you'll share it with me.'

The grin had widened, becoming positively lascivious, and belatedly Saffron became aware of her naked state, her embarrassment made all the worse by the fact that the bronze and gold scarf which she had tied round her throat still remained at her neck, like some long-ago slave necklace.

'I don't think that's a good idea.' Hastily she reached for her robe and pulled it on. 'It's late already, and if I don't get on it will be midnight before we eat.'

It was foolish to feel so awkward, now, after all the intimacies they had shared, but the truth was that she had no experience of anything like this, and the sight of Niall, so dark and strong, so devastatingly *male*, in the intimacy of her white and gold bedroom, where no man had ever set foot before, had put her completely off-balance.

'OK.' Niall's agreement came with surprising equanimity when she had nerved herself for something more. 'You're probably right,' he added with a swift glance at the clock. 'But I will take that shower, if you don't mind—'

'Be my guest.'

Saffron's heart was starting to race uncomfortably. Niall's movement, small as it was, had made the covers drop from the muscled lines of his chest down to his narrow waist. If he sat up any more, then the whole of his magnificent body would be revealed… With an effort she dragged her eyes away, turning to the door.

'There are fresh towels in the airing cupboard—'

Get a grip! she told herself as she hurried downstairs.

Niall was a sophisticated man of the world. He must have been in this situation many times—it was nothing new to him! He would treat it simply as a natural development—and would expect her to do the same. She had no chance of convincing him that she could handle the sort of casual affair he clearly wanted if she didn't show a little more sophistication herself.

She had set the kitchen table, prepared a salad, put tiny new potatoes on to boil and was busy beating eggs for a substantial omelette by the time she heard Niall's footsteps descending the stairs.

'Won't be a minute,' she said, putting her head round the door, and immediately wishing she hadn't as the sight of Niall, fresh from his shower, with his jet-black hair still damp and showing a disconcerting tendency to curl at his temples and the nape of his neck, was thoroughly disturbing to her carefully imposed mental equilibrium. 'Would you like a drink?'

'No thanks.'

He was looking around him with interest, taking in the details of her living-room.

'Do you realise that this is the first time I've really seen your home properly? The other times I've been in this room we haven't exactly stayed around for long.'

His smile was one of sensual satisfaction, like the expression of a well-fed tiger, so that she knew he was recalling just why they hadn't lingered.

'I like your home, Saffron. It may only be small but it has character.' His gesture indicated the embroidered shawl draped over the settee, the toning pastel cushions.

'It didn't look at all like this when I moved in—it was a real dump then. I did all the painting myself, and made the curtains,' she added with a touch of pride. 'Mum and a couple of my sisters wanted to come and help, or at least do some of the sewing, but I wanted it to be all my own. They would have hated my choice of colours—or tried to pass on things from their homes that they thought I could use. Sometimes being the baby of the family can be a real pain.'

'They won't let you grow up?'

'That's about it—that's why I could never have stayed in Lincolnshire. There were too many Ruanes—too much family. I had to find myself—develop my own individuality.'

Niall glanced round the room again. 'It looks like you've managed to do that.'

'Mmm.' Saffron's smile was full of satisfaction. 'I've just about got it how I want— What's wrong?' she asked, seeing the way his head had suddenly turned and he seemed to be listening hard.

'Is there something cooking that could—?' He didn't have to finish the sentence.

'The potatoes!'

Niall followed as she dashed back into the kitchen and turned down the heat under the pan, leaning one hip up against the worktop and watching her as she wiped up the spilled water and then poured the egg mixture into a pan. A glossy magazine lay on the windowsill and he picked it up, studying it for a moment.

'Do you have a subscription to every magazine under the sun? Or have you raided a newsagent's lately? The magazines—' he added when she turned a puzzled frown on him '—you must have half a dozen on the coffee-table in there—and—'

'Oh, that's a weakness of mine.' Saffron concentrated fiercely on her cooking. 'Another result of being one of six.'

'How?' Niall questioned curiously. 'I don't quite follow the logic.'

'Well, bedrooms weren't the only things we had to share. There wasn't a lot of money to go around so treats like magazines were fairly strictly rationed. We did get them, but never one each. So there was a strict rota—one week Mollie got it first, then Karis, and so on. It was great when you were number one or two, but when you had to wait until *everyone* had read it—that could take all week. Some of my sisters were very slow readers! So now, my idea of a treat is a brand-new, pristine, glossy magazine—untouched by human hand.'

She slipped the finished omlettes on to warmed plates and put them on the table.

'Supper's ready—'

She broke off in surprise and shock as Niall moved, but not to sit down. Instead, he slid a hand under her chin, lifting her face to his, and placed a swift, firm kiss on her half-open mouth.

'Wh-what was that for?'

'Just wanted to.' Niall laughed at her stunned expression. 'This looks good,' he went on, settling himself in a chair and reaching for the bowl of salad. 'And I suppose that you'll justify all those clothes upstairs in much the same way as the magazines?'

'Well, if you'd spent as much of your life in hand-me-downs as I have—'

Saffron stopped dead at the realisation of what his remark meant, the pan falling from her hand and landing in the sink with a clatter.

'You've been poking round my bedroom?'

'Oh, come on Saffron.' His tone mocked her indignation. 'I'd have to be completely blind to miss the fact that your one small wardrobe is bursting at the seams. I didn't have to look inside.'

'I'd still prefer it if you respected my privacy.'

'My, I have ruffled your feathers, haven't I? Don't worry, sweetheart, I'm not like your family—I'm not about to take over and dictate how you run your life or decorate your precious nest. What's really bugging you, Saffron?' he went on, when she continued to glare at him. 'It can't just be that you're worried about what I might think of your clothes. After all, I'm already well aware of the fact that what you were wearing on our first meeting isn't exactly typical of your usual style.'

'But you would say it was more revealing of my character.'

'Well, let's say that it was an interesting pointer to a side of you that perhaps isn't quite so obvious to everyone.'

'And that's the side—'

'Damn it, no it isn't!' Niall broke in on her angrily, anticipating what she had been about to say. 'I am not so shallow as to make up my mind about you—or anyone—on the strength of a first impression.'

Reaching out, he caught hold of her hand and drew her gently towards him, his strength making a nonsense of her stubborn determination to resist.

'And I'm well aware of the fact that there's more to you than met the eye at our first meeting.'

Deliberately he let his silver gaze slide to the point at the neck of her robe where her breasts curved under the towelling, and when he lifted his eyes to her face again his smile was hard to resist.

'So, is it so terrible that I want to know as much as I can about you?'

Put like that, she could hardly say yes, could she?

'No, of course not.' She managed to smile, sitting down opposite him. 'And I admit to loving new clothes. Though, of course, I'll have to stop buying them now—'

'Why's that?'

'Can't afford them. Most of what's in my wardrobe was bought during the first heady months, when A Movable Feast was actually making a profit. And, of course, some were presents—'

'From Owen?' Niall put in, when a reluctance to bring the other man's name into the conversation made her hesitate.

Saffron nodded. 'I realise that really they were bought more for his sake than mine—Owen liked to project the right sort of image—we were always out somewhere. So of course I had to look the part.'

'I always knew the man was a fool,' Niall growled.

'But I think it's your turn now.' Saffron wanted to get well away from the subject of Owen. 'You know about my family—it's time you told me about yours.'

'Nothing so interesting or numerous as your crowd,' Niall said, helping himself to potatoes. 'I only have one brother.'

'The one who married the girl—I'm sorry.' Saffron cursed herself for her foolishness in touching on the prickly subject again.

'No problem. I told you, it's over—she chose the right brother.'

'Is he older or younger than you?' she asked, simply for something to say.

'Older—but only by eighteen months. My parents fully intended to stop at one, but nature thought otherwise, and I was what Mother calls her happy accident. Andrew looks a lot like me but we're very different characters— chalk and cheese. Andy's a university lecturer—in philosophy—and he's happily settled into marriage with a two-year-old daughter and twins on the way.'

'Twins!' Saffron choked on a mouthful of omelette. 'Do twins run in your family?'

'My father has a twin sister—but you needn't worry.' The grey eyes looked deep into her stunned brown ones. 'I'll always make sure you're protected—as I did tonight. There'll be no risk.'

He had seen her consternation, the tangle of emotions in her face, and had misinterpreted her reaction. Saffron knew that she ought to feel thankful that he had no inkling of the real reason for her distress. He must never know that she had suddenly been prey to a weak and foolish longing to know what Niall's children would look like— twin boys or girls, with his black hair and clear, light-coloured eyes...

'Are you sure you won't have a drink?' It was an effort to speak naturally. 'There's wine—'

'Not when I'm driving, thanks.'

'Oh, but—driving?' The full impact of what he had said hit home. 'Where—'

'I have to get back to the hotel. My secretary has probably left all sorts of messages for me. I only took the time to let her know where I was staying before I came on here.'

But he had done that. Saffron's appetite suddenly deserted her.

'I'm surprised you didn't phone Owen while you were at it—perhaps arrange a few meetings...'

Her voice was tart, disguising the hurt she felt. For a brief space of time she had let herself live in a delusion, allowed herself to think he put her first in his life, and it was only now, when it had been stripped away from her, that she saw just how much that dream had meant to her.

'I am here to work, Saffron. Officially, this trip is business, not pleasure.'

'And me? What heading do I come under?'

Niall's lips curved into a smile that warmed the rather cool expression that had made his face distant a moment before.

'You know you could never be anything other than pleasure.' The smile grew, becoming sensual in a way that matched the gleam that turned those silver eyes translucent. 'So much so that my hotel bed is going to feel hellishly empty without you.'

'I could always come with you,' Saffron suggested, her sense of hurt slightly appeased by his huskily seductive words.

But Niall shook his head with a decisiveness that left no room for further argument.

'I never mix business and pleasure—it's a combination that just doesn't work. Besides, I thought we agreed to keep things private. If you turned up at my hotel the whole town would soon be talking. Now, where did I leave my jacket?'

'In my room—'

It was at the foot of her bed, discarded in the heat of their passion—a passion that seemed to have cooled so very rapidly, on Niall's part at least. But then, almost every action, every word he said, drove home to her the fact that his feelings were nothing like her own. With a struggle she schooled her features into a detachment to match Niall's as he came back down the stairs, the leather jacket slung over one shoulder.

'I'll be in touch.'

She couldn't believe the lightness of his tone. Was this the same man who had held her so close, whose voice, raw and rough with desire, had whispered such erotic compliments in her burning ears only an hour or so before? If he had ever felt that blazing desire, now it was well damped-down and totally under control.

'You know where I am.' Her smile switched on and off like a neon sign, and she fumbled with the handle as she opened the door.

'Hey—don't look like that. I'll only be a few miles down the road. We have a couple of very exciting months ahead of us.'

A couple of months—and then what? Did she have to ask? He'd made it only too plain from the start.

'Come here—'

Reaching out, Niall caught hold of the bronze scarf that she had forgotten was still round her throat. Pulling gently on it, he drew her near enough to kiss her thoroughly, then let her go, running one strong hand through the tumbled dark hair that fell in wild abandon on to her shoulders.

'Sleep well, sweetheart...' And with a careless wave he was gone.

'Sleep well'! 'Only a few miles down the road'! Saffron felt that never before had she understood the meaning of so near and yet so far. Niall was here in Kirkham, with her and yet not truly *with* her. She was just a passing fancy to him, another of those things that he wanted and so was determined to have—and, like a fool, she was weak enough to accept that little from him.

Slowly, with an empty ache deep inside her, Saffron locked up and headed upstairs, unable to face the washing-up until morning. The sight of her untidy bed, the tangled sheets and covers evidence of the passionate activity that had filled the early hours of the evening, made her push her hand into her mouth, biting down hard on her fingers against the cry of pain that almost escaped her.

She had told herself that she could cope with the sort of affair Niall wanted, but now she was prey to terrible doubts on that score. Could she really go through with this? And yet, as she felt the soft cotton of her towelling robe brush against skin still sensitised by the urgent touch of Niall's hands, nipples still faintly raw from his kisses, she knew there was no way she could deny herself the excitement, the fulfilment she had felt in his arms.

She tidied up the damp towels Niall had used, steeling her senses against the sensual impact of the scent of his body that still lingered on them, and moved to open the wash-basket, meaning only to drop them in and close the lid. But the sight of the scarlet strips of silk, the basque, suspender belt and lacy panties that still lay at the bottom of the container, thrown there in haste two weeks before and never touched since then, stopped her dead.

She had known something was missing from her life, and had decided, quite rationally, that passion—or at least sex—was the vital element things lacked. And so she had bought those ridiculous garments—seductive underwear as unsubtle as a stripper's provocative outfit—and decked herself out in them in order to play a part, and the truth was that a part was all it had been.

'The sacrifical lamb,' Kate had called her, and looking back at herself, sitting in this house, decked out in all her tawdry glory, waiting for Owen, Saffron was appalled at how accurate the description was. She had been prepared to give herself to Owen in a sense of sacrifice, to fill an emptiness that she had thought meant she needed more from him, when in fact it should have told her quite the opposite. She had tried to force herself to feel something she could never feel, and she could only be thankful that she had never actually gone through with it. How much more empty she would have felt then.

With Niall, it had been so very different. With him, she hadn't needed any of those 'props', any fancy dress, and when the time had come there had been no hesitation, no doubts, and even now, whatever the future held, she had no regrets.

So what made the difference? Standing there, clutching the damp towels to her like some sort of talisman, she found that her heart actually seemed to stop for a moment as she faced a truth that was at once so simple and yet so desperately, hopelessly complicated that it would affect the rest of her life, for better or worse.

She had had no doubts, no fears with Niall because he was the man she loved—the man to whom she had given her heart and soul in the same moment that she had given him her body.

CHAPTER TEN

'NOT another bookshop!'

Saffron's voice was full of a resigned exasperation that had Niall pausing in mid-stride, his foot on the step up to the shop doorway.

'We must have been into every one in the city.'

'Just this one. I want to look for—'

'Oh, go on!'

Saffron laughed her defeat. It would take a far harder heart than she possessed to refuse him anything when he turned on that boyishly appealing charm, that devastating smile, even though she knew only too well that it was deliberately calculated to have just that affect.

'But don't expect me to stand around and wait while you become lost in some musty old tome.'

'There won't be any musty tomes in here!' Niall protested. 'We've exhausted all the secondhand shops.'

'Exhausted is the word. And they were definitely dusty, if not musty—as I know to my cost,' Saffron grumbled, rueful eyes going to the dark streak which marred her ivory cotton sleeveless tunic and skirt. Niall, however, had managed to keep his cool linen suit and black T-shirt immaculate as always. 'My feet are aching and I'm dying of thirst.'

'Then the next stop will be somewhere for tea—I promise.'

'Betty's?' Saffron asked cajolingly, her spirits lifting. 'You really can't come to York and not have tea at

Betty's. I tell you what,' she added at Niall's nod of agreement, 'we'll probably have to queue for a table—it's always packed, even this late on in the summer—so why don't I go on ahead and you can meet me there? Davygate, remember? Bottom of this street and turn left.'

The queue inside the famous tearooms was every bit as long as she had anticipated, spilling out on to the pavement, but, knowing how efficiently the staff dealt with things, clearing tables and seating people as soon as possible, she was content to wait outside, enjoying the warmth of the late August sun.

As she leaned back against the wall, she let her mind drift back over the past three months—months that had brought her some of the best moments of her life. Being able to spend time with Niall, to see him, talk to him, to make love with him and, above all else, to love him, had filled her days with a joy and brightness, a sense of purpose such as she had never known before.

But in order for it to do so, she had had to accept the limitations Niall put on the relationship. That first night in her cottage had set the tone for the way things were to be. Business and pleasure were strictly defined areas, and one never mixed with the other, and as he often worked late into the evening that meant that she rarely saw him except for a belated meal.

'Wouldn't it be easier if I came to you?' she had asked one evening when he hadn't arrived at her home until ten. 'After all, I do work in Kirkham, and it would save you the long drive out.'

'I don't mind,' Niall had returned. 'It helps me wind down at the end of the day—gives me time to think—'

'About work?' Saffron couldn't erase the tart note from her voice.

'That and other things. Don't sulk, Saffron, it doesn't suit you.'

'I'm not sulking—it's just, I never see you—'

'I know, but these meetings are important.'

'Well, then—' inspiration put a gleam in her eye '—surely the people you're talking to have to eat some time. Couldn't we kill two birds with one stone?'

'No.' It was flat, emotionless, and totally decisive. 'I thought we agreed to keep our relationship private—that you didn't want people talking.'

'I know—but—'

But sometimes it seemed that Niall's insistence on privacy worked more in his favour than her own. He dictated the terms, decided when or not he could see her, and she was reduced to sitting at home, waiting for him.

'I thought you'd had enough of that with Richards—whose mama, incidentally, is still spitting acid over the way she thinks you ditched him.'

'You'd think she'd be relieved. After all, she was convinced that all I was after was the family fortune. But I suppose that, considering herself the nearest thing Kirkham has to a local aristocracy, she believes that it reflects badly on her reputation to have a mere working girl turn down her precious son and heir.'

'All the more reason not to let her know that you've replaced him with me.'

'True.' Saffron gave a faint shudder at the thought of Agnes Richards' vindictiveness if she was to find out.

'Besides—' Niall's glance at her was seductively enticing, the colour of his eyes deepening to the soft tones of antique pewter '—I much prefer it this way. In Kirkham, and at the factory, I have to be polite to so many people. When I'm here I can relax...'

His hand was sliding up her spine, stroking the delicate skin of her back, making her arch like a sensual cat.

'There's just the two of us, and I have you all to myself.'

The smile grew, becoming as warm as his caresses, drawing her to him as irresistibly as the deceptively gentle pressure of his hands.

'And that's just the way I want it. How could I ever work with you? I wouldn't be able to concentrate. When I looked at you, all I'd be able to think of would be doing this—' His mouth drifted along the side of her cheek. 'And this—'

As his lips captured hers, Saffron abandoned any thought of arguing with him further, the explosion of sensual awareness that he could set alight simply by touching her driving everything else from her mind. She loved and wanted Niall more than she had ever wanted any other man in her life and, that being so, she knew that she had no alternative but to accept his unspoken conditions, no matter how personally unsatisfactory she found them, to accept only the passionate sexual pleasure and easy companionship that was all Niall was prepared to offer, without asking for any more.

'Well, this is a surprise! I never expected to meet you here!' The unexpected sound of a man's voice jolted Saffron back to the present and she glanced up swiftly, squinting into the sun.

'Hello, Owen,' she said carefully. 'How are things with you?'

'OK.' Owen didn't sound as enthusiastic as she might have expected. 'But no thanks to that bastard Forrester. Did you know he did me out of thousands?'

'Hardly.' Saffron didn't trouble to erase the tartness

from her voice. After several months away from him, Owen sounded even more like a spoiled child to her than she remembered. 'You were asking way over the odds for the factory.'

'No more than he could afford—but, no, he'd rather spend his money on some bimbo who's caught his fancy. You didn't know about that?' he asked, seeing Saffron's start and misinterpreting the reason for it.

'I'd not heard anything.'

And she was frankly surprised that Owen had either. Niall had been so determined to keep their relationship from becoming general knowledge that they had never actually been out together in Kirkham, heading further afield for such trips to restaurants or theatres that they had been on. But the truth was that they had spent more time in Saffron's cottage—more often than not in her bed—than anywhere else.

'Oh, well, I don't expect she'll last much longer.' Owen hadn't noticed her abstracted silence. 'From what I hear, they never do. Forrester isn't noted for the length of his attachments, and Ron Bassett tells me he's not renewing the lease on his flat after September.'

Saffron managed another choked sound that might have been a response, unable to hide her relief when Owen moved on. She had forgotten that one of his friends owned the building where Niall had found a short-term let, and so, presumably, would be well aware of his future plans.

And more aware of them than she was, apparently. Niall had said nothing to her about leaving Kirkham.

Owen had barely disappeared round the corner when Niall appeared, triumphantly brandishing a bulging carrier bag.

'I found exactly what I was looking for. There's a particular historical saga my mother's deeply into—something about a Scottish adventurer in the sixteenth century—and she's been desperately hunting for volumes four and five. I got them both. Saffron?'

'Oh, sorry...' Saffron dragged her thoughts away from Owen's disturbing comments with an effort, and forced herself to switch on a bright smile. 'That's great. There's nothing worse than being part-way through something totally absorbing and not being able to find the next volume.'

'Especially when she's already bought part six—the final one—and has been struggling not to open it until she's filled in the missing bits.'

When he smiled like that her very soul lit up, Saffron thought, the sting of Owen's sneering comments easing in her heart. After all, he hadn't told her anything she didn't already know or suspect, so why should she let it get her down? But the problem was that what Owen had said had brought to the forefront of her mind something that she had been trying to avoid confronting for the past couple of weeks.

Niall's time in Kirkham wouldn't last forever. He had already spent over three months here, and according to local gossip the changes he had set in motion at Richards' were almost complete. Inevitably, sooner rather than later, he would be thinking of returning to London, and what would happen to her then?

'Why the solemn face?' Niall asked, but before Saffron could think of an answer to give him the queue moved forward suddenly and, because those in front of them wanted seats for more than two, they found themselves unexpectedly shown to the first available table, and the awkward moment passed without comment.

'I'm glad we're here and not downstairs,' Saffron said, looking around at the huge plate glass windows, decorated at the top with a stained glass design of green and gold leaves, that surrounded the ground floor of the café. 'Of course, the food is wonderful wherever you sit, but being downstairs can seem a bit enclosed.'

'Well, if you recommend this place, it must be good. I've enough experience of your cooking to value your opinion. So, tell me, what do you suggest I try?'

'Well, a Yorkshire Fat Rascal is a speciality. That's like a rich scone made with butter, spices, almonds, citrus peel and cherries. Or they do a dark and light chocolate torte that would turn a saint into a sinner. And then there are the chocolate or coffee éclairs—'

'Hang on!' Niall protested laughingly. 'You'll make it impossible to choose.'

'Then pick one for now, and we'll buy a selection of the others to take home—'

She caught herself up sharply on that revealing 'home', but luckily Niall appeared too absorbed in the menu to notice, and at that moment a smiling waitress appeared to take their order.

'I didn't think you'd be able to resist a Fat Rascal,' she commented when they were alone again. 'Though I suspected it might be a toss-up between that and the chocolate torte.'

Niall nodded, his smile a sensual curl of his lips, silver eyes gleaming wickedly.

'I'm going to follow your suggestion and take some home.' The smile grew, his eyes seeming translucent in the afternoon sunlight. 'Then I'm going to feed it to you bit by bit—while undressing you between each mouthful—'

'Niall!' Saffron whispered sharply, well aware of the fiery colour that had rushed into her cheeks. 'Behave!'

His words sounded particularly indecent in the very proper surroundings of the elegant tearooms, with the clink of china teacups and the subdued murmur of polite conversation acting as a backdrop.

'Can I help it if your beauty would turn a saint into a sinner?' he asked in mock innocence, echoing her own comment of a few moments earlier.

'Flatterer! And I very much doubt that you were ever any sort of saint!'

'Maybe not, but now that I've found those books for my mother, that's at least one person who'll consider me a candidate for canonisation. And I expect Jayne will be pleased too—she'd started on volume one the last time I saw her— What is it?'

Disturbingly, those sharp grey eyes had caught Saffron's change of expression, the way she had shifted uncomfortably in her chair at the mention of the woman he had once cared about.

'Isn't it difficult for you to see her like that? I mean— married to your brother and pregnant with his children?'

If the roles were reversed, and she had to see Niall married to someone else, she didn't think she would be able to bear it.

'Not at all,' Niall returned calmly. 'Looking back, I don't think I ever loved Jayne at all. It was just that I got misled by the fact that she was a rare sort of woman who liked me for myself and not just for the money I earned. Anyway, as I told you, she and Andy are perfect for each other.'

'So you do believe in love for other people?' Saffron

looked down at her plate to hide the pain she knew must show in her eyes.

'With my parents celebrating forty years of marriage just before Christmas I'd be a fool not to—it's just that I've no experience of the emotion myself to judge by. In all my life I've never found anything I couldn't turn my back on in the end.'

'And just walk away.' She couldn't completely erase the uneven note from her voice. Was this a warning? Was he telling her that before too long he would turn his back on her and walk out of her life?

'Usually it's kinder that way.' The cool detachment of his tone sent an icy shiver down her spine. He sounded as if he was already halfway out of the door, mentally at least.

His tone reminded her sharply of the way he had spoken some weeks before, when, just in case she had had any doubts about the limitations he put on their relationship, he had made his position painfully clear.

'That damn place needs more work than I'd ever anticipated to get it put right, and it won't be done in a couple of weeks,' he had told her a couple of days after he had finally taken over the factory. 'I'm going to have to stay in Kirkham for much longer than I thought at first—possibly even until November.'

It had cost Saffron a great deal of effort to school her face into an expression that hid the stabbing disappointment she felt at the thought that, as always, it was business that would keep him in Kirkham, not any commitment to her.

'Will you stay at the Swan all that time?' she had asked carefully, and Niall had shaken his dark head in rejection of the idea.

'I'll have to find a temporary base somewhere for the next five months. I'm certainly not prepared to put up with hotel accommodation for that long.'

'There's always this place,' she had suggested, aiming for what she hoped was casual indifference, so that he wouldn't suspect any of the emotional baggage that went along with the offer.

For a long second he had seemed to consider the idea, but a moment later she was intensely relieved that she had made the offer sound as if it didn't matter to her one way or the other as he shook his head in firm rejection of her suggestion.

'I don't think so. I need to be nearer the factory, in case anyone wants to contact me. Somewhere in Kirkham would be better.'

Of course it would, Saffron had told herself on a wave of bitter disappointment, recognising a careful cover-up when she saw one. He wouldn't want the sort of commitment implied by moving in with her, even for a short space of time. After all, he still didn't even want their relationship to be generally known.

'Saffron?' Belatedly she became aware that Niall had spoken and she hadn't heard a word.

'I—I'm sorry—'

'I was just saying that talking of my parents has reminded me—it's Dad's birthday at the end of next week and I really should get him a present before I forget. He'd be fascinated to read about your father's work—so would Andy...'

'Is this an excuse to go back to the bookshop?' Saffron didn't know how she kept her voice so light. She even managed a smile.

'Just for a minute—five at the most—but you said you wanted to visit the Minster, so I could see you there.'

It was a good job that she had privately added an extra ten minutes to the five that Niall had promised he would be, Saffron reflected almost twenty minutes later, as she wandered around the cool, echoing aisles of the ancient Minster. Once inside a bookshop, he completely lost all track of time.

A sudden prickle of awareness alerted her to the fact that she was being watched, and, looking up, she saw the subject of her thoughts standing just inside the main doorway, watching her with a strange, unreadable look on his face. As soon as he realised that she had seen him, he switched on a smile that disturbed and disconcerted her by the speed with which it came and went, like a flashing neon sign.

'Did you get what you wanted?'

Silently Niall shook his dark head, seeming disinclined to speak.

'Oh, well, you'll find it somewhere else, I'm sure.'

She wasn't really surprised by his sudden silence. The Minster had had that effect on her too, the first time she had set foot inside it. She had felt as if her tongue had frozen in her mouth in awe at the sight of the spectacular, soaring columns, the glorious stained glass windows.

'It's all been beautifully restored, hasn't it? You'd never know there'd ever been that terrible fire. Niall?' This was more than just stunned appreciation. 'Is there something wrong?'

He seemed to drag himself back from a long way away.

'Sorry—my mind was somewhere else.'

Somewhere none too pleasant, to judge from his expression, Saffron told herself. His eyes were clouded, the muscles around his mouth drawn tight. But he clearly didn't want to talk about it, and she knew it was best not to try and probe too deeply. To do so was to risk setting a match to the mental equivalent of a keg of gunpowder. So she confined her conversation to innocuous facts about the Minster and the turbulent history of York itself, finding the effort of maintaining a flow of trivial chatter harder and harder in the face of Niall's monosyllabic unresponsiveness, until finally she turned to him in exasperation as they walked down the narrow cobbled street called the Shambles.

'Have you had enough history—is that it? Because if so we might as well go home.'

'Fine,' was Niall's only response, and without another word he turned on his heel and set off towards the car park, his long stride covering the ground at such a pace that Saffron was forced to break into a trot to catch him up.

'Just what is the matter?' she demanded breathlessly as Niall bent to unlock the car.

'Matter?' he sounded as if he didn't understand what the word meant. But then a moment later he seemed to give himself another mental shake. 'Like you said—too much history.'

That smile flashed across his face again, looking even more unconvincing in the sunlight.

'I've OD'd on medieval and Roman facts,' he said brusquely, getting into the car.

Niall's silence persisted throughout the journey back to Saffron's cottage, any attempt at conversation effectively prevented by the way he put on a cassette tape of Carreras singing selections from popular operas at the sort of volume that drowned any other sound. As a result, by the time they drew up outside the tiny house, her nerves were so tightly stretched that she felt they would snap if she didn't find out soon just what was behind the uncomfortable change in his mood, even if, as she feared, it was a prelude to his breaking off their relationship.

'Are you coming in for supper? You said you wanted to watch that film on television.'

She had to ask, even though she very much suspected she knew what the answer was going to be. So much for feeding her chocolate torte bit by bit, she thought on a wave of disappointment.

'No—yes—' he corrected himself sharply. 'But nothing to eat, thanks. I couldn't manage anything after that Fat Rascal.'

For a brief moment a touch of rueful humour showed in his eyes and Saffron's heart lifted. Perhaps he'd got over whatever had annoyed him. Most likely, it was just not being able to find the book that he wanted. But when Niall dumped the bookshop carrier bag on the kitchen table, the first thing that slid out of it was an all too familiar volume.

'Dad's book! But you said—'

'Yeah—well—I was thinking of something else.'

'Obviously!'

'I saw Owen in York.'

Saffron's tart comment and Niall's quiet statement clashed in the air and then there was a sudden, taut silence during which her brain was suddenly thrown into overdrive. Was this what had put him into such a foul mood? Alarm-bells were going off inside her head.

'So did I.'

Her response was careful. She was thoroughly disconcerted by the way Niall's eyes narrowed suddenly, and he watched her closely, as if he expected her to say something more, but then abruptly his mood seemed to change.

'I'm parched—how about a drink?'

'There's lager in the fridge—and mineral water. Or I—'

'Water's fine.' He poured himself a large glassful and drank it down with obvious relish.

It *was* hot, Saffron reflected. Hot and close. The warmth of the late summer afternoon was turning to a sticky, sultry evening that seemed to threaten a coming storm.

'How's business at A Movable Feast these days?' Niall asked abruptly.

'No better. Not good—bloody awful, in fact.' The past months had seen no improvement in her financial position and things were getting close to desperate.

'Would a contract help?'

He was lounging back against one of the white-painted units, one long-fingered hand toying idly with his now empty glass, but he looked anything but relaxed. Saffron had been about to suggest that they go into the livingroom and sit down, but something about his attitude made her pause. There was a tension, an aura of danger about him that made her think worryingly of the ominously dark clouds now gathering thickly on the horizon.

'Would it! You bet. You don't happen to have one hidden up your sleeve—I'll bite your hand off for it if you do.'

She wished he would look at her. It was thoroughly disconcerting trying to conduct a conversation with someone whose eyes were fixed firmly on the opposite wall.

'I've been thinking about the factory,' Niall went on inconsequentially. 'Everyone's worked damned hard on the improvements, and they deserve some sort of celebration—something everyone can join in. So, as November the fifth seems appropriate, I was thinking of a mammoth bonfire and fireworks display—open to all of Kirkham. It would combine enjoyment with some good publicity. We might even make it an annual event. We'd need food, of course—and that's where you come in.'

'You want us to do it?' All Saffron's earlier sense of constraint vanished under the rush of enthusiasm. 'Oh, yes please! Just tell me what you want. And I don't suppose you've thought about staff lunches at the factory—or at least sandwiches.' Her smile was pleading, cajoling. 'We could do those too…'

No, she'd pushed a bit too hard there—a mistake. She knew from the way Niall's face changed, the overly precise way he replaced his empty glass on the worktop. It doesn't matter—forget the idea, she was about to say, but just then Niall did look at her, and immediately she wished that he hadn't, because there was no warmth in those light eyes, only the cold, expressionless gleam of hard ice.

'Did you ever consider taking on another partner in your business—if only a sleeping one? Someone who would invest enough money to keep you afloat during this rough patch?'

Why did she suddenly feel like some small, vulnerable animal, sensing a hunter's trap but not knowing exactly where it might be?

'Well, actually, I did ask Owen if he'd consider doing just that when he sold the factory—if he got the price he wanted for it. But of course it didn't work out like that.'

No matter how hard she tried to iron out the rather breathless note in her voice, it still showed through her words. She knew that her heart was racing, not just at the hope of saving her little company, but more at the thought that if she and Niall were partners he could not just disappear out of her life.

'You could always find someone else.'

'You?' It slipped out before she could catch it back.

'Don't tell me you hadn't thought of it before now.'

Something in Niall's tone jarred, killing the rush of delight she had felt at his suggestion and replacing it with something much more uncomfortable—a cold, creeping sensation as if something slimy was crawling over her skin.

'I—had hoped...' What was the point in denying it? 'That perhaps you'd become part of my life.'

'Your business life?'

If that was all. 'Well, yes—I—'

'Of course you did,' he cut in harshly. 'After all, the money you had hoped for from Owen wasn't forthcoming—nor was the wedding-ring you were angling for—so you needed another wealthy benefactor.'

Saffron gasped in shock as the sardonic echoing of her own words hit her like a slap in the face. They had only been meant half seriously, and certainly not aimed at him, but coming from Niall they sounded like evidence for the prosecution.

'Who told you this?' she demanded sharply.

'Who do you think?' Niall flung back at her, but even as he spoke she could hear one particularly petulant voice speaking the unpleasant words.

'Owen,' she said bleakly, no room for doubt in her mind. Owen, who had made it plain that he had nothing good to say about anyone—so why should he have been any different when he had met up with Niall?

'Owen,' Niall confirmed harshly.

'And you'd believe him?' Bitterness made her voice

hard. 'You never had much time for him in the past, and isn't this so obviously sour grapes?'

Unless, of course, Owen had given Niall just what he had been looking for—an excuse to turn and walk away—a reason for leaving. The thought made her feel suddenly despairingly weak.

'But Owen doesn't know he has anything to be jealous about, does he? Besides, I could have worked it out for myself. What was more obvious than that when Owen didn't come through you'd turn to someone else—someone with even more money than your little suburban entrepreneur? After all, what you needed was someone who was boring as hell and oily with it—someone who had nothing to recommend him but his money.'

'Oh, God!'

The cry of shock escaped her in the same moment that all colour fled from her cheeks as she recognised her own foolish words, shouted down the stairs to Kate all those weeks ago, on the day that Niall had first called at her office. He had heard them, and they had obviously stuck in his mind, festering like some open wound, until now they seemed to confirm the awful things Owen had accused her of.

'I didn't mean it quite like that—'

'No? Then how did you mean it?' His tone lashed her harshly. 'Forgive me if I find it difficult to think of any other interpretation of the words than a determination to find someone to finance you, or at the very least hand you a fortune on a plate. Are you going to deny that you took every opportunity to push your company's plight in my face?'

'N-no—but—'

'Even now, you can still think of nothing else other

than some way of finding a rescue package for your damn business.' He flung the words in her face, the light-coloured eyes burning incandescent with rage. 'That's all I ever was to you, wasn't it? You're just like all the others—only after one thing—'

The pain was indescribable; she felt as if her heart was tearing slowly in two. She no longer cared whether Niall actually believed in the things he had accused her of or was simply using them as an excuse.

'Not just one thing—'

She didn't care what she was saying either, wanting only to lash out at Niall, hurt him as he was hurting her by even listening to Owen's sordid little slander.

'Though, of course, at first I didn't know that you had other skills. I never expected that we would be so good in bed together—'

She broke off sharply, silenced by his savage expletive. For a terrifying moment Niall's hands clenched into fists at his sides, but then he seemed to regain control of his temper and drew in a long, ragged breath.

'So, if I was to tell you that you haven't a hope in hell,' he said, in a voice that was so unnaturally calm that it was far more frightening than if he had shouted at her, 'that the business partnership you've been hoping for will never exist?'

'Then I'd ask you—ever so politely, of course—to stop wasting my time and get out of my life.'

If he really believed her capable of such mercenary motives, then she was better off without him. And she had always known that this moment must come sooner or later, so it was probably better to deal with it right here and now. Better a swift, sharp breaking off than a slow, agonising fraying of the fragile ties that had held them together.

'After all, you were the one who said that when something was finished it was best to go quicky, without a backward glance.'

To cover her own private pain she made her voice as cold and hard as she could, not recognising the hateful, brittle tones as her own, wanting only to drive him out, make him go so that she could break her heart in peace.

'Fine.'

She had succeeded only too well; she knew that as soon as she saw the cold gleam in those translucent eyes. His voice was icy too—freezingly, hatefully calm.

'That suits me too,' Niall said, and then he turned on his heel and strode swiftly to the door.

He didn't look back—but then, of course, she had never expected he would. But even though she had known that was how it would be, she still forced her spine to stay unnaturally stiff, willing her legs to support her, her head to lift defiantly high, until the door slammed shut behind him. Only when she knew that he had really gone, that he couldn't see her, did she let herself sink weakly into a chair, her tear-stained face in her hands.

It was supposed to hurt less if you cut something off sharply, with a single blow, she told herself despairingly. It was supposed to be much less painful than letting it wear away slowly—so why did she feel such agony? Why did she feel that there was nothing left inside her, that it had all shattered into tiny, jagged splinters? She had known that this was coming, had tried to anticipate it from the start, so why did she feel as if her world had come to a terrible, explosive end?

Because the man she loved had gone out of her life

forever, and she didn't know how—or even if she could start to build up the fragmented pieces of her existence over again. In her mind, like a mockery, a nagging, throbbing ache, she heard Niall's voice saying, 'Looking back is just a waste of time...the only way is forward.' And, as if to emphasise the point, just at the moment that his car roared into life and sped off down the road, the storm which had been threatening all evening finally broke overhead, with a deafening crash of thunder and a flare of lightning that seemed to split the sky.

CHAPTER ELEVEN

THE rain that had started with the thunderstorm on the night Niall had walked out had continued almost without stopping through the following month, making the atmosphere outside as miserable and bleak as the feeling inside Saffron's heart, and now it pounded down on her head, plastering her dark hair against her skull until it hung in unflattering rats' tails around her neck and shoulders.

Miserably Saffron made a feeble attempt to wipe away the wetness from her face, heedless of the way the futile action smudged her mascara into dark panda rings around her eyes. She didn't care what she looked like anyway. Her impulsive journey to London had all been to no avail, and the house across the street from where she now stood—Niall's house—was dark and empty and securely locked. There was no one at home to respond to her desperate knock on the door.

It had been Kate who had urged her to come, persuading her against her own better instincts.

'You look dreadful,' she had said when, after days without sleep, Saffron had finally been unable to pretend any longer and had admitted to the pain that Niall's rejection had inflicted on her. 'You can't go on like this.'

'I can't do anything else,' Saffron had protested. 'Niall wants nothing more to do with me—he actually believes all that filth that Owen told him.'

'But only because you let him. You didn't even deny it—or give him a chance to say anything else.'

'Probably because there wasn't anything he wanted to say.'

But, once implanted in her mind, the doubts had taken root, proving immovable in spite of every attempt she made to drive them away. Convinced in her own mind that Niall had been preparing to end their affair, had she jumped in too quickly, pushed him into going when perhaps that hadn't been what he meant?

'You'll never know unless you ask,' had been Kate's pragmatic advice. 'Face him, Saff. Tell him why you reacted as you did. Perhaps he's feeling every bit as miserable as you.'

And Saffron had allowed herself to be persuaded, letting a tiny, weak flame of hope light up in her bruised heart. That flame had flickered slightly when, after trying to contact Niall at the factory, she had learned that he no longer lived in Kirkham but had gone back to London within twenty-four hours of walking out on her.

No backward glances. The words seemed to ring in her ears, warring with the hope she had clung to so desperately. She couldn't go back now, she knew. The only way to cope with this was to talk to Niall face to face—because there was no way this could be done over the phone.

And so she had come to London. Knowing that she didn't have the courage to set foot in the headquarters of Forrester Leisure, she had tracked down his home address by the simple expedient of forcing it out of Owen—her fury at the story he had told Niall had stunned him into handing it over without very much persuasion—and then she had taken the night train down to the capital, arriving so early in the morning that even Niall couldn't possibly be at work yet. Her heart had been beating high up in her throat, hope buzzing through her veins, as she had run up the steps to the black-painted door and pressed the bell firmly.

But there was no answer. No one had responded to her summons, no light had been switched on inside the elegant town-house, which had remained shuttered and unwelcoming as before. In the end she had had to admit that her journey had been in vain.

'You're an idiot!' she told herself fiercely when, in spite of everything, she found herself unable to leave, but lingered, miserable and uncomfortable in the steady downpour, on the opposite side of the road. 'What would a man who lives in a house like that want with a very ordinary girl like you?'

Except for the obvious, stern realism forced her to add, and she knew there was no denying it. Niall had had what he wanted from her, and now it was over.

She was finally turning away, preparing to leave, when the sound of tyres splashing down the wet street towards her made her freeze, shrinking back against the wall. There was no mistaking the sleek grey car, and her heart lurched painfully as she watched it pull up outside the house.

'Niall—'

His name escaped her lips on a whisper as her eyes went to the dark, masculine figure she so longed to see. But a moment later she could only be deeply thankful for the fact that she hadn't called it out loud or made any gesture to attract his attention as she saw that there were, in fact, two people in the car, and that the person in the driving-seat was a tall, elegant blonde who was very definitely female.

Looking back is just a waste of time. Niall's words sounded in her head like a death-knell to her foolish hopes. He certainly hadn't wasted any time that way. She couldn't even convince herself, though she knew that Niall was an early riser, that this scenario was more innocent than it appeared, because as he pushed open his door—and she was surprised to find that he *was* in the passenger seat, the blonde actually doing the driving—it became apparent that he was wearing evening dress.

The elegant black jacket and trousers seemed to have been tailored on to his lithe form, and the whiteness of his shirt formed a stark contrast to the jet darkness of his hair. At some point he had dragged off his bow tie and loosened the top couple of buttons of his shirt—or the blonde had done that for him—Saffron reflected bitterly, recognising an uncharacteristically rumpled edge to Niall's appearance that brought her hard up against the painful but unavoidable possibility that he had undressed earlier and then hastily and none too carefully pulled on his clothes again in order to make the journey home.

Huddled into a corner, trying desperately to become invisible, Saffron heard Niall's low voice as it carried clearly across the silent street, the unmistakable note of intimate warmth in his words stabbing like a brutal knife into her already wounded heart.

'Are you sure you won't come in for coffee—or anything else?'

The blonde's reply was indistinct, though obviously negative, but Saffron caught the warmth in her voice that softened her refusal.

'Besides,' she added more clearly as Niall swung his long legs on to the glistening tarmac, 'you need to get into bed. After a night like last night, you'll need some sleep.'

'You too,' Niall retorted laughingly, the implication of his words burning like bitter acid in Saffron's mind, and she was grateful for the hot tears that stung her eyes, blurring the image of his dark head lowering to press a farewell kiss on the woman's cheek. 'I'll be round to collect the car this evening. Take care, Jay, love—drive safely.'

Through a haze of misery Saffron heard the car door slam and Niall's hurried footsteps running up the steps to his door, where he paused to wave after the departing car.

If she kept absolutely still, she told herself, then perhaps he wouldn't notice her. It was barely light, and the gloom of the rain, her black coat, might just conceal her. But in the end her own weakness betrayed her. She couldn't stop herself from turning her head, couldn't resist the temptation to take one last bittersweet look at his beloved face, the long, lean lines of his body as he stood in his doorway.

That tiny movement was her downfall. Catching it out of the corner of his eye, Niall swiftly turned his attention in her direction, those steely grey eyes, almost the same colour as the rain-clouds above them, fixing on her face with a laser-like intensity that she could feel even across the street which separated them.

For a long, long moment, he froze, staring at her, and she could have sworn that his lips moved, forming the sound of her name, and that he took a single step forward—towards her. But then abruptly he stopped, shaking his head so hard that it sent that errant lock of jet-black hair flying forward on to his forehead as it had done so often in the past.

But this time there was no hope that he would let her brush it back; she knew that in the moment that his expression changed, his face hardening before he turned from her, thrusting his key into the lock with a haste that revealed only too clearly how keen he was to get away from her. The sound of the glossy black door slamming shut behind him drove the point home like a brutal blow in her face. He had made his decision, and she knew she had no hope of appeal.

So now she knew. The tiny hope was gone, killed off once and for all by the hard-faced indifference he had shown her. Niall didn't want her. He had found someone else, someone with whom he had obviously just spent a very intimate and satisfying night. He might have wanted her once, and, true to his declaration, had gone straight for what he wanted—but he had also warned her how he would react when he grew bored.

This was the second time he had shown her that he had meant what he said, that he was perfectly capable of turning his back and walking away without looking back. She wasn't so much of a fool that she needed the message driving home any more forcefully. With desperate tears blending into the raindrops on her cheeks, she turned and ran stumblingly away.

The sound of her doorbell ringing on and on dragged Saffron from the heavy sleep of exhaustion into which she had fallen an hour or so before. At least, she had thought it was only an hour—two at the most—but a hasty glance at her alarm clock told her that it was, in fact, eight times that. Worn out by the stress of recent weeks, her body had finally succumbed to the need for the oblivion that had escaped it for so long.

'Go away!' she groaned, putting her fingers into her ears to drown out the sound, but the childish action failed to obliterate the persistent noise, and suddenly remembering that she had promised to ring Kate as soon as possible, to let her know what had happened, she was overcome with guilt at the thought that her friend had probably called round in a state of some concern.

'All right—I'm coming!'

Snatching up her white towelling dressing-gown, she stumbled downstairs, eyes still blurred with sleep, her hair a tangled mess, and unlocked the door in a rush.

'Kate—I'm sorry. But honestly there's nothing to report. I saw Niall and—'

The words died on her lips as her gaze focused on the tall, dark, very masculine form of the last person she had expected to see—and he was very definitely *not* Kate.

'You saw Niall, and—?' he drawled sardonically. 'So it *was* you.'

'Of course it was!' His change of tone on the last four words bothered her. She couldn't interpret what lay behind it. 'You know it was—you saw me.'

The pain of that moment stabbed at her again, and acting on a purely reflex action she made a move to slam the door shut in his face. But Niall anticipated her response, blocking the movement by the simple expedient of ramming one booted foot hard up against the door and wedging it open.

'I didn't realise—not at first. I'd had a—very heavy night, and I wasn't thinking at all straight. I really thought that I was seeing things—that I was still drunk.'

'You really know how to make me feel small!' Saffron flung at him bitterly. 'You thought I was just a figment of your intoxicated imagination!'

'I was inside the house before I started thinking clearly, and when I looked again you'd gone. Look, do you think you could let me in, just for a minute? I'm getting soaked out here.'

Niall's sudden appearance seemed to have fogged her brain. She hadn't even noticed that it was raining again, the same sort of steady downpour that had drenched her the day before. Niall's hair was already wet, flattened to his skull in a way that reminded her painfully of so many occasions when she had seen him fresh from taking a shower—or sharing one with her.

It would serve him right if she left him outside, or turned away from him as he had done to her, she told herself, but something in his face, a strangely diffident expression that was quite unlike the Niall she knew, twisted something sharply in her too-vulnerable heart.

'Please—' Niall had seen the change in her face.

'Well...'

'Oh, come on, Saffron, surely it's better to talk in comfort. Besides, you'll freeze if you stay there much longer, dressed like that.'

Saffron gave a shocked gasp as Niall's words brought home to her the fact of her half-dressed state. Frozen in shock at the sight of him on her doorstep, she now realised that she still had only one arm in the dressing-gown's sleeve—the other was hanging loose at her back. The robe itself hung open, revealing her short yellow satin nightdress to his coldly appraising gaze. Hastily she pulled the white towelling round her, shoving her hand into the sleeve and belting the robe firmly around her slim waist.

'You'd better come in,' she muttered ungraciously, pushing a nervous hand through the tangled mane of her dark hair in a vain attempt to restore it to some sort of order. 'I'll make some coffee.'

She could do with a drink herself, she reflected as she filled the kettle and switched it on. It might make her brain start functioning at last. She had just registered fully exactly what Niall must have meant by a 'heavy night' and it brought a foul taste into her mouth.

'Why were you there?' Niall asked suddenly. 'What did you come all the way to London for?'

'I could ask the same of you,' Saffron told him sharply, distracting herself by collecting mugs, teaspoons, coffee-granules and milk from the fridge as she spoke. 'After all, you can't expect me to believe that you've driven a couple of hundred miles to Kirkham simply to find out what I wanted when you could just have picked up a phone.'

He must have left almost as soon as he had sobered up—once he'd collected his car from the beautiful Jay. The thought of the elegant blonde was a slash of pain that had her hand clenching on the neck of the milk bottle.

'Why did you come?' Niall ignored her tirade.

'Perhaps I wanted to see how the other half lives.'

No, flippancy was a definite mistake; Niall's dark scowl told her that. He looked tired, she thought regretfully, pale and drained, with shadows under those spectacular eyes. His jaw was dark with the day's growth of beard, and the black T-shirt and jeans he wore under a loose denim jacket seemed to emphasise the fact. Probably worn out by too many 'heavy nights', she told herself tartly, pushing away the weak sympathy that had tried to sneak into her mind.

'Actually, I wanted to talk to you about Bonfire Night.' She took refuge behind the excuse she had thought up as an explanation for her presence in London if she had managed to speak to him.

'What about Bonfire Night?'

Saffron drew a deep breath and brought it out in a rush. 'I think you'd better get someone else to do the catering.'

'Why the hell should I do that?' Niall demanded harshly.

'Isn't it obvious?'

'Not to me.' He was being deliberately awkward. 'We had a contract—'

'An agreement only—and that was before we—you—'

'Our personal lives have no bearing on this whatsoever.' She couldn't believe how cold and distant his voice was, and his eyes were as bleak and unrevealing as the North Sea on a winter's day. 'And I happen to think that your company will be perfect for the sort of thing I want.'

'Well, I won't do it! I can't. A Movable Feast is going out of business—I'm closing it down.'

'You'd do that rather than work for me?'

'It's not a question of choice, damn you!'

It was as if she had slapped him hard in the face. Niall took a step backwards, his hard features losing colour, his eyes clouding.

'You—God, Saffron, I never wanted that!'

'It's not your fault!' Saffron put in swiftly, driven by strict honesty. 'It's this damned recession—there just isn't the business out there.'

'But have you tried advertising—a leaflet campaign? You could—'

'Niall, please!' Saffron's voice was thick and choked. She found it an unbearably bitter irony that when he had once been so determined to have nothing to do with her business, now he was apparently keen to help. 'I've tried everything I can think of and I can see no way out.'

Suddenly, belatedly, she became aware of the way that the rainwater was dripping from his hair, falling in damp patches onto his jacket and the T-shirt beneath it, flattening it against the strong lines of his chest, reminding her of how, in the past, she had peeled it off him...

'Oh, for heaven's sake!' Exasperation hid the other, more complicated feelings in her voice. 'Take that jacket off and hang it near the boiler—it'll dry out there. And get a towel to see to your hair.'

The kettle boiled while he did as he was told, and she was grateful for the fact that he had his back to her because it meant that he didn't see the way her hand shook as she reached for it.

'About the business—I could—'

'No!' Saffron couldn't bear to let him continue. 'You can't do anything because I won't accept anything from you. I— Oh, no!'

She broke off on a cry of pain as the kettle swung in her unsteady grip and boiling water splashed over her hand.

'Saffron!'

Reacting with instinctive speed, Niall pulled her towards the sink, wrenching on the cold tap as he did so. Saffron gave a shaky sigh of relief as the icy water poured on to her hand, soothing the pain of her injured fingers. In spite of her efforts to hold them back, a couple of weak tears slid from the corners of her eyes and trickled down her cheeks.

'Oh, God, Saffron!' Niall said, in a new and very different tone, one that shattered what little was left of her peace of mind, the unexpected thread of concern rocking her belief in his total indifference to her feelings.

'It doesn't hurt so much now,' she managed unevenly, and had no idea, even in her own mind, whether she meant her scalded hand or the cruelty of his rejection of her.

She wished that he would move away, or that she had never told him to take off his jacket. His nearness, the feel of that muscular body so close to hers, firm and hard underneath the clinging softness of his T-shirt, was almost more than she could bear. She could breathe in the scent of him with a sensuality that was almost shocking, the soft sound of his breathing played havoc with her already sensitive nerves and the temptation to lean back against him, feel those strong arms enfold her, was only just resistible.

'Saffron...' Niall said, and his voice had changed once

again. This time there was a suggestion of hesitation, something she might almost have described as tentativeness, that was so unexpected it made her turn stunned brown eyes on his face, only to find that once she had met the smoky force of his heavy-lidded gaze she couldn't look away again.

He was going to kiss her, she told herself. He wanted to kiss her, and she, weak fool that she was, was going to let him, because she couldn't resist him. She had never had the strength to hold out against the sexual appeal of his beautiful male body, the strongly carved features of his face, the startling contrast of the softness of his hair.

One kiss, she told herself. Just one, and then she'd put a stop to this.

But she'd reckoned without the physical fireworks, the explosive detonation that simply touching Niall could set off in her body, every nerve suddenly seeming electrically charged. Behind her, the water gushed unheeded into the sink, completely forgotten as she swayed against him, her mouth opening softly to allow the tantalising enticement of his tongue.

'Saffron, sweetheart,' he murmured against her lips. 'Why do we let other things get in the way of this—?'

He should never have spoken. The sound of his voice, touched with the same husky warmth that had shaded it when he spoke to the blonde in his car, slashed through the haze of delight that was clouding her senses, and when his hands moved over her body, pushing the white robe aside, reminding her of how little she had on, she snapped back to reality with a jarring suddenness, jerking backwards as his fingers moved to slide the delicate lacy straps of her nightdress down over her shoulders.

'*No!*' Her hands pushed frantically at his hard chest. 'Niall—I said no!'

'Saffron, honey, you don't mean that.'

He was using the snake-charmer's voice again, effortlessly weaving a spell around her mind in the same way that his kisses, his touch, had enchanted her body.

'We both know what this leads to—how good it can be—'

'No!'

With a movement that wrenched at her heart as much as her body, she tore herself away from him. On the day they had first met, at the restaurant, she had thought of the yearning he could awaken in her in the form of a coiled, sleeping snake, and now she saw that, as with a real serpent, awakening her sexuality had created something that was both beautiful and dangerous. Her desire for Niall had been a source of great delight at first, but blinded by that pleasure she had been unable to see that its bite was in fact lethally destructive in the way that it weakened her, putting her at his mercy.

'I can't believe you're such a sexual opportunist—that you'd try it on in this way. What about your new woman—the one I saw you with—your blonde—?'

'My blonde?'

Suddenly, amazingly, he was laughing, his dark head thrown back, silver eyes gleaming in genuine amusement.

'Oh, God, Saffron, this is such a cliché! That was Jayne.'

'Jayne?' The name rang faint bells, but she couldn't quite remember...

'My sister-in-law. The one who got away and married my brother. If you'd been able to see into the car properly you'd have realised how pregnant she is.'

Saffron's head was spinning. 'But how—why?'

'I'd been to a dinner party with Andy and Jayne. During the evening I—I drank more than was wise, and very sensibly Jayne refused to let me drive home. She even confiscated my keys so that I had to spend what little was left of the night in their spare bedroom. Then, in the morning, because she knew I was still not one hundred per cent, she drove me home and, being the determined lady she is, held on to my car until *she* was sure I was fit to drive.'

'It must have been one hell of a night.'

'Believe me, it was,' Niall admitted wryly. 'So you see, sweetheart, you don't have to worry about Jayne.'

He meant the words to be reassuring and, on the surface at least, they were. But it was hearing them in that dismissive tone that brought home to Saffron just why she really *did* have to worry.

'Oh, but I do.'

Jayne might not matter in the present, but it was what she had been to Niall in the past that made her so important. He had believed himself to be in love with Jayne, but when she had chosen his brother instead he had had no trouble in getting over that awkward feeling and moving on. 'It was how little it bothered me that was worrying,' he had said, and she would be more than wise to take warning from that now.

'You walked out on me once, Niall; how long before you do so again? Do you have another brother you can pass me on to when you grow tired?'

'It won't be like that—'

'No, it won't, because I'm not going to let it happen. I'm not prepared to go through that again.'

'You won't have to—'

Niall reached out and drew her close again, his lips on her face, trailing burning kisses over the soft skin of her cheek, down the slender line of her throat, coming perilously close to the pale curves exposed by the deeply scooped neckline of her nightdress.

'I said *no*!'

It took all her strength to say it, all her courage to look into his face and see those clear eyes cloud over in genuine confusion and disbelief. He had been so sure of himself—of her. He had never imagined that she might actually turn him down.

'You might be able to dismiss those ugly accusations you flung at me, but I can never forget that you believed them in the first place. I thought you hated me because I was only after your money.'

Niall's shrug dismissed her objection with a lack of concern that further convinced her she had made the right decision.

'Would you believe, I don't care any more?'

'Oh, yes. I can believe that only too easily. You can forget them *now*, when it suits you. You can dismiss them just like that.'

A dreary, deadly sense of despair told her that in just this way would he dismiss *her* when he decided he had had enough.

'The fireworks you said we lit between us might be enough for you to compensate for such a lack of trust—they might even have made a brilliant display at first.'

And she could hardly deny that with her body aching, yearning, needing his touch so desperately. Drawing a deep, uneven breath, she forced herself to ignore the physical pain, concentrating instead on the mental one.

'But, like all pyrotechnics, they have only a very temporary glory. As far as I'm concerned, they've burned themselves out, leaving only a blackened, smoking stub!'

'You don't mean that—'

'Oh, yes, I do!'

Resolutely ignoring the protest from every nerve, the agonising pain in her heart, she wrenched herself away and struggled to restore some order to her appearance, hampered by the way she seemed to have lost control over her hands.

'And I mean this even more—you may say that you don't care, but I do. I care that you even thought I was capable of something so low, so despicable! So, let me tell you something once and for all, Mr Wealthy Benefactor Forrester! I don't want your money, or your influence, or your help. I don't want your company, or your—lovemaking.'

The word threatened to destroy her control, sticking in her throat and almost choking her, but she forced it out with a ruthless determination that she hadn't known she possessed.

'I don't want *you*! So will you please get out of my life and leave me alone? I never want to see you again!'

For one dreadful moment she thought that he was going to refuse to go. His face had closed up, his eyes becoming blank and dead, as if steel shutters had slammed shut behind them, and the muscles around his mouth and jaw were drawn tight over the strong bones. But then he gave a curt nod and moved deliberately away from her.

'I'll go, Saffron,' he said, and the terrible coldness of his voice seemed to freeze the blood in her veins. 'For now. But I won't leave you alone. You see, I want you to provide the food for the Bonfire Night celebrations, and I won't have anyone else.'

'You can't force me!'

'No, I can't.' The mildness of his agreement was somehow more frightening than if he had raged at her. 'But if you won't do it, no one else will. I'll cancel the whole thing.'

'Oh, but you can't do that!' Saffron was appalled. 'It's already been announced. Everyone in Kirkham's looking forward to it. All the children are so excited—you can't disappoint them!'

'I can and I will, unless you fulfil your part of the bargain,' Niall stated inflexibly. 'It won't do you any harm—it might even do some good. Think of it as a publicity venture—a last-ditch attempt to save A Movable Feast.'

She couldn't find a word to say, either to agree or refuse. He was just using this to torment her, perhaps in some cruel way to get back at her for damaging his macho pride by turning him down. She couldn't really have any hope that all the publicity in the world would finally drag her business out of the swamp of near-bankruptcy.

'What about Kate and your other workers? Don't they deserve one last attempt to save their jobs—their livelihood?'

'You really know how to twist the knife,' Saffron flung at him bitterly. It would always be on her conscience if she took Kate and the others down with her.

'Oh, come on, Saffron! Is it really so very much to ask? You co-operate with me on this for just a few short weeks, and before you know it I'll be gone—back to London—leaving you in peace.'

Privately, Saffron doubted that the future held any sort of peace for her, whether Niall was here or in London. Loving him the way she did, and knowing that he felt only a temporary physical desire for her, had drained all light, all joy from her life.

'Well—will you do it? Or do I cancel the event?' Niall demanded harshly.

Which, of course, left her with only one possible reply.

He had her in a cleft stick, and he was well aware of that fact.

'You don't leave me any choice,' she said resignedly. 'You know I have to do it.'

CHAPTER TWELVE

'SAUSAGES—hundreds of them—rolls, baked potatoes...'

Saffron ticked off items on her check-list as each carefully packed box was carried from the kitchen into the waiting van.

'Gingerbread men—sorry—gingerbread *persons*! Toffee apples... Kate, I thought there were going to be more—'

'Right here!' Her friend's voice was calm and reassuring. 'Don't panic. Everything's under control.'

With regard to the food, at least, that was true, Saffron thought unhappily. If only the rest of her life could be as easily organised and positive. Instead it seemed to be falling to pieces around her, and there was nothing she could do to stop it.

She didn't really know how she had got through the past five weeks. Once she had agreed to provide the food for the bonfire, she had thought that Niall would then leave her strictly alone to do just that, while he concentrated on the other details. She had also assumed that he wouldn't be staying in Kirkham any longer than he actually had to, but would spend most of his time in London, sending instructions by telephone or fax, and only appearing on the big day itself, when his presence as the new owner of Richards' Rockets would naturally be required, and that as a result she wouldn't see very much of him.

She couldn't have been more wrong. At times it now seemed that she was in his company more than she had ever been when they had been together. Certainly, she was seen more often in public with him.

For some reason, Niall seemed to have appointed her not only to the position of caterer, but also consultant on all matters relating to the likes and dislikes of the people of Kirkham, so that, no matter how much she protested, she was always being roped in to give her opinion on the choice of music, the design of the displays—anything at all. He also seemed to change his mind about the food to be provided with a frequency that both infuriated and bewildered her, and had the circumstances been different, and Niall just an ordinary client, she would have handed in her notice and walked away without hesitation.

But Niall was no ordinary client, and because he was who he was, the very existence of the Bonfire Night celebrations depended on her. She could have no doubt that if she backed out Niall would carry out his threat to cancel everything, and as the days passed and the excitement grew she knew she could never let that happen. And so she pushed to one side the ill-effects of nights without sleep, the lack of appetite that kept her from eating, tacked a wide, bright smile on to her face and forced herself to endure the torment of days spent with Niall in an existence that brought home to her the true, bitter meaning of 'so near and yet so far'.

'That's the lot.' Kate sighed with relief. 'It's been a mammoth task, but we've done it. We can certainly pat ourselves on the back this time. And its done us no harm on the business front, either—all that publicity for one thing. We'll be raking in the profits soon.'

'Maybe.' Saffron smiled rather wanly at her friend's enthusiasm. 'It's a little too early to be counting any chickens yet, let alone any profits. But all the free advertising has helped get our name known.'

She had to admit that Niall had been more than fair in the way that he had made sure that every poster, every hand-out, every newspaper report on the coming event always featured the words, 'Catering by A Movable Feast' displayed in a prominent position. As a result, there had been a sudden rush of interest in her business that had given a much-needed boost to her hopes of keeping it going after all.

'And perhaps we'll take some more orders tonight. We've got a lot to thank your Niall for.'

'Not *my* Niall,' Saffron corrected automatically.

'Still no chance of making up?' Kate enquired gently, and Saffron shook her head, her unhappiness showing on her face.

'I realised I'm not cut out for a temporary affair, after all. I am like my sisters, Kate; I do need love and marriage, or at least commitment—I can't settle for less.'

'Not even for Niall Forrester?'

Particularly not for Niall Forrester, Saffron thought later that evening as she watched Niall ceremonially set light to the enormous bonfire that had been built in the middle of a huge field on the outskirts of the town. If Niall loved her, she would go through hell and high water for him; she would probably not even ask for the commitment she had said she wanted, but take each day at a time and be content with that—if he loved her.

But she knew that his relationship with her had come under the heading of things he wanted, nothing more, and, loving him the way she did, that would never be enough. She couldn't live her life with a man who didn't trust her, who had wanted to keep their relationship hidden, driving home his emotional independence from her by setting up a completely separate home, turning down her offer to share her cottage. He hadn't even known how much that offer had cost her. With a sigh she turned away, and tried to concentrate her attention on the huge trestle tables laden with food.

'Everything OK?'

Niall had come up behind her, his casual question making her jump nervously.

'Fine.' She fiddled unnecessarily with a pile of napkins, unable to make herself look at him, afraid of what her own face might reveal.

'You've done a brilliant job—' She sensed rather than saw the tilt of his dark head that indicated the display of food. 'There's enough here to feed several armies and still have plenty to take home. You managed to get all the extra staff you needed?'

Saffron nodded silently, still keeping her face averted.

'There were plenty of wives and girlfriends of the factory workers who were only too willing to help.'

'And the sweatshirts were all right?'

'They were fabulous!' Genuine delight overcame the rigid restraint she was imposing on her voice and she swung round in a gesture of spontaneous enthusiasm, a smile breaking through her control.

It had been Niall's suggestion that the women who staffed the refreshment tables should wear some sort of uniform, and he had taken it on himself to have sweatshirts made in an assortment of colours, all decorated with an attractive print of a picnic basket filled to overflowing, and the words 'A Movable Feast' in clear, white lettering. She was wearing one of them now, the rich, golden yellow a foil for her dark hair and pale skin.

'It was a brilliant idea! Thank you for...'

Her voice trailed off, her stomach lurching painfully as

she realised that, without thinking, she had caught hold of Niall's arm to emphasise her point.

For the first time since he had come up to her, she looked directly at Niall, her breath catching in her throat as she saw the way his strong profile was etched against the firelight, the flames casting flickering, changeable shadows across the hard bones and planes of his face, their glow reflected warmly in the pale depths of his eyes. Like her, he was dressed casually, aiming for comfort and warmth in jeans and a rich blue sweater, and as her eyes dropped nervously to where her fingers encircled the strength of his arm she had a sudden agonising recollection of just how it had felt to be held in those arms, to feel them close around her... With a wordless sound of distress, she snatched her hand away again, reacting as sharply as if she had been burned by the heat of his skin.

'My pleasure.' Niall's tone was dry, so much so that she wasn't exactly sure that he was referring to her comment about the sweatshirts. 'They should help to get the name of your business known anyway—all good publicity.'

'We've certainly had plenty of that,' she told him, struggling to impose some degree of control on her voice. 'The advertising has resulted in all sorts of enquiries. We've got a couple of definite contracts and plenty of interest.'

'I'm glad.' Niall's voice was low and slightly husky. 'I've tried every damn thing I could think of to put custom your way.'

'*You* have!' Saffron turned wide, startled brown eyes on his shadowed face. 'Why?'

'I wanted to make sure that you didn't lose your business.'

'You did that? For me?'

'It was the only way I could be sure that you wouldn't need me as a partner.'

Behind Saffron's back a newly lit rocket soared upwards into the pitch-black sky, exploding with a shriek into a hail of multicoloured stars, and she could only be thankful that the way that the unexpected sound had made her jump like a startled cat had hidden the agonising distress that had stabbed home at Niall's words.

He still didn't trust her. He still thought that her only interest in him was financial, that all she had ever wanted from him was a rescue package for A Movable Feast.

'Well, you've certainly managed that.'

The moment's respite had given her a chance to impose a rigid control on her voice, and she was relieved to find that it sounded reasonably light-hearted, even though deep inside she felt as if she was breaking up, shattering into tiny, desolate fragments.

'And now I suppose you think I should be suitably grateful?'

'Grateful? Why the hell should you be grateful? Look—I know you wanted to sort things out on your own, and all I've done is simply point people in your direction. *You're* the one who's impressed them enough to want to employ you. The way you've tackled the catering for tonight is evidence enough of your flair and efficiency. That's why people have decided to use A Movable Feast, not because of any pressure from me.'

Saffron found it hard to believe what she was hearing. If Niall had understood her double-edged use of the word 'grateful', then obviously he had deliberately ignored it, instead offering her the sort of unpatronising praise that any human being would love to hear, and that sent a warm glow through her bruised heart.

'I have something for you.'

Saffron stared at the white envelope Niall had pulled from his pocket, eyeing it warily, as if it was a rat that might bite.

'Take it—you've earned it.'

Saffron's hands were slightly unsteady as she ripped the letter open, but even before she had fully unfolded the single sheet of paper it enclosed she knew with a sense of distress just what it was. And she was right. There before her, perfectly typed and formally spelled out, was an offer to employ A Movable Feast to provide business lunches at Richards' Rockets...

She read no further, but, screwing the letter up into a tight, crumpled ball, marched determinedly towards the fire and flung it as far from her as she could, watching with intense satisfaction the swift flare of flame that devoured it.

'I know exactly how it feels,' Niall murmured behind her. 'You have just that effect on me, too.'

'*What*?'

Not knowing whether she was furious or flattered, Saffron whirled round, her dark hair flying.

'What are you trying to do to me, Niall?' she demanded. 'You bully me into doing the food for this damn bonf—'

'Yes, I know. I'm sorry about that, but it was the only thing I could think of.'

Niall's voice was disturbingly different, and his expression was as penitent as his tone. Blinking hard in shock, Saffron stared into his eyes, seeing the flicker of the fire reflected in them, the changing shadows suddenly making him look so unlike the man she thought she knew, the confident, controlled, ruthless Niall Forrester she had first met.

'And—and then you try to bribe me—'

'No, not bribe,' Niall cut in sharply. 'I told you—you'd earned it. And the letter—the contract didn't come from me. I've put a manager in charge at Richards'—a good man...'

He didn't need to go on. In her mind, Saffron could see the letter as clearly as if it was before her eyes, and even in the brief survey she had given it she had subconsciously absorbed the fact that it had not been Niall's firm slash of a signature at the bottom of the typewritten page.

'But he does as you say—'

'It's his opinion that counts on local matters, Saffron. I don't have time to attend to every last little detail for all my companies—that's what I employ a manager for.'

He couldn't have used an argument more guaranteed to convince her. Did she really think that Niall Forrester, head of Forrester Leisure, would bother about trivial matters like who cooked his employees' lunches?

'So, you've finished your job here.' Saffron's heart twisted at the thought that his words were also evidence of just how much Niall was moving away from Kirkham.

'Richards' is up and running, yes.'

'You'll be heading back to London...'

'There's one more thing I have to see to first. Saffron, I have something else for you.'

A new tension in the long powerful body before her, the way a muscle moved in his jaw, alerted her to the fact that this was something very different from the business contract.

'I don't want—' she began, but Niall brushed her protest aside.

'But, believe me, if you throw this in the fire, then I'll go right in after it.'

'You'll—' The husky intensity in his voice frightened her. 'What do you mean?'

'Saffron—'

Niall broke off suddenly, interrupted by a sound that began as a sort of intrigued murmur, then grew in volume and strength, gathering force like a wave rushing in to the shore. His eyes went to something behind Saffron's back, and a look of shock and consternation crossed his face.

'Oh, God!' he muttered. 'Damn them—I said nine-thirty. Saffron—'

The noise around them was increasing so quickly that she could hardly hear Niall speak, and then, slowly, through the din and confusion, she became aware that everyone was shouting a single word—her own name.

'Saffron! *Saffron!*'

'What is it?'

Spinning round in response, she was momentarily dazzled by the flare of light from a huge set-piece firework display erected at the far end of the field, slightly raised above the rest so that no one could miss it.

'Saffron—' Niall said again, a touch of desperation in his voice, but by now her vision had cleared, so that she could focus properly—though when she realised what was before her she had to doubt whether she was, in fact, seeing what was really there or just imagining things.

MARRY ME, SAFFRON!

The huge, brilliant letters blazed out of the night sky, spelling out their message for everyone to see.

Marry me, Saffron! Her brain reeled in shock. It couldn't be true; she was imagining things.

Dazedly she turned back to Niall, seeing the strain on his face, the hand he had taken from his pocket, the tiny, square jeweller's box on his palm...

'You— But— *You!*'

Silently he nodded, his eyes never leaving her face.

'You— You did that?'

'It wasn't supposed to be set off until I'd had a chance to ask you privately,' he said hurriedly. 'And it was meant to say *please*—but obviously one of the damn fuses didn't light properly.'

To Saffron's astonished eyes he looked suddenly very boyish, impossibly young, and disturbingly vulnerable.

'Saffron! Saffron?'

The crowd was calling her name. Friendly faces were all around her, eyes gleaming with curiosity in the firelight.

'Saffron—tell us. What's your answer?'

She could only turn to Niall, unable to speak, even to think. Her face had lost all colour and her brown eyes were just dark pools of shock.

'Oh, God!' Niall's exclamation was low and harsh and he caught hold of her arm in a grip that bruised. 'Let's get out of here!'

Dazedly Saffron let him lead her away, his arm coming round her waist, drawing her close into the protective warmth of his body. She was vaguely aware of the light touch with which he parried questions, deflected curious bystanders, answered laughing comments, but couldn't make herself focus on anything. All around her the noise of the celebrations, the crash and fizz of fireworks, the crackle of the fire, the murmur of the crowds, seemed to blur into a whirling, multicoloured haze.

And then at last they were well away from the fire, and suddenly it was quiet, and very dark, and there was only the two of them. Sure-footed on the uneven grass, Niall led her across the field to the deserted spot where his car was parked, releasing her only to unlock the door.

Still too numbed to think for herself, Saffron let herself be manoeuvred into the front seat and waited in silence, staring straight in front of her, until Niall moved round to the driver's side and got in beside her. The slam of the car door cut off the last traces of sound from outside, enclosing them in their own private world.

After a long silent moment Niall moved to switch on the reading light above them before turning to take both her hands in his.

'Saffron—I'm sorry. I should have thought. I didn't mean—'

Didn't mean—! Pain seared through Saffron at his words. What was this, then? Some sick, cruel joke?

'I didn't think. I just wanted to do something spectacular to show you how much I love you, but I should have realised—'

Saffron stirred at last, her trance shattered by the sight of Niall Forrester, a man she had never known at a loss for words, suddenly fumbling for them, stumbling over each phrase. And *had* he said—?

'Love?' she croaked, and at the sound of her voice Niall froze into sudden stillness then, with a swift, muttered curse, pushed rough hands through the black sleekness of his hair.

'I'm doing this all wrong—I'm sorry. I should have told you that first, but the man I left in charge of the firework display obviously got itchy fingers—'

'Tell me now.'

That stopped him dead. He looked at her, silver eyes touched with doubt, then drew a deep, ragged breath.

'Saffron Ruane, I love you,' he stated, so slowly and clearly that there could be no possible doubt as to exactly what he had said.

'But you don't believe in love.'

'Didn't believe,' he corrected gently. 'And that was quite simply because I'd never experienced it. I might have thought I knew about it, and perhaps I came close with the way I felt about Jayne, but I only cared about her as much as I could for a potential sister-in-law, not someone with whom I wanted to spend the rest of my life.'

'You could still walk away.' Saffron's voice was low and uncertain, but he caught it and nodded slowly, his expression serious.

'But I can't walk away from you. I tried it once and it almost destroyed me.'

'And yet you believed Owen—'

'No—yes— Sweetheart, I feel so bad about that. I can only say that I was so off-balance I didn't really know what I was doing. I'd already realised that I was in so deep—deeper than I'd ever been before—that, quite honestly, it scared me. I'd never let anything have that much control over me before. I'd built myself a world that I liked—one that worked perfectly—and suddenly it was all turned upside-down and I wasn't in the driving-seat any more. Then Richards came along with his vicious tongue, like the serpent in the Garden of Eden—'

He broke off abruptly, shaking his dark head as if in despair at his own behaviour.

'I didn't want to believe him—I *shouldn't* have believed him—but I'd been there before. I'd had my fill of women who were only interested in my money. I wanted to believe you weren't like that, but there were so many things you'd said, and the thought that *you* could do that to me blew me right off course. I couldn't think straight—and when I challenged you—'

'The way I reacted seemed to confirm what Owen had said,' Saffron put in sombrely. 'I was so convinced that you were preparing to leave me that I didn't even bother to fight.' She had given him a push out of the door, in fact. 'I behaved like the person you thought I was.'

'Exactly—and I couldn't forget our first meeting—'

Saffron groaned aloud, colour flaring in her cheeks. She could just imagine how she had seemed to him.

'That was such a mistake—but I was so angry. I wanted to shock Owen. Instead, I shocked you, appearing to be bold and mercenary, brittle and demanding, just like the person I pretended to be when you told me what Owen had said. It was all just a front,' she said sadly. 'I'm sorry—I must have hurt you.'

'And made me mad as hell,' Niall admitted ruefully. 'So mad I couldn't think straight for weeks. I took off to London because I told myself I couldn't bear to be in the same town as you, but I felt as if I'd been torn in two. It was as if we weren't two separate people any more, as if we'd fused together to form a sort of third entity—something stronger—bigger—more beautiful than we could ever be on our own. And without you I was less than half a person.'

For a man who hadn't believed in love, he'd just given an incredibly powerful description of that emotion, Saffron thought dazedly, tears of joy pricking at her eyes.

'That was why you saw me with Jayne—'

The grin Niall turned on her was boyishly shamefaced.

'I was losing my grip on things, and at that damn dinner party I was drinking to try to forget about you. I ended up completely out of my head—so much so that Jay decided to take me in hand. She sat me down and listened while I poured everything out—we talked until five the next morning. When I'd finished she gave me her advice—to get myself sobered up and get back to you as quickly as possible to sort things out. You were so much on my mind—that was why I thought I was seeing things when I got out of the car and there you were. And when

I realised it hadn't been my imagination and looked again you'd gone.'

He shuddered violently, remembering, and Saffron twisted her hand in his until she was holding him, squeezing his fingers tight in compassion.

'I drank a gallon of black coffee in order to sober up fast, and then I broke every speed limit in the country driving up here—'

'Only to have me reject you because I was convinced I meant nothing to you.'

'Why the hell did you think that?' Niall's voice was raw.

'You were so determined that no one would know about us. You kept so much of your life separate—had your own flat—'

'Of course I did! You made it plain how much your privacy meant to you—and after the way you'd grown up I could see that for myself. Your cottage was your first private space—I couldn't invade that.'

'But I invited you!'

Even as she protested, she felt she knew what he was going to say.

'But you weren't ready for that, were you? Be honest, sweetheart—the first day we made love you were like a cat on hot bricks, terribly defensive about your home, edgy as hell because I was in your private haven.'

'I'd never done anything like that before—'

'I know—' his smile was infinitely gentle '—I *know*. And that was why I had to give you space, wait until you really wanted me—'

'But I did—' Saffron caught herself up sharply, remembering the way she'd felt at the time. 'You're right,' she admitted. 'I wanted to share my life with you, but I hadn't realised just what that meant in terms of giving up my privacy again.'

But Niall had. He had understood her better than she had herself, and had acted out of consideration for her feelings.

'And now?' he questioned softly.

'Niall—I love you more than life itself. I want to share my life with you—my hopes, my dreams, my body—and my home. If you really think you could exist in a doll's house.'

'If I was with you, anywhere would be a palace,' he assured her, in a voice that was husky with feeling.

One hand slid upwards to cup her cheek, drawing her face towards his for a kiss that was long and sweet and so tender that when he lifted his head again Saffron found that her cheeks were actually wet with tears of joy, tears she hadn't even been aware of having shed.

'I have to admit that I didn't just want to keep things quiet for your sake,' Niall told her. 'I needed time and peace in which to think about this feeling that had crept up on me so suddenly. I felt as if I'd been hit over the head by it—and I certainly didn't need the sort of hassle Owen Richards was likely to subject us to if he found out. And I'm sorry if I ruined things tonight. I should have kept it the way it was—kept it private—'

'No...' Saffron laid a gentle hand over his mouth to silence him. 'It was wonderful—magical.'

'Are you sure?'

'Positive.'

How could she not be sure? She might have worried about his desire to keep their affair secret, but how much more public could you get than tonight? How could she have any lingering doubts about a man who had wanted to display his love to the world?

'Perhaps this will convince you,' she whispered, pulling him towards her again, her arms lacing themselves around his neck, her lips soft and enticing.

'I'm convinced,' Niall sighed at last. 'But I may need to have that reinforced later.'

'Any time,' Saffron assured him lovingly. 'But now I think we'd better get back to the bonfire.'

'What the hell for?'

'I have a job to do.'

'Forget the food—'

'It's not the food.'

'Then, what—?'

'I have to find enough fireworks to spell out the word "YES" in letters five miles high.'

The glow that lit in his eyes was brighter than the blaze of the bonfire that could still be seen through the back window of the car.

'No need for fireworks,' he said when he had kissed her again. 'I'll take that as my answer.'

'But everyone from Kirkham will be wanting to know—'

'Damn everyone from Kirkham!' Niall declared dismissively. A moment later a wicked, teasing grin crossed his face. 'Anyway, don't you think that everyone will already have guessed what your answer was?'

His hands moved lower, sliding under the bright cotton of her sweatshirt and finding the soft warmth of her skin.

'What the hell do you think they suspect we've been up to all this time?'

The sensual touch of his hands, the look in those molten silver eyes, the thickness of his voice, told Saffron exactly what was in his mind, and excitement feathered across her skin, making her shiver in anticipation, her breathing quickening in time with the rapid beat of her heart.

'But Mr Forrester,' she teased softly, 'I thought you told me you were too old to make out in cars.'

'Too old?' he growled in her ear, pulling her close with a strength that communicated more of the way he was feeling than words ever could. 'Just try me—'

'Oh, I will...' she sighed, surrendering to an embrace that promised the sort of private firework display beside which the one still going on in the field behind them would pale into insignificance.

MILLS & BOON®

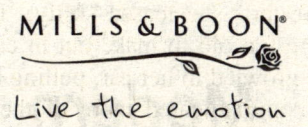

Live the emotion

The Tycoon's Love Child

They were making more than just love…

In April 2005, By Request brings back three favourite romances by our bestselling Mills & Boon authors:

The Italian's Runaway Bride
by Jacqueline Baird
Savage Innocence *by Anne Mather*
The Paternity Affair *by Robyn Donald*

Make sure you buy these passionate stories, on sale 1st April 2005

Available at most branches of WHSmith, Tesco, ASDA, Martins, Borders, Eason, Sainsbury's and all good paperback bookshops.

www.millsandboon.co.uk

MILLS & BOON®
Live the emotion

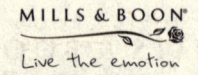

Modern
romance™

POSSESSED BY THE SHEIKH by Penny Jordan

After being stranded in the desert, Katrina was rescued by a Sheikh and taken back to his luxury camp. He decided to marry her, though he thought her a whore. Then he discovered – first hand – that she was a virgin…

THE DISOBEDIENT BRIDE by Helen Bianchin

Their marriage was perfect – and then billionaire Tyler Benedict's wife left! Now he wants her back. Beautiful Lianne Marshall can't refuse his deal – but this time she won't play fair. However, Tyler is after more than a business arrangement!

HIS PREGNANT MISTRESS by Carol Marinelli

Australian billionaire Ethan Carvelle left Mia Stewart years ago. Now Mia's pregnant – claiming Ethan's late brother is the father! Torn between duty and desire, he decides to make her his mistress. But he knows nothing of the secret Mia is hiding…

THE FUTURE KING'S BRIDE by Sharon Kendrick

Prince Gianferro Cacciatore is heir to the throne of Mardivino and his father, the King, is dying. The pressure is on Gianferro to find a wife and his heart is set on English aristocrat Millie de Vere. But Millie hardly knows the prince…

Don't miss out…
On sale 1st April 2005

Available at most branches of WHSmith, Tesco, ASDA, Martins, Borders, Eason, Sainsbury's and all good paperback bookshops.

Visit www.millsandboon.co.uk

MILLS & BOON®

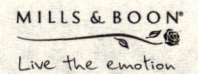

Live the emotion

Modern
romance™

IN THE BANKER'S BED by Cathy Williams

When Melissa Lee works for Elliot Jay, she expects their relationship to be strictly business. He is seriously sexy, but he keeps his emotions in the deep freeze! Melissa is soon getting Elliot hot under the collar, and now he has a new agenda: getting her into his bed!

THE GREEK'S CONVENIENT WIFE by Melanie Milburne

When her brother's exploits leave Maddison Jones at the mercy of billionaire Demetrius Papasakis, the last thing she expects is a proposal. But Demetrius knows she has to agree to a marriage of convenience – and Maddison finds herself unable to resist!

THE RUTHLESS MARRIAGE BID by Elizabeth Power

Taylor's time as Jared Steele's wife was short, but not sweet. Within weeks she discovered that he had a mistress and that she was pregnant. She lost the baby *and* her marriage. Now she is stunned by Jared's return – and his claim that he wants her back!

THE ITALIAN'S SEDUCTION by Karen van der Zee

It sounded like heaven: an apartment in a small Italian town. But after a series of mishaps Charli Olson finds herself stranded – until gorgeous Massimo Castellini offers her a room in his luxurious villa. Though he's vowed never to love again, Massimo finds Charli irresistible.

Don't miss out...
On sale 1st April 2005

Available at most branches of WHSmith, Tesco, ASDA, Martins, Borders, Eason, Sainsbury's and all good paperback bookshops.

Visit www.millsandboon.co.uk

Extra

Favourite, award-winning or bestselling authors. Bigger reads, bonus short stories, new books or much-loved classics. *Always* fabulous reading!

Don't miss:

EXTRA passion for your money! (March 2005)
Emma Darcy – Mills & Boon Modern Romance
NEW *Mistress to a Tycoon* and **CLASSIC** *Jack's Baby*

EXTRA special for your money! (April 2005)
Sherryl Woods – Silhouette Special Edition –
Destiny Unleashed. This **BIG** book is about a woman who is finally free to choose her own path…love, business or a little sweet revenge?

EXTRA tender for your money! (April 2005)
Betty Neels & Liz Fielding – Mills & Boon
Tender Romance – **CLASSIC** *The Doubtful Marriage* and **BONUS**, *Secret Wedding*
Two very popular writers write two very different, emotional stories on the always-bestselling wedding theme.

Available at most branches of WHSmith, Tesco, ASDA, Martins, Borders, Eason, Sainsbury's and all good paperback bookshops.

www.silhouette.co.uk

0305/024/MB120

MILLS & BOON

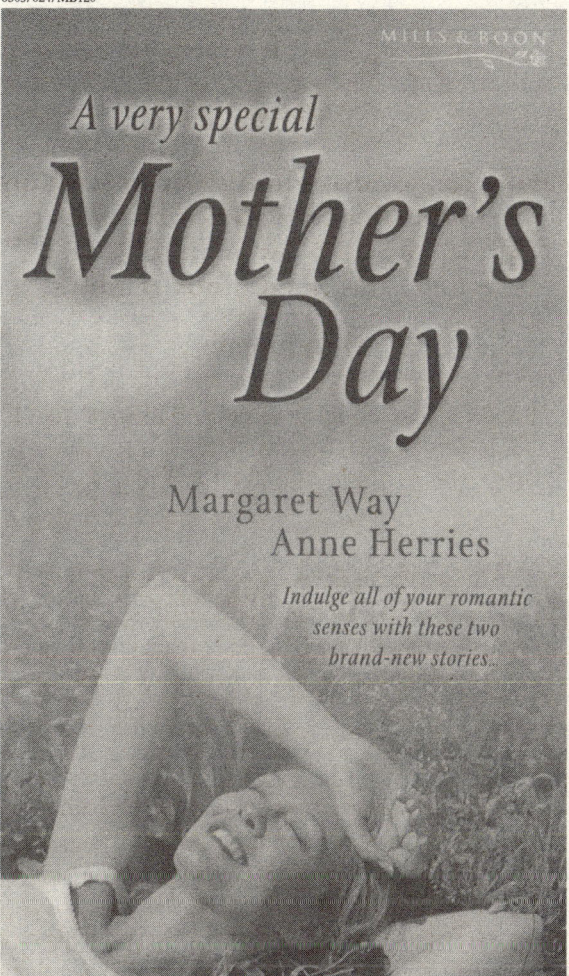

A very special

Mother's Day

Margaret Way
Anne Herries

*Indulge all of your romantic
senses with these two
brand-new stories..*

On sale 18th February 2005

*Available at most branches of WHSmith, Tesco, ASDA, Martins, Borders,
Eason, Sainsbury's and all good paperback bookshops.*

MILLS & BOON

All in a Day

What a difference a day makes…

CAROLE MORTIMER

REBECCA WINTERS

JESSICA HART

On sale 4th February 2005

Available at most branches of WHSmith, Tesco, ASDA, Martins, Borders, Eason, Sainsbury's and all good paperback bookshops.

Paris or Bust!

Kate Hoffmann

Jacqueline Diamond

Jill Shalvis

MILLS & BOON

WIN a romantic weekend in PARIS
SEE INSIDE FOR DETAILS

Three brand-new stories

Falling in love has never been this exciting...or unpredictable!

On sale 6th May 2005

Available at most branches of WHSmith, Tesco, ASDA, Martins, Borders, Eason, Sainsbury's and all good paperback bookshops.

Blaze

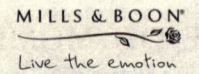

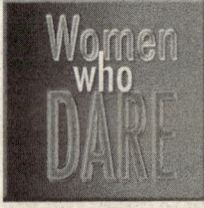

Women who DARE

Don't miss Karen Anders's
exciting new series featuring three friends who dare each other to taste the forbidden—and get a souvenir!

Hers to Take
January 2005

Yours to Seduce
February 2005

Mine to Entice
April 2005

www.millsandboon.co.uk

LIVE THE MOMENT
with our intense new series from

MILLS & BOON®

Medical romance™

24:7

The cutting edge of Mills & Boon Medical Romance

The emotion is deep, The drama is real, The intensity is fierce

Experience our new wave of Medical Romance stories. Look out for:

NURSE IN RECOVERY *by Dianne Drake*
March 2005

DANGEROUS ASSIGNMENT *by Fiona McArthur*
April 2005

THE DOCTOR'S LATIN LOVER *by Olivia Gates*
May 2005

THE MEDICINE MAN *by Dianne Drake*
June 2005

WHERE THE HEART IS *by Kate Hardy*
August 2005

**24:7
Feel the heat -
every hour...every minute...every heartbeat**

MILLS & BOON

Volume 10 on sale from 2nd April 2005

Lynne Graham

International Playboys

Bond of Hatred

Available at most branches of WHSmith, Tesco, Martins, Borders, Eason, Sainsbury's and all good paperback bookshops.

Published 18th March 2005

New York Times Bestselling Author

Jennifer Crusie

Charlie All Night

"Crusie has a gift for concocting nutty scenarios and witty one-liners..." —*People* magazine

MIRA

M404

Published 17th December 2004

Susan Wiggs

THE CHARM SCHOOL

From wallflower to belle of the ball...

"...an irresistible blend of *The Ugly Duckling* and *My Fair Lady*. Jump right in and enjoy yourself."—*Catherine Coulter*

Look out for next month's *EXTRA* Special Edition

USA Today from bestselling author
SHERRYL WOODS

A woman who is finally free to choose her own path..... will she choose love, business or a little sweet revenge?

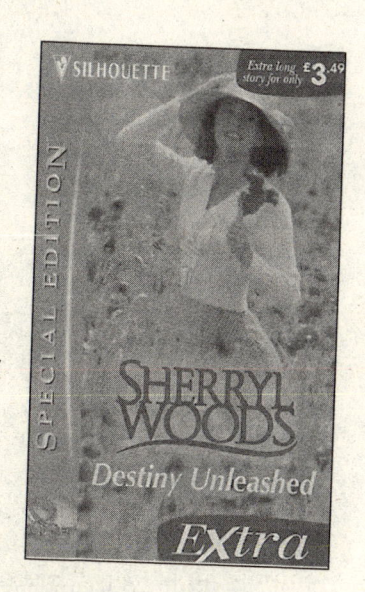

Don't miss out on this fabulous book which will be on sale from 18th March 2005

Available at most branches of WHSmith, Tesco, ASDA, Martins, Borders, Eason, Sainsbury's and all good paperback bookshops.

From This Day Forward

SILHOUETTE

Marie Ferrarella
Emilie Richards

On sale 18th March 2005

Available at most branches of WHSmith, Tesco, ASDA, Martins, Borders, Eason, Sainsbury's and all good paperback bookshops.